F. PAUL WILSON

MIDNIGHT MASS

TOR®

A TOM DOHERTY ASSOCIATES BOOK
NEW YORK

This is a work of fiction. All the characters and events portrayed in this book are either products of the author's imagination or are used fictitiously.

MIDNIGHT MASS

Copyright © 2004 by F. Paul Wilson

Edited by David G. Hartwell

A Tor Book
Published by Tom Doherty Associates, LLC
175 Fifth Avenue
New York, NY 10010

www.tor.com

Tor® is a registered trademark of Tom Doherty Associates, LLC.

ISBN 0-765-34634-6
EAN 978-0-765-34634-6

First edition: April 2004
First mass market edition: November 2005

Printed in the United States of America

0 9 8 7 6 5 4 3 2 1

Vampires have always existed in secret in Central Europe, not just as legends and imaginary menaces but as predators that feed on human blood. But with the fall of Communism and the turmoil throughout the continent, they took bold steps to take ove̲r̲ ̲ ̲ ̲ ̲ ̲ ̲ ̲ ̲ ̲ ̲ ̲ ̲:asing portions of the v̲ ̲ ̲ ̲ ̲ ̲ ̲ ̲ ̲ ̲ all of Europe, India, the̲ ̲ ̲ ̲ ̲ ̲ ̲ ̲ ̲ ̲:h and South America.

PRAISE FOR *MIDNIGHT MASS*

"This one starts big ... Far-out, fresh, and gripping. And better than the movie."   —*Kirkus Reviews*

"In Wilson's creepy, terrifying thriller, vampires are rapidly taking over the planet ... Wilson makes his vampires truly frightening and the eerie atmosphere of the book not unlike that of the movie *28 Days Later*. The undead might have every advantage, but the likable, compelling mortals in this gripping read aren't giving up easily.   —*Booklist*

PRAISE FOR REPAIRMAN JACK

"Repairman Jack is one of the most original and intriguing characters to arise out of contemporary fiction in ages. His adventures are hugely entertaining."   —Dean Koontz

"*The Tomb* is one of the best all-out adventure stories I've read in years."
—Stephen King (President of the Repairman Jack fan club)

AUTHOR'S NOTE

Midnight Mass was born out of my dissatisfaction with the tortured romantic aesthetes who have been passing lately for vampires. Stephen King gave us the real deal in *'Salem's Lot,* but what gives since then? I wanted to get back to the roots—go retro, if you will—and write about the soulless, merciless, parasitic creatures we all knew and loved.

My premise going in was that all the legends about the undead were true: they feared crosses, were killed by sunlight (all right, I'm told that one originated with F. W. Murnau's *Nosferatu,* so it's not really legend, but it *has* become part of the lore), were burned by holy water and crucifixes, cast no reflection, etcetera. You know them as well as I do.

I also adopted the position that all the Catholic Church's mythology is true as well. Vampire lore has been inextricably entwined with Catholic imagery. I was raised a Catholic and, though now in recovery, I feel very much at home with its icons.

Then I took Ted Sturgeon's advice and started asking the next question. The mythic power of the cross over the undead led me to a concept I'd touched on in *The Keep,* and I decided to explore it further.

I've known since I began writing in the early 1970s that some day I'd have to do one, so here it is: my vampire novel. (No, *The Keep* was a *pseudo*vampire novel. This one's the real deal.)

ACKNOWLEDGMENTS

Thanks to Kim Newman for allowing me to borrow his usage of the word "get" as it pertains to vampires and those they've transformed into their own kind (though I've burdened the concept with more plot weight here). There are equivalent terms in the language, but certainly none with such a perfect Old World feel. If you haven't read Kim's wonderful *Anno Dracula* novels, you are missing a rare treat. To Blake Dollens for his keen eye.

And, of course, a special nod to Richard Matheson, who first tilled this soil with *I Am Legend*.

PART ONE

OPUS DEI

ZEV . . .

Gasping in horror and revulsion, Zev Wolpin stumbled away from St. Anthony's Church. He stretched his arms before him, reaching into the dark for something, anything, to support him before he fell.

Leaves slapped his face, twigs tugged at his graying beard as he plowed into foliage. His bike . . . where was his bike? He thought he'd left it in a clump of bushes, but obviously not this clump. Had to find it, had to get away from this place. But the dark made him disoriented . . . the dark, and what he'd just witnessed.

He'd heard whispers, stories he couldn't, wouldn't, believe, so he'd come to see for himself, to prove them wrong. Instead . . .

Zev bent at the waist and retched. Nothing but a bubble of bile and acid came up, searing the back of his throat.

The whispers were only partly true. The truth was worse. The truth was unspeakable.

He straightened and looked around in the darkness. Wan light from the crescent moon in the cloud-streaked sky made the shadows deeper, and Zev feared the shadows. Then he spotted a curving glint of light from the chrome on his bike's front wheel. He ran to it, yanked it by the handlebars from its hiding place, and hopped on.

His aging knees protested as he pedaled away along dark and silent streets lined with dark and silent houses, heading south when he should have been going west, but *away* was all that mattered now.

Lakewood was a small town, maybe ten miles from the Atlantic Ocean; a place where the Rockefeller family was said to have vacationed. So it didn't matter much if he headed south or north, he wouldn't be far from the place he now called home. The town was once home to fifty thousand or more before the undead came. Now he'd be surprised if there were a thousand left. He'd heard it was the same all up and down the East Coast.

The exertion helped clear his mind. He had to be careful. Prudent he hadn't been. In fact, he'd been downright reckless tonight, venturing out after sundown and sneaking up on St. Anthony's. *Schmuck!* What had he been thinking? He prayed he didn't pay for it with his life. Or worse.

He shuddered at the thought of ending up the victim in a ceremony like the one he'd witnessed tonight. He had to find temporary shelter until dawn. Even then he wouldn't be safe, but at least there wouldn't be so many shadows.

The blue serge suit coat that had once fit rather snugly now hung loose on his half-starved frame and flapped behind him as he rode. He'd had to punch new holes in his belt to hold up the pants. He'd complained so often about not being able to lose weight. Nothing to it, really. Simply don't eat.

His ever-hungry stomach rumbled. How could it think of food after what he'd just seen?

A shadow passed over him.

A blast of cold dread banished any concern about his next meal. His aging neck protested as he glanced up at the sky, praying to see a cloud near the moon. But the glowing crescent sat alone in a clear patch of night.

No! Please! He increased his speed, his legs working like pistons against the pedals. Not a flying one!

Zev heard something like a laugh above and behind him. He ducked, all but pressing his face to the handlebars. Something swooped by, clawing at the back of his coat as it passed. Its grip slipped but the glancing impact was enough to disrupt Zev's balance. His front wheel wobbled, the bike tipped to the left and hit the curb, sending him flying.

Zev landed hard on his left shoulder, his lungs emptying with a grunt. His momentum carried him onto his back. What he saw circling above him made him forget his pain. He rolled over and struggled to his feet. He instinctively checked the yarmulke clipped to his thinning gray hair, then gripped the cross dangling from a string around his neck. That might save him in close quarters, but not from a creature that could swoop down from any angle. He felt like a field mouse under the cold gaze of a hawk.

He started running. He didn't know where he was going but knew he had to move. The bike was no good. He needed a tight space where his back was protected and he could use the cross to keep his attacker at bay. One of these houses, maybe. A basement, even a sewer drain—anyplace but out here in the open where—

"Here! Over here!"

A woman's voice, calling in a stage whisper to his left. Zev looked across an overgrown lawn, saw only a large tree, a pine of some sort with branches almost brushing the ground.

"Quick! In the tree!"

A trap maybe. A team this could be—a winged one driving prey into the arms of another on the ground. He'd never heard of anything like it, but that meant nothing.

A glance over his shoulder showed him that the creature had half folded its wings and was diving his way from above. No choice now. Zev veered left for the tree and whatever waited within its shadowed branches.

He was almost there when the woman's voice shouted, "Down!"

Zev obeyed, diving for the grass. He heard a hiss of rage, felt the wind from the creature's wings as it hurtled past no more than a foot or two above him. He lurched back to his feet and staggered forward. Pale hands reached from the branches and pulled him into the shadows.

"Are you all right?" the woman said.

He couldn't see her—she was a shadow among the shadows—but her voice sounded young.

"Yes. No. If you mean am I hurt, no."

But all right? No, he was not all right. Never again would he be all right.

"Good." She grabbed his hands and pressed them against a tree limb. "Hold on to this branch. Steady it while I try to break it. Quick, before it makes another pass."

The dead branch sat chest high and felt about half an inch in diameter. With Zev steadying it, the woman threw her weight hard against it. The wood snapped with a loud crack.

"What are you—?"

She shushed him. "It's coming back."

She moved to the edge of the trees, carrying the branch with her. Zev watched her, silhouetted against the moonlit lawn. Average height, short dark hair were all he gained about her looks. He saw her crouch, then hurl her branch like a spear at the creature as it swooped by on another pass. She missed and high-pitched derisive laughter trailed into the sky.

She returned to Zev, stopped on the other side of the broken branch, and patted the front of his shirt. She pulled him close and whispered in his ear.

"Your cross—tuck it away."

"No! It will—"

"Do as I say. They can see in the dark. And try to look frightened."

Try? Who had to try?

She put an arm around him to hold him close, keeping the branch between them.

Another whisper: "Pull out that cross when I tell you."

Zev had no idea what she was up to but had nowhere else to turn, so . . .

Her grip on him tightened. "Here it comes. Ready . . ."

Zev could see it now, a dark splotch among the shadows of the branches, wings spread, gliding in low, arms stretched out before it.

". . . ready . . ."

Suddenly it folded its wings and shot at them like a missile. "Now!"

As Zev pulled out the cross he felt the woman shove him away. He lost his balance and tumbled back, saw her fall in the other direction, felt a clawed hand grip his shoulder, heard the creature's screech of triumph rise into a wail of shock and agony as it slammed against the trunk of the tree.

Zev regained his feet amid the frantic and furious struggling of the hissing creature. Its charging attack had opened a passage through the branches, lightening the shadows. As he ducked its thrashing wings he realized it had impaled itself on the broken branch. It flopped back and forth like a speared fish, then pushed away from the trunk, trying to dislodge itself from the wood that had pierced its chest.

Zev turned to run. Now was his chance to get away from this thing. But what of the woman? He couldn't abandon her.

He spotted her standing behind the creature. She'd hiked up her already short skirt and kicked at the thing's back, shoving it further onto the branch. The creature howled and thrashed, and in its struggles broke the branch off the trunk with a gunshot crack.

Free now, it whirled and staggered out into the moonlight. Its wings flapped but couldn't seem to lift it. Perhaps ten feet beyond the branches it dropped to its knees. The woman was right behind it, giving it another kick. It rolled onto its back, clawing at the wooden shaft that jutted two or three feet from its chest. Its movements were weaker now, its wings lay crumpled beneath it. Howling and writhing in agony, it gripped the branch and started to slide it out of its chest.

"No, you don't!" the woman cried.

She gripped the upper end, shoving it back down and leaning on it to hold it in place.

"This is for Bern!" she screamed, naked fury rawing her voice. "This is what you made me do to her! How does it feel? How does it *feel*?"

For an instant Zev wondered who was more frightening, this screeching woman or the struggling monster she held pinned to the earth.

The creature clawed and kicked at her, almost knocking her over. He had to help. If that thing got free . . .

Mouth dry, heart pounding, Zev forced himself from the shadows and added his own weight to the branch. He felt it punch deeper into the thing's chest. Then a sickening scrape as it thrust past ribs and into the ground beneath.

The creature's struggles became abruptly feebler. He saw now that it was a female. It might have been beautiful once, but the sickly pallor and the bared fangs robbed it of any attractiveness.

Finally it shuddered and lay still. Zev watched in amazement as its wings shriveled and disappeared.

"*Gevalt!*" he whispered, although he didn't know why. "You did it! You killed one!"

He'd heard they could be killed—all the old folk tales said they could be—but he'd never actually seen one die, never even met anyone who had.

It was good to know they could be killed.

"*We* did." She finally released her grip on the branch but her gaze remained locked on the creature. "If you have a soul," she said, "may God have mercy on it."

What was this? Like a harpy, she screeches, then she blesses the thing. A madwoman, this was.

She faced him. "I'm sorry for my outburst. I . . . it's just . . ." She seemed to lose her train of thought, as if something had distracted her. "Anyway, thank you for the help."

"You saved my life, young lady. It's me who should be thanking."

She was staring at him. "You're Rabbi Wolpin, aren't you."

Shock stole his voice for a few heartbeats. She knew him?

"Why . . . yes. But I don't recognize . . ."

She laughed. A bitter sound. "Please, God, I hope not."

He could see her now. Nothing familiar about her features, no particular style to her short dark hair. He noticed a tiny crescent scar on the right side of her chin. Heavy on the eye makeup—very heavy. A tight red sweater and even tighter short black skirt hid little of her slim body. And were those fishnet stockings?

A prostitute? In these times? Such a thing he never would have dreamed. But then he remembered hearing of women selling themselves to get food and favors.

"So, you know me how?"

She shrugged. "I used to see you with Father Cahill."

"Joe Cahill," Zev said, feeling a burst of warmth at the mention of his friend's name. "I was just over at his church. I saw . . ." The words choked off.

"I know. I've—" She waved her hand before her face. "She's starting to stink already. Must be an older one."

Zev looked down and saw that the creature was already in an advanced state of rot.

"We'd better get out of here," the woman said, backing away. "They seem to know when one of their kind dies. Get your bike and meet me by the tree."

Zev continued to stare at the corpse. "Are they always so hard to kill?"

"I don't think the branch went all the way through the heart at first."

"*Nu*? You've done this before?"

Her expression was bleak as she looked at him. "Let's not talk about it."

When Zev wheeled his bike back to the tree he found her standing beside a child's red wagon, an old-fashioned Radio Flyer. A book bag emblazoned with *St. Anthony's School* lay in the wagon. He hadn't noticed either earlier. She must have had them hidden among the branches.

She said, "You mentioned you were at St. Anthony's. Why?"

"To see if what I'd heard was true." The urge to retch gripped Zev again. "To think that was Father Cahill's church."

"He wasn't the pastor."

"Not in name, maybe, but they were his flock. He was the glue that held them together. Someone should tell him what's going on."

"Oh, yes. That would be wonderful. But nobody knows where he is, or if he's even alive."

"I do."

Her hand shot out and gripped his arm, squeezing. "He's alive?"

"Yes," Zev said, taken aback by her intensity. "At least I think so."

Her grip tightened. "Where?"

He wondered if he'd made a mistake telling her. He tried not to sound evasive. "A retreat house. Have I been there? No. But it's near the beach, I'm told."

True enough, and he knew the address. After Joe had been moved out of St. Anthony's rectory to the retreat house, he and Zev still shared many phone conversations. At least until the creatures came. Then the phones stopped working and Zev's time became devoted more to survival than to keeping up with old friends.

"You've got to find him! You've got to tell him! He'll come back when he finds out and he'll make them pay!"

"A *mensch*, he is, I agree, but only one man."

"No! Many of his parishioners are still alive, but they're afraid. They're defeated. But if Father Joe came back, they'd have hope. They'd see that it wasn't over. They'd regain the will to fight."

"Like you?"

"I'm different," she said, the fervor slipping from her voice. "I never lost the will to fight. But my circumstances are special."

"How?"

"It's not important. *I'm* not important. But Father Joe is.

Find him, Rabbi Wolpin. Don't put it off. Find him tomorrow and tell him. When he hears what they've done to his church he'll come back and teach them a lesson they'll never forget!"

Zev didn't know about that, but it would be good to see his young friend again. Searching him out would be a *mitzvah* for St. Anthony's, but might be good for Zev as well. It might offer some shape to his life . . . a life that had devolved to mere existence, an endless, mind-numbing round of searching for food and shelter while avoiding the creatures by night and the human slime who did their bidding during the day.

"All right," Zev said. "I'll try to find him. I won't promise to bring him back, because such a decision will not be mine to make. But I promise to look for him."

"Tomorrow?"

"First light. And who should I say sent me?"

The woman turned away and shook her head. "No one."

"You won't tell me your name?"

"It's not important."

"But you seem to know him."

"Once, yes." Her voice grew thick. "But he wouldn't recognize me now."

"You can be so sure?"

She nodded. "I've fallen too far away. There's no coming back for me, I'm afraid."

She'd been through something terrible, this one. So had everyone who was still alive, including Zev, but her experience, whatever it was, had made her a little *meshugeh*. More than a little, maybe.

She started walking away, looking almost silly dragging that little red wagon behind her.

"Wait . . ."

"Just find him," she said without turning. "And don't mention me."

She stepped into the shadows and was gone from sight, with only the squeaks of the wagon wheels as proof that she hadn't evaporated.

Father Joe Cahill and a prostitute? Zev couldn't believe it.

But even if it were true, it was far less serious than what Joe had been accused of.

Maybe she hadn't sold herself in the old days. Maybe it was something she had to do to survive in these new and terrible times. Whatever the truth, he blessed her for being here to help him tonight.

But who is she? he wondered. Or perhaps more important, who *was* she.

CAROLE . . .

Carole hid the red wagon behind the bushes along the side of the house, then climbed the rickety stairs to the front porch, unlocked the door, and stepped inside. That was when the voice spoke. It had been silent the whole long walk home. Now it started in again.

<Home sweet home. Is that what you're after thinking now, Carole? And don't be thinking that the good deed you did tonight will be offsetting the mortal sins you committed earlier this evening. It won't. Not by a long shot!>

"Quiet," Carole muttered. "I need to listen."

She'd been in this house two weeks now, and she'd made it as secure as possible. As secure as anything could be since her world ended last month.

Last month? Yes . . . six weeks this coming Friday. It seemed a lifetime ago. She never would have believed everything could fall apart so fast. But it had.

Despite her security measures, she held her breath, listening for the sound of someone—or some*thing*—else in the house besides her. She heard nothing but the breeze stirring the curtains in the upstairs bedroom. It had been warm when she'd left but the night had grown chilly. May was such an untrustworthy month.

She fished the flashlight out of her shoulder bag and turned it on, then off again—just long enough to orient herself. She wasn't worried about the light being seen from outside—the blankets draped over the windows would prevent that. She wanted to save her batteries, a rare and precious commodity. When she reached the stairs she flicked the light on again so she could step over the broken first tread. She noticed little splatters of blood on the banister and newel post. She'd clean them up in the morning, when she could use natural light.

When she reached the bedroom she closed the window and quickly undressed.

<Sure and you may be able to remove those whore clothes, Carole, but you can't remove the stain of what you did in them.>

Carole had no illusions about that. She pulled on a baggy gray sweatsuit and slipped beneath the covers, praying the voice would let her sleep tonight. The night's labors had exhausted her.

She thought of Rabbi Wolpin, and that made her think of Father Cahill, and that led to thoughts of St. Anthony's and the school where she'd taught, and the convent where she'd lived . . .

She thought of her last nights there, less than six weeks ago, just days before Easter, when everything had been so different . . .

GOOD FRIDAY . . .

"The Holy Father says there are no such things as vampires," Sister Bernadette Gileen said.

Sister Carole Hanarty glanced up from the pile of chemistry tests on her lap—tests she might never be able to return to her sophomore students—and watched Bernadette as she drove through town, working the shift on the old Datsun like a long-haul trucker. Her dear friend and fellow Sister of Mercy was thin, almost painfully so, with large blue eyes and short red hair showing around the white band of her wimple. As she peered through the windshield, the glow of the setting sun ruddied the clear, smooth skin of her round face.

Sister Carole shrugged. "If His Holiness said it, then we must believe it. But we haven't heard anything from him in so long. I hope . . ."

Bernadette turned toward her, eyes wide with alarm.

"Oh, you wouldn't be thinking anything's happened to His Holiness now, would you, Carole?" she said, the lilt of her native Ireland elbowing its way into her voice. "They wouldn't dare!"

Momentarily at a loss as to what to say, Carole gazed out the side window at the budding trees sliding past. The sidewalks of this little Jersey Shore town were empty, and hardly any other cars were on the road. She and Bernadette had had to try three grocery stores before finding one with anything to sell. Between the hoarders and delayed or canceled shipments, food was getting scarce.

Everybody sensed it. How did that saying go? By the pricking in my thumbs, something wicked this way comes . . .

Or something like that.

She rubbed her cold hands together and thought about Bernadette, younger than she by five years—only twenty-six—with such a good mind, such a clear thinker in so many ways. But her faith was almost childlike.

She'd come to the convent at St. Anthony's two years ago and the pair of them had established instant rapport. They shared so much. Not just a common Irish heritage, but a certain isolation as well. Carole's parents had died years ago, and Bernadette's were back on the Auld Sod. So they became sisters in a sense that went beyond their sisterhood in the order. Carole was the big sister, Bernadette the little one. They prayed together, laughed together, walked together. They took over the convent kitchen and did all the food shopping together. Carole could only hope that she had enriched Bernadette's life half as much as the younger woman had enriched hers.

Bernadette was such an innocent. She seemed to assume that since the Pope was infallible when he spoke on matters of faith or morals he somehow must be invincible too.

Carole hadn't told Bernadette, but she'd decided not to believe the Pope on the matter of the undead. After all, their existence was not a matter of faith or morals. Either they existed or they didn't. And all the news out of Europe last year had left little doubt that vampires were real.

And that they were on the march.

Somehow they had got themselves organized. Not only did they exist, but more of them had been hiding in Eastern Europe than even the most superstitious peasant could have imagined. And when the communist bloc crumbled, when all the former client states and Russia were in disarray, grabbing for land, slaughtering in the name of nation and race and religion, the undead took advantage of the power vacuum and struck.

They struck high, they struck low, and before the rest of the world could react, they controlled all Eastern Europe.

If they had merely killed, they might have been containable. But because each kill was a conversion, their numbers increased in a geometric progression. Sister Carole understood geometric progressions better than most. Hadn't she spent years demonstrating them to her chemistry class by dropping a seed crystal into a beaker of supersaturated solution? That one crystal became two, which became four, which became eight, which became sixteen, and so on. You could watch the lattices forming, slowly at first, then bridging through the solution with increasing speed until the liquid contents of the beaker became a solid crystalline mass.

That was how it had gone in Eastern Europe and Russia, then spreading into the Middle East and India, then China. And last fall, into Western Europe.

The undead became unstoppable.

All of Europe had been silent for months. Officially, at least. But a couple of the students at St. Anthony's High who had shortwave radios had told Carole of faint transmissions filtering through the transatlantic night recounting ghastly horrors all across Europe under undead rule.

But the Pope had declared there were no vampires. He'd

said it, but shortly thereafter he and the Vatican had fallen silent along with the rest of the continent.

Washington had played down the immediate threat, saying the Atlantic Ocean formed a natural barrier against the undead. Europe was quarantined. America was safe.

Then had come reports, disputed at first, and still officially denied, of undead in Washington, DC, running rampant through the Pentagon, the legislators' posh neighborhoods, the White House itself. Then New York City. The New York TV and radio stations had stopped transmitting. And now . . .

"You can't really believe vampires are coming to the Jersey Shore, can you?" Bernadette said. "I mean, that is, if there were such things."

"It is hard to believe, isn't it?" Carole said, hiding a smile. "Especially since no one comes to Jersey unless they have to."

"Oh, don't you be having on with me now. This is serious."

Bernadette was right. It was serious. "Well, it fits the pattern my students have heard from Europe."

"But dear God, 'tis Holy Week! 'Tis Good Friday, it is! How could they dare?"

"It's the perfect time, if you think about it. There will be no Mass said until the first Easter Mass on Sunday morning. What other time of the year is daily mass suspended?"

Bernadette shook her head. "None."

"Exactly." Carole looked down at her cold hands and felt the chill crawl all the way up her arms.

The car suddenly lurched to a halt and she heard Bernadette cry out. "Dear Jesus! They're already here!"

Half a dozen black-clad forms clustered on the corner ahead, staring at them.

"Got to get out of here!" Bernadette said and hit the gas.

The old car coughed and died.

"Oh, no!" Bernadette wailed, frantically pumping the gas pedal and turning the key as the dark forms glided toward them. "No!"

"Easy, dear," Carole said, laying a gentle hand on her arm. "It's all right. They're just kids."

Perhaps "kids" was not entirely correct. Two males and four females who looked to be in their late teens and early twenties, but carried any number of adult lifetimes behind their heavily made-up eyes. Grinning, leering, they gathered around the car, four on Bernadette's side and two on Carole's. Sallow faces made paler by a layer of white powder, kohl-crusted eyelids, and black lipstick. Black fingernails, rings in their ears and eyebrows and nostrils, chrome studs piercing cheeks and lips. Their hair ranged the color spectrum, from dead white through burgundy to crankcase black. Bare hairless chests on the boys under their leather jackets, almost-bare chests on the girls in their black push-up bras and bustiers. Boots of shiny leather or vinyl, fishnet stockings, layer upon layer of lace, and everything black, black, black.

"Hey, look!" one of the boys said. A spiked leather collar girded his throat; acne lumps bulged under his whiteface. "Nuns!"

"Penguins!" someone else said.

Apparently this was deemed hilarious. The six of them screamed with laughter.

We're *not* penguins, Carole thought. She hadn't worn a full habit in years. Only the headpiece.

"Shit, are *they* gonna be in for a surprise tomorrow morning!" said a buxom girl wearing a silk top hat.

Another roar of laughter by all except one. A tall slim girl with three large black tears tattooed down one cheek, and blond roots peeking from under her black-dyed hair, hung back, looking uncomfortable. Carole stared at her. Something familiar there . . .

She rolled down her window. "Rosita? Rosita Hernandez, is that you?"

More laughter. " 'Rosita'?" someone cried. "That's Wicky!"

The girl stepped forward and looked Carole in the eye.

"Yes, Sister. That used to be my name. But I'm not Rosita anymore."

"I can see that."

She remembered Rosita. A sweet girl, extremely bright, but so quiet. A voracious reader who never seemed to fit in with the rest of the kids. Her grades plummeted as a junior. She never returned for her senior year. When Carole had called her parents, she was told that Rosita had left home. She'd been unable to learn anything more.

"You've changed a bit since I last saw you. What is it—three years now?"

"You talk about *change*?" said the top-hatted girl, sticking her face in the window. "Wait'll tonight. Then you'll *really* see her change!" She brayed a laugh that revealed a chrome stud in her tongue.

"Butt out, Carmilla!" Rosita said.

Carmilla ignored her. "They're coming tonight, you know. The Lords of the Night will be arriving after sunset, and that'll spell the death of your world and the birth of ours. We will present ourselves to them, we will bare our throats and let them drain us, and we'll join them. Then we'll rule the night with them!"

It sounded like a canned speech, one she must have delivered time and again to her black-clad troupe.

Carole looked past Carmilla to Rosita. "Is that what you believe? Is that what you really want?"

The girl shrugged her high thin shoulders. "Beats anything else I got going."

Finally the old Datsun shuddered to life. Carole heard Bernadette working the shift. She touched her arm and said, "Wait. Just one more moment, please."

She was about to speak to Rosita when Carmilla jabbed her finger at Carole's face, shouting.

"Then you bitches and the candy-ass god you whore for will be fucking extinct!"

With a surprising show of strength, Rosita yanked Carmilla away from the window.

"Better go, Sister Carole," Rosita said.

The Datsun started to move.

"What the fuck's with you, Wicky?" Carole heard Carmilla scream as the car eased away from the dark cluster. "Getting religion or somethin? Should we start callin you *Sister* Rosita now?"

"She was one of the few people who was ever straight with me," Rosita said. "So fuck off, Carmilla."

By then the car had traveled too far to hear more.

↑ ↑ ↑

"What awful creatures they were!" Bernadette said, staring out the window in Carole's convent room. She hadn't been able to stop talking about the incident on the street. "Almost my age, they were, and such horrible language!"

The room was little more than a ten-by-ten-foot plaster box with cracks in the walls and the latest coat of paint beginning to flake off the ancient embossed tin ceiling. She had one window and, for furnishings, a crucifix, a dresser and mirror, a work table and chair, a bed, and a night stand. Not much, but she gladly called it home. She took her vow of poverty seriously.

"Perhaps we should pray for them."

"They need more than prayer, I'd think. Believe me you, they're heading for a bad end." Bernadette removed the oversized rosary she wore looped around her neck, gathering the beads and its attached crucifix in her hand. "Maybe we could offer them some crosses for protection?"

Carole couldn't resist a smile. "That's a sweet thought, Bern, but I don't think they're looking for protection."

"Sure, and lookit after what I'm saying," Bernadette said, her own smile rueful. "No, of course they wouldn't."

"But we'll pray for them," Carole said.

Bernadette dropped into a chair, stayed there for no more than a heartbeat, then was up again, moving about, pacing the confines of Carole's room. She couldn't seem to sit still.

She wandered out into the hall and came back almost immediately, rubbing her hands together as if washing them.

"It's so quiet," she said. "So empty."

"I certainly hope so," Carole said. "We're the only two who are supposed to be here."

The little convent was half empty even when all its residents were present. And now, with St. Anthony's School closed for the coming week, the rest of the nuns had gone home to spend Easter Week with brothers and sisters and parents. Even those who might have stayed around the convent in past years had heard the rumors that the undead might be moving this way, so they'd scattered. Carole's only living relative was an aunt, her mother's sister Joyce, who lived in Harrisburg and usually invited her to spend Easter and the following week with her; but she hadn't invited her this year, and wasn't answering her phone. She had a son in California; maybe she'd gone to stay with him. Lots of people were leaving the East Coast.

Bernadette hadn't heard from her family in Ireland for months. Carole feared she never would.

So that left just the two of them to hold the fort, as it were. The convent was part of a complex consisting of the church itself, the rectory, the grammar school and high school buildings, the tiny cemetery, and the sturdy old two-story rooming house that was now the convent. She and Bernadette had taken second-floor rooms, leaving the first floor to the older nuns.

Carole wasn't afraid. She knew they'd be safe here at St. Anthony's, although she wished there were more people left in the complex than just Bernadette, herself, and Father Palmeri.

"I don't understand Father Palmeri," Bernadette said. "Locking up the church and keeping his parishioners from making the stations of the cross on Good Friday. Who's ever heard of such a thing, I ask you? I just don't understand it."

Carole thought she understood. She suspected that Father Alberto Palmeri was afraid. Sometime this morning he'd locked up the rectory, barred the door to St. Anthony's, and hidden himself in the church basement.

God forgive her for thinking it, but to Sister Carole's mind Father Palmeri was a coward.

"Oh, I do wish he'd open the church, just for a little while," Bernadette said. "I need to be in there, Carole. I *need* it."

Carole knew how Bern felt. Who had said religion was an opiate of the people? Marx? Whoever it was, he hadn't been completely wrong. For Carole, sitting in the cool, peaceful quiet beneath St. Anthony's gothic arches, praying, meditating, and feeling the presence of the Lord were like a daily dose of an addictive drug. A dose she and Bern had been denied today. Bern's withdrawal pangs seemed worse than Carole's.

The younger nun paused as she passed the window, then pointed down to the street.

"And now who in God's name would they be?"

Carole rose and stepped to Bernadette's side. Passing on the street below was a cavalcade of shiny new cars—Mercedes Benzes, BMW's, Jaguars, Lincolns, Cadillacs—all with New York plates, all cruising from the direction of the Parkway.

The sight of them in the dusk tightened a knot in Carole's stomach. The lupine faces she spied through the windows looked brutish, and the way they drove their gleaming luxury cars down the center line . . . as if they owned the road.

A Cadillac convertible with its top down passed below; four scruffy occupants lounged on the seats. The driver wore a cowboy hat, a woman in leather sat next to him. Both were drinking beer. When Carol saw the driver glance up and look their way, she tugged on Bern's sleeve.

"Stand back! Don't let them see you!"

"Why not? Who are they?"

"I'm not sure, but I've heard of bands of men who do the vampires' dirty work during the daytime, who've traded their souls for the promise of immortality later on, and for . . . other things now."

"Sure and you're joking, Carole!"

Carole shook her head. "I wish I were."

"Oh, dear God, and now the sun's down." She turned frightened blue eyes toward Carole. "Do you think maybe we should . . . ?"

"Lock up? Most certainly. I know what His Holiness said about there not being any such things as vampires, but maybe he's changed his mind since then and just can't get word to us."

"Sure and you're probably right. You close these and I'll check down the hall." She hurried out, her voice trailing behind her. "Oh, I do wish Father Palmeri hadn't locked the church. I'd dearly love to say a few prayers there."

Sister Carole glanced out the window again. The fancy new cars were gone, but rumbling in their wake was a convoy of trucks—big, eighteen-wheel semis, lumbering down the center line. What were they for? What did they carry? What were they delivering to town?

Suddenly a dog began to bark, and then another, and more and more until it seemed as if every dog in town was giving voice.

To fight the unease rising like a flood tide within her, Sister Carole concentrated on the simple manual tasks of closing and locking her window and drawing the curtains.

But the dread remained, a sick, cold certainty that the world was falling into darkness, that the creeping hem of shadow had reached her corner of the globe, and that without some miracle, without some direct intervention by a wrathful God, the coming night hours would wreak an irrevocable change on her life.

She began to pray for that miracle.

| | |

Carole and Bernadette had decided to leave the convent of St. Anthony's dark tonight.

And they decided to spend the night together in Carole's room. They dragged in Bernadette's mattress, locked the door, and doubled-draped the window with the bedspread. They lit the room with a single candle and prayed together.

Yet the music of the night filtered through the walls and the doors and the drapes, the muted moan of sirens singing antiphon to their hymns, the muffled pops of gunfire punctuating their psalms, reaching a crescendo shortly after midnight, then tapering off to . . . silence.

Carole could see that Bernadette was having an especially rough time of it. She cringed with every siren wail, jumped at every shot. Carole shared Bern's terror, but she buried it, hid it deep within for her friend's sake. After all, Carole was older, and she knew she was made of sterner stuff. Bernadette was an innocent, too sensitive even for yesterday's world, the world before the undead. How would she survive in the world as it would be after tonight? She'd need help. Carole would provide as much as she could.

But for all the imagined horrors conjured by the night noises, the silence was worse. No human wails of pain and horror had penetrated their sanctum, but imagined cries of human suffering echoed through their minds in the ensuing stillness.

"Dear God, what's happening out there?" Bernadette said after they'd finished reading aloud the Twenty-third Psalm.

She huddled on her mattress, a blanket thrown over her shoulders. The candle's flame reflected in her frightened eyes and cast her shadow, high, hunched, and wavering, on the wall behind her.

Carole sat cross-legged on her bed. She leaned back against the wall and fought to keep her eyes open. Exhaustion was a weight on her shoulders, a cloud over her brain, but she knew sleep was out of the question. Not now, not tonight, not until the sun was up. And maybe not even then.

"Easy, Bern—" Carole began, then stopped.

From below, on the first floor of the convent, a faint thumping noise.

"What's that?" Bernadette said, voice hushed, eyes wide.

"I don't know."

Carole grabbed her robe and stepped out into the hall for a better listen.

"Don't you be leaving me alone, now!" Bernadette said, running after her with the blanket still wrapped around her shoulders.

"Hush," Carole said. "Listen. It's the front door. Someone's knocking. I'm going down to see."

She hurried down the wide, oak-railed stairway to the front foyer. The knocking was louder here, but still sounded weak. Carole put her eye to the peephole, peered through the sidelights, but saw no one.

But the knocking, weaker still, continued.

"Wh-who's there?" she said, her words cracking with fear.

"Sister Carole," came a faint voice through the door. "It's me . . . Rosita. I'm hurt."

Instinctively, Carole reached for the handle, but Bernadette grabbed her arm.

"Wait! It could be a trick!"

She's right, Carole thought. Then she glanced down and saw blood leaking across the threshold from the other side.

She gasped and pointed at the crimson puddle. "That's no trick."

She unlocked the door and pulled it open. Rosita huddled on the welcome mat in a pool of blood.

"Dear sweet Jesus!" Carole cried. "Help me, Bern!"

"What if she's a vampire?" Bernadette said, standing frozen. "They can't cross the threshold unless you ask them in."

"Stop that silliness! She's hurt!"

Bernadette's good heart won out over her fear. She threw off the blanket, revealing a faded blue, ankle-length flannel nightgown that swirled just above the floppy slippers she wore. Together they dragged Rosita inside. Bernadette closed and relocked the door immediately.

"Call 9-1-1!" Carole told her.

Bernadette hurried down the hall to the phone.

Rosita lay moaning on her side on the foyer tiles, clutching her bleeding abdomen. Carole saw a piece of metal, coated with rust and blood, protruding from the area of her navel. From the faint fecal smell of the gore Carole guessed that her intestines had been pierced.

"Oh, you poor child!" Carole knelt beside her and cradled her head in her lap. She arranged Bernadette's blanket over Rosita's trembling body. "Who did this to you?"

"Accident," Rosita gasped. Real tears had run her black eye makeup over her tattooed tears. "I was running . . . fell."

"Running from what?"

"From *them*. God . . . terrible. We searched for them, Carmilla's Lords of the Night. Just after sundown we found one. Looked just like we always knew he would . . . you know, tall and regal and graceful and seductive and cool. Standing by one of those big trailers that came through town. My friends approached him but I sorta stayed back. Wasn't too sure I was really into having my blood sucked. But Carmilla goes right up to him, pulling off her top and baring her throat, offering herself to him."

Rosita coughed and groaned as a spasm of pain shook her.

"Don't talk," Carole said. "Save your strength."

"No," she said in a weaker voice when it eased. "You got to know. This Lord guy just smiles at Carmilla, then he signals his helpers who pull open the back doors of the trailer." Rosita sobbed. "Horrible! Truck's filled with these . . . *things!* Look human but they're dirty and naked and act like beasts. They like *pour* out the truck and right off a bunch of them jump Carmilla. They start biting and ripping at her throat. I see her go down and hear her screaming and I start backing up. My other friends try to run but they're pulled down too. And then I see one of the things hold up

Carmilla's head and hear the Lord guy say, 'That's right, children. Take their heads. Always take their heads. There are enough of us now.' And that's when I turned and ran. I was running through a vacant lot when I fell on . . . this."

Bernadette rushed back into the foyer. Her face was drawn with fear. "911 doesn't answer! I can't raise anyone!"

"They're all over town." Rosita said after another spasm of coughing. Carole could barely hear her. She touched her throat—so cold. "They've been setting fires and attacking the cops and firemen when they arrive. Their human helpers break into houses and drive the people outside where they're attacked. And after the things drain the blood, they rip the heads off."

"Dear God, why?" Bernadette said, crouching beside Carole.

"My guess . . . don't want any more undead. Maybe only so much blood to go around and—"

She moaned with another spasm, then lay still. Carole patted her cheeks and called her name, but Rosita Hernandez's dull, staring eyes told it all.

"Is she . . . ?" Bernadette said.

Carole nodded as tears filled her eyes. You poor misguided child, she thought, closing Rosita's eyelids.

"She's died in sin," Bernadette said. "She needs anointing immediately! I'll get Father."

"No, Bern," Carole said. "Father Palmeri won't come."

"Of course he will. He's a priest and this poor lost soul needs him."

"Trust me. He won't leave that church basement for anything."

"But he must!" she said almost childishly, her voice rising. "He's a priest."

"Just be calm, Bernadette, and we'll pray for her ourselves."

"We can't do what a priest can do," she said, springing to her feet. "It's not the same."

"Where are you going?"

"To . . . to get a robe. It's cold."

My poor, dear, frightened Bernadette, Carole thought as she watched her scurry up the steps. I know exactly how you feel.

"Bring my prayer book back with you," she called after her.

Carole pulled the blanket over Rosita's face and gently lowered her head to the floor.

She waited for Bernadette to return . . . and waited. What was taking her so long? She called her name but got no answer.

Uneasy, Carole returned to the second floor. The hallway was empty and dark except for a pale shaft of moonlight slanting through the window at its far end. Carole hurried to Bern's room. The door was closed. She knocked.

"Bern? Bern, are you in there?"

Silence.

Carole opened the door and peered inside. More moonlight, more emptiness.

Where could—?

Down on the first floor, almost directly under Carole's feet, the convent's back door slammed. How could that be? Carole had locked it herself—deadbolted it at sunset.

Unless Bernadette had gone down the back stairs and . . .

She darted to the window and stared down at the grassy area between the convent and the church. The high, bright moon had made a black-and-white photo of the world outside, bleaching the lawn below with its stark glow, etching deep ebony wells around the shrubs and foundation plantings. It glared from St. Anthony's slate roof, stretching a long wedge of night behind its Gothic spire.

And scurrying across the lawn toward the church was a slim figure wrapped in a long raincoat, the moon picking out the white band of her wimple, its black veil a fluttering shadow along her neck and upper back—Bernadette was too old-country to approach the church with her head uncovered.

"Oh, Bern," Carole whispered, pressing her face against the glass. "Bern, don't!"

She watched as Bernadette ran up to St. Anthony's side entrance and began clanking the heavy brass knocker against the thick oak door. Her high, clear voice filtered faintly through the window glass.

"Father! Father Palmeri! Please open up! There's a dead girl in the convent who needs anointing!"

She kept banging, kept calling, but the door never opened. Carole thought she saw Father Palmeri's pale face float into view to Bern's right through the glass of one of the church's few unstained windows. It hovered there for a few seconds, then disappeared.

But the door remained closed.

That didn't seem to faze Bern. She only increased the force of her blows with the knocker, and raised her voice even higher until it echoed off the stone walls and reverberated through the night.

Carole's heart went out to her. She shared Bern's need, if not her desperation.

Why doesn't Father Palmeri at least let her in? she thought. The poor thing's making enough racket to wake the dead.

Sudden terror tightened along the back of Carole's neck.

. . . wake the dead . . .

Bern was too loud. She thought only of attracting the attention of Father Palmeri, but what if she attracted . . . others?

Even as the thought crawled across her mind, Carole saw a dark, rangy figure creep onto the lawn from the street side, slinking from shadow to shadow, closing in on her unsuspecting friend.

"Oh, dear God!" she cried, and fumbled with the window lock. She twisted it open and yanked up the sash.

Carole screamed into the night. "Bernadette! Behind you! There's someone coming! Get back here now, Bernadette! NOW!"

Bernadette turned and looked up toward Carole, then stared around her. The approaching figure had dissolved into the shadows at the sound of the shouted warnings. But Bernadette must have sensed something in Carole's voice, for she started back toward the convent.

She didn't get far—ten paces, maybe—before the shadowy form caught up to her.

"NO!" Carole screamed as she saw it leap upon her friend.

She stood frozen at the window, her fingers clawing the molding on each side as Bernadette's high wail of terror and pain cut the night.

For the span of an endless, helpless, paralyzed heartbeat, Carole watched the form drag her down to the silver lawn, tear open her raincoat, and fall upon her, watched her arms and legs flail wildly, frantically in the moonlight, and all the while her screams, oh, dear God in Heaven, her screams for help were slim, white-hot nails driven into Carole's ears.

And then, out of the corner of her eye, Carole saw the pale face appear again at the window of St. Anthony's, watch for a moment, then once more fade into the inner darkness.

With a low moan of horror, fear, and desperation, Carole pushed herself away from the window and stumbled toward the hall. *Someone* had to help. Along the way she snatched the foot-long wooden crucifix from Bernadette's wall and clutched it against her chest with both hands. As she picked up speed, graduating from a lurch to a walk to a loping run, she began to scream—not a wail of fear, but a long, seamless ululation of rage.

Something was killing her friend.

The rage was good. It shredded the fear and the horror and the loathing that had paralyzed her. It allowed her to move, to keep moving. She embraced the rage.

Carole hurtled down the stairs and burst onto the moonlit lawn—

And stopped, disoriented for an instant. She didn't see Bern. Where was she? Where was her attacker?

And then she saw a patch of writhing shadow on the grass ahead of her near one of the shrubs.

Bernadette?

Clutching the crucifix, Carole ran for the spot, and as she

neared she realized it was indeed Bernadette, sprawled face down, but not alone. Another shadow sat astride her, hissing like a reptile, gnashing its teeth, its fingers curved into talons that tugged at Bernadette's head as if trying to tear it off.

Carole reacted without thinking. Screaming, she launched herself at the creature, ramming the big crucifix against its exposed back. Light flashed and sizzled and thick black smoke shot upward in oily swirls from where cross met flesh. The thing arched its back and howled, writhing beneath the cruciform brand, thrashing wildly as it tried to wriggle out from under the fiery weight.

But Carole stayed with it, following its slithering crawl on her knees, pressing the flashing cross deeper and deeper into its steaming, boiling flesh, down to the spine, into the vertebrae. Its cries became almost piteous as it weakened, and Carole gagged on the thick black smoke that fumed around her, but her rage would not allow her to slack off. She kept up the pressure, pushed the wooden crucifix deeper and deeper in the creature's back until it penetrated the chest cavity and seared into its heart. Suddenly the thing gagged and shuddered and then was still.

The flashes faded. The final wisps of smoke trailed away on the breeze.

Carole abruptly released the shaft of the crucifix as if it had shocked her. She ran back to Bernadette, dropped to her knees beside the still form, and turned her over onto her back.

"Oh, no!" she screamed when she saw Bernadette's torn throat, her wide, glazed, sightless eyes, and the blood, so much blood smeared all over the front of her.

Oh no. Oh, dear God, please no! This can't be! This can't be real!

A sob burst from her. "No, Bern! Nooooo!"

Somewhere nearby, a dog howled in answer.

Or was it a dog?

Carole realized she was defenseless now. She had to get back to the convent. She leaped to her feet and looked around. Nothing moving. A dozen feet away she saw the crucifix still buried in the dead thing.

She hurried over to retrieve it, but recoiled from touching the creature. She could see now that it was a man—a naked man, or something that very much resembled one. But not quite. Some indefinable quality was missing.

Was it one of *them*?

This must be one of the undead Rosita had warned about. But could this . . . this *thing* . . . be a vampire? It had acted like little more than a rabid dog in human form.

Whatever it was, it had mauled and murdered Bernadette. Rage bloomed again within Carole like a virulent, rampant virus, spreading through her bloodstream, invading her nervous system, threatening to take over. She fought the urge to batter the corpse.

She choked back the bile rising in her throat and stared at the inert form prone before her. This once had been a man, someone with a family, perhaps. Surely he hadn't asked to become this vicious night thing.

"Whoever you were," Carole whispered, "you're free now. Free to return to God."

She gripped the shaft of the crucifix to remove it but found it fixed in the seared flesh like a steel rod set in concrete.

Something howled again. Closer.

She had to get back inside, but she couldn't leave Bern out here.

Swiftly she returned to Bernadette's side, worked her hands through the grass under her back and knees, and lifted her into her arms. She staggered under the weight. Dear Lord, for such a thin woman she was heavy.

Carole carried Bernadette back to the convent as fast as her rubbery legs would allow. Once inside, she bolted the door, then tried to carry her up the steep stairway. She stopped on the third step. She'd intended to take Bern's body back to her room, but who knew when the poor girl would be buried? Might be days. And the second floor got warm during the day. Better to lay her out in the cellar where it was cooler.

With Bernadette in her arms she struggled down the narrow stairwell to the cellar, almost falling twice along the way. She stretched her out on an old couch. She straightened Bern's thin legs, crossed her hands over her blood-splattered chest, and arranged her torn nightgown and raincoat around her as best she could. She adjusted the wimple on her head. Then she ran up to Bernadette's room and returned with her bedspread. She draped her from head to toe, then knelt beside her.

Looking down at that still form under the quilt she had helped Bernadette make, Carole sagged against the couch and began to cry. She tried to say a requiem prayer but her grief-racked mind had lost the words. So she sobbed aloud and asked God why? How could He let this happen to a dear, sweet innocent who had wished only to spend her life serving Him? WHY?

But no answer came.

When Carole finally controlled her tears, she forced herself to her weary feet and made her way back to the main floor. When she saw the light on in the front foyer, she knew she should turn it off. She stepped over the still form of Rosita under the blood-soaked blanket. Two violent deaths here on the church grounds, a place devoted to God. How many more beyond these grounds?

She knew she should carry Rosita to the basement as well, but lacked the strength—of either will or body.

Tomorrow . . . first thing tomorrow morning, Rosita. I promise.

She turned off the light and raced through the dark back up to her own room where she huddled shivering in her bed.

CAROLE . . .

Carole awoke in a cold sweat. Good Friday again. How many times must she relive that night?

She pushed herself up from the mattress and stumbled to

the bathroom. She poured an inch of water from the tap into a glass and drank it down. Didn't want to risk drinking too much without boiling it first.

At least the water was still running. Was that the vampires' doing? Carole wouldn't be surprised. Water was one of the necessities of life. It seemed to her the vampires wanted a certain number of the living to survive, but not to communicate. Which would explain why the electricity and the telephones went out that first weekend. Keep people isolated and insulated from any message of hope.

She found her way back to the bed and buried her head under the pillow. She needed sleep—dreamless sleep that would allow her to wake up refreshed instead of exhausted. She didn't want to dream of Good Friday again, or worse, the following day . . . the worst day of her life.

HOLY SATURDAY . . .

Carole awoke to the wail of sirens. She sat up in bed, blinking in the morning light.

A dream . . . please, God, show me that last night was all a dream.

But her throat tightened at the sight of Bernadette's empty mattress on the floor beside her bed. No . . . not a dream. A living nightmare.

She'd stayed up till dawn, then she'd pulled the bedspread from the window and fallen into exhausted sleep.

The sirens . . . closer now. She crept to the window and peeked at the street below. Two police cars, red and blue lights flashing, roared past the front of the convent and made squealing turns into the church parking lot.

The police! They've come!

Carole rose and hurried across the hall to Bern's room in time to see them slow to a stop before the church.

Thank you, God, she thought. All is not lost. The police are still on the job.

Before pushing away from the window she searched the lawn to the left of the church for the remains of the vampire she'd killed last night. A bright, clear, unconscionably beautiful morning, with a high trail of brown smoke drifting from the east. She couldn't find the vampire, but she spotted Bernadette's wooden cross lying in a man-shaped puddle of brown ooze on the grass. Could that be all that remained of—?

Can't worry about that now, she thought as she dashed back into the hall and down the rear stairs. She had to get to the police, tell them about Bernadette. They'd take her to a morgue or a funeral home where Carole could arrange for a proper burial.

She reached the rear door and had just turned back the deadbolt when she glanced through the glass. The sight of a lean, wolfish man, all in denim, uncoiling from the front passenger seat of the first car froze her heart. He settled a cowboy hat over his long brown hair and looked around, smirking as if he owned the world. A tattooed blond woman in a leather vest got out of the driver seat while two more men in rough clothes slithered from the second car. The first wore his long black hair in a single braid down the middle of his back; the second was sandy haired and balding, wearing a scraggly beard to compensate for what he'd lost on his scalp. All four wore wraparound sunglasses and had silvery earrings dangling from their right lobes.

Carole ducked away from the door and jammed her hands against her mouth. She'd seen these people before, last night, leading the caravan of trucks carrying the undead into town. It seemed so long ago, a lifetime. But this could only mean that the police had lost. The undead and their caretakers were in control now.

But what were they doing here at St. Anthony's?

She crept away from the door and down the hall toward the kitchen. The windows over the sink looked out toward the church. She could watch from there and see without being seen. She needed to know what they were up to. She leaned over the big double sink and cranked the window open an inch or two, just enough to hear what they were saying.

She sniffed the air that wafted through the opening. Something burning somewhere . . . smelled like some sort of meat. She glanced at the brown smoke trailing across the sky. Could that be—?

A car door slammed. She watched the one in the cowboy hat heft a crowbar as he walked from his police car to the side door of the church. Swinging it like a baseball bat he started bashing the hooked end against the doorknob. The clang of metal on metal echoed like a church bell through the eerie silence of the morning. Then he reversed his grip and rammed the tip of the long end between the door and the frame. A few hard yanks and the door popped open.

The woman and the two other men ran inside while the cowboy returned to the police car. He leaned against the fender and lit a cigarette; he carelessly bounced the crowbar against the hood, denting it with every bounce.

A few minutes later the two other men emerged, dragging Father Palmeri between them. The priest had a bloody nose and was blubbering in fear, begging them to let him go.

The sandy-haired man laughed. "Found him hiding in the basement! Lookit him! Peed his pants!"

Carole shook her head in dismay when she saw the darker stain on Father Palmeri's black cassock. God forgive her, she'd never liked the man, and after last night when he could have saved Bernadette simply by letting her into the church, well, she liked him even less. He was a man of God. He was supposed to set an example.

Then the woman appeared. She'd draped herself in Father Palmeri's long white chasuble and came out dancing and skipping behind the whimpering priest.

Carole felt her anger begin to boil. How dare this . . . this tramp sully holy vestments like that. It was sacrilege.

"You like basements, priest?" the cowboy said, grinning.

"Good. 'Cause you're gonna be seeing a lot of them from now on."

Carole's stomach dropped. What did that mean? Were they going to turn him into a vampire? Oh, no. They couldn't do that. Not to a priest.

She had to help him, but what could she do? She was one woman and there were four of them. She watched as they locked Father Palmeri in the caged rear compartment of one of the cars. Then they started toward the convent, the cowboy in the lead, the crowbar on his shoulder.

No! Not here! Not now! And she'd unlocked the door.

Hide! The basement? No. She had to pass the rear door to reach it. They'd see her for sure. She could make it to the second floor but couldn't think of anyplace to hide up there.

She did a quick turn and her gaze came to rest on the big institutional-size oven to her left. She yanked down the door and looked inside. Could she fit? Maybe, maybe not. But even if she did fit, the plate glass window in the door would give her away. But no. A closer look showed that it was fogged with baked-on grease. Bless old Sister Mary Margaret's bad eyes. Last week was her turn to clean the oven. She never did a good job, for which Carole was now grateful.

Moving as quickly as she could without causing a racket, she slid out the two metal racks and slipped them between the oven and the neighboring cabinet. She pulled a long-handled metal spatula from the wall rack and bent the end into an acute angle. Then she sidled into the close space, her flannel nightgown sticking to the grease-splattered surfaces, and tucked her knees against her chest.

She fit. Barely. Now to get the door closed. She reached out with the spatula, hooked its bent end around the upper edge of the oven door, and pulled. It barely budged. These old oven doors were heavy. Straining her muscles, she managed to pull it a quarter of the way closed when the spatula slipped off. The door fell back with a clank.

She felt her heart kick into a higher gear as she tried

again. The cowboy and his gang would be walking in any—

She heard the back door slam open and a woman's voice say, "Nice of them to leave the place unlocked."

"Probably means it's empty," said a voice she recognized as the cowboy's. "Check it out anyway. See if we can put a nun on Gregor's plate, too."

The woman snickered. "Yeah! A priest-and-nun combo platter!"

"A three-way!" someone else said.

Lots of laughter at that. But for Carole, only terror clawing at her gut. She had to close this door. Now.

She stretched out and again hooked the spatula end over the edge. The handle slipped in her sweaty palm. She tightened her grip and began to pull.

"I'll take this floor," said the cowboy's voice. "Al, you and Kenny check out upstairs. Jackie, you take the basement."

Carole heard feet moving, some away, some pounding up the stairs, and one set moving closer, toward the kitchen. The oven door was a third of the way up now. Her arm was aching. If only she could use both hands. She set her teeth and gave the door a yank. To her shock it snapped toward her once it passed the halfway mark and she had to release the spatula to keep it from slamming shut. She eased it closed just as someone walked into the room.

Carole closed her eyes and shuddered with relief, but that vanished when she opened them again and saw the spatula still hooked on the door.

She stifled a bleat of terror. The business end was sticking outside.

She looked through the grimy glass and saw a pair of denim-clad legs enter the kitchen and stop directly before the oven. The cowboy—had he spotted the spatula?

Sweet Jesus, don't let him see it!

Carole almost wept when the legs moved on.

"Let's see what we got here," she heard him say.

She heard cabinet doors swing open, heard their contents

hit the floor, heard drawers pulled from their slots and dropped. He couldn't be looking for a person—not in those spaces. What was he after?

"Ay, here we go."

More footsteps. Father Palmeri's white chasuble stopped in front of the oven. The woman.

"Whatcha got there, Stan?"

"First, whatcha find in the basement?"

"Dead nun. Least I'm pretty sure she's a nun. She's wearin a tore-up nightie and a raincoat, but she's got one of those veil hats on her head. And she was bit."

"And she still got her head?"

"Yeah. Think she ran into that dead feral outside?"

"Dunno, but someone sure kicked his ass, huh?"

"True that." The woman moved out of view of the oven glass. "So whatcha got there?"

"Homemade chocolate chip cookies. Still fresh."

"Ooh, gimme!"

Carole bit back a sob. She and Bernadette had baked those yesterday afternoon, and now these human slime were eating them.

"Yo, Stan," said a male voice. "Nobody upstairs but we got a dead goth chick in the front hall."

"Was she bit?"

"Nah. Some kinda steel pipe stickin from her gut."

"Whoa! What kinda weird shit went down here last night? Sounds like my kinda party."

They laughed and then went silent. Stuffing their faces with her cookies, Carole supposed.

Finally the cowboy said, "All right. The priest house is next. We'll take these with us. Somebody remind me we gotta come back for the bit one. We should toss her on the pile before sunset."

With that they shuffled out, leaving Carole alone and cramped and sweating in the oven. She closed her eyes and pretended she was sitting on a pew in the cool open spaces

of St. Anthony's, savoring the peaceful air as she waited for
mass to begin.

† † †

Carole waited more than an hour before she dared to leave
the oven. After slowly straightening her cramped back, the
first thing she did was peek through the kitchen window. She
sagged against the sink with relief when she saw the police
cars gone.

Next she ran up to her room and exchanged her grease-
spotted nightgown for a plaid blouse and khaki slacks. Usually she'd wear a skirt, but not today.

She looked around. Now . . . what?

She couldn't stay here in the convent. She had to move
somewhere else. But where? And how could she leave
Bernadette here to be hauled off by those human animals so
they could "toss her on the pile," whatever that meant?

Carole knew she had to do something. But what?

Since joining the convent a dozen years ago, straight out of
high school, all important decisions had been taken out of her
hands. The Sisters of Mercy had put her through college at
Georgian Court where she'd earned her teaching degree. All
along she'd followed the instructions of Sister Superior. A
calm, contemplative existence of poverty, chastity, and obedience, devoted to prayer and study and doing the Lord's work.

Now *she* had to decide. She wanted to hide Bernadette's
body, but couldn't think of a single safe place. She wanted to
move Rosita's body down to the basement but didn't dare:
The cowboy would know someone was here.

So she spent the day in a state of mental and emotional
paralysis. She prayed for guidance, she walked the halls, she
sat on her bed and stared out the window, watching for the
cowboy and his gang, dreading the moment they returned.

The only decision she made was to hide under her bed
when they did.

But they didn't return. The afternoon dragged into evening, and then the sun was down. Carole allowed herself the faint hope that they'd forgotten about Bernadette or had become involved in more pressing matters.

She draped her window, lit a candle, and began to pray.

She didn't know what time the power went out. She had no idea how long she'd been kneeling beside her bed when she glanced at the digital alarm clock on her night table and saw that its face had gone dark.

Not that a power failure mattered. She noticed barely an inch of the candle left. She held her watch face near the flame. Only 2 A.M. Would this night ever end?

She was tempted to lift the bedspread draped over the window and peek outside, but was afraid of what she might see.

How long until dawn? she wondered, rubbing her eyes. Last night had seemed endless, but this—

Beyond her locked door, a faint creak came from somewhere along the hall. It could have been anything—the wind in the attic, the old building settling—but it had sounded like floorboards creaking.

And then she heard it again.

Carole froze, still on her knees, hands still folded in prayer, elbows resting on the bed, and listened. More creaks, closer, and something else . . . a rhythmic shuffle . . . in the hall . . . approaching her door . . .

Footsteps.

With her heart punching frantically against the wall of her chest, Carole leaped to her feet and stepped close to the door, listening with her ear almost touching the wood. Yes. Footsteps. Slow. And soft, like bare feet scuffing the floor. Coming this way. Closer. Right outside the door now.

Carole felt a sudden chill, as if a wave of icy air had penetrated the wood, but the footsteps didn't pause. They passed her door, moving on.

And then they stopped.

Carole had her ear pressed against the wood now. She

could hear her pulse pounding through her head as she strained for the next sound. And then it came, more shuffling outside in the hall, almost confused at first, and then the footsteps began again.

Coming back.

This time they stopped directly outside Carole's door. The cold was back again, a damp, penetrating chill that reached for her bones. Carole backed away from it.

And then the nob turned. Slowly. The door creaked with the weight of a body leaning against it from the other side, but Carole's bolt held.

Then a voice. Hoarse. A single whispered word, barely audible, but a shout could not have startled her more.

"Carole?"

Carole didn't reply—*couldn't* reply.

"Carole, it's me. Bern. Let me in."

Against her will, a low moan escaped Carole. No, no, no, this couldn't be Bernadette. Bernadette was dead. Carole had left her cooling body lying in the basement. This was some horrible joke . . .

Or was it? Maybe Bernadette had become one of *them*, one of the very things that had killed her.

But the voice on the other side of the door was not that of some ravenous beast . . .

"Please let me in, Carole. I'm frightened out here alone."

Maybe Bern *is* alive, Carole thought, her mind racing, ranging for an answer. I'm no doctor. I could have been wrong about her being dead. Maybe she survived . . .

She stood trembling, torn between the desperate, aching need to see her friend alive, and the wary terror of being tricked by whatever creature Bernadette might have become.

"Carole?"

Carole wished for a peephole in the door, or at the very least a chain lock, but she had neither, and she had to do something. She couldn't stand here like this and listen to that plaintive voice any longer without going mad. She had to *know*. Without giving herself any more time to think, she snapped back the bolt and pulled the door open, ready to face whatever awaited her in the hall.

She gasped. "Bernadette!"

Her friend stood just beyond the threshold, swaying, stark naked.

Not completely naked. She still wore her wimple, although it was askew on her head, and a strip of cloth had been layered around her neck to dress her throat wound. In the wan, flickering candlelight that leaked from Carole's room, she saw that the blood that had splattered her was gone. Carole had never seen Bernadette unclothed before. She'd never realized how thin she was. Her ribs rippled beneath the skin of her chest, disappearing only beneath the scant padding of her small breasts with their erect nipples; the bones of her hips and pelvis bulged around her flat belly. Her normally fair skin was almost blue white. The only other colors were the dark pools of her eyes and the orange splotches of hair on her head and her pubes.

"Carole," she said weakly. "Why did you leave me?"

The sight of Bernadette standing before her, alive, speaking, had drained most of Carole's strength; the added weight of guilt from her words nearly drove her to her knees. She sagged against the door frame.

"Bern . . ." Carole's voice failed her. She swallowed and tried again. "I—I thought you were dead. And . . . what happened to your clothes?"

Bernadette raised her hand to her throat. "I tore up my nightgown for a bandage. Can I come in?"

Carole straightened and opened the door further. "Oh, Lord, yes. Come in. Sit down. I'll get you a blanket."

Bernadette shuffled into the room, head down, eyes fixed on the floor. She moved like someone on drugs. But then, after losing so much blood, it was a wonder she could walk at all.

"Don't want a blanket," Bern said. "Too hot. Aren't you hot?"

She backed herself stiffly onto Carole's bed, then lifted

her ankles and sat cross-legged, facing her. Mentally, Carole explained the casual, blatant way she exposed herself by the fact that Bernadette was still recovering from a horrific trauma, but that made it no less discomfiting.

Carole glanced at the crucifix on the wall over her bed, above and behind Bernadette. For a moment, as Bernadette had seated herself beneath it, she thought she had seen it glow. It must have been reflected candlelight. She turned away and retrieved a spare blanket from the closet. She unfolded it and wrapped it around Bernadette's shoulders and over her spread knees, covering her.

"I'm thirsty, Carole. Could you get me some water?"

Her voice was strange. Lower pitched and hoarse, yes, as might be expected after the throat wound she'd suffered. But something else had changed in her voice, something Carole could not pin down.

"Of course. You'll need fluids. Lots of fluids."

The bathroom was only two doors down. She took her water pitcher, lit a second candle, and left Bernadette on the bed, looking like an Indian draped in a serape.

When she returned with the full pitcher, she was startled to find the bed empty. She spied Bernadette by the window. She hadn't opened it, but she'd pulled off the bedspread drape and raised the shade. She stood there, staring out at the night. And she was naked again.

Carole looked around for the blanket and found it . . . hanging on the wall over her bed . . .

Covering the crucifix.

Part of Carole screamed at her to run, to flee down the hall and not look back. But another part of her insisted she stay. This was her friend. Something terrible had happened to Bernadette and she needed Carole now, probably more than she'd needed anyone in her entire life. And if someone was going to help her, it was Carole. *Only* Carole.

She placed the pitcher on the nightstand.

"Bernadette," she said, her mouth as dry as the timbers in these old walls, "the blanket . . ."

"I was hot," Bernadette said without turning.

"I brought you the water. I'll pour—"

"I'll drink it later. Come and watch the night."

"I don't want to see the night. It frightens me."

Bernadette turned, a faint smile on her lips. "But the darkness is so beautiful."

She stepped closer and stretched her arms toward Carole, laying a hand on each shoulder and gently massaging the terror-tightened muscles there. A sweet lethargy began to seep through Carole. Her eyelids began to drift closed . . . so tired . . . so long since she'd had any sleep . . .

No!

She forced her eyes open and gripped Bernadette's cold hands, pulling them from her shoulders. She pressed the palms together and clasped them between her own.

"Let's pray, Bern. With me: Hail Mary, full of grace . . ."

"No!"

". . . the Lord is with thee. Blessed art thou . . ."

Her friend's face twisted in rage. "I said, NO, damn you!"

Carole struggled to keep a grip on Bernadette's hands but she was too strong.

". . . amongst women . . ."

And suddenly Bernadette's struggles ceased. Her face relaxed, her eyes cleared, even her voiced changed, still hoarse, but higher in pitch, lighter in tone as she took up the words of the prayer.

"And Blessed is the fruit of thy womb . . ." Bernadette struggled with the next word, unable to say it. Instead she gripped Carole's hands with painful intensity and loosed a torrent of her own words. "Carole, get out! Get out, oh, please, for the love of God, get out now! There's not much of me left in here, and soon I'll be like the ones that killed me and I'll be after killing you! So run, Carole! Hide! Lock yourself in the chapel downstairs but get away from me *now!*"

Carole knew now what had been missing from Bernadette's

voice—her brogue. But now it was back. This was the real
Bernadette speaking. She was back! Her friend, her sister was
back! Carole bit back a sob.

"Oh, Bern, I can help! I can—"

Bernadette pushed her toward the door. "*No one* can help
me, Carole!" She ripped the makeshift bandage from her
neck, exposing the jagged, partially healed wound and the
ragged ends of the torn blood vessels within it. "It's too late
for me, but not for you. They're a bad lot and I'll be one of
them again soon, so get out while you—"

Suddenly Bernadette stiffened and her features shifted.
Carole knew immediately that the brief respite her friend
had stolen from the horror that gripped her was over. Something else was back in command.

Carole turned and ran.

But the Bernadette-thing was astonishingly swift. Carole
had barely reached the threshold when a steel-fingered hand
gripped her upper arm and yanked her back, nearly dislocat-
ing her shoulder. She cried out in pain and terror as she was
spun about and flung across the room. Her hip struck hard
against the rickety old spindle chair by her desk, knocking it
over as she landed in a heap beside it.

Carole groaned with the pain. As she shook her head to
clear it, she saw Bernadette approaching, her movements
swift, more assured now, her teeth bared—so many teeth,
and so much longer than the old Bernadette's—her fingers
curved, reaching for Carole's throat. With each passing second there was less and less of Bernadette about her.

Carole tried to back away, her frantic hands and feet slipping on the floor as she pressed her spine against the wall.
She had nowhere to go. She pulled the fallen chair atop her
and held it as a shield against the Bernadette-thing. The face
that had once belonged to her dearest friend grimaced with
contempt as she swung her hand at the chair. It scythed
through the spindles, splintering them like matchsticks,
sending the carved headpiece flying. A second blow cracked

the seat in two. A third and fourth sent the remnants of the chair hurtling to opposite sides of the room.

Carole was helpless now. All she could do was pray.

"Our Father, who art—"

"Too late for that to help you now, *Carole*!" she rasped, spitting her name.

". . . hallowed be Thy Name . . ." Carole said, quaking in terror as frigid undead fingers closed on her throat.

And then the Bernadette-thing froze, listening. Carole heard it too. An insistent tapping. On the window. The creature turned to look, and Carole followed her gaze.

A face was peering through the glass.

Carole blinked but it didn't go away. This was the second floor! How—?

And then a second face appeared, this one upside down, looking in from the top of the window. And then a third, and a fourth, each more bestial than the last. And as each appeared it began to tap its fingers and knuckles on the window glass.

"NO!" the Bernadette-thing screamed at them. "You can't come in! She's mine! No one touches her but *me*!"

She turned back to Carole and smiled, showing those teeth that had never fit in Bernadette's mouth. "They can't cross a threshold unless invited in by one who lives there. *I* live here—or at least I did. And I'm not sharing you, Carole."

She turned again and raked a clawlike hand at the window. "Go aWAY! She's MINE!"

Carole glanced to her left. The bed was only a few feet away. And above it—the blanket-shrouded crucifix. If she could reach it . . .

She didn't hesitate. With the mad tapping tattoo from the window echoing around her, Carole gathered her feet beneath her and sprang for the bed. She scrambled across the sheets, one hand outstretched, reaching for the blanket—

A manacle of icy flesh closed around her calf and roughly dragged her back.

"Oh, no, bitch," said the hoarse, unaccented voice of the Bernadette-thing. "Don't even *think* about it!"

It grabbed two fistfuls of fabric at the back of Carole's blouse and hurled her across the room as if she weighed no more than a pillow. The wind whooshed out of Carole as she slammed against the far wall. She heard ribs crack. She fell among the splintered ruins of the chair, pain lancing through her right flank. The room wavered and blurred. But through the roaring in her ears she still heard that insistent tapping on the window.

As her vision cleared she saw the Bernadette-thing's naked form gesturing again to the creatures at the window, now a mass of salivating mouths and tapping fingers.

"Watch!" she hissed. "Watch me!"

With that, she loosed a long, howling scream and lunged, arms curved before her, body arcing toward Carole in a flying leap. The scream, the tapping, the faces at the window, the dear friend who now wanted only to slaughter her—it all was suddenly too much for Carole. She wanted to roll away but couldn't get her body to move. Her hand found the broken seat of the chair by her hip. Instinctively she pulled it closer. She closed her eyes as she raised it between herself and the horror hurtling toward her.

The impact drove the wood of the seat against Carole's chest; she groaned as new stabs of pain shot through her ribs. But the Bernadette-thing's triumphant feeding cry cut off abruptly and devolved into a coughing gurgle.

Suddenly the weight was released from Carole's chest, and the chair seat with it.

And the tapping at the window ceased.

Carole opened her eyes to see the naked Bernadette-thing standing above her, straddling her, holding the chair seat before her, choking and gagging as she struggled with it.

At first Carole didn't understand. She drew her legs back and inched away along the wall. And then she saw what had happened.

Three splintered spindles had remained fixed in that half of the broken seat, and those spindles were now firmly and deeply embedded in the center of the Bernadette-thing's chest. She wrenched wildly at the chair seat, trying to dislodge the oak daggers but succeeded only in breaking them off at skin level. She dropped the remnant of the seat and swayed like a tree in a storm, her mouth working spasmodically as her hands fluttered ineffectually over the bloodless wounds between her ribs and the slim wooden stakes out of reach within them.

Abruptly she dropped to her knees with a dull thud. Then, only inches from Carole, she slumped into a splay-legged squat. The agony faded from her face and she closed her eyes. She fell forward against Carole.

Carole threw her arms around her friend and gathered her close.

"Oh Bern, oh Bern, oh Bern," she moaned. "I'm so sorry. If only I'd got there sooner!"

Bernadette's eyes fluttered open and the darkness was gone. Only her own spring-sky blue remained, clear, grateful. Her lips began to curve upward but made it only halfway to a smile, then she was gone.

Carole hugged the limp cold body closer and moaned in boundless grief and anguish to the unfeeling walls. She saw the leering faces begin to crawl away from the window and she shouted at them though her tears.

"Go! That's it! Run away and hide! Soon it'll be light and then *I'll* come looking for *you*! For *all* of you! And woe to any of you that I find!"

She cried over Bernadette's body a long time. And then she wrapped it in a sheet and held and rocked her dead friend in her arms until sunrise on Easter Sunday.

CAROLE . . .

The voice yanked her from sleep, the voice that sounded like
Bernadette's but robbed of all her sweetness and compassion.

   *<That was when you turned your back on the Lord, Car-
ole. That was when you began your life of sin.>*

After the horrors of Easter weekend had come loneliness.
Carole had begun talking to herself in her head—just for
company of sorts—to ease her through the long empty
hours. But the voice had taken on a life of its own, becoming
Bernadette's. In a way, then, Bern was still alive.

"Yes," Carole said, sitting up on the side of the bed and
peering out the window at the lightening sky. "I suppose that
was when it began."

She'd walked out of the tomb of St. Anthony's convent on
Easter morning and left the old Sister Carole Hanarty behind. That gentle soul, happy to spend her days and nights in
the service of the Lord, praying, fasting, teaching chemistry
to reluctant adolescents, and holding to her vows of poverty,
chastity, and obedience, was dead.

In her place was a new Sister Carole, tempered in the
forge of that night and recast into someone relentlessly
vengeful and fearless to the point of recklessness.

And perhaps, she admitted with no shame or regret, more
than a little mad.

She'd departed St. Anthony's and begun her hunt. She'd
been hunting ever since.

Carole stretched and glanced around the room. The walls
had been decked with family pictures of weddings and children when she'd moved herself in. She'd removed those
and lain the ones on the bureau and dresser face down. All
those smiling children . . . she couldn't bear their eyes
watching her.

She knew their names. The Bennetts—Kevin, Marie, and
their twin girls. She hadn't known them before, but Carole

felt she knew them now. She'd seen their family photos, seen the twins' bedroom.

She knew from the state of the empty house when she'd found it that the owners hadn't moved out. They'd been driven out. She hoped for the sake of their souls that they were dead now. Truly dead.

<*It's not too late to be turning back. You can start following the rules again. You can become a good person again and go back to doing the Lord's work.*>

"But the rules have changed," Carole whispered.

Being a good person meant something different than it had then. And doing the Lord's work . . . well, it was an entirely different sort of work now.

2

ZEV . . .

It had been almost a full minute since he'd slammed the brass knocker against the heavy oak door. That should have been proof enough. After all, wasn't the knocker in the shape of a cross? But no, they had to squint through their peephole and peer through the sidelights that framed the door.

Zev sighed and resigned himself to the scrutiny. He couldn't blame people for being cautious, but this seemed overly so. The sun was in the west and shining full on his back; he was all but silhouetted in it. What more did they want?

I should maybe take off my clothes and dance naked?

He gave a mental shrug and savored the salt tang of the sea air. The bulk of this huge Tudor mansion stood between him and the Atlantic, but the ocean's briny scent and rhythmic rumble were everywhere. He'd bicycled from Lakewood, which was only ten miles inland from here, but the warm May day and the bright sun beating on his dark blue suit coat had sweated him up. It had taken him longer than he'd planned to find this retreat house.

Spring Lake. The Irish Riviera. An Irish Catholic seaside

resort since before the turn of the century. He looked around at its carefully restored Victorian houses, the huge mansions facing the beach, the smaller homes set in neat rows running straight back from the ocean. Many of them were still occupied. Not like Lakewood. Lakewood was an empty shell.

Oh, they'd been smart, those bloodsuckers. They knew their easiest targets. Whenever they swooped into an area they went after officialdom first—the civic leaders, the cops, the firemen, the clergy. But after that, they attacked the non-Christian neighborhoods. And among Jews they picked the Orthodox first of the first. Smart. Where else would they be less likely to run up against a cross? It worked for them in Brooklyn and Queens, and so when they came south into New Jersey, spreading like a plague, they headed straight for the town with one of the largest collections of yeshivas in North America.

But after the Bensonhurst and Kew Gardens holocausts, the people in the Lakewood communities should not have taken quite so long to figure out what was going to happen. The Reformed and Conservative synagogues started handing out crosses at Shabbes—too late for many but it saved a few. Did the Orthodox congregations follow suit? No. They hid in their homes and shuls and yeshivas and read and prayed.

And were liquidated.

A cross, a crucifix—they held power over the undead, drove them away. Zev's fellow rabbis did not want to accept that simple fact because they could not face its devastating ramifications. To hold up a cross was to negate two thousand years of Jewish history, it was to say that the Messiah had come and they had missed him.

Did it say that? Zev didn't know. For all he knew, the undead predated Christianity, and their fear of crosses might be related to something else. Argue about it later—people were dying. But the rabbis had to argue it then and there. And as they argued, their people were slaughtered like cattle.

How Zev had railed at them, how he'd pleaded with them! Blind, stubborn fools! If a fire was consuming your house, would you refuse to throw water on it just because you'd always been taught not to believe in water? Zev had arrived at the rabbinical council wearing a cross and had been thrown out—literally sent hurtling through the front door. But at least he had managed to save a few of his own people. Too few.

He remembered his fellow Orthodox rabbis, though. All the ones who had refused to face the reality of the vampires' fear of crosses, who had forbidden their students and their congregations to wear crosses, who had watched those same students and congregations die en masse. And soon those very same rabbis were roaming their own community, hunting the survivors, preying on other yeshivas, other congregations, until the entire community was liquidated and its leaders incorporated into the brotherhood of the undead.

This was the most brilliant aspect of the undead tactics: Turn all the community leaders into their own kind and set them loose among the population. What could be more dismaying, more devastating than seeing the very people who should have been leading the resistance become enthusiastic participants in the slaughter?

The rabbis could have saved themselves, could have saved their people, but they would not bend to the reality of what was happening around them. Which, when Zev thought about it, was not at all out of character. Hadn't they spent generations learning to turn away from the rest of the world?

But now their greatest fear had come to pass: they'd been assimilated—with a vengeance.

Those early days of anarchic slaughter were over. Now that the undead held the ruling hand, the bloodletting had become more organized. But the damage to Zev's people had been done—and it was irreparable. Hitler would have been proud. His Nazi "final solution" was an afternoon picnic compared to the work of the undead. In a matter of months, in Israel and Eastern Europe, the undead did what Hitler's Reich could not do in all the years of the Second World War. Muslims and Hindus had fared just as poorly, but that was not Zev's concern. His heart did not bleed for Islam and India.

There's only a few of us now. So few and so scattered. A final Diaspora.

For a moment Zev was almost overwhelmed by grief, but he pushed it down, locked it back into that place where he kept his sorrows, and thought of how fortunate it was for his wife Chana that she died of natural causes before the horror began. Her soul had been too gentle to weather what had happened to their community.

Forcing himself back to the present, he looked around. Not such a bad place for a retreat, he thought. He wondered how many houses like this the Catholic Church owned.

A series of clicks and clacks drew his attention back to the door as numerous bolts were pulled in rapid succession. The door swung inward, revealing a nervous-looking young man in a long black cassock. As he looked at Zev his mouth twisted and he rubbed the back of his wrist across it to hide a smile.

"And what should be so funny?" Zev asked.

"I'm sorry. It's just—"

"I know," Zev said, waving off any explanation as he glanced down at the wooden cross slung on a cord around his neck. "I know."

A bearded Jew in a baggy serge suit wearing a yarmulke and a cross. Hilarious, no?

Nu? This was what the times demanded, this was what it came down to if he wanted to survive. And Zev did want to survive. Someone had to live to carry on the traditions of the Talmud and the Torah, even if there were hardly any Jews left alive in the world.

Zev stood on the sunny porch, waiting. The priest watched him in silence.

Finally Zev said, "Well, may a wandering Jew come in?"

"I won't stop you," the priest said, "but surely you don't expect me to invite you."

Ah, yes. Another precaution. The undead couldn't cross the threshold of a home unless invited, so don't invite. A good habit to cultivate, he supposed.

He stepped inside and the priest immediately closed the door behind him, relatching all the locks one by one. When he turned around Zev held out his hand.

"Rabbi Zev Wolpin, Father. I thank you for allowing me in."

"Brother Christopher, sir," he said, smiling and shaking Zev's hand. His suspicions seemed to have been allayed. "I'm not a priest yet. We can't offer you much here, but—"

"Oh, I won't be staying long. I just came to talk to Father Joseph Cahill."

Brother Christopher frowned. "Father Cahill isn't here at the moment."

"When will he be back?"

"I—I'm not sure. You see—"

"Father Cahill is on another bender," said a stentorian voice behind Zev.

He turned to see an elderly priest facing him from the far end of the foyer. White-haired, heavyset, also wearing a black cassock.

"I'm Rabbi Wolpin."

"Father Adams," the priest said, stepping forward and extending his hand.

As they shook Zev said, "Did you say he was on 'another' bender? I never knew Father Cahill to be much of a drinker."

The priest's face turned stony. "Apparently there was a lot we never knew about Father Cahill."

"If you're referring to that nastiness last year," Zev said, feeling the old anger rise in him, "I for one never believed it for a minute. I'm surprised anyone gave it the slightest credence."

"The veracity of the accusation was irrelevant in the final

analysis. The damage to Father Cahill's reputation was a fait accompli. The bishops' rules are clear. Father Palmeri was forced to request his removal for the good of St. Anthony's parish."

Zev was sure that sort of attitude had something to do with Father Joe being on "another bender."

"Where can I find Father Cahill?"

"He's in town somewhere, I suppose, making a spectacle of himself. If there's any way you can talk some sense into him, please do. Not only is he killing himself with drink but he's become a public embarrassment to the priesthood and to the Church."

Zev wondered which bothered Father Adams more. And as for embarrassing the priesthood, he was tempted to point out that too many others had done a bang-up job of that already. But he held his tongue.

"I'll try."

He waited for Brother Christopher to undo all the locks, then stepped toward the sunlight.

"Try Morton's down on Seventy-one," the younger man whispered as Zev passed.

I I I

Zev rode his bicycle south on route 71. So strange to see people on the streets. Not many, but more than he'd ever see in Lakewood again. Yet he knew that as the undead consolidated their grip on the rest of the coast, they'd start arriving with their living minions in the Catholic communities like Spring Lake, and then these streets would be as empty as Lakewood's.

He thought he remembered passing a place named Morton's on his way in. And then up ahead he saw it, by the railroad track crossing, a white stucco one-story box of a building with "Morton's Liquors" painted in big black letters along the side.

Father Adams' words echoed back to him . . . *on another bender* . . .

Zev pushed his bicycle to the front door and tried the

knob. Locked up tight. A look inside showed a litter of trash, broken bottles, and empty shelves. The windows were barred; the back door was steel and locked as securely as the front. So where was Father Joe?

Then, by the overflowing trash Dumpster, he spotted the basement window at ground level. It wasn't latched. Zev went down on his knees and pushed it open.

Cool, damp, musty air wafted against his face as he peered into the Stygian darkness. It occurred to him that he might be asking for trouble by sticking his head inside, but he had to give it a try. If Father Cahill wasn't here, Zev would begin the return trek to Lakewood and write off this whole trip as wasted effort.

"Father Joe?" he called. "Father Cahill?"

"That you again, Chris?" said a slightly slurred voice. "Go home, will you? I'm all right. I'll be back later."

"It's me, Joe. Zev. From Lakewood."

He heard shoes scraping on the floor and then a familiar face appeared in the shaft of light from the window.

"Well I'll be damned. It *is* you! Thought you were Brother Chris come to drag me back to the retreat house. Gets scared I'm gonna get stuck out after dark. So how ya doin', Reb? Glad to see you're still alive. Come on in!"

Zev noted Father Cahill's glassy eyes and how he swayed ever so slightly, like a skyscraper in the wind. His hair was uncombed, and his faded jeans and worn Bruce Springsteen *Tunnel of Love* Tour sweatshirt made him look more like a laborer than a priest.

Zev's heart twisted at the sight of his friend in such condition. Such a *mensch* like Father Joe shouldn't be acting like a *shikker*. Maybe it was a mistake coming here.

"I don't have that much time, Joe. I came to tell you—"

"Get your bearded ass down here and have a drink or I'll come up and drag you down."

"All right," Zev said. "I'll come in but I won't have a drink."

He hid his bike behind the Dumpster, then squeezed

through the window. Joe helped him to the floor. They embraced, slapping each other on the back. Father Joe was a bigger man, a giant from Zev's perspective. At six-four he was ten inches taller, at thirty-five he was a quarter-century younger; he had a muscular frame, thick brown hair, and—on better days—clear blue eyes.

"You're grayer, Zev, and you've lost weight."

"Kosher food is not so easily come by these days."

"All kinds of food are getting scarce." He touched the cross slung from Zev's neck and smiled. "Nice touch. Goes well with your *zizith*."

Zev fingered the fringe protruding from under his shirt. Old habits didn't die easily.

"Actually, I've grown rather fond of it."

"So what can I pour you?" the priest said, waving an arm at the crates of liquor stacked around him. "My own private reserve. Name your poison."

"I don't want a drink."

"Come on, Reb. I've got some nice hundred-proof Stoli here. You've got to have at least *one* drink—"

"Why? Because you think maybe you shouldn't drink alone?"

Father Joe winced. "Ouch!"

"All right," Zev said. "*Bisel*. I'll have *one* drink on the condition that you *don't* have one. Because I wish to talk to you."

The priest considered that a moment, then reached for the vodka bottle.

"Deal."

He poured a generous amount into a paper cup and handed it over. Zev took a sip. He was not a drinker and when he did imbibe he preferred his vodka ice cold from a freezer. But this was tasty. Father Cahill sat back on a case of Jack Daniel's and folded his arms.

"*Nu?*" the priest said with a Jackie Mason shrug.

Zev had to laugh. "Joe, I still say that somewhere in your family tree is Jewish blood."

For a moment he felt light, almost happy. When was the

last time he had laughed? Probably at their table near the back of Horovitz's deli, shortly before the St. Anthony's nastiness began, well before the undead came.

Zev thought of the day they'd met. He'd been standing at the counter at Horovitz's waiting for Yussel to wrap up the stuffed derma he'd ordered when this young giant walked in. He towered over the rabbis and yeshiva students in the place, looking as Irish as Paddy's pig, and wearing a Roman collar. He said he'd heard this was the only place on the whole Jersey Shore where you could get a decent corned beef sandwich. He ordered one and cheerfully warned that it better be good. Yussel asked him what could he know about good corned beef and the priest replied that he'd grown up in Bensonhurst. Well, about half the people in Horovitz's on that day—and on any other day, for that matter—had grown up in Bensonhurst, and before you knew it they were all asking him if he knew such-and-such a store and so-and-so's deli.

Zev then informed the priest—with all due respect to Yussel Horovitz behind the counter—that the best corned beef sandwich in the world was to be had at Shmuel Rosenberg's Jerusalem Deli in Bensonhurst. Father Cahill said he'd been there and agreed one hundred percent.

Yussel served him his sandwich then. As the priest took a huge bite out of the corned beef on rye, the normal *tumel* of a deli at lunchtime died away until Horovitz's was as quiet as a shul on Sunday morning. Everyone watched him chew, watched him swallow. Then they waited. Suddenly his face broke into this big Irish grin.

"I'm afraid I'm going to have to change my vote," he said. "Horovitz's of Lakewood makes the best corned beef sandwich in the world."

Amid cheers and warm laughter, Zev led Father Cahill to the rear table that would become theirs, and sat with this canny and charming gentile who had so easily won over a roomful of strangers and provided such a *mechaieh* for Yussel. He learned that the young priest was the new assistant to Father Palmeri, the pastor at St. Anthony's Catholic Church at the northern end of Lakewood. Father Palmeri had been there for years but Zev had never so much as seen his face. He asked Father Cahill—who wanted to be called Joe—about life in Brooklyn these days and they talked for an hour.

During the following months they would run into each other so often at Horovitz's that they decided to meet regularly for lunch, on Mondays and Thursdays. They did so for years, discussing religion—oy, the religious discussions!—politics, economics, philosophy, life in general. During those lunchtimes they solved most of the world's problems. Zev was sure they'd have solved them all if the scandal at St. Anthony's hadn't resulted in Father Joe's removal from the parish.

But that was in another time, another world. The world before the undead took over.

Zev shook his head as he considered the current state of Father Joe in the dusty basement of Morton's Liquors.

"It's about the vampires, Joe," he said, taking another sip of the Stoli. "They've taken over St. Anthony's."

Father Joe snorted and shrugged.

"They're in the majority now, Zev, remember? They've taken over the whole East Coast. Why should St. Anthony's be different from any other parish?"

"I didn't mean the parish. I meant the church."

The priest's eyes widened slightly. "The church? They've taken over the building itself?"

"Every night," Zev said. "Every night they are there."

"That's a holy place. How do they manage that?"

"They've desecrated the altar, destroyed all the crosses. St. Anthony's is no longer a holy place."

"Too bad," Father Joe said, looking down and shaking his head sadly. "It was a fine old church." He looked up again. "How do you know about what's going on at St. Anthony's? It's not exactly in your neighborhood."

"A neighborhood I don't exactly have any more."

Father Joe reached over and gripped his shoulder with a huge hand.

"I'm sorry, Zev. I heard your people got hit pretty hard over there. Sitting ducks, huh? I'm really sorry."

Sitting ducks. An appropriate description.

"Not as sorry as I, Joe," Zev said. "But since my neighborhood is gone, and since I have hardly any friends left, I use the daylight hours to wander. So call me the Wandering Jew. And in my wanderings I meet some of your old parishioners."

The priest's face hardened. His voice became acid.

"Do you, now. And how fare the remnants of my devoted flock?"

"They've lost all hope, Joe. They wish you were back."

He barked a bitter laugh. "Sure they do! Just like they rallied behind me when my name and honor were being dragged through the muck. Yeah, they want me back. I'll bet!"

"Such anger, Joe. It doesn't become you."

"Bullshit. That was the old Joe Cahill, the naive turkey who believed all his faithful parishioners would back him up. But no. A child points a finger and the bishop removes me. And how do the people I dedicated my life to respond? They all stand by in silence as I'm railroaded out of my parish."

"It's hard for the commonfolk to buck a bishop."

"Maybe. But I can't forget how they stood quietly by while I was stripped of my position, my dignity, my integrity, of everything I wanted to be . . ."

Zev thought Joe's voice was going to break. He was about to reach out to him when the priest coughed and squared his shoulders.

"Meanwhile, I'm a pariah over here in the retreat house, a goddamn leper. Some of them actually believe—" He broke off in a growl. "Ah, what's the use? It's over and done. Most of the parish is dead anyway, I suppose. And if I'd stayed there I'd probably be dead too. So maybe it worked out for the best. And who gives a shit anyway?"

"Last night I met someone who does. She saved me from one of the winged ones."

"You were out at night?"

"Yes. A long story. She was dressed rather provocatively and knew me because she'd seen me with you."

Joe looked interested now. "What was her name?"

"She wouldn't say. But she begged me to find you and bring you back."

"Really." His interest seemed to be fading.

"Yes. She said when you heard what they've done to your church you'd come back and teach them a lesson they'll never forget."

"Sounds like you ran into an escaped mental patient," Joe said as he reached for the bottle of Glenlivet next to him.

"No-no!" Zev said. "You promised!"

Father Joe drew his hand back and crossed his arms across his chest.

"Talk on. I'm listening."

Joe had certainly changed for the worse. Morose, bitter, apathetic, self-pitying.

"They've taken over your church, just as they've taken over my temple. But the temple they use only for a dormitory. Your church, they've desecrated it. Each night they further defile it with butchery and blasphemy. Doesn't that mean anything to you?"

"It's Palmeri's parish. I've been benched. Let him take care of it."

"Father Palmeri is their leader."

"He should be. He's their pastor."

"No. He leads the undead in the obscenities they perform in the church."

Joe stiffened and the glassiness cleared from his eyes.

"Palmeri? He's one of them?"

Zev nodded. "More than that. He's one of the local leaders. He orchestrates their rituals."

Zev saw rage flare in the priest's eyes, saw his hands ball into fists, and for a moment he thought the old Father Joe was going to burst through.

Come on, Joe. Show me that Cahill fire.

But then he slumped back.

"Is that all you came to tell me?"

Zev hid his disappointment and nodded. "Yes."

"Good." He grabbed the Scotch bottle. "Because I need a drink."

Zev wanted to leave, yet he had to stay, had to probe deeper and see how much of his old friend was left, and how much had been replaced by this new, bitter, alien Joe Cahill. Maybe there was still hope. So they talked on.

┬ ┬ ┬

Zev looked up at the window and saw that it was dark.

"*Gevalt!* I didn't notice the time!"

Father Joe seemed surprised too. He stepped to the window and peered out.

"Damn! Sun's down!" He turned to Zev. "Lakewood's out of the question for you, Reb. Even the retreat house is too far to risk now. Looks like we're stuck here for the night."

"We'll be safe?"

He shrugged. "Why not? As far as I can tell I'm the only one who's been in here for weeks, and only in the daytime. Be pretty odd if one of those leeches decided to wander in here tonight."

"We'd have to invite it in, right?"

He shook his head. "Doesn't seem to work that way with stores. Only homes."

Zev's *guderim* twisted. "That's not good."

"Don't worry. We're okay if we don't attract attention. I've got a flashlight if we need it, but we're better off sitting here in the dark and shooting the breeze till sunrise." Father Joe smiled and picked up a huge silver cross, at least a foot in length, from atop one of the crates. "Besides, we're armed. And frankly, I can think of worse places to spend the night."

He stepped over to the case of Glenlivet and opened a fresh bottle. His capacity for alcohol was enormous.

Zev could think of worse places too. In fact he had spent a number of nights in much worse places since the Lakewood holocaust. He decided to put the time to good use.

"So, Joe. Maybe I should tell you some more about what's happening in Lakewood."

COWBOYS . . .

King of the world.

Al Hulett leaned back in the passenger seat of the big Cadillac convertible they'd just driven out of somebody's garage, burning rubber all the way, and let the night air mess with his spiky black hair.

As usual, Stan was driving with Jackie riding shotgun. Al and Kenny had the back seat with Heinekens in their fists, Slipknot's *Iowa* CD in the slot, and "Skin Ticket" blasting through the speakers. Al finished his Heinie and tossed the empty over his shoulder so it landed on the trunk top. He heard a faint, frightened yelp from within, then a crash as the bottle bounced off and shattered on the asphalt behind them.

He leaned back and pounded a fist on the trunk. "Ay, shuddup up in there! You're messin with my meditation!"

This brought a howl of laughter from Kenny, which didn't necessarily mean it was real funny, just that Kenny was always a good audience.

He and the Kenman had been together since grammar school. How many years was that now? Ten? Twelve? Couldn't be more than a dozen. No way. Whatever, the two of them had stuck together through it all, never breaking up, even when Kenny pulled that short jolt in Yardville on a B&E. Even when the whole world went to hell.

But they'd come through it all like gold. They'd hired out to the winners. Joined the best hunting pack around.

Coulda turned out different. He and Kenny coulda had their throats chewed out and their heads ripped off just like a bunch of guys they knew, but they happened to be the right guys in the right place at the right time.

The right place was a bar they'd broken into, and the right time had been Easter morning—didn't know it was Easter then, only learned that later.

Al and Kenny and some friends had started partying Friday afternoon in this old shotgun shack back in the pines. By Sunday morning they'd run out of booze, so they rode their Harleys out to Route 9. That was when they learned about all the shit that had went down the past two nights. So they'd broke into this bar-package store and were helping themselves to some liquid refreshment when this dude in a cowboy hat walked in. Said his name was Stan. Said he saw their Harleys outside and was wondering if they was the kinda guys who might like to go to work for the winners.

Al and Kenny weren't too sure about that at first, so Stan said the chai-slurpin, Chardonnay-sippin, Gap-wearin, hummus-dippin, classic-rock-listenin world that had thought "loser" every time it looked at them and had never given them a chance was on its knees now and did they want to help bust a coupla caps in its fuckin head to put it down for good?

That Stan, man, he had a way with words.

Still . . . workin for the vampires . . .

Then Stan had made them an offer they couldn't refuse.

So that was why Al was riding in a Caddy tonight 'stead of on a Harley.

King of the fucking world.

Well, not king, really. But at least a prince . . . when the sun was up.

Night was a whole different story.

If you could get used to the creeps you were working for, it wasn't too bad a set-up. Could have been worse, Al knew—a *lot* worse.

Like being cattle, for instance.

Pretty smart, those bloodsuckers. America thought it was ready for them but it wasn't. They hit high, they hit low, and before you knew it, they was in charge of the whole East Coast.

Well, almost in charge. They did whatever they damn well pleased at night, but they'd never be in charge around the clock because they couldn't be up and about in the daylight. They needed somebody to hold the fort for them between sunrise and sunset.

That was where Al and Kenny and the other cowboys came in. They'd all been made the same offer.

They could be cattle, or they could be cowboys and drive the cattle.

Not much of a choice as far as Al could see.

You see, the bloodsuckers had two ways of killing folks. They had the usual way of ripping into your neck and sucking out your blood. If they got you that way, you became one of them come the next sundown. But once they had the upper hand, they changed their feeding style. Smart, those bloodsuckers. If they got too many of their kind wandering around, they'd soon have nobody to feed on—a world full of chefs with nothing to cook. So after they were in control, they got the blood a different way, one that didn't involve sucking it out. You died unsucked, you stayed dead. Something they called true death.

But they'd offered Al and Stan and the guys *un*death. Be their cowboys, herd the cattle and take care of business between sunrise and sunset, be their muscle during the day, do a good job for ten years, and they'd see to it that you got done in the old-fashioned way, the way that left you like them. Undead. Immortal. One of the ruling class.

"Ay-yo, Al," Kenny shouted over the howl of "Disasterpiece." "What kinda vampire you gonna be?"

Not again, Al thought. They'd worked this over too many times for Al's taste. It was getting real old. But Kenny never seemed to tire of gnawing this particular bone.

Kenny had this pale cratered skin. Even though he was in his twenties he still got pimples. Looked like the man in the moon now, but in the old days he'd been a real pizza face.

Once he almost killed a guy who'd called him that. And he had this crazy red hair that used to stick out in all directions when he didn't cut it, but even when he did it Mohican style, like now, all shaved off on the sides and showing the ugly knobs on his skull, it looked crazier than ever. Made *Kenny* look crazier than ever. And Kenny was pretty crazy as it was.

"I can tell you what kind I ain't gonna be," Al said, "and that's one of them ferals."

"Ay, I'm down wit that. I'm gonna be a pilot, man. Get me some wings."

Jackie turned down the music and swiveled in the front seat. She was thin and blonde, with a left nostril ring and a stud through her right eyebrow, and she had this tat of a devil face sticking out a Gene Simmons-class tongue on her left delt. She dangled an arm over the back near Al's knees and sneered.

"Wings? You'll be lucky if you get a plate of Buffalo wings."

Stan seemed to think this was real funny. Even Al had to laugh a little.

Kenny made this sour face. "Funny. Real fuckin funny."

"How many kinds of vampires are there, anyway?" Al said.

He wasn't just trying to take the heat off Kenny, he really wanted to know. In the weeks since he'd joined the posse he'd noticed that some of the bloodsuckers could sprout wings and fly. Most just walked around like everybody else—only at night, of course—and looked like everybody else, although some had faces that seemed to turn uglier and uglier as time went on.

Then there was the kind that were pretty much like animals. These were scary. Al had only seen a couple of them from a distance and that was plenty close enough. Hardly nothing human left in their faces or the way they moved. Couldn't even talk. The other bloodsuckers called them "ferals" and they were like vampire shock troops. These were the guys they let loose when they first blew into a town. Al gathered they must be kinda hard to control because the other vampires kept them locked up pretty much of the time.

Good thing. Al had a feeling if he ran into a feral at night the thing would be on him and chompin on his windpipe before it noticed he was wearing a cowboy earring.

That special earring—a dangly silver crescent-moon thing—said you were working for them. It gave you a free pass if you ran into one of them at night.

Because the night was theirs.

Being a cowboy wasn't so bad, really. You could be assigned to keep an eye on their nests, make sure no save-the-world types—Stan liked to call them rustlers—got in there and started splashing holy water around and driving stakes into their cold little hearts. Or you could be part of a posse, which meant you spent the day riding around hunting strays. One good way to earn brownie points with the bloodsuckers was to have a stray cow or two ready for them after sundown.

They had a cow in the trunk right now. Some old bitch who'd scratched and clawed at them when they rounded her up. Deserved what she had comin to her. Plus she was good for brownie points.

Those points weren't nothing to sneer at. Earn enough of them and you got to spend some stud time on one of their cattle ranches—where all the cows were human. And young.

Neither Al or Kenny or any of their pack had been to one of the farms yet, but they'd all heard it was like incredible. You came back *sore*, man.

Al didn't particularly like working for the vampires. But then he couldn't remember ever liking anybody he'd worked for. The bloodsuckers gave him the creeps, but what was he supposed to do? If you can't beat 'em, join 'em. Plenty of guys felt the same way.

Another thing that didn't set too well was being at the bottom of the pecking order. Seemed he had to take orders from everybody except Kenny. Stan said that would change. Told them how he'd started at the bottom too. Learned the ropes and soon got to be leader of his own posse.

Stan and Jackie was some sorta team. A good one. Al

looked at Jackie. Not the greatest looking piece with that wild bottle-blond hair all black at the roots, but considering the severe lack of poontang around these parts lately, she was starting to look drop-dead gorgeous. Al could've really used a piece of her, but he knew if he went for it he'd wind up on the wrong end of that Bowie knife Stan kept strapped to his belt.

Jackie might cut him too. Just for fun. One tough broad, that Jackie. But her real talent was smoking out the ladies. Like the old bitch in the trunk. Jackie pulls out her piercings, gets dressed up in clothes that hide her tats, then goes knocking door to door, pretending to be looking for her little girl. Nobody figures a broad's gonna be working for the bloodsuckers, so sooner or later one of them answers the door and then *blammo*, the posse's there like coons on an open garbage can.

Al just wished the old bitch was younger. Then he coulda had a little fun with her before—

"Hail, hail, the gang's all here," Jackie said as they rounded a corner and pulled up before St. Anthony's. "And there's Gregor." She grinned at Kenny. "Maybe you should go ask him what you gotta do to earn your wings. I'm sure he'll be glad to sit down and chat about it."

Kenny didn't say nothing.

The old church was like the unofficial meeting place for Stan's posse and Gregor, the numero uno bloodsucker in charge of the Jersey Shore. One mean son of an undead bitch, that Gregor. Even the other vampires seemed to be like afraid of him. He was big, with these wide shoulders, long dark hair, ice cold blue eyes, and square pale face. But then all the bloodsuckers had pale faces. It was his smile that got to Al. Most times it looked painted on, but with all those sharp teeth of his it managed to make him look both happy and very, very hungry at the same time.

The posses had to meet with Gregor every night and tell him how things had gone while he was cutting his Z's or whatever it was the bloodsuckers did when the sun was up. It was part of the job. Al's least favorite part of the job. He didn't know what it was that made his skin crawl every time he got near one. Wasn't their looks, their dirty clothes, their stink. Something else, something you couldn't see or smell. Something you *felt*.

Al spotted Gregor by the church steps with his guards. He was dressed as usual in a dark suit, white shirt, no tie. Always the same, like he was going to a business meeting or something. Which put him a cut above most vampires, who never changed their clothes. Ever.

Hey, this was weird. Usually he had one or two undead goons guarding him. Tonight he had four. What was up?

Al didn't get the bodyguard thing. Like who'd ever mess with Gregor? But he didn't seem to go anywhere without them. They didn't look like the typical pumped-up guard dog types, but all four carried Glocks and razor-sharp machetes on their belts.

The local undead bigshots stood around Gregor: Mayor Davis, Councilwoman Ellis, Rabbi Goldstein, and the only black face in sight, big fat Reverend Dalton.

Al had lived around Lakewood for years and never knew any of these people's names—like he needed to know who was mayor, right?—but he knew them now.

He looked around for the priest, Palmeri, who was usually with Gregor, but didn't see him. Just as well. *There* was a bad dude. Almost as creepy as Gregor.

As Stan eased the car into the curb, one of the bodyguards came over. He wore black jeans, a black shirt crusted with old blood, and a worried expression.

"No report tonight," he said in some sort of fag British accent. "Do you 'ave something for Gregor?"

Here was another thing not to like about the vampires. All the high-ups were one kind of foreigner or another. Gregor looked like John Travolta but sounded like Bela Lugosi. His guard here sounded like Mick Jagger.

"Yeah," Stan said. "Got a cow in the trunk. What's up?"

"Not your concern. I'll bring 'er to Gregor."

"Okay. Al, you and Kenny wanna get her out?"

They did that. The ride in the trunk seemed to have taken most of the fight out of the old broad. She had to be sixty-five or seventy and she didn't look so hot at first, but she came to life, screaming and yelling when she saw the bloodsuckers.

The bodyguard made a face when he saw her. "'Ere now, what's this? She the best you could do?"

"We hit a dry neighborhood. We'll do better tomorrow."

"See that you do." He grabbed the old broad's arm and she fainted. He barely seemed to notice. "Move on. Get to your 'omes and stay inside. We'll wake you at the usual time."

As Gregor's guard dragged the unconscious broad toward the church, Stan peeled away from the curb.

"Somethin's up," Jackie said.

Stan nodded. "Wonder what's eatin them?"

"You don't think another one of us bought it, do you?" Kenny said looking all nervous.

Al knew how he felt. Someone had been offing cowboys lately. Nothing big scale, just one here, one there, but enough to make you start looking over your shoulder.

"Nah," Stan said. "They'd tell us that. This is somethin else."

As Stan cranked up Slipknot again, Al looked back at the receding church. The local undead were carrying the old broad up the church steps. Gregor stayed on the sidewalk, his guards tight around them.

What could get vampires shook up enough that they didn't want their own posses near them? It gave him a crawly feeling in his gut.

As they turned a corner Al thought he saw a female vampire with her own set of bodyguards step out of the shadows and move toward Gregor.

GREGOR . . .

His get-guards tensed and turned at Olivia's approach but
Gregor did not acknowledge it. He'd been informed of her
arrival from New York an hour ago and had been aware of
her presence in the shadows, watching him. He waited till
she spoke.

"Good evening, Gregor," she said with a light French accent.

He whirled and smiled. "Why, Olivia. What a wonderful
surprise!"

It appeared she'd dressed for the occasion: a red gown—
plucked from the window of a Fifth Avenue designer shop,
no doubt—and an elaborate Marie Antoinette wig over her
own hair which Gregor knew to be short and mousy brown.

Their guards—she'd brought six with her—stood around
and between them.

She smiled. "I'm sure." She waved her hand. "Step back,
gentlemen. Gregor and I have private matters to discuss."

They did, albeit reluctantly.

Gregor shook his head as he watched the ten form a rough
circle around Olivia and him. Considering recent events, he
should have taken comfort in the number. That didn't make
them any less of an inconvenience. One or two get-guards at
all times were a nuisance, but four—he felt strangled. And
Olivia with six tonight. How did she manage?

"You've come about Angelica, I suppose," he said in a low
voice.

She nodded. "You knew Franco would send someone."

Yes, he had. Somehow, some way, someone had killed
Angelica last night. Gregor—over the objections of his
get—had personally tracked down her remains before dawn
and had them removed to a place where they could be
burned. Secretly burned. It wouldn't do to let the cattle know

that one of the undead elite had been brought down while on the wing.

But Angelica's death was no secret among the undead. Gregor had been expecting an emissary from New York tonight, but Olivia of all people. Raw ambition from a rival get-line. This would not do.

"It could have been an accident, you know."

"I doubt that," Olivia said. "Angelica was too experienced."

Angelica—Gregor had never liked her, and hated her now. The old bitch had to go out and hunt alone. Not that any of her get-guards could have accompanied her—none of them had wings. No reason for Angelica to hunt. With her status she could have had cattle brought to her every night.

Gregor pressed his point. "It's not as if Angelica was shot down with a crossbow or the like. She was pierced with a tree branch, one that was snapped off a tree not a dozen feet from where we found her. It was quite evident that she flew into the tree and—"

Olivia smiled, showing her fangs. "I certainly don't believe that, Gregor. And neither, I dare say, do you. The situation around here has been precarious for some time, what with some sort of vigilante group running around killing your serfs. How many dead now—four?"

Gregor stiffened. "Where do you get your information?"

"That's not important. Franco is concerned that the situation is getting out of hand."

"Nothing of the sort." He was sure she was overstating Franco's concern. "Everything is under control. As for these so-called vigilantes—"

"Four serfs in four weeks, Gregor. Not just killed—their throats are slit and then they're strung up for all to see. Bad enough. But now these vigilantes have taken down Angelica."

"We don't know if it was the same group."

"That's the trouble. You don't know a thing about the perpetrators, do you."

Too true. Whatever group was killing the serfs—an older

term; Gregor had become used to calling them cowboys—wasn't announcing itself. No fliers, no graffiti, no name, no identity. Just a corpse twisting in the wind. They did their dirty work and then faded away.

"Some of the killings could be by copycats," Gregor offered.

"Even worse! Our hold is fragile, Gregor. We need our serfs. We can't have the night if they don't hold the day for us. The carrot-and-the-stick approach is usually sufficient, but they're as loyal as cockroaches, and if someone else comes along with a bigger stick, our carrot may not be enough."

"Scum," Gregor growled.

"Of course they are. Who but scum would sell out their own kind? But they're *our* scum. And we need them. Without them guarding our daysleep, we're vulnerable. If we can't protect them, they won't protect us."

"I hardly need a lecture on this, Olivia."

"Maybe you do." She pointed a long-nailed finger at him. "Because if you don't straighten this out, I'll have to do it for you."

Gregor glared at her. He knew what that meant: he'd be sent back to New York where Franco would demote him to some sort of low-level functionary.

He was a veteran of the battle of the Vatican, damn it. No one could humiliate him like that.

His thoughts drifted back. What a week that had been. Vatican City was immune to the ferals because of the plethora of crosses—crosses everywhere, on the walls, the ceilings, even the floors. The priests and the Swiss Guard had fought valiantly against the serfs. It was not until turned military commanders and soldiers began shelling the buildings with tanks and artillery that they made any progress. Vatican City eventually was reduced to rubble. That was the good news. The bad news was that the Pope had died in the shelling. It would have been such a coup to turn him and make him an icon for the Catholic undead.

Gregor missed those good old days of head-on assault:

Prague, Berlin, Rome, Paris, London. They'd all fallen in days. But that approach had run into unforeseen problems. Franco was trying a new tack. Gregor agreed that it made more sense, but it lacked the heady rush of the blitzkrieg. And it allowed upstarts like Olivia to rise.

If Olivia had her way and Gregor was called back to New York, she would remove all his get—which now included the mayor, the councilwoman, the priest, and the reverend among others—and install her own in their place. Olivia's domain would expand while his would contract to near zero.

Gregor would not allow that. These vigilantes would be found and run to ground if he had to do it himself.

ZEV . . .

After a few hours their talk died of fatigue. Father Joe gave Zev the flashlight to hold, then stretched out across a couple of crates to sleep. Zev tried to get comfortable enough to doze but found sleep impossible. So he listened to his friend snore in the dusty darkness of the cellar.

Poor Joe. Such anger in the man. But more than that—hurt. He felt betrayed, wronged. And with good reason. But with everything falling apart as it was, the wrong done to him would never be righted. He should forget about it already and go on with his life, but apparently he couldn't. Such a shame. He needed something to pull him out of his funk. Zev had thought news of what had happened to his old parish might rouse him, but it seemed only to make him want to drink more. Father Joseph Cahill, he feared, was a hopeless case.

Zev closed his eyes and tried to rest. He found it hard to get comfortable with the cross dangling in front of him so he took it off but laid it within easy reach. He was drifting toward a doze when he heard a noise outside. By the dumpster. Metal on metal.

My bicycle!

He slipped to the floor and tiptoed over to where Joe slept. He shook his shoulder and whispered.

"Someone's found my bike!"

The priest snorted but remained sleeping. A louder clatter outside made Zev turn, and as he moved his elbow struck a bottle. He grabbed for it in the darkness but missed. The sound of smashing glass echoed through the basement like a cannon shot. As the odor of Scotch whiskey replaced the musty ambiance, Zev listened for further sounds from outside. None came.

Maybe it had been an animal. He remembered how raccoons used to raid his garbage at home . . . when he'd had a home . . . when he'd had garbage . . .

Zev stepped to the window and looked out. Probably an animal.

A pale, snarling demonic face, baring its fangs and hissing, suddenly filled the window. Zev fell back as the thing rammed its hand through the glass, reaching for his throat, its curved fingers clawing at him, missing. It pushed up the window, then launched itself the rest of the way through, hurtling toward Zev.

He tried to dodge but was too slow. The impact knocked the flashlight from his grasp and it rolled across the floor. Zev cried out as he went down under the snarling thing. Its ferocity was overpowering, irresistible. It straddled him and lashed at him, batting his fending arms aside, its clawed fingers tearing at his collar to free his throat, stretching his neck to expose the vulnerable flesh, its foul breath gagging him as it bent its fangs toward him. Zev screamed out his helplessness.

JOE . . .

Father Joe Cahill awoke to cries of terror.

He shook his head to clear it and instantly regretted the move. His head weighed at least two hundred pounds, and his mouth was stuffed with foul-tasting cotton. Why did he keep doing this to himself? What was the point in acting out the drunken Irish priest cliché? Not only did it leave him feeling lousy, it gave him bad dreams. Like now.

Another terrified shout, only a few feet away.

He looked toward the sound. In the faint light from the flashlight rolling across the floor he saw Zev on his back, fighting for his life against—

Jesus! This was no dream!

He leaped over to where the creature was lowering its fangs toward Zev's throat. He grabbed it by the back of the neck and lifted it clear of the floor. It was surprisingly heavy but that didn't slow him. Joe could feel the anger rising in him, surging into his muscles.

"Rotten piece of filth!"

He swung the vampire by its neck and let it fly against the cinderblock wall. It impacted with what should have been bone-crushing force, but bounced off, rolled on the floor, and regained its feet in one motion, ready to attack again. Strong as he was, Joe knew he was no match for this thing's power. He turned, grabbed his big silver crucifix, and charged the creature.

"Hungry? Eat this!"

As the creature bared its fangs and hissed at him, Joe shoved the long lower end of the cross's upright into the gaping maw. Blue-white light flickered along the silver length of the crucifix, reflecting in the creature's startled, agonized eyes as its flesh sizzled and crackled. The vampire let out a strangled cry and tried to turn away but Joe wasn't through with it yet. He was literally seeing red as rage poured out of a hidden well and swirled through him. He rammed the cross farther down the thing's gullet. Light flashed deep in its throat, illuminating the pale tissues from within. It tried to grab the cross and pull it out but the flesh of its fingers burned and smoked wherever it came in contact with it.

Finally Joe stepped back and let the thing squirm and

scrabble up the wall and out the window into the night. Then he turned to Zev. If anything had happened—

"Hey, Reb!" he said, kneeling beside the older man. "You all right?"

"Yes," Zev said, struggling to his feet. "Thanks to you."

Joe slumped onto a crate, momentarily weak as his rage dissipated. This is not what I'm about, he thought. But it had felt so damn good to let loose on that vampire. Almost too good.

I'm falling apart . . . like everything else in the world.

"That was too close," Joe said, giving the older man's shoulder a fond squeeze.

"For that vampire, too close for sure." Zev replaced his yarmulke. "And would you please remind me, Father Joe, that in the future if ever I should maybe get my blood sucked and become undead that I should stay far away from you."

Joe laughed for the first time in too long. It felt good.

3

JOE . . .

They climbed out of Morton's basement shortly after dawn. Joe carried an unopened bottle of Scotch—for later. He stretched his cramped muscles and shielded his eyes from the rising sun. The bright light sent stabs of pain through his brain.

"Oy," Zev said as he pulled his hidden bicycle from behind the dumpster. "Look what he did."

Joe inspected the bike. The front wheel had been bent so far out of shape that half the spokes were broken.

"Beyond fixing, Zev."

"Looks like I'll be walking back to Lakewood."

Joe looked around, searching the ground. "Where'd our visitor go?"

He knew it couldn't have got far. He followed drag marks in the sandy dirt around to the far side of the dumpster, and there it was—or rather what was left of it: a rotting, twisted corpse, blackened to a crisp and steaming in the morning sunlight. The silver crucifix still protruded from between its teeth.

"Three ways we know to kill them," Zev said. "A stake through the heart, decapitation, or exposing them to sunlight. I believe Father Cahill has just found a fourth."

Joe approached and gingerly yanked his cross free of the foul remains.

"Looks like you've sucked your last pint of blood," he said and immediately felt foolish.

Who was he putting on the macho act for? Zev certainly wasn't going to buy it. Too out of character. But then, what *was* his character these days? He used to be a parish priest. Now he was a nothing. A less than nothing.

He straightened and turned to Zev.

"Come on back to the retreat house, Reb. I'll buy you breakfast."

But as Joe turned and began walking away, Zev stayed and stared down at the corpse.

"They say most of them don't wander far from where they spent their lives," Zev said. "Which means it's unlikely this fellow was Jewish if he lived around here. Probably Catholic. Irish Catholic, I'd imagine."

Joe stopped and turned. He stared at his long shadow. The hazy rising sun at his back cast a huge hulking shape before him, with a dark cross in one shadow hand and a smudge of amber light where it poured through the bottle of Scotch in the other.

"What are you getting at?" he said.

"The *Kaddish* would probably not be so appropriate so I'm just wondering if someone should maybe give him the last rites or whatever it is you people do when one of you dies."

"He wasn't one of us," Joe said, feeling the bitterness rise in him. "He wasn't even human."

"Ah, but he used to be before he was killed and became one of them. So maybe now he could use a little help."

Joe didn't like the way this was going. He sensed he was being maneuvered.

"He doesn't deserve it," he said and knew in that instant he'd been trapped.

"I thought even the worst sinner deserved it," Zev said.

Joe knew when he was beaten. Zev was right. He shoved the cross and bottle into Zev's hands—a bit roughly, perhaps—then went and knelt by the twisted cadaver. He administered a form of the final sacrament. When he was through he returned to Zev and snatched back his belongings.

"You're a better man than I am, Gunga Din," he said as he passed.

"You act as if they're responsible for what they do after they become undead," Zev said hurrying along beside him, panting as he matched Joe's pace.

"Aren't they?"

"No."

"You're sure of that?"

"Well, not exactly. But they certainly aren't human anymore, so maybe we shouldn't hold them accountable on human terms."

Zev's reasoning tone flashed Joe back to the conversations they used to have in Horovitz's deli.

"But Zev, we know there's some of the old personality left. I mean, they stay in their home towns, usually in the basements of their old houses. They go after people they knew when they were alive. They're not just dumb predators, Zev. They've got the old consciousness they had when they were alive. Why can't they rise above it? Why can't they . . . resist?"

"I don't know. I've never had the opportunity to sit down with one and discuss it. Maybe they can't resist. To tell the truth, the question has never occurred to me. A fascinating concept: an undead refusing to feed. Leave it to Father Joe to come up with something like that. We should discuss this on the trip back to Lakewood."

Joe had to smile. So *that* was what this was all about.

"I'm not going back to Lakewood."

"Fine. Then we'll discuss this now. Maybe the urge to feed is too strong to overcome."

"Maybe. And maybe they just don't try hard enough."

"This is a hard line you're taking, my friend."

"Maybe I'm a hard-line kind of guy."

"You didn't used to be, but it seems you've become one."

Joe felt a flash of unreasoning anger and gave him a sharp look. "You don't know what I've become."

Zev shrugged. "Maybe true, maybe not. But did you see the face of the one that attacked me? I'm sure he didn't look like that before he was turned. They seem to change, at least some of them, on the outside. Maybe on the inside they change too."

"If they acted like mindless beasts, I'd agree. But they're intelligent, they can reason. That means they can choose."

"Do you truly think you'd be able to resist?"

"Damn straight."

Joe wasn't sure why he said it, didn't even know if he meant it. Maybe he was mentally preparing himself for the day when he might find himself in that situation.

After walking a block or so in silence, Joe said, "What I don't get is how these undead get away with breaking all the rules."

"Meaning what? Laws?"

"Not civil laws—the laws of physics and chemistry and God knows what else. I've never had a problem reconciling science and belief. God designed creation to run by certain rules; science is merely man's attempt to use his God-given intelligence to understand those rules."

"So you don't take Genesis literally."

"Of course not. It's not natural science. It was never meant to be. The Bible is the story of a people and their relationship with their God."

"A God who seems very far away lately."

Joe sighed at the truth of that. He'd felt abandoned for some time now. The air cooled as they neared the ocean, the briny on-shore breeze carrying the eternal rumble of the breakers and the calls of the seagulls as they wheeled over the jetties. Some things, at least, hadn't changed.

"It seems the undead are exempt from the rules God laid down for creation. The flying ones, for instance. You said you were attacked by one the other night. I've seen one or two gliding around on a moonlit night. How do you explain them? I'm no expert on aerodynamics, but those wings shouldn't be able to support them, yet they do. And where do the wings go when they're not using them?"

Zev shrugged. "These are questions I can't answer."

"Here's another. I was around when a gang of locals chased one down. He'd ripped up a woman's throat but he didn't get away fast enough. They blinded him with holy water, held him down with crosses, and drove a stake through his heart. Then they cut off his head."

"The traditional method, as opposed to the new Cahill method. And of course he was dead then. Truly dead."

"Right. But he didn't bleed."

"So?"

"If he doesn't have blood to feed his muscles, how do they move?"

"A mystery."

"It's as if the laws of our world have been suspended where the undead are concerned."

"Suspended by whom? Or what?"

"*There's* a question I'd like answered."

"All very interesting," Zev said as they climbed the front steps of the retreat house. "Well, I'd better be going. A long walk I've got ahead of me. A long, *lonely* walk all the way back to Lakewood. A long, lonely, possibly *dangerous* walk back for a poor old man who—"

"All right, Zev! All *right!*" Joe said, biting back a laugh. "I get the point. You want me to go back to Lakewood. Why? What's it going to prove?"

"I just want the company," Zev said with pure innocence.

"No, really. What's going on in that Talmudic mind of yours? What are you cooking?"

"Nothing, Father Joe. Nothing at all."

Joe stared at him. Damn it all, his interest was piqued. What was Zev up to? And what the hell—why not go? He had nothing better to do.

"All right, Zev. You win. I'll come back to Lakewood with you. But just for today. Just to keep you company. And I'm not going anywhere near St. Anthony's, okay? Understood?"

"Understood, Joe. Perfectly understood."

"I'm not getting involved with my old parish again, is that clear?"

"That such a thing should ever enter my mind. *Feh!*"

"Good. Now wipe that smile off your face and we'll get something to eat."

† † †

Later, under the climbing sun, they walked south along the deserted beach, barefooting through the wet sand at the edge of the surf. Joe had his sneakers slung over his shoulder, Zev carried a black shoe in each hand, and acted like a little kid, laughing at the chill of the water as it sloshed over his ankles.

"I can't believe you've never been to the beach," Joe said. "Not even as a kid?"

"Never."

Joe shook his head in dismay and gestured at the acres of sand. "This is Manasquan Beach. You should have seen this place on a summer weekend. Wall-to-wall people. Probably never see that again. Probably be as empty as this even on the Fourth of July."

"Your Independence Day. We never made much of secular holidays. Too many religious ones to observe. What would people do here besides swim?"

"Lie in the sun and work on their skin cancers."

"Really? I imagine that sunbathing is maybe not the fad it used to be."

Joe laughed. "Ah, Zev. Still the master of the understatement. I'll say one thing, though: The beach is cleaner than I've ever seen it. No beer cans or hypodermics."

Zev pointed ahead. "But what's that?"

As they approached the spot, Joe saw a pair of naked bodies stretched out on their backs on the sand, one male, one female, both young and short-haired. Their skin was bronzed and glistened in the sun. The man lifted his head and stared at them. A blue crucifix was tattooed in the center of his forehead. He rolled over, reached into the backpack beside him, and withdrew a huge, gleaming, nickel-plated revolver.

"Just keep walking," he said.

"Will do," Joe said. "Just out for a stroll."

As they passed the couple, Joe noticed a similar tattoo on the girl's forehead.

"A very popular tattoo," he said.

"Clever idea. That's one cross you can't drop or lose. Probably won't help you in the dark, but if there's a light on it might give you an edge."

He noticed the rest of the girl too. Small firm breasts jutting straight up despite the fact that she was on her back, dark fuzz on her pubes. He felt a stir within and looked away.

"How do you do that?" Zev said.

"What?"

"Look away from such a beautiful sight."

Are you watching me that closely? Joe wondered.

"Practice, practice, practice."

"How do you turn it off? Or does it just die?"

"Believe me, the sexual impulse doesn't die. I've always had one. I remember having crushes as a kid. I remember one girl, Eleanor Jepson, that I was infatuated with. I'd think about her night and day, I'd write poems to her—which I'd immediately tear up for fear someone would find them. I'd ride my bike past her house at least ten times a day hoping to catch a glimpse of her; I learned her schedule at school and I'd run through the halls so I could just happen to be passing her locker when she'd stop there between classes.

"But as a priest I'd do just the opposite. As soon as I felt an attraction starting I'd turn away from it. You learn to do that—to not think about something. It's different from saying, 'Don't think about a pink unicorn.' Instead you turn your mind away, you learn to not think about what you don't want to think about. Trust me, it can be done. And instead of looking for 'chance' meetings, you avoid contact except in the most public of situations. No tête-à-têtes or in-depth, one-on-one meetings, no lingering glances, no touches on the arm or shoulder. The key is to recognize the spark and douse it before it can ignite."

"Such a way to live. Pardon me, but it's unnatural."

"Tell me about it."

Celibacy hadn't been easy. How he'd ached for one particular woman, but he'd put his calling above that longing. Besides, she'd had her own vows. And nestled within him had been the hope that the new Pope might lift the ban on marriage for priests. But no one had heard from the Pope since last year.

Zev laughed. "The woman two nights ago, the one dressed like a prostitute who saved this sorry hide, for an instant there I thought, Father Joe and a prostitute . . . ?"

"What did she look like?"

"Short dark hair, blue eyes, might have been prettier if she hadn't looked so haggard. I sensed she knew you. In fact I'm sure she did. The only way she knew me was because she'd seen me with you." He touched his chin. "Oh, yes. And she had a little scar right here. A tiny crescent."

Joe stopped walking. No. It couldn't be. "You could almost be describing . . ." He shook his head. "No. Not dressed like that."

"Who were you thinking of?"

"One of the nuns. Sister Carole. She was . . . special."

Oh, was she ever. His heart lightened at just the thought of her.

"What? Someone was special to you and I know nothing? I thought we discussed everything."

Almost everything, Joe thought. But not this. Not Carole.

"She wasn't special just to me, she was special to everyone who knew her, or met however briefly. You would have taken to her, I know it. She was one of those people who lights up a room simply by entering it."

"Then your Sister Carole this was certainly not. Darken a room, that's what this one would do. This woman was very grim, frightening in a way; the only time she brightened was when she mentioned your name."

"No. My Carole—" He caught himself. "St. Anthony's Sister Carole, would have been out of town when the undead struck—back with her family in Pennsylvania."

He'd thought about her countless times since Good Friday. *She's safe . . . I pray she's safe. She's too delicate, too sensitive for that kind of horror. She never would have survived.*

"Since the mystery woman wasn't your paramour or your Sister Carole," Zev said, "I assume we can get back to priestly celibacy. I read once where priests had been allowed to marry until sometime during the Middle Ages. Why was that changed?"

"For financial reasons. Priests were accumulating wealthy estates and leaving them to their families instead of the Church. So one of the Popes instituted the no-marriage rule. It came around and bit the Church on its ass."

"Oy, did it ever."

"Yeah. The priesthood became attractive to too many who were ambiguous about their sexuality or to those who saw the Church as a sanctuary from their darker impulses; it wasn't. The impulses only became stronger. Seems to me that early entrance to a seminary interferes with normal maturation, and because of that you wind up with a percentage of priests with arrested sexual development."

Joe thanked God that he'd yielded to his vocation later in life. The love of God had always been strong in him, but he hadn't seen himself as a priest until after his graduation from Brooklyn College. The idea took hold and wouldn't let go. He'd entered the seminary at age twenty-three, but not as a virgin.

"The arrested types," he said, "they're the ones who became pedophiles, and their presence tainted the rest of us. We all got smeared with the same brush. Look at me. I'm a prime example."

"No one who knows you," Zev said, "believed a word of that."

"Didn't matter. As soon as something like that gets out, you're ruined. Guilty or innocent, who you are and whatever good you've done is canceled out." He ground his teeth. "The only feeling I've ever experienced looking at a child was the desire to see him or her grow into a God-loving adult."

Zev put a hand on his arm. "I know, Joe. I know."

They walked on in silence.

ZEV . . .

Eventually they turned west and made their way inland, finding Route 70 and following it into Ocean County via the Brielle Bridge.

"I remember nightmare traffic jams right here every summer," Joe said as they trod the bridge's empty span. "Never thought I'd miss traffic jams."

They cut over to Route 88 and followed it toward Lakewood. Along the way they found a few people out and about in Bricktown, furtively scurrying between houses. They walked a gauntlet of car dealerships, the stock sitting dirty and idle in the lots beneath waving pennants, the broken showroom windows carrying signs promising deals that would never be closed.

Zev noticed how Joe's steps seemed to grow heavier with every mile. But he had to show him something that would make his steps—and his heart—even heavier.

At the corner of New Hampshire Avenue, he turned them south.

"But it's shorter this way," Joe said, pointing down 88.

"I know. But we'll end up in the same spot, and along the way there's something you must see."

They trod the undulating pavement until they came to a baseball field, the former home of the Lakewood Blue Claws.

Joe smiled. "This brings back memories. Remember the games we used to go to?"

"I do," Zev said. The Blue Claws, a class-A minor league team, maybe, but those games had been fun. The stadium even served Kosher food. "But what I want to show you here, baseball's got nothing to do with."

"I don't think I like the sound of that." Joe pointed to the unusual number of gulls and crows circling the field. "And I *know* I don't like the look of that."

Zev knew as they climbed the grassy slope to the fence that whatever uneasy premonitions Joe was feeling, even the worst he could imagine would leave him unprepared for the sight that awaited him on the other side.

He remembered his recent look onto the playing field. At first he hadn't been sure what he was seeing: a huge pile of blackened debris occupying most of the diamond and spreading into the outfield. Then he'd started picking out limbs and torsos, and there, piled high where home plate used to be . . . skulls. Innumerable skulls.

Joe stared at the charred, rotting mounds for maybe ten seconds, then closed his eyes and swallowed.

"What in the name of God . . . ?"

"Hardly in the name of God," Zev said. "On those first few nights of the invasion they committed wholesale slaughter. They loosed a horde of bestial creatures—undead, yes, but only vaguely human—who beheaded their prey after drinking their blood. A way to keep down the undead population, I assume. It makes sense that they wouldn't want too many of their kind concentrated in one area. Like too many carnivores in one forest—when the herds of prey are wiped out, the predators starve. And just to make sure none of those early victims would be rising from the grave, they brought their bodies and their heads here, soaked them with kerosene, and struck a match."

"Jesus."

"Him I doubt had much to do with it either. They fed the fire for days, the smoke dirtied the sky. And when the wind blew the wrong way—oy. Even now . . ." He sniffed the air. "Luckily we're upwind."

"But they were also killing off their future food supply."

"Enough of us they left to hunt down and feed on, but far too few to offer resistance of any consequence."

They walked the rest of the way into Lakewood in silence. When they entered the town . . .

"A real ghost town," the priest said as they walked Forest Avenue's deserted length.

"Ghosts," Zev said, nodding sadly. It had been a long walk and he was tired. "Yes. Full of ghosts."

In his mind's eye he saw the shades of his fallen brother rabbis and all the yeshiva students, beards, black suits, black hats, crisscrossing back and forth at a determined pace on weekdays, strolling with their wives on Shabbes, their children trailing behind like ducklings.

Gone. All gone. Victims of the undead. Undead themselves now, some of them. It made him sick at heart to think of those good, gentle men, women, and children curled up in their basements now to avoid the light of day, venturing out in the dark to feed on others, spreading the disease . . .

He fingered the cross slung from his neck. *If only they had listened!*

And then he heard the grating sound of a heavily distorted guitar. He grabbed Joe's arm.

"Quick. Into the bushes!"

They ducked behind a thick stand of rhododendrons along the foundation of the nearest house and watched a convertible glide by. Zev counted four in the car, three men and a blond woman, all scruffy and unwashed, lean and wolfish, in cut-off sweatshirts or denim jackets, the driver wearing a big Texas hat, someone in the back with a red Mohican, all guzzling beer. The thumping blast of their music dopplered in and out. Thank God they liked to play it at ear-damaging levels. It acted as an early warning system.

"Chazzers," Zev muttered.

When they'd passed, Joe stepped out of the bushes and stared after them.

"Who the hell were they?"

"Scum of the earth. They like to call themselves cowboys. I call them Vichy."

"Vichy? Like the Vichy French?"

"Yes. Very good. I'm glad to see that you're not as culturally illiterate as the rest of your generation. Vichy humans—that's what I call the collaborators. They should all die of pox." He looked around. "We should get off the street. I know a place near St. Anthony's where we can hide."

"You've traveled enough today, Reb. And I told you, I don't care about St. Anthony's. I'll get you situated, then head back."

"You can't leave yet, Joe," Zev said, gripping the young priest's arm. He'd coaxed him this far; he couldn't let him get away now. "Stay the night. See what Father Palmeri's done."

"If he's one of them he's not a priest anymore. Don't call him Father."

"*They* still call him Father."

"Who?"

"The undead."

Zev watched Father Joe's jaw muscles bunch.

Joe said, "Maybe I'll just take a quick trip over to St. Anthony's myself—"

"No. It's different here. The area is thick with Vichy and undead. They'll get you if your timing isn't just right. I'll take you."

"You need rest, pal."

Father Joe's expression showed genuine concern. Zev was detecting increasingly softer emotions in the man since their reunion last night. A good sign perhaps?

"Rest I'll get when we reach where I'm taking you."

CAROLE . . .

<And what are you doing, Carole? What are you DOING? You'll be after killing yourself! You'll be blowing yourself to pieces and then you'll be going straight to hell. HELL, Carole!>

"But I won't be going alone," Carole muttered.

She had to turn her head away from the kitchen sink now. The fumes stung her nose and made her eyes water, but she kept on stirring the pool chlorinator into the hot water until it was completely dissolved. She wasn't through yet. She took the beaker of No Salt she'd measured out before starting the process and added it to the mix in the big Pyrex bowl. Then she stirred some more. Finally, when she was satisfied that she was not going to see any further dissolution at this temperature, she put the bowl on the stove and turned up the flame.

A propane stove. She'd seen the big white tank out back last week when she was looking for a new home; that was why she'd chosen this old house. With New Jersey Natural Gas in ruins, and GPU no longer sending electricity through the wires, propane and wood stoves were the only ways left to cook.

I really shouldn't call it cooking, she thought as she fled the acrid fumes and headed for the living room. Nothing more than a simple dissociation reaction—heating a mixture of calcium hypochlorate with potassium chloride. Simple, basic chemistry. The very subject she'd taught bored juniors and seniors for years at St. Anthony's School.

"And you all thought chemistry was such a useless subject!" she shouted to the walls.

She clapped a hand over her mouth. There she was, talking out loud again. She had to be careful. Not so much because someone might hear, but because she worried she might be losing her mind.

Maybe she'd already lost it. Maybe all this was merely a delusion. Maybe the undead hadn't taken over the entire civilized world. Maybe they hadn't defiled her church and convent, slaughtered her best friend. Maybe it was all in her mind.

<Sure and you'd be wishing it was all in your mind, Carole. Of course you would. Then you wouldn't be sinning!>

Yes, she truly did wish she were imagining all this. At least then she'd be the only one suffering, and all the rest would still be alive and well, just as they'd been before she went off the deep end.

But if this was a delusion it was certainly an elaborate, consistent one. Every time she woke up—she never allowed herself to sleep too many hours at once, only catnaps—it was the same: quiet skies, vacant houses, empty streets, furtive, scurrying survivors who trusted no one, and—

What's that?

Sister Carole froze as her ears picked up a sound outside. Music. She hurried in a crouch to the front door and peered through the sidelight. A car. A convertible. Someone was out driving in—

She ducked when she saw who was in it. She recognized that cowboy hat. She didn't have to see their earrings to know who—what—they were.

They were headed east. Good. They'd find a little surprise waiting for them down the road.

As it did every so often, the horror of what her life had become caught up to Carole then, and she slumped to the floor of the Bennett house and began to sob.

Why? Why had God allowed this to happen to her, to His Church, to His world?

Better question: Why had she allowed these awful events to change her so? She had been a Sister of Mercy.

<Mercy! Do you hear that, Carole? A Sister of MERCY!>

She had taken vows of poverty, chastity, and obedience, had vowed to devote her life to teaching and doing the Lord's work. But now there was no money, no one worth losing her virginity to, no Mother Superior or Church to be obedient to, and no students left to teach.

All she had left was the Lord's work.

<Believe me you, Carole, I'd hardly be calling the making of plastic explosive and the other horrible things you've been doing the Lord's work. It's killing! It's a SIN!>

Maybe Bernadette's voice was right. Maybe she would go to hell for what she was doing. But somebody had to make those rotten cowboys pay.

COWBOYS . . .

"Shit! Goddam shit!"

Stan's raging voice and the sudden braking of the car yanked Al from the edge of a doze. A few beers, nice warm sunlight . . . he'd been on his way to catching a Z or two. He opened his eyes.

"Yo, what the fu—"

Then he saw him. Or, rather, it. Dead ahead. *Dead* ahead. A body, hanging by its feet from a utility pole.

"Oh, shit," Kenny said from beside him. "Another one."

Jackie turned off the music. The sudden silence was creepy.

Al squinted at the body. "Who is it?"

"I dunno," Stan said. Then he looked back at Al from under the wide brim of his cowboy hat. "Whyn't you go see."

Al swallowed. He'd turned out to be the best climber, so he'd wound up the second-story man of the team. But he didn't want to make this climb.

"What's the use?" Al said. "Whoever he is, he's dead."

"See if he's one of us," Stan said.

"Ain't it *always* one of us?"

"Then see *which* one of us it is, okay?"

Stan had been pissing Al off today with his hot-shit 'tude. He was posse leader, yeah, but give it a rest now and then, okay? But this time he was right: Somebody had to go see who'd got unlucky last night.

Al hopped over the door and headed for the pole. What a pain in the ass. The rope around the dead guy's feet was looped over the first climbing spike. He shimmied up to it and got creosote all over himself in the process. The stuff was a bitch to get off. And besides, it made his skin itch. On the way up he'd kept the pole between himself and the body. Now it was time to look. He swallowed. He'd seen one of these strung-up guys up close before and—

He spotted the earring, a blood-splattered silvery crescent moon dangling on a fine chain from the brown-crusted earlobe, an exact replica of the one dangling from Al's left ear, only this one was dangling the wrong way.

"Yep," he said, loud so's the car could hear it. "It's one of us."

"Damn!" Stan's voice. "Anyone we know?"

Stan and the rest jumped out of the car and stared up at him.

Al squinted at the face but with the gag stuck in its mouth, and the head so encrusted with clotted blood and crawling with buzzing, feeding flies darting in and out of the gaping wound in the throat, he couldn't make out no features.

"Can't tell."

"Well, cut him down then."

This was the part Al hated most of all. It seemed almost like a sin. Not that he'd ever been religious or nothing, but someday, if he didn't watch his ass, this could be him.

He pulled his K-BAR from its scabbard and sawed at the rope above the knot on the climbing spike. It frayed, jerked a couple of times, then parted. He closed his eyes as the body tumbled downward. He hummed Metallica's "Sandman" to blot out the sound it made when it hit the pavement. He especially hated the sick, wet *plop* of the head if it landed first. Which this one did.

"Looks like Benny Gonzales," Jackie said.

Kenny was nodding. "Yep. No doubt about it. That's Benny. Shit."

They dragged his body over to the curb and drove on, but the party mood was gone.

"I'd love to catch the bastards who're doin this shit," Stan said as he drove. "They've gotta be close by around here somewhere."

"They could be anywhere," Al said. "They found Benny back there, killed him there—you saw that puddle of blood under him—and left him. Then they cut out."

"They're huntin us like we're huntin them," Jackie said.

"But I wanna be the one to catch 'em," Kenny said.

Jackie sneered. "Yeah? And what would you do if you did?"

Kenny said nothing, and Al knew that was the answer. Nothing. He'd bring them in and turn them over. The bloodsuckers didn't like you screwing with their cattle.

But something had to be done. Lots of the cattle they roped in called Al and company traitors and collaborators and worse. Lately it looked like some of them had gone beyond name-calling and graduated to throat-slitting.

Benny Gonzales was the fifth one in a month.

Seemed the guys behind this wanted to make it look like the vampires themselves was doing the killings, but it didn't wash. Too messy. These bodies had blood all over them, and a puddle beneath them. When the bloodsuckers slit somebody's throat, they didn't let a drop of it go to waste. They licked the platter clean, so to speak.

"We gotta start being real careful," Stan was saying. "Gotta keep our eyes open."

"And look for what?" Kenny said.

"For a bunch of guys who hang out together—a bunch of guys who ain't cowboys."

Jackie started singing that Willie Nelson song "Mama, Don't Let Your Babies Grow up to Be Cowboys," and it set Stan off.

"Knock it off, goddamn it! This ain't funny! One of us could be next! Now keep your fucking eyes open!"

Al studied the houses drifting by as they cruised into Point Pleasant Beach. Cars sat quietly along the curbs of the empty streets and the houses appeared deserted, their empty, blind windows staring back at him. But every so often they'd pass a yard that looked cared for, and those houses would be defiantly studded with crosses and festooned with garlands of garlic. And every so often you could swear you saw somebody peeking out from behind a window or through a screen door.

"You know, Stan," Al said. "I'll bet those cowboy killers are hiding in one of them houses with all the garlic and crosses."

"Maybe, Stan said. "But I kinda doubt it. Those folks tend to stay in after sundown. Whoever's behind this is working at night."

That made sense to Al. The folks in those houses hardly ever came out. They were loners. Dangerous loners. *Armed* loners. The vampires couldn't get in because of all the garlic and crosses, and the cowboys who'd tried to get in, or even take off some of the crosses, usually got shot up. The vampires had said to leave them be for now. Sooner or later they'd run out of food and have to come out. *Then* they'd get them.

Smart, those bloodsuckers. Al guessed they figured they had plenty of time to outwait the loners. All the time in the world.

They was cruising Ocean Avenue by the boardwalk area now, barely a block from the Atlantic. What a difference. Last year, on a nice spring day like this, you'd see all sorts of people, locals and day-trippers, hanging out. Now it was deserted. The sun was high and warm but it was like winter had never ended.

They was gliding past the empty, frozen rides when Al caught a flash of color moving between a couple of the boardwalk stands.

"Pull over," he said, tapping Stan's shoulder. "I think I just saw something."

The tires screeched as Stan made a sharp turn into Jenkinson's parking lot.

"What kinda something?"

"Something blond. With tits, I think."

Kenny let out a cowboy whoop and tossed his Heineken empty high. It smashed on the asphalt in a glittery green explosion.

"Shut the fuck up!" Stan said. "You tryin to queer this little round-up or what?"

"Hey, no, man," Kenny said. "I was just—"

"Just keep quiet and listen. You and Jackie head down two blocks and work your way back up on the boards."

"I don't wanna go with him," Jackie said, jutting her chin at Kenny.

"He needs someone with more experience along. Me and Al'll go up here and work our way down. Get goin and don't blow this. I don't wanna be bringin Gregor no old lady again tonight."

Jackie didn't look happy but she went. As she and Kenny trotted back to the Risden's Beach bath houses, Stan squared his ten-gallon hat on his head and pointed toward the miniature golf course at the other end of the parking lot. Al took the lead and Stan followed.

Arnold Avenue ended here in a turretlike police station, still boarded up from the winter, but its big warning sign was still up, informing anyone who passed that alcoholic beverages and dogs and motorbikes and various other goodies were prohibited in the beach and boardwalk area by order of the mayor and city council of Point Pleasant Beach.

Al smiled. The beach and the boardwalk and the sign were still here, but the mayor and the city council were long gone.

Pretty damn depressing up on the boards. The big glass windows of Jenkinson's arcade was smashed and it was all dark inside. The lifeless video games stared back with dead eyes. All the concession stands was boarded up, the paralyzed rides just rusting and peeling, and it was *quiet*. No barkers shouting, no kids laughing, no squealing babes in bikinis running in and out of the surf. Just the monotonous pounding of the waves against the deserted beach.

And the birds. The seagulls was doing what they'd always done. Probably the only thing they missed was the garbage the crowds used to leave behind.

Al and Stan headed south, checking all the nooks and crannies as they moved. The only other humans they saw was Kenny and Jackie coming up the other way from the South Beach Arcade.

"Any luck?" Stan called.

"Nada," Jackie said.

"Ay-yo, Al!" Kenny said. "How many Heinies you have anyway? You seein things now? What was it—a blond *seagull*?"

But Al knew he'd seen something moving up here, and it hadn't been no goddamn seagull. But where . . .

"Jackie," Stan said. "Take Kenny under the boards and see if anyone's hidin down there."

Kenny put on this big shit-eating grin. "Aaaaay, under the boardwalk with Jackieeee. Cooool."

Stan ignored him and spoke to Jackie. "If it's a girl like Al thinks he saw, see if you can talk her out. I ain't up for no foot race, know what I'm sayin?"

Jackie nodded. "Gotcha." She turned to Kenny and snapped her fingers, like she was talking to a dog. "C'mon, boy. We're goin for a walk."

"Ooooh. Under the boardwalk with—"

"Don't"—she jabbed a finger within an inch of his nose— "even think about it!"

Kenny, his tongue hanging out like a dog, followed her down the wooden steps to the sand. That Kenny. What a pisser.

"Let's go back to Jenk's," Stan said. "She might be hidin inside."

They'd turned and were heading back up the boards when Al took one last look back . . . and saw something moving. Something small and red, rolling across the boards toward the beach from between one of the concession stands.

A ball.

He tapped Stan on the shoulder, put a finger to his lips, and pointed. Stan's eyes widened. He glanced toward the beach, probably looking to signal Jackie and Kenny, but they were out of sight. So the two of them crept toward the spot where the ball had rolled from.

As they got closer, Al realized why they'd missed this spot on the first pass. It was really two concession stands—a frozen yogurt place and a saltwater taffy shop—with boards nailed up over the space between to make them look like a single building.

Stan tapped Al on the shoulder and pointed to the roof of the nearer concession stand. Al nodded. He knew what he wanted: The second-story man had to do his thing again.

Al got to the top of the chain link fence behind the concession stands and from there it was easy to haul himself up to the roof. His sneakers made barely a sound as he crept across the tar of the canted roof to the far side.

The girl must have heard him coming, because she was already looking up when he peeked over the edge. She had one of them cross tattoos on her forehead.

That ain't gonna help you against me, honey.

Al felt a surge of satisfaction when he saw her blond ponytail and long thick bangs. Nice.

He felt something else when he saw the tears streaming down her cheeks from her pleading eyes, and her hands raised, palms together, as if praying to him. She wanted him to see nothin—she was *begging* Al to see nothing.

For an instant he was tempted. The fear in those frightened blue eyes reached deep inside and touched something there, disturbed a part of him so long unused he'd forgotten it belonged to him.

And then he saw she had a little boy with her, maybe seven years old, dark haired but with eyes as blue as hers, with a tattoo on *his* forehead. She was pleading for the kid as much as herself. Maybe more than herself. And with good reason. The vampires *loved* little kids. Al didn't get it. Kids were smaller, had less blood than adults. Maybe their blood was purer, sweeter. Someday, when he was undead himself, he'd know.

But even with the kid there, Al might have done something stupid, might have called down to Stan that there was nothing here but some old tom cat who'd probably taken a swat at that ball and rolled it out. But when he saw that she was knocked up—*very* knocked up, as in start-boiling-the-water knocked up—he knew he had to turn her in.

As much as the bloodsuckers loved kids, they went *crazy* for babies. Infants were like the primo delicacy among the vampires. Al once had seen a couple of them fighting over a newborn.

That had been a sight.

He sighed and said, "Too bad, honey, but you're packin too many points." He turned and called down toward the boardwalk. "Bingo, Stan. We struck it rich."

She screamed and the little boy began to cry.

Al shook his head as he watched her cower and hold the kid tight against her. Sorry babe. It ain't always a pleasant job, but a cowboy's gotta do what a cowboy's gotta do.

And besides, all these brownie points were gonna bring him that much closer to some stud time at the nearest cattle farm.

LACEY . . .

Lacey Flannery heard them coming before she saw them. Coming her way. They weren't talking, which was a bad sign. Could mean they were on the hunt. She had a faint hope that maybe they were wanderers like her, but she wasn't about to lay any money on it.

She'd motorboated down from the Sandy Hook area last night. The water tended to be pretty safe, even at night. The suckers stayed off it. She'd abandoned the boat at first light on the inlet jetty and sacked out here under the boardwalk. She'd been awake for about half an hour now. She'd packed up her stuff and had been ready to move out when she heard footsteps on the boards above. A bunch of feet—could have been four, six, maybe eight people. So she'd stayed put, figuring they'd move on.

But instead they were coming to her.

Lacey squatted with her back against a double piling and wondered what to do. Her sleeping bag and duffel were stacked before her on the sand. Better play it safe. She dipped into her bag of tricks, briefly considered her .38, but decided against it. She didn't have many bullets and didn't know what kind of trouble the noise of a shot would bring down on her. She chose her nunchucks instead. Two twelve-inch steel rods connected by a three-inch chain.

Yeah. That'll do.

She slipped out of her black leather jacket and her bare arms goosebumped in the breeze off the water. The tight black tank top she wore beneath wasn't much for warmth but at least it wouldn't get in her way. She looked down and noticed her nipples poking at the thin fabric. She hadn't worn a bra in three years and didn't miss it now. She rubbed her nipples to make them stick out even more. Hey, girl—use *all* your weapons. Then she stuck the nunchucks inside the waistband of her jeans at the small of her back. The chain was cold between her cheeks. Thong panties didn't cover much.

Her mouth felt a little dry, her palms a little moist. Let's hope they're friendly, she thought. If not, then let's hope there's no more than two of them.

She rose and peeked around the piling.

Shit. One was a woman. She was going to be harder to distract. And worse, they were wearing cowboy earrings. The good news was there were only two of them.

Lacey stepped out and faced them. "How's it going?"

The stopped dead, staring.

"Ooooh, Jackie," said the dumb-looking guy with the bad skin and the red Mohican as his eyes fixed on Lacey's chest. "This ain't Al's blonde, but she'll do. Oh, baby, will she do."

"Shut up, Kenny."

The skinny, pierced-up, white-trash blonde gave her an up and down; she seemed more interested in checking to see if Lacey's hands were empty. She looked thirty-five but was probably thirty. Not at all Lacey's type.

She fixed Lacey with her squinty brown eyes. "What're you doin down here?"

"Catching some Z's," Lacey said. "How about you two?"

"Lookin for loooove," Kenny said, grinning. "In all the wrong places." He stepped closer. "Hey, ain't you somethin. Look at those muscles, Jackie. And she got tats too."

Lacey looked down at her upper arms and the black Celtic knots that encircled each just between the sleek, well-cut bulges of her biceps and deltoids. She'd spent a lot of time on those muscles.

"Want to see them wiggle like snakes?"

She began contracting and relaxing the muscles, making them dance under the Celtic knots which in turn undulated like, well, snakes.

"Tits and tats and ripped to boot," he said, easing another step closer. "I think I'm in love. Think we can have her join the posse, Jacks?"

"No way. Besides, that ain't for us to decide."

"They look so hard," he said. "You mind if I give one a little squeeze?"

Lacey smiled. "You're talking about my muscles but you're staring at my nips."

He laughed. "Oh, I do like this one, Jackie." He looked at her. "We gotta—"

That was when Lacey kicked him. She knew how to kick, had taken classes in it, and she lashed out her foot as hard as she could, putting a lot of her lower body behind it. She landed a good one, right square in his balls. He made a breathy noise, something like *"Hommf!"* as he went knock-kneed and dropped to the sand. Jackie stared at him stupidly, as if trying to figure out what had just happened, while Lacey grabbed for her nunchucks. She had a grip on one end and was snapping the other in a sidearm arc when Jackie looked back at her. Her mouth was opening, starting to shout, when the steel bar caught her across the left side of her head. She tumbled to her right and hit the sand, still conscious but just barely, holding her head and groaning. Blood seeped between her fingers.

Lacey turned back to Kenny. He was down on his knees with his hands jammed between his thighs, clutching his jewels, his face gray, his mouth working.

"You fucking bitch!" he managed. "You're gonna wish—"

Lacey kicked him again, in the stomach this time, high, a bull's eye into his solar plexus. He doubled over. Kenny wouldn't be threatening Lacey or anybody else for a while.

Five seconds later she was back in her jacket and booking south with her duffel and her sleeping bag. Behind and above her she thought she heard a woman's voice cry out. The blond the two creeps had mentioned? Lacey stopped and listened. She heard another cry and looked up at a seagull coasting overhead on the breeze. It squawked again. Had that been what she'd heard?

She dropped her load and grabbed the edge of the boardwalk. The ends of the weathered boards rasped against her palms as she pulled herself up for a look—all those chin-ups at the gym were finally paying off. She held her eyes at board level. No one in sight.

She dropped back to the sand, grabbed her things, and started walking again.

No time to waste. She'd come to find her uncle.

CAROLE . . .

Sister Carole checked the Pyrex bowl on the stove. A chalky layer of potassium chloride had formed in the bottom. She turned off the heat and immediately decanted the boiling upper fluid, pouring it through a Mr. Coffee filter into a Pyrex brownie pan. She threw out the scum in the filter and put the pan of filtrate on the windowsill to cool.

She heard the sound of a car again and rushed to a window. It was the same car, the convertible, with the same occupants—

No, wait. There had been only four before. Now there were three squeezed into the rear. The woman who had been in the front earlier was in the back; she looked as if she might be sick; the man with the red Mohican seemed to be struggling with a newcomer, a young woman with long blond hair. She looked—

Jesus, Mary, and Joseph, the poor thing was pregnant!

Sister Carole suddenly felt as if something were tearing apart within her chest. Was there no justice, was there no mercy anywhere?

She dropped to her knees and began to pray for her, but in the back of her mind she wondered why she bothered. None of her prayers had been answered so far.

<Sacrilege, Carole! That's SACRILEGE! Now tell me why you'd be thinking the Lord would answer the prayers of such a SINNER? I know you were taught that he does, but believe me you, he doesn't!>

Maybe not, Carole thought. But if He'd answered *somebody's* prayers somewhere along the line, maybe she wouldn't have been forced to turn the Bennett's kitchen into an anarchist's laboratory.

The Lord helped those who helped themselves, didn't He? Especially when they were doing the Lord's work.

COWBOYS . . .

"Please leave me alone," the blonde whimpered, pushing Kenny's hand away as he tried to unbutton her top. She'd been nothing but a blubbering basket case since Al had put her kid in the trunk. "I want my little boy. Please let him out. Please!"

Al was sitting shotgun while Stan drove. Her whining was getting on Al's nerves. And so was Kenny. He turned around and checked out the back seat. Jackie was slumped on the driver side, holding an old sweatshirt against the side of her head. The bleeding had stopped but she looked pale and sick. The pregnant cow had the middle seat, and Kenny was nuzzling up against her from the other side.

Al said, "I still can't believe you got kayo'd by a girl."

Kenny kept his eyes on the cow. "I told you, man, she suckered me. I was slippin up on her, real casual like, gettin ready to make my move, and she's lookin like she's fallin for it when she punts me."

Kenny had been in sad shape for about ten or fifteen minutes, but he'd snapped back. He walked a little funny but the kick hadn't seemed to take the steam out of his usual horniness.

Jackie was another story. She'd puked once on the boardwalk, and another time in the parking lot. Al hoped she didn't puke up the car. You just didn't find a Cadillac convertible every day.

The cow started wailing about her kid again. "Please let my little boy out of the trunk! He'll suffocate!"

"Look!" Stan shouted, speaking for the first time since they'd left Point—he'd been real pissed at Kenny and Jackie for losing a girl. "I'll get your brat outta the trunk, all right. I'll tie a rope around his feet and *drag* him back to Lakewood if you don't shut up!"

She sobbed but didn't say anything more.

Al remembered the little kid lookin up at him as he

shoved him into the trunk. "Don't let them hurt my mommy," he'd said. Kinda reminded Al of his little brother when they were kids. Never could stand his little brother.

Kenny started toyin with the cow again. "C'mon. Show ol' Kenny those pretty pregnant titties."

"Ease up, Kenny."

Kenny didn't look at him. "Mind your own fucking business, Al."

Stan looked at Al and jerked his head toward the back seat. "Straighten out your friend, will ya?"

Al grabbed Kenny's arm. "Lay off her, man."

Kenny slammed his hand away. "Yeah? What for? To save her for you? Bull*shit!*"

Kenny could be a real asshole at times.

"We're not saving her for me," Al said. "For Gregor. You remember Gregor, don't you, Kenny?"

Some of Kenny's tough-guy act faded.

"Course I do," he said. "But I don't wanna suck her blood, man." He jammed his hand down between the cow's legs. "I got other things in mind. It's been a long time, man—a *long* time—and I gotta—"

"What if you screw up the baby?" Al said. "What if she starts having the baby and it's born dead? All because of you? What're you gonna tell Gregor then, Kenny? How you gonna explain that to him?"

"Who says he has to know?"

"You think he won't find out?" Al said. "I tell you what, Kenny. You wanna to get your jollies with this broad, fine. Go ahead. But if that's what you're gonna do, we're droppin you and her here—right here—and drivin away. Am I right, Stan?"

Stan nodded. "Fuckin ay."

"And then you can explain any problems to Gregor yourself tonight when we meet. Okay?"

"Gregor-Gregor-Gregor! Let up, huh? You just about piss your pants every time we get near him. He ain't so tough. Gimme a stake and a hammer and show me where he snoozes and I'll show you how tough he is. Fuckin leech is what he is. Stake him through his heart, cut off his head, and then we won't have to worry bout no more fuckin shit from Gregor. Do it to alla them. Show 'em all."

"Yeah?" Stan said, smilin but lookin straight ahead. "Then what?

"Then we'll be fuckin heroes, man."

"Heroes to who? These Saab-drivin, gel-haired, sprout-chewin faggots hiding behind their crosses and garlic? You wanna be heroes to them, go ahead. But what happens when word of what you done gets out to the other bloodsuckers and they come a-knockin? What then? You know how many of them there is out there, man? Zillions. They'll come back with a truckload of those ferals and rip us all to shreds. That what you want, asshole?"

Sounded to Al like Stan had already given Kenny's idea some thought and had shit-canned it.

Kenny said, "Hey, no, but—"

"Then shut the fuck up. And leave the cow alone."

Kenny pulled his hand away from the blonde and sat on it.

"Jesus, guys. It's been a long time. I need some."

"Hey, I need some too," Al told him. "But I ain't ready yet to get killed for a little pregnant poontang, know what I mean?"

Stan said, "Look at it this way. We gotta take some shit now and then, but you know anybody else got it better? We hold the fort, man. We hold the fort for them till we get to join up." He grinned. "Then we'll have assholes holding the fort for *us*."

Stan seemed to think that was real funny. He laughed about the rest of the way into Lakewood.

CAROLE . . .

Sister Carole finished her prayers at sundown and went to check on the cooled filtrate. The bottom of the pan was layered with potassium chlorate crystals. Potent stuff. The Germans had used it in their grenades and land mines during World War One.

She got a clean Mr. Coffee filter and poured the contents of the pan through it, but this time she saved the residue in the filter and let the liquid go down the drain.

<Lookit after what you're doing now, Carole! You're a sick woman! SICK! You've got to be stopping this and praying to God for guidance! Pray, Carole! PRAY!>

Sister Carole ignored the voice and spread out the crystals in the now-empty pan. She set the oven on LOW and placed the pan on the middle rack. She had to get all the moisture out of the potassium chlorate before it would be of any use to her.

So much trouble, and so dangerous. If only her searches had yielded some dynamite, even a few sticks, everything would have been so much easier. She'd searched everywhere—hunting shops, gun stores, construction sites. She'd found lots of other useful items, but no dynamite. Only some blasting caps. She no choice but to improvise.

This was her third batch. She'd been lucky so far. She hoped she survived long enough to get a chance to use it.

GREGOR . . .

"You've outdone yourselves this time, boys."

Gregor stared at the three cowboys. Ordinarily he found it doubly difficult to be near them. Not simply because the crimson thirst made a perpetual test of proximity to a living font of hot, pulsing sustenance when he'd yet to feed, urging him to let loose and tear into their throats; but also because these four were so common, such low-lifes.

Gregor couldn't wait until he was moved up and would no longer be forced to deal directly with flotsam such as these. Living collaborators were a necessary evil, but that didn't mean he had to like them.

Tonight, however, he could almost say that he enjoyed

their presence. He'd been unhappy about the news of a fifth slain cowboy, but was ecstatic with the prizes they had brought with them.

He had shown up shortly after sundown at the customary meeting place outside St. Anthony's church. Of course, it didn't look much like a church now, what with all the crosses broken off. He'd found the scurvy trio waiting for him as usual, but they had with them a small boy and—dare he believe his eyes—a pregnant woman. His knees had gone weak at the double throb of life within her.

"Where's your companion?" he asked. "The woman?"

"Jackie's not feeling so hot so we left her home," said the one in the cowboy hat.

What was his name? So many of these roaches to keep track of. This one was called Stan. Yes, that was it.

"Well, I'm extremely proud of all of you."

"We thought you'd appreciate it," Stan said.

Gregor felt his grin grow even wider.

"Oh, I do. Not just for the succulence of the prizes you've delivered, but because you've vindicated my faith in you. I knew the minute I saw you that you'd make a good posse leader."

An outright lie. But it cost him nothing to heap the praise on Stan, and perhaps it would spur him to do as well next time. Maybe better. Although what could be better than this?

"Anything for the cause," the redheaded one said.

The one with the spiked dark hair—Al, Gregor remembered—gave his partner a poisonous look, as if he wanted to kick him for being such a boot-lick.

"And your timing could not be better," Gregor told them. "We have a special guest visiting from New York." He didn't mention that she was here because someone was exterminating their fellow slugs. "I will present this gravid cow to her as a gift. She will be enormously pleased."

At least Gregor hoped so. He was relying on the gift to take the edge off her reaction when she learned that another cowboy was dead.

"Is that the lady I saw you with last night?"

Al's words startled Gregor. Had this cowboy been spying on him? He felt his lips pulling back, baring his fangs.

"When was this?"

Al took half a step back. "When we was driving away after droppin off that old lady. I saw her like come up behind you."

Gregor relaxed. "Yes, that was her. These gifts will be good for me. And trust me, what is good for me will eventually prove to be good for you. I won't forget your efforts."

Partly true. The little boy would go to the local nest leader who'd been pastor of St. Anthony's during his life and had a taste for young boys. The priest had become the de facto leader of Gregor's local get. Over the decades Gregor had noted that the newly turned took to the undead existence with varying degrees of aptitude. Father Palmeri seemed a natural. He'd adapted to his new circumstances with amazing gusto. Perhaps zeal was a better term. Some people, one might say, were born to be undead.

He'd save the boy for tomorrow since the priest already had a bloodsource lined up for tonight. The pregnant female would indeed go to Olivia. But the rest was a laugh. As soon as Gregor was moved out of here, he'd never give these walking heaps of human garbage another thought.

But he smiled as he turned away.

"As always, may your night be bountiful."

CAROLE . . .

A little after sundown, Sister Carole removed the potassium chlorate crystals from the oven. She poured then into a bowl and then gently, carefully, began to grind them down to a fine power. This was the touchiest part of the process. A little too much friction, a sudden shock, and the bowl would blow up in her face.

<You'd like that, wouldn't you, Carole. Sure, and you'll be thinking that would solve all your problems. Well, it won't,

*Carole. It will merely start your REAL problems! It will send
you straight to HELL!>*

Sister Carole made no reply as she continued the grinding. When the powder was sifted through a four-hundred-
mesh screen, she spread it onto the bottom of the pan again
and placed it back in the oven to remove the last trace of
moisture. While that was heating she began melting equal
parts wax and Vaseline, mixing them in a small Pyrex bowl.

When the mix had reached a uniform consistency she dissolved it in some camp stove gasoline. She removed the
potassium chlorate powder from the oven and stirred in three
percent aluminum powder to enhance the flash effect. Then
she poured the Vaseline-wax-gasoline solution over the powder. She slipped on rubber gloves and began stirring and
kneading everything together until she had a uniform, gooey
mess. This went on the windowsill to cool and to speed the
evaporation of the gasoline.

Then she went to the bedroom. Soon it would be time to
go out and she had to dress appropriately. She stripped to her
white cotton underpants and laid out the tight black skirt and
red blouse she'd lifted from the shattered show window of
that deserted shop down on Clifton Avenue. She slipped her
small breasts into a heavily padded bra, then began squeezing into a fresh pair of black pantyhose.

*<You're getting into THOSE clothes again, are you? You
look cheap, Carole! You look like a WHORE!>*

I know, she thought. That's the whole idea.

JOE . . .

Father Joe Cahill watched the moon rise over the back end
of his old church and wondered about the wisdom of coming
back. The casual decision made in the full light of day now
seemed reckless and foolhardy in the dark.

But no turning back now. He'd followed Zev to the second
floor of this three-story office building across the street from

the rear of St. Anthony's, and here they'd waited for dark. It must have been a law office once. The place had been vandalized, the windows broken, the furniture trashed, but an old Temple University Law School degree hung askew on the wall, and the couch was still in one piece. So while Zev caught some Z's, Joe sat, sipped a little of his Scotch, and did some heavy thinking.

Mostly he thought about his drinking. He'd done too much of that lately, he knew; so much so that he was afraid to stop cold. So he was allowing himself just a touch now, barely enough to take the edge off. He'd finish the rest later, after he came back from that church over there.

He'd been staring at St. Anthony's since they'd arrived. It too had been extensively vandalized. Once it had been a beautiful little stone church, a miniature cathedral, really, very Gothic with all its pointed arches, steep roofs, crocketed spires, and multifoil stained glass windows. Now the windows were smashed, the crosses that had topped the steeple and each gable were gone, and anything resembling a cross on its granite exterior had been defaced beyond recognition.

As he'd known it would, the sight of St. Anthony's brought back memories of Gloria Sullivan, the young, pretty church volunteer whose husband worked for United Chemical International in New York; he commuted to the city every day, trekked overseas a little too often. Joe and Gloria had seen a lot of each other around the church offices and had become good friends. But Gloria had somehow got the idea that what they had went beyond friendship, so she showed up at the rectory one night when Joe was there alone. He tried to explain that as attractive as she was, she was not for him. He had taken certain vows and meant to stick by them. He did his best to let her down easy but she'd been hurt. And angry.

That might have been that, but then her five-year-old son Kevin had come home from altar boy practice with a story about a priest making him pull down his pants and touching him. Kevin was never clear on who the priest had been, but Gloria Sullivan was. Obviously it had been Father Cahill—any man who could turn down the heartfelt offer of her love and her body had to be either a queer or worse. And a child molester was worse.

She took it to the police and to the papers.

Joe groaned softly at the memory of how swiftly his life had become hell. But he had been determined to weather the storm, sure that the real culprit eventually would be revealed. He had no proof—still didn't—but if one of the priests at St. Anthony's was a pederast, he knew it wasn't him. That left Father Alberto Palmeri, St. Anthony's fifty-five-year-old pastor.

Before Joe could get to the truth, however, the bishop had stepped in and removed Joe from the parish. Joe left under a cloud that had followed him to the retreat house in the next county and hovered over him till this day. The only place he'd found even brief respite from the impotent anger and bitterness that roiled under his skin and soured his gut every minute of every day was in the bottle—and that was sure as hell a dead end.

So why had he agreed to come back here? To torture himself? Or to get a look at Palmeri and see how low he had sunk?

Maybe that was it. Maybe seeing Palmeri wallowing in his true element would give Joe the impetus to put the whole St. Anthony's incident behind him and rejoin what was left of the human race—which needed all the help it could get.

And maybe it wouldn't.

Getting back on track was a nice thought, but over the past few months Joe had found it increasingly difficult to give much of a damn about anyone or anything.

Except maybe Zev. The old rabbi had stuck by him through the worst of it, defending him to anyone who would listen. But an endorsement from an Orthodox rabbi hadn't meant diddly in St. Anthony's.

Yesterday Zev had biked all the way to Spring Lake to see him. Old Zev was all right.

And he'd been right about the number of undead here too. Lakewood was *crawling* with the things. Fascinated and re-pelled, Joe had watched the streets fill with them shortly after sundown.

But what had disturbed him more were the creatures he'd seen *before* sundown.

The humans. Live ones.

The collaborators. The ones Zev called Vichy.

If there was anything lower, anything that deserved true death more than the undead themselves, it was the still-living humans who worked for them.

A hand touched his shoulder and he jumped. Zev. He was holding something out to him. Joe took it and held it up in the moonlight: a tiny crescent moon dangling from a chain on a ring.

"What's this?"

"An earring. The local Vichy wear them. The earrings identify them to the local nest of undead. They are spared."

"Where'd you get it?"

Zev's face was hidden in the shadows. "The previous owner . . . no longer needs it.

"What's that supposed to mean?"

Zev sighed. He sounded embarrassed. "Some group has been killing the local Vichy. I don't know how many they've eliminated, but I came across one in my wanderings. Not such a pleasant task, but I forced myself to relieve the body of its earring. Just in case."

Joe found it hard to imagine the old pre-occupation Zev performing such a grisly task, but these were different times.

"Just in case what?"

"In case I needed to pretend to be one of them."

Joe had to laugh. "I can't see that fooling them for a sec-ond."

"Maybe a second is all I'd need. But it will look better on you. Put it on."

"My ear's not pierced."

A gnarled hand moved into the moonlight. Joe saw a

long needle clasped between the thumb and index finger.

"That I can fix," Zev said.

† † †

"On second thought," Zev whispered as they crouched in the deep shadows on St. Anthony's western flank, "maybe you shouldn't see this."

Puzzled, Joe squinted at him in the darkness.

"You lay a guilt trip on me to get me here, you make a hole in my ear, and now you're having second thoughts?"

"It is horrible like I can't tell you."

Joe thought about that. Certainly there was enough horror in the world outside St. Anthony's. What purpose did it serve to see what was going inside?

Because it used to be my church.

Even though he'd been an associate pastor, never fully in charge, and even though he'd been unceremoniously yanked from the post, St. Anthony's had been his first parish. He was back. He might as well know what they were doing inside.

"Show me."

Zev led him to a pile of rubble under a smashed stained glass window. He pointed up to where faint light flickered from inside.

"Look in there."

"You're not coming?"

"Once was enough, thank you."

Joe climbed as carefully, as quietly as he could, all the while becoming increasingly aware of a growing stench like putrid, rotting meat. It was coming from inside, wafting through the broken window. Steeling himself, he straightened and peered over the sill.

For a moment he felt disoriented, like someone peering out the window of a Brooklyn apartment and seeing the rolling hills of a Kansas farm. This could not be the interior of St. Anthony's.

In the flickering light of dozens of sacramental candles he

saw that the walls were bare, stripped of all their ornaments, including the plaques for the Stations of the Cross; the dark wood was scarred and gouged wherever there had been anything remotely resembling a cross. The floor too was mostly bare, the pews ripped from their neat rows and hacked to pieces, their splintered remains piled high at the rear under the choir balcony.

And the giant crucifix that had dominated the space behind the altar—only a portion remained. The cross pieces on each side had been sawed off so that an armless, life-size Christ now hung upside down against the rear wall of the sanctuary.

Joe took in all that in a flash; then his attention gravitated to the unholy congregation that peopled St. Anthony's this night. The collaborators—the Vichy humans—made up the periphery of the group. Some looked like bikers and trailer-park white trash, but others looked like normal, everyday people. What bonded them was the crescent-moon earring dangling from every right earlobe.

But the rest, the group gathered in the sanctuary—Joe felt his hackles rise at the sight of them. They surrounded the altar in a tight knot. He recognized some of them: Mayor Davis, Reverend Dalton, and others, their pale, bestial faces, bereft of the slightest trace of human warmth, compassion, or decency, turned upward. His gorge rose when he saw the object of their rapt attention.

A naked teenage boy—his hands tied behind his back, was suspended over the altar by his ankles. He was sobbing and choking, his eyes wide and vacant with shock, his mind all but gone. The skin had been flayed from his forehead—apparently the Vichy had found an expedient solution to the cross tattoo—and blood ran in a slow stream across his abdomen and chest from his freshly truncated genitals. And beside him, standing atop the altar, a bloody-mouthed creature dressed in a long cassock. Joe recognized the thin shoulders, the graying hair trailing from the balding crown, but was shocked at the crimson vulpine grin he flashed to the things clustered below him.

"Now," said the creature in a lightly accented voice Joe had heard a thousand times from St. Anthony's pulpit.

Father Alberto Palmeri.

From the group a hand reached up with a straight razor and drew it across the boy's throat. As the blood sprang from the vessels and flowed down over his face, those below squeezed and struggled forward like hatchling vultures to catch the falling drops and scarlet trickles in their open mouths.

Joe fell away from the window and vomited. He felt Zev grab his arm and lead him away. He was vaguely aware of crossing the street and heading back toward the ruined legal office.

ZEV . . .

"Why in God's name did you want me to see that?"

Zev looked across the office toward the source of the words. He could make out a vague outline where Father Joe sat on the floor, his back against the wall, the open bottle of Scotch in his hand. The priest had taken one drink since their return, no more.

"I thought you should know what they were doing to your church." He felt bad about the immediate effect on Joe, but he was hoping the long-term consequences would benefit him and others.

"So you've said. But what's the reason behind that one?"

Zev shrugged in the darkness. "I'd gathered you weren't doing well, that even before everything else began falling apart, you had already fallen apart. So when this woman who saved me urged me to find you, I took up the quest and came to see you. Just as I expected, I found a man who was angry at everything and letting it eat up his *guderim*. I thought maybe it would be good to give that man something very specific to be angry at."

"You bastard!" Father Joe whispered. "Who gave you the right?"

"Friendship gave me the right, Joe. I should know that you are rotting away and do nothing? I have no congregation of my own anymore so I turned my attention on you. Always I was a somewhat meddlesome rabbi."

"Still are. Out to save my soul, ay?"

"We rabbis don't save souls. Guide them maybe, hopefully give them direction. But only you can save your soul, Joe."

Silence hung in the air for a while. Suddenly the crescent-moon earring Zev had given Father Joe landed in the puddle of moonlight on the floor between them. He noticed a speck of crimson on the post.

"Why do they do it?" the priest said. "The Vichy—why do they collaborate?"

"The first ones are quite unwilling, believe me. They co-operate because their wives and children are held hostage by the undead. But before too long the dregs of humanity begin to slither out from under their rocks and offer their services in exchange for the immortality of vampirism."

"Why bother working for them? Why not just bare your throat to the nearest bloodsucker?"

"That's what I thought at first," Zev said. "But as I witnessed the Lakewood holocaust I detected their pattern. After the immediate onslaught—and the burning of the bodies of their first victims—they change tactics. They can choose who joins their ranks, so after they've fully infiltrated a population, they start to employ a different style of killing. For only when the undead draws the life's blood from the throat with its fangs does the victim become one of them. Anyone drained as in the manner of that boy in the church tonight dies a true death. He's as dead now as someone run over by a truck. He will not rise tomorrow night."

"So the Vichy work for them for the opportunity of getting their blood sucked the old-fashioned way."

"And joining the undead ranks."

Zev heard no humor in the soft laugh that echoed across the room from Father Joe.

"Great. Just great. I never cease to be amazed at our fellow human beings. Their capacity for good is exceeded only by their ability to debase themselves."

"Hopelessness does strange things, Joe. The undead know that. So they rob us of hope. That's how they beat us. They transform our friends and neighbors and leaders into their own, leaving us feeling alone, completely cut off. Some can't take the despair and kill themselves."

"Hopelessness," Joe said. "A potent weapon."

After a long silence, Zev said, "So what are you going to do now, Father Joe?"

Another bitter laugh from across the room.

"I suppose this is the place where I declare that I've found new purpose in life and will now go forth into the world as a fearless vampire killer."

"Such a thing would be nice."

"Well screw that. I'm only going as far as across the street."

"To St. Anthony's?"

Zev saw Father Joe take a swig from the Scotch bottle and then screw the cap on tight.

"Yeah. To see if there's anything I can do over there."

"Father Palmeri and his nest might not like that."

"I told you, don't call him Father. And screw *him*. Nobody can do what he's done and get away with it. I'm taking my church back."

In the dark, behind his beard, Zev smiled.

COWBOYS . . .

Al had the car out on his own. He wasn't supposed to, gas being hard to come by and all, but he needed to be alone, or at least away from Kenny. Yeah, sure, they'd been friends forever but they'd never been together 24–7. Usually the four of them played cards and did some drinking before turning in. But Jackie was out of commission and Stan was still pissed and wasn't playing cards with nobody, so that left Al with just Kenny.

They all lived together in one of the big mansions off Hope Road. Stan liked to brag that one of the Mets used to live there. Big deal. The place had all the comforts of home: electricity from a generator, videotapes and DVDs—with a good selection of porn—and a fridge full of beer. But sometimes Kenny could wear you out, man. Big time. Like tonight.

Al was feeling better already, banging his head in time to Insane Clown Posse's "Cemetery Girl" as he cruised the dark streets.

He looked up. Clouds hid the moon. He wished it was out and full. Amazing how dark a residential street could be when there was no traffic, no street lights. At least he had his headlights and—

Whoa. He hit the brakes. He'd just passed someone on the sidewalk. Someone female looking. And not too old.

He quick took off his earring and flipped the Caddy into reverse. He kept the earring palmed, ready to flash it if the lady turned out to be one of the bloodsuckers, but otherwise keeping it out of sight just in case this was somebody looking for a new cowboy to kill.

He did a slow backup while he searched the shadows and moonlit patches. Nothing. Shit. Either he was seeing things or he'd spooked her.

He was just about to slam back into DRIVE when he heard a voice. A woman's voice.

"Hey, mister."

Al grabbed his flashlight from the passenger seat and beamed it toward the voice.

A woman half hiding behind a tree in the bushes. Not undead. Maybe thirty, skinny but not bad looking. He played the light up and down her. Short dark hair, lots of eye makeup, a red sweater tight over decent-size boobs, a short black skirt very tight over black stockings.

Despite the alarm bells going off in his brain, Al ignored

them as he felt his groin start to swell. He left the car in the
middle of the street—like he had to worry about getting a
ticket, right?—and walked over to her.

"Who're you?"

She smiled. No, not bad looking at all.

"My name's Carole," she said. "You got any food?"

"Some." Yeah, she looked like she could use a few good
meals. "But not a whole helluva lot."

Actually, he had a *lot* of food, but saw no reason to let her
know that.

"Can you spare any?"

"I might be able to help you out some. Depends on how
many mouths we're talking about."

"Just me and my kid."

The words jumped out of his mouth before he could stop
them: "You got a kid?"

She waved her hands in quick, nervous moves. "Don't
worry. She's only four. She don't eat much."

A four-year-old. Two kids in one day. Almost too good to
be true.

His brain kicked into overdrive. How to play this? For a
while now he'd had this little scheme of keeping a piece on
the side, with neither the bloodsuckers or the posse knowing
nothing about her. He'd get her a house, keep her fed, keep
her protected. But it sounded like this Carole already had
herself a house. Even better. She could stay where she was
and he'd visit her whenever he could get away. She treated
him right, they could play house for a while. She gave him
any trouble, like holding out on him, she and her brat became gifts to Gregor. That was where they were going to
wind up anyway, but no reason Al couldn't get some use out
of her before she became some bloodsucker's meal or
wound up on a cattle farm.

And maybe he'd get *real* lucky. Maybe she'd get pregnant
before he turned her in.

"Well . . . all right," he said, trying to sound reluctant.
"Bring her out where I can see her."

"She's home asleep."

"Alone?" Al was like immediately pissed. He already considered that kid his property. He didn't want no bloodsucker sneaking in and robbing him of what was rightfully his. "What if—?"

"Don't worry. I've got her surrounded by crosses."

"Still, you never know." He paused, thinking. "Here's the deal. I got food but I got this tiny little rundown place that ain't fit for the cockroaches that live there. Maybe I could like spend some time at your place. That way I could guard you and your kid from those cowboys. They'd love nothing better'n hauling a little kid into the bloodsuckers."

Did that sound concerned enough?

A hand flew to her mouth. "Oh dear!" Her voice softened. "You must be a good man."

"Oh, I'm the best," he said.

And I've got this friend behind my fly who's just dying to meet you.

"I'll show you my place," she said. "It's not much but there's room for you."

Yeah, babe. Right on top of you.

She got in the car and directed him to the corner and around to the middle of the next block to an old two-story colonial set back among some tall oaks on an overgrown lot. He nodded with growing excitement when he saw a child's red wagon parked against the front steps.

"You live here? Hell, I musta passed this place a couple of times already today."

"Really?" she said. "We usually stay hidden in the basement."

"Good thinkin."

He followed her up the steps and through the front door. Inside there was a couple of candles burning but the heavy drapes hid them from outside.

"Lynn's sleeping upstairs," she said. "I'll just run up and check on her."

Al watched her black-stockinged legs hungrily as she

bounded up the bare wooden stairway, taking the steps two at a time. He adjusted his jeans for a little more comfort. Man, he was hard as a rock. Couldn't wait to get her out of that miniskirt and himself into—

And then it hit him: Why wait till she came back down? What was he doing standing around down here when he could be upstairs getting himself a preview of what was to come?

"Yoo-hoo," he said softly as he put his foot on the first step. "Here comes Daddy."

But the first step wasn't wood. Wasn't even a step. His foot went right through it, like it was made of cardboard or something. As Al looked down in shock he saw that it *was* made of cardboard—painted cardboard. His brain was just forming the question *Why*? when a sudden blast of pain like he'd never known in his whole life shot up his leg from just above the ankle.

He screamed, lunged back, away from the false step, but the movement tripled his agony. He clung to the newel post like a drunk, weeping and moaning for God knew how long, until the pain eased for a second. Then slowly, gingerly, accompanied by the metallic clanking of uncoiling chain links, he lifted his leg out of the false tread.

Al let loose a stream of curses through his pain-clenched teeth when he saw the bear trap attached to his leg. Its sharp, massive steel teeth had sunk themselves deep into the flesh of his lower leg.

But fear began to worm through the all-enveloping haze of his agony.

The bitch set me up!

Kenny had wanted to find the guys who were killing the cowboys. But now Al had done just that, and it scared him shitless. What a dumbass he was. Baited by a broad—the oldest trick in the book.

Gotta get outta here!

He lunged for the door but the chain caught and brought him up short with a blinding blaze of agony so intense his scream damn near shredded his vocal cords. He toppled to the floor and lay there whimpering like a kicked dog until the pain became bearable again.

Where were they? Where were the rest of the cowboy killers? Upstairs, laughing as they listened to him howl? Waiting until he wore himself out so he'd be easy pickings?

He'd show them.

Al pulled himself to a sitting position and reached for the trap. He tried to spread its jaws but they were locked tight on his leg. He wrapped his hand around the chain and tried to yank it free from where it was fastened below but it wouldn't budge.

Panic began to grip him now. Its icy fingers were tightening on his throat when he heard a sound on the stairs. He looked up and saw her.

A nun.

He blinked and looked again.

Still a nun. He squinted and saw that it was the broad who'd led him in here. She was wearing a bulky sweater and loose slacks, and all the makeup had been scrubbed off her face, but he knew she was a nun by the thing she wore on her head: a white band up front with a black veil trailing behind.

And suddenly, amid the pain and panic, Al was back in grammar school, back in St. Mary's before he got expelled, and Sister Margaret was coming at him with her ruler, only this nun was a lot younger than Sister Margaret, and that was no ruler she was carrying, that was a baseball bat—an *aluminum* baseball bat.

He looked around. Nobody else, just him and the nun.

"Where's the rest of you?"

"Rest?" she said.

"Yeah. The others in your gang. Where are they?"

"There's only me."

She was lying. Had to be. One crazy nun killing all those cowboys? No way! But still he had to get out of here. He tried to crawl across the floor but the fucking chain wouldn't let him.

"You're makin a mistake!" he cried. "I ain't one a them!"

"Oh, but you are," she said, coming down the stairs.

"No. Really. See?" He touched his right ear lobe. "No earring."

"Maybe not now, but you had one earlier." She stepped over the gaping opening of the phony tread and circled to his left.

"When? *When*?"

"When you drove by earlier today. You told me so yourself."

"I lied!"

"No, you didn't. But I lied. I wasn't in the basement. I was watching through the window. I saw you and your three friends in that car." Her voice suddenly became cold and brittle and sharp as a straight razor. "And I saw that poor woman you had with you. Where is she now? What did you do with her?"

She was talking through her teeth now, and the look in her eyes, the strained pallor of her face had Al ready to pee his pants. He wrapped his arms around his head as she stepped closer with the bat.

"Please!" he wailed.

"What did you do with them?"

"Nothin!"

"Lie!"

She swung the bat, but not at his head. Instead she slammed it with a heavy metallic clank against the jaws of the trap. As he screamed with the renewed agony and his hands automatically reached for his injured leg, Al realized that she must have done this sort of thing before. Because now his head was completely unprotected and she was already into a second swing. And this one was aimed much higher.

CAROLE . . .

<You've done it again, Carole! AGAIN! I know they're a bad lot, but look what you've DONE!>

Sister Carole looked down at the unconscious man with the bleeding head and trapped, lacerated leg. She sobbed.

"I know," she said aloud.

She was so tired. She'd have liked nothing better now than to go upstairs and cry herself to sleep. But she couldn't spare the time. Every moment counted now.

She tucked her feelings—her mercy, her compassion—into the deepest, darkest pocket of her being, where she couldn't see or hear them, and got to work.

The first thing she did was tie the cowboy's hands good and tight behind his back. Then she got a washcloth from the downstairs bathroom, stuffed it in his mouth, and secured it with a tie of rope around his head. That done, she grabbed the crowbar and the short length of two-by-four from where she kept them on the floor of the hall closet; she used the bar to pry open the jaws of the bear trap and wedged the two-by-four between them to keep them open. Then she worked the cowboy's leg free. He groaned a couple of times during the process but he never came to.

She bound his legs tightly together, then grabbed the throw rug he lay upon and dragged him and the rug out to the front porch and down the steps to the red wagon she'd left there. She rolled him off the bottom step into the wagon bed and tied him in place. Then she slipped her arms through the straps of her heavily loaded backpack and she was ready to go. She grabbed the wagon's handle and pulled it down the walk, down the driveway apron, and onto the asphalt. From there on it was smooth rolling.

Sister Carole knew just where she was going. She had the spot all picked out.

She was going to try something a little different tonight.

COWBOYS . . .

Al screamed and sobbed against the gag. If he could just talk to her he knew he could change her mind. But he couldn't get a word past the cloth jammed against his tongue.

And he didn't have long. She had him upside down, strung up by his feet, swaying in the breeze from one of the climbing spikes on a utility pole, and he knew what was coming next. So he pleaded with his eyes, with his soul. He tried mental telepathy.

Sister, Sister, Sister, don't do this! I'm a Catholic! My mother prayed for me every day and it didn't help, but I'll change now, I promise! I swear on a stack of fuckin bibles I'll be a good boy from now on if you'll just let me go this time!

Then he saw her face in the moonlight and realized with a final icy shock that he was truly a goner. Even if he could make her hear him, nothing he could say was going to change this lady's mind. The eyes were empty. No one was home. The bitch was on autopilot.

When he saw the glimmer of the straight razor as it glided above his throat, there was nothing left to do but wet himself.

CAROLE . . .

When Sister Carole finished vomiting, she sat on the curb and allowed herself a brief cry.

<Go ahead, Carole. Cry your crocodile tears. A fat lot of good it'll do you come Judgment Day. No good at all. What'll you say then, Carole? How will you explain THIS?>

She dragged herself to her feet. She had two more things to do. One of them involved touching the fresh corpse. The second was simpler: starting a fire to attract other cowboys and their masters.

GREGOR . . .

Gregor stood amid his get-guards and watched as cowboy Kenny ran in circles around his dead friend's swaying, up-ended corpse.

"It's Al! The bastards got Al! I'll kill 'em all! I'll tear 'em to pieces!"

How Gregor wished somebody would do just that. He'd heard about these deaths but this was the first he'd seen—an obscene parody of the bloodletting rituals he and his night-brothers performed on the cattle. This was acutely embar-rassing, especially with Olivia newly arrived from New York.

"Come out here!" Kenny screamed into the darkness. "Come out and fight like men!"

Stan, the head of this posse, was stamping out the brush fire at the base of the utility pole.

"We should be getting back, Gregor," one of his guards whispered. "It's too open out here. Not safe."

All four of them had their pistols drawn and were eyeing the night, their heads rotating back and forth like radar dishes.

Gregor ignored him and called out, "Someone cut him down."

Stan pointed to Kenny. "Climb up there."

"Hey, no—"

"He was your bud," Stan said. "You do it."

Kenny reluctantly climbed the pole.

"I want to let him down easy!" he yelled when he'd reached the rope.

"Just cut the rope," Stan said.

"Dammit, Stan. Al was one of *us!* I'll cut it slow and you ease him down."

"Oh, fuck, all right," Stan said. "C'mere, Jackie, and help me."

The woman stood back by one of the cars that had brought them all here. Not the fancy convertible the posse had been using recently—Al had apparently taken that for a drive and never come back. She had a bandage around her head over a blackened left eye. Gregor wondered what had happened to her. Beaten by one of her own posse perhaps?

He looked at Jackie and remembered lusting after women for their bodies; now he cared only for the red wine running through them. Sexual lust was a dim memory. He hadn't had an erection since he was turned, seventy years ago.

Blood . . . always blood. Gregor was glad he had supped before accompanying these cowboys to their dead friend.

This made six dead. Two in the past three days. The pace was accelerating. Olivia would be on the warpath.

Jackie shook her head. "No way," she said, her voice faint. "I can't."

"Get your skinny ass over here!"

"He's comin down!" Kenny shouted.

"Damn fuck!" Stan shouted as the body slumped earthward. He reached up to grab it and—

The flash was noonday bright, the blast deafening as the shock wave knocked Gregor to the ground. His first instinct was to leap to his feet again, but he realized he couldn't see. The bright flash had fogged his night vision with a purple, amebic afterimage. He lay quiet until he could see again, then rose to his feet.

He heard wailing sounds. The woman crouched beside the car, screaming hysterically; the cowboy who had climbed the pole lay somewhere in the bushes, crying out about his back, how badly it hurt and how he couldn't move his legs. But the other two—Stan and the murdered Al—were nowhere to be seen.

His get-guards were struggling to their feet, enclosing him in a tight, four-man circle. "Are you all right, Gregor?" one said.

"Of course I'm all right," he snapped. "You wouldn't be asking that question if I weren't."

Gregor shook his head. He tried to choose carefully for his get, emphasizing intelligence. Sometimes they fell short.

Gregor began to brush off his clothes as he looked around, then froze. He was wet, covered with blood and torn flesh. The entire street glistened, littered with bits of bone, muscle, skin, and fingernail-size pieces of internal organs, leaving no way of telling what had belonged to whom.

Gregor shuddered at the prospect of explaining this to Olivia.

His fury exploded. The first killing tonight had been embarrassing enough by itself. But now another cowboy had been taken out, and still another crippled to the point where he'd have to be put down—all right in front of him. This had passed beyond embarrassment into humiliation.

When he caught these vigilantes he'd deal with them personally. And see that it took them days to die.

CAROLE . . .

Sister Carole saw the flash and heard the explosion through the window over the sink in the darkened kitchen of the Bennett house. No joy, no elation. This wasn't fun. But she did find a certain grim satisfaction in learning that her potassium chlorate plastique had worked.

The gasoline had evaporated from the latest batch and she was working with that now. The moon provided sufficient illumination for the final stage. Once she had the right amount measured out, she didn't need much light to pack the plastique into soup cans. All she had to do was make sure she maintained the proper loading density.

That done, she stuck a number-three blasting cap in the end of each cylinder and dipped it into the pot of melted wax she had on the stove. And that did it. She now had waterproof block charges with a detonation velocity comparable to forty-percent-ammonia dynamite.

"All right," she said aloud to the night through her kitchen window. "You've made my life a living hell. Now it's your time to be afraid."

GREGOR . . .

"Three in one night!"

Olivia's eyes seemed to glow with red fire in the gloom of the Post Office basement. She'd taken up temporary residence in the old granite building.

"They booby-trapped the body." Gregor knew it sounded lame but it was the truth.

Olivia's voice was barely a whisper as she pierced him with her stare. "You've disappointed me, Gregor."

"It is a temporary situation, I assure you."

"So you keep saying, but it has lasted far too long already. The dead serfs total seven now. Seven! Wait till Franco hears!"

Gregor quailed at the thought. "He doesn't have to hear. Not yet."

"You're losing control, Gregor. You don't seem to realize that besides our strength and our special powers, we have two weapons: fear and hopelessness. We cannot control the cattle by love and loyalty, so if we are to maintain our rule, it must be through the terror we inspire in them and the seeming impossibility of ever defeating us. What have the cattle witnessed in your territory, Gregor?"

Gregor knew where this was headed. "Olivia, please, I—"

"I'll tell you what they've witnessed," she said, her voice rising. "They've witnessed your inability to protect the serfs we've induced to herd the cattle and guard the daylight hours for us. And trust me, Gregor, the success of one vigilante group will give rise to a second, and then a third, and before long it will be open season on our serfs. And then you'll have no control. Because the cattle herders are cowardly swine, Gregor. The lowest of the low. They work for us only because they see us as the victors and they want to be on the winning side at any cost. But if we can't protect them, if they get a sense that we might be vulnerable and that our continued dominance might *not* be guaranteed, they'll turn on us in a flash."

"I know that, and I'm—"

"Fix it, Gregor." Her voice sank to a whisper again. "I will give you till dawn Friday to remedy this. If not, you'll awaken Friday night to find yourself heading back to New York to face Franco. Is that clear?"

Dawn Friday? Gregor could scarcely believe what he was hearing. Here it was Thursday morning with only a few hours until dawn—too late to take any action now. That left him one night to catch these marauding swine. And to think he'd just made her a gift of the pregnant cow's baby. The ungrateful—

He swallowed his anger.

"Very clear."

"Good. I expect you to have a plan by sundown."

"I will."

"Leave me now."

As Gregor turned and hurried up the steps he heard a new-born begin to cry in the darkness. The sound made him hungry.

4

Joe yawned and stretched his limbs in the morning light. He'd stayed up most of the night and let Zev sleep. The old guy needed his rest. Sleep would have been impossible for Joe anyway. He was too wired. So he'd sat up, staring at the back of St. Anthony's.

The undead had left before first light, dark shapes drifting out the doors and across the grass like parishioners leaving a predawn service. Joe had felt his teeth grind as he scanned the group for Palmeri, but he couldn't make him out in the dimness. He might have gone out the front. By the time the sun had begun to peek over the rooftops and through the trees to the east, the streets outside were deserted.

He woke Zev and together they walked around to the front of the church. The heavy oak and iron doors, each forming half of a pointed arch, were closed. Joe pulled them open and fastened the hooks to hold them back. Then, taking a breath, he walked through the vestibule and into the nave.

Even though he was ready for it, the stench backed him up a few steps. When his stomach settled, he forced himself ahead, treading a path between the two piles of shattered and splintered pews. Zev walked beside him, a handkerchief pressed over his mouth.

Last night he had thought the place a shambles. He saw now that it was worse. The light of day poked into all the corners, revealing everything that had been hidden by the warm glow of the candles. Half a dozen rotting corpses hung from the ceiling—he hadn't noticed them last night—and others were sprawled on the floor against the walls. Some of the bodies lay in pieces. Behind the chancel rail a headless female torso was draped over the front of the pulpit. To the left stood the statue of Mary. Someone had fitted her with foam rubber breasts and a huge dildo. And at the rear of the sanctuary was the armless Christ hanging head down on the upright of his cross.

"My church," he whispered as he moved along the path that had once been the center aisle, the aisle once walked by daily communicants and brides with their proud fathers. "Look what they've done to my church!"

Joe approached the huge block of the altar. When he'd first arrived at St. Anthony's it had been backed against the far wall of the sanctuary, but he'd had it moved to the front so that he could celebrate Mass facing his parishioners. Solid Carrara marble, but you'd never know it now. So caked with dried blood, semen, and feces it could have been made of styrofoam.

His revulsion was fading, melting away in the growing heat of his rage, drawing the nausea with it. He had intended to clean up the place but there was too much to be done, too much for two men. It was hopeless.

"Fadda Joe?"

He spun at the sound of the strange voice. A thin figure stood uncertainly in the open doorway. A timid-looking man of about fifty edged forward.

"Fadda Joe, that you?"

Joe recognized him now. Carl Edwards. A twitchy little man who used to help pass the collection basket at 10:30 Mass on Sundays. A transplantee from Jersey City—hardly anyone around here was originally from around here. His face was sunken, his eyes feverish as he stared at Joe.

"Yes, Carl. It's me."

"Oh, thank God!" He ran forward and dropped to his knees before Joe. He began to sob. "You come back! Thank God, you come back!"

Joe pulled him to his feet.

"Come on now, Carl. Get a grip."

"You come back to save us, ain'tcha? God sent you here to punish him, didn't He?"

"Punish whom?"

"Fadda Palmeri! He's one a them! He's the worst of alla them! He—"

"I know," Joe said. "I know."

"Oh, it's so good to have ya back, Fadda Joe! We ain't knowed what to do since the suckers took over. We been prayin for someone like you and now ya here. It's a freakin miracle!"

Joe wanted to ask Carl where he and all these people who seemed to think they needed him now had been when he was being railroaded out of the parish. But that was ancient history.

"Not a miracle, Carl," Joe said, glancing at Zev. "Rabbi Wolpin brought me back." As Carl and Zev shook hands, Joe said, "And I'm just passing through."

"Passing through? No. Don't say that! Ya gotta stay!"

Joe saw the light of hope fading in the little man's eyes and something twisted within, tugging at him.

"What can I do here, Carl? I'm just one man."

"I'll help! I'll do whatever ya want! Just tell me!"

"Will you help me clean up?"

Carl looked around and seemed to see the cadavers for the first time. He cringed and turned a few shades paler.

"Yeah . . . sure. Anything."

Joe looked at Zev. "Well? What do you think?"

Zev shrugged. "I should tell you what to do? My parish it's not."

"Not mine either."

Zev jutted his beard at Carl. "I think maybe he'd tell you differently."

Joe did a slow turn. The vaulted nave was utterly silent except for the buzzing of the flies around the cadavers. A massive cleanup job. But if they worked all day they could make a decent dent in it. And then—

And then what?

Joe didn't know. He was playing this by ear. He'd wait and see what the night brought.

"Can you get us some food, Carl? I'd sell my soul for a cup of coffee."

Carl gave him a strange look.

"Just a figure of speech, Carl. We'll need some food if we're going to keep working."

The man's eyes lit again.

"That means ya staying?"

"For a while."

"I'll getcha some food," he said excitedly as he ran for the door. "And coffee. I know someone who's still got coffee. She'll part with some of it for Fadda Joe." He stopped at the door and turned. "Ay, and Fadda, I never believed any of them things was said aboutcha. Never."

Joe tried but he couldn't hold it back.

"It would have meant a lot to have heard that from you then, Carl."

The man lowered his eyes. "Yeah. I guess it woulda. But I'll make it up to ya, Fadda. I will. You can take that to the bank."

Then he was out the door and gone. Joe turned to Zev and saw the old man rolling up his sleeves.

"*Nu?*" Zev said. "The bodies. Before we do anything else, I think maybe we should move the bodies."

ZEV . . .

By early afternoon, Zev was exhausted. The heat and the heavy work had taken their toll. He had to stop and rest. He sat on the chancel rail and looked around. Nearly eight hours work and they'd barely scratched the surface. But the place did look and smell better.

Removing the flyblown corpses and scattered body parts had been the worst of it. A foul, gut-roiling task that had taken most of the morning. They'd carried the corpses out to the small graveyard behind the church and left them there. Those people deserved a decent burial but there was no time for it today.

Once the corpses were gone, Father Joe had torn the defilements from the statue of Mary and then they'd turned their attention to the huge crucifix. It took a while but they finally found Christ's plaster arms in the pile of ruined pews. Both still were nailed to the sawed-off crosspieces of the crucifix. While Zev and Joe worked at jury-rigging a series of braces to reattach the arms, Carl found a mop and bucket and began the long, slow process of washing the fouled floor of the nave.

Now the crucifix was intact again—the life-size plaster Jesus had his arms reattached and was once again nailed to his refurbished cross. Joe and Carl had restored him to his former position of dominance. The poor Nazarene was upright again, hanging over the center of the sanctuary in all his tortured splendor.

A grisly sight. Zev never could understand the Catholic attachment to these gruesome statues. But if the undead loathed them, then Zev was for them all the way.

His stomach rumbled with hunger. At least they'd had a good breakfast. Carl had returned from his food run this morning with fresh-baked bread, peanut butter, and two thermoses of hot coffee. He wished now they'd saved some. Maybe there was a crust of bread left in the sack.

He headed back to the vestibule to check and found an aluminum pot and a paper bag sitting by the door. The pot was hot and full of beef stew, the sack contained three cans of Pepsi.

He poked his head out the doors but saw no one on the street outside. It had been that way all day—he'd spy a figure or two peeking in the front doors; they'd hover there for a moment as if to confirm that what they had heard was true, then they'd scurry away.

He looked down at the meal that had been left. A group of the locals must have donated from their hoard of canned stew and precious soft drinks to fix this. Zev was touched.

He was about to call out to Joe and Carl when a shadow fell across the floor. He looked up and saw a young woman in a leather jacket standing in the doorway. The first thing he did was check for her right ear for one of those cursed crescents. Easy enough to see with her close-cropped, almost boyish brown hair. She didn't. Such a relief.

"Yes?" He straightened and faced her. "Can I help you?"

"Isn't this St. Anthony's church?" she said, making a face as she looked around at the destruction.

"It was. We're trying to make it so again."

Her gaze had come to rest on his yarmulke. "But you're a—"

"A rabbi, yes. Rabbi Zev Wolpin, at your service." He gestured around him at the church. "Such a long story, you wouldn't believe."

She smiled. A pretty smile. "I'll bet. I'm looking for my uncle. He was a priest here but he left. I need to find him."

Zev felt a lightness in his chest. "His name wouldn't happen to be Cahill, would it?"

Her smile broadened. "Yeah. Father Joe Cahill. You know where he might be?"

"I believe I do." He turned and called into the nave. "Father Joe! You have company!"

LACEY . . .

Lacey totally lost it when she recognized the tall, broad-shouldered man striding toward her through the rubble of the church. He needed a shave, he needed a haircut, and his faded jeans and flannel shirt were anything but priestly, but she knew those blue eyes and the smile that lit his face when he saw her.

"Uncle Joe!"

She found herself running forward and flinging herself at him, sobbing unashamedly and uncontrollably as she clung to him like a drowning sailor to a rock.

"Lacey, Lacey," he cooed, holding her tight against him. "It's all right. It's all right."

Finally she got hold of herself and eased her deathgrip on him. She wiped her eyes.

"Sorry about that. It's just . . ."

"I know," he said, taking her hands in his.

Lacey looked up at her uncle. Did he? Did he realize what she'd been through to get here? She'd thought she was tough, but the trip from Manhattan had taken her longer than she could have imagined, and put to shame every nightmare she'd ever had.

"How are your mom and dad?" he asked.

She saw the forlorn hope in his eyes—her mother was his older sister—but had to shake her head.

"I don't know. I tried to contact them when the shit hit the—I mean, when everything went to hell, but the lines were down and everything was chaos. I got to wondering if they'd even bothered trying to get in touch with me."

"I'm sure they did," Uncle Joe said. "Of course they did."

"How can you be so sure? They've refused to speak to me for years."

"But they love you."

"Funny way of showing it."

"They're not rejecting you, Lacey, just your lifestyle."

"One's pretty much wrapped up in the other, don't you think. At least you kept talking to me."

She'd been moved as a kid from Brooklyn to New Jersey when her father landed a job with a big pharmaceutical company in Florham Park, but New York had remained in her blood. When it came time for college her first and last choice had been NYU, for reasons beyond what it offered academically. Its location in Greenwich Village had been equally important.

Because somewhere along her years in high school Lacey Flannery had realized she wasn't like the other girls. She needed an accepting atmosphere, a place where anything goes, to stretch her boundaries and find out about herself, learn who she really was.

In her second year at NYU she moved into an off-campus apartment with a senior named Janey Birnbaum. At the time her folks thought they were just roommates. Three years ago, right after her graduation with a BA in English, she came out.

And that was when her folks stopped speaking to her. She'd tried to visit them, tried to explain, but they hadn't wanted to see or speak to her.

The one person in the family she'd found she could talk to was, of all people, her uncle the Catholic priest. Uncle Joe hadn't approved but he didn't turn her away. He'd tried to act as go-between but her folks stood firm: either get counseling and get cured—like she was mentally ill or something!—or stay away.

She had a feeling her father was behind the hard line, but she couldn't be sure. Now she might never know.

The rabbi said, "So may I ask, what is it, this lifestyle, that your parents reject but a priest doesn't?"

"I'm a dyke."

The rabbi blinked. Probably the first time anyone had

ever put it to him that bluntly. She also noticed her uncle's grimace. Obviously he didn't like the word. Lacey hadn't liked it either at first, but Janey and her more radical friends encouraged her to use to it because they were taking it back.

That was all fine back then, but now . . . take it back from whom?

"Doesn't that mean a lesbian?" the rabbi said.

"Through and through."

"Oh. I see."

"Not just a garden-variety lesbian," Uncle Joe said. His wry smile looked forced. "A radical lesbian feminist, and an outspoken one at that."

"You forgot to mention atheist."

His smile faded a little. "I try to forget that part."

It had taken Lacey awhile to come out, but when she did she decided not to be out partway. She wasn't ashamed of who she was or how she felt and was ready to get in the face of anyone who tried to give her grief about it.

She'd started writing articles and reviews for the underground press—the radical, the gay, even the entertainment freebies—with the hope of eventually moving above ground. Her role model was Norah Vincent, who'd been writing a regular column for the *Village Voice*—back when there'd been a *Village Voice*. Lacey didn't always agree with her views but she envied her pulpit. She'd vowed that someday she'd have a column like that.

But that dream was gone now, along with so many others . . .

"Anyway," she said, "I hadn't been able to contact Mom and Dad, so I decided to check up on them."

She'd been all alone then. Janey had gone out one day, scrounging for food, and never come back. After spending a week looking for her, Lacey had to face the unthinkable: Janey was either dead or had been turned into an undead. Crushed, grieving, and with New York becoming more dangerous every day, she'd decided to go home. She fought her way through the Holland Tunnel—the living collaborators hadn't closed it off yet—and made it to her folks' place in Union, New Jersey.

"When I got to their house, I found the front door smashed in and blood on the living-room rug." She felt herself puddling up, her throat tightening like a noose. "I don't think they made it."

She hoped they were alive or dead, anything but in between. They'd rejected her, they'd caused her untold pain—though she'd probably given as good as she got on that score—but they were still her parents and the thought of her mother and father prowling the night, sucking blood . . .

She'd nurtured the hope that with time they'd have come to accept her as she was—she'd never expected approval, but maybe just enough acceptance to invite her back for dinner some night. It didn't look like that was ever going to happen now.

Uncle Joe wrapped an arm around her shoulders. "I . . ." His voice choked off and the two of them stood still and silent.

"This was your brother, Joe?" the rabbi said.

"My big sister. Cathy."

"I'm so sorry."

"Yeah," Uncle Joe said. "So am I." He cleared his throat. "But we can hope for the best, can't we? And in the meantime, lunch is getting cold. Are you hungry, Lacey?"

She was famished.

ZEV . . .

"Tastes like Dinty Moore," Joe said around a mouthful of the stew.

"It is," Lacey said. "I ate a lot of this before I turned vegan. I recognize the little potatoes."

Zev found the stew palatable but much too salty. He wasn't about to complain, though.

They were feasting in the sacristy, the small room off the sanctuary where the priests had kept their vestments—a clerical Green Room, so to speak. Joe and Lacey sat side by side. Carl and Zev sat apart.

"What's vegan?" he asked.

"Someone who eats only veggies," Lacey said.

"But—"

"I know. Being a vegan was a luxury. Now I eat whatever I can find."

Carl laughed. "Fadda, the ladies of the parish must be real excited about you coming back to break into their canned goods like this."

Zev said, "I don't believe I've ever had anything like this before."

"I'd be surprised if you had," said Joe. "I doubt very much that something that calls itself Dinty Moore is kosher."

Zev smiled but inside he was suddenly filled with a great sadness. Kosher . . . how meaningless now seemed all the observances that he had allowed to rule and circumscribe his life. Such a fierce proponent of strict dietary laws he'd been in the days before the Lakewood holocaust. But those days were gone, just as the Lakewood community was gone.

And Zev was a changed man. If he hadn't changed, if he were still observing, he couldn't sit here and sup with these two men and this young woman. He'd have to be elsewhere, eating special classes of ritually prepared foods off separate sets of dishes. But really, hadn't division been the main thrust of holding to the dietary laws in modern times? They served a purpose beyond mere observance of tradition. They placed another wall between observant Jews and outsiders, keeping them separate even from fellow Jews who didn't observe.

Zev took another big bite of the stew. Time to break down all the walls between people . . . while there was still enough time and people left alive to make it matter.

"You okay, Zev?" Joe asked.

Zev nodded silently, afraid to speak for fear of sobbing. Despite all its anachronisms, he missed his life in the good old days of a few months ago. Gone. It was all gone. The rich traditions, the culture, the friends, the prayers. He felt adrift—in time and in space. Nowhere was home.

And then there was the matter of the cross . . . the power of the cross over the undead . . .

He'd sneaked a copy of *Dracula* to read when he was a boy, and he'd caught snatches of vampire movies on TV. The undead were always portrayed as afraid of crosses. But that had been fiction. Vampires weren't real—or so he'd thought—and so he'd never examined the broader implications of that fear of the cross. Now . . .

"You sure?" Joe seemed genuinely concerned.

"Yes, I'm okay. As okay as you could expect me to feel after spending the better part of the day repairing a crucifix and eating non-kosher food. And let me tell you, that's not so okay."

He put his bowl aside and straightened from his chair.

"Come on, already. Let's get back to work. There's much yet to do."

JOE . . .

"Almost sunset," Carl said.

Joe straightened from scrubbing the marble altar and stared west through one of the smashed windows. The sun was out of sight behind the houses there.

"You can go now, Carl," he said to the little man. "Thanks for your help."

"Where you gonna go, Fadda?"

"I'll be staying right here."

Carl's prominent Adam's apple bobbed convulsively as he swallowed.

"Yeah? Well then, I'm staying too. I told you I'd make it up to ya, didn't I? An' besides, I don't think the suckers'll like the new, improved St. Ant'ny's too much when they come back tonight. I don't think they'll even get through the doors."

Joe smiled at the man, then looked around. Luckily it was May and the days were growing longer. They'd had time to make a difference here. The floors were clean, the crucifix was restored and back in its proper position, as were most of the Stations of the Cross plaques. Zev had found them under the pews and had taken the ones not shattered beyond recognition and rehung them on the walls. Lots of new crosses littered those walls. Carl had found a hammer and nails and had made dozens of them from the remains of the pews.

"You're right. I don't think they'll like the new decor one bit. But there's something you can get us if you can, Carl. Guns. Pistols, rifles, shotguns, anything that shoots."

Carl nodded slowly. "I know a few guys who can help in that department."

"And some wine. A little red wine if anybody's saved some."

"You got it."

He hurried off.

"You're planning Custer's last stand, maybe?" Zev said from where he was tacking the last of Carl's crude crosses to the east wall.

"More like the Alamo."

"Same result," Zev said with one of his shrugs.

"I've got a gun," Lacey said.

Joe stared at her. She'd been helping him scrub the altar. "You do? Why didn't you say something?"

"It's only got two bullets left."

"Where are the rest?"

She met his gaze evenly. "I had to leave them behind in a couple of people who tried to stop me. It was a tough trip getting here."

"Are you okay with that?"

She nodded. "Better than I thought I'd be. You do what you have to do."

What an amazing young woman, he thought. Who'd have thought Cathy's little girl could turn out so tough and resilient.

He remembered Lacey as a teen. She'd always been a little different from her peers. On the surface she seemed like a typical high-school kid—she dated, though she had no serious crushes, played soccer and field hockey with abandon—but on holidays and family gatherings, she'd stay in the background. Joe would make a point of sitting down with her; he'd draw her out, and then another Lacey would emerge.

The other Lacey was a thinker, a questioner. She had doubts about religion, about government. She burned with an iconoclastic fire that urged her to question traditions and break with them whenever possible. She was fascinated by the old anarchists and dug up all their works. He remembered her favorite was *No Treason* by someone named Lysander Spooner. Instead of hanging posters of the latest teenage heartthrob boy band in her room, Lacey had pictures of Emma Goldman and Madelyn Murray O'Hare.

Joe's sister and her husband tolerated her views with a mixture of humor and apprehension. If this was the shape and scope of Lacey's teenage rebellion, they'd live with it. It was just a phase, they'd say. She'll grow out of it. Better than drunk driving or drugs or getting pregnant.

But it wasn't a phase. It was Lacey. And later, when she came out as a lesbian, they turned their backs on her. Joe had tried to talk them out of slamming the family door, but this was more than they could take.

"Who taught you to shoot?" he asked.

"A friend." She smiled. "A *guy* friend, believe it or not. It was a self-defense thing. He took me out to the range until I got comfortable with pulling the trigger. I'm not a great shot, but if you're within ten feet of me and you're looking for trouble, you're gone."

Joe had to smile. "Never let it be said you're not full of surprises, Lacey."

She laughed softly. "No one's *ever* said that."

They turned back to scrubbing the altar. They'd been at it for over an hour now. Joe was drenched with sweat and figured he smelled like a bear, but he couldn't stop until it was clean.

But it wouldn't come clean.

"What did they do to this altar?" Lacey asked.

"I don't know. This crud . . . it seems part of the marble now."

The undead must have done something to the blood and foulness to make the mixture seep into the surface as it had.

"Let's take a break."

He turned sat on the floor with his back against the altar and rested. He didn't like resting because it gave him time to think. And when he started to think he realized that the odds were pretty high against his seeing tomorrow morning.

At least he'd die well fed. Their secret supplier had left them a dinner of fresh fried chicken by the front doors. Even the memory of it made his mouth water. Apparently someone was *really* glad he was back.

Lacey settled next to him. She'd shed her leather jacket hours ago. Her bare arms were sheened with perspiration.

"That talk about Custer's last stand and the Alamo," she said. "You're not planning to die here, are you?"

To tell the truth, as miserable as he'd been, he wasn't ready to die. Not tonight, not any night.

"Not if I can help it."

"Good. Because as much as I can appreciate self-immolating gestures, I don't think I'm ready to take part in a Jersey Shore version of the Alamo or Little Big Horn."

"Well, the cry of 'Remember the Alamo!' did spur a lot of people to action, but I agree. Going down fighting here will not solve anything."

"Then what's the plan? We should have some sort of plan."

Good question. Did he have a plan?

"All I want to do is hold off the undead till dawn. Keep them out of St. Anthony's for one night. That's all. That will be a statement—*my* statement. *Our* statement if you want to stay on."

And if he found an opportunity to ram a stake through Palmeri's rotten heart, so much the better. But he wasn't counting on that.

"That's it?" Lacey said. "One night?"

"One night. Just to let them know they can't have their way everywhere with everybody whenever they feel like it. We've got surprise on our side tonight, so maybe it will work." One night. Then he'd be on his way. "You shouldn't feel you have to stay just because you're my niece."

"I don't. But if I—"

"What the fuck have you *done*?"

Joe looked up at the shout. A burly, long-haired man in jeans and a cut-away denim jacket stood in the vestibule staring at the partially restored nave. As he approached, Joe noticed his crescent moon earring.

A Vichy.

Joe balled his fists but didn't move.

"Hey, I'm talking to you, asshole. Are you responsible for this?"

When all he got from Joe was a cold stare, he turned to Zev and fixed on his yarmulke.

"Hey, you! Jew! What the hell you think *you're* doing here?" He started toward Zev. "You get those fucking crosses off—"

"Touch him and I'll break you in half," Joe said in a low voice.

The Vichy skidded to a halt and stared at him.

"Are you crazy? Do you know what Father Palmeri will do to you when he gets here?"

"*Father* Palmeri? Why do you still call him that?"

"It's what he *wants* to be called. And he's going to call you *dog meat* when he gets through with you!"

Joe pulled himself to his feet and looked down at the Vichy. Suddenly the man didn't seem so sure of himself.

"Tell him I'll be waiting." Joe gave him a hard, two-handed shove against his chest that sent him stumbling back. Damn, that felt good. "Tell him Father Cahill is back."

"You're a priest? You don't look like one."

Joe slapped him across the face. Hard. It snapped the creep's chin toward his shoulder. *That* felt even better.

"Shut up and listen. Tell him Father Joe Cahill is back—and he's pissed. Tell him that." Another chest shove. "Now get out of here while you still can."

Rubbing his cheek, the man backpedaled and hurried out into the growing darkness. Joe turned to Zev and found him grinning through his beard.

" 'Father Joe Cahill is back—and he's pissed.' I like that."

"It'll make a great bumper sticker," Lacey said, her eyes wide with admiration. "You were great! I never knew my uncle the priest was such a tough dude. Maybe we've got more than a prayer tonight."

Joe didn't know about that. He hoped so.

"I think I'll close the front doors," he said. "The criminal element is starting to wander in. While I'm doing that, see if we can find some more candles. It's getting dark in here."

On the front steps he unhooked the left door and closed it. He was unhooking the right when he heard a woman's voice behind him.

"Father Cahill? Is that you?"

He turned and in the dying light saw a lone figure standing by a children's red wagon at the bottom of the steps.

"Yes. Do I know you?"

He heard her sob. "Oh, it *is* you! You've come back!"

Joe hurried down to the sobbing woman. "Are you all right?"

"I've been praying for your return but I'm such a sinner I thought God had turned his back on us all. But you're back! Thank God!"

Something familiar about her voice . . . but she kept her head down. Joe reached out, and tilted her chin so he could see her.

He gasped when he saw her tear-stained face. He barely recognized her. Her skin was pale, her cheeks sunken, but he knew her.

"Sister Carole!"

Impulsively he threw his arms around her and pulled her against him in a hug. He wanted to laugh but feared if he opened his mouth he'd burst out crying. Sweet emotions roiled through him, making him weak. She was here, she was alive. He wanted to tell her how he'd missed her— missed knowing she was in the neighboring building, missed seeing her walk back and forth to the school, missed the smile she would flash him whenever they crossed paths.

"It's so good to see you, Carole!" He pushed her back and looked at her, hoping to see that smile. But her eyes were different, haunted. "Dear God, what's happened to you?" Immediately he thought: Stupid question. The same thing that's happened to us all. "Why are you here? I thought you'd gone to Pennsylvania for Easter."

She shook her head. "I had to stay behind . . . with Sister Bernadette . . . they . . . I had to . . ." She loosed a single, agonized sob. "How could I stay in the convent after that?"

Joe wasn't following. Her speech was so disjointed. This wasn't like Carole. He'd always known her as a woman of quiet intelligence, with a sharp, organized mind. Everyone left alive had suffered, but what had she experienced to leave her so shattered?

"Where have you been staying?"

She looked away. "Here and there."

"Well, you're staying here now." He took her arm. "Come inside. We've got—"

She pulled away. "I can't. I've too many sins."

"We're all sinners, Carole."

"But these are terrible sins. *Mortal* sins. So many mortal sins."

"This is where sins are forgiven. I'm going to try to say mass later."

"Mass?" Her lip quivered. "Oh, that would be wonderful. But I can't. Even though it's a Holy Day, I—"

"What Holy—?" And then he remembered. With all that had been going on, it had slipped his mind. "Oh, God, it's Ascension Thursday, isn't it."

Sister Carole nodded. "But I'll just have to add missing Mass on a Holy Day of Obligation to my list of sins."

"Come inside, Carole. Please. I'll hear your confession."

"No." She paused, as if she were listening for something. "To receive absolution I must be sorry for my sins and promise to sin no more." She shook her head and something flashed in her eyes, something hard and dangerous. "I'm not. And I won't."

Joe stared at her, trying to fathom . . .

"I don't follow you, Carole."

"Please don't, Father. It's not a path you want to tread." She bent and grabbed the handle of her little red wagon, then turned and started away. "God bless you, Father Cahill."

Joe hurried after her. He couldn't let her go. It was too dangerous, but more than that, he wanted her near, where he could talk to her, be with her. He grabbed her arm.

"I can't let you go."

She snatched her arm free and kept moving. "You can't make me stay. Don't try. I won't. I can't." The last word was couched in a sob that damn near broke his heart.

"Carole, please!"

But she hurried on into the shadows without looking back. Joe started after her again, then stopped. Short of picking her up and carrying her back to the church—and he couldn't see himself doing that—what could he do?

Suddenly weary, he turned and climbed the steps. As he finished closing the front doors, he took one last longing look at the night.

Carole . . . what's happened to you? Please be safe.

He closed the door and wished the lock hadn't been

smashed. He turned and found Lacey and Zev standing in the vestibule.

"We were getting worried about you," Lacey said.

"I ran into one of the nuns who used to teach in St. Anthony's school."

Zev's eyebrows arched. "And you didn't let her in?"

"Wouldn't come in. But she reminded me that this is a Holy Day: Ascension Thursday."

Zev shrugged. "Which means?"

"Supposedly," Lacey said, "forty days after Easter, Jesus ascended into Heaven to sit at the right hand of God." She smiled. "An ingenious way to dodge all those inconvenient questions about the state and whereabouts of the remains of the 'Son of God.'"

Joe looked at her. "Lacey, you can't still be an atheist."

She shrugged. "I never really was. I call myself that because it's such an in-your-face term. Like dyke. But atheism implies that you consider the question of a provident god important enough to take seriously. I don't. At heart I'm simply a devout agnostic."

Joe was glad Carl wasn't here to hear this. He wouldn't understand or appreciate Lacey's outspokenness. But that was Lacey. No excuses, no sugar coating: Here I am, here's what I think, take it or leave it. Through the years she'd made him angry at times, but then she'd smile and he'd see his sister Cathy in her face and his anger would fade away.

He pointed to the gold crucifix hanging from her neck. "But you wear a cross. Didn't you once tell me you'd die before wearing anything like that?"

"I damn near did die because I *wasn't* wearing one. So now I wear one for perfectly pragmatic reasons. I've never been one for fashion accessories, but if it chases vampires, I want one."

"But you've got to take the next step, Lacey. You've got to ask *why* the undead fear it, *why* it sears their flesh. There's something *there*. When you face that reality, you won't be an atheist or agnostic anymore."

Lacey smiled. "Did I mention I'm a devout empiricist too?"

"Like a worm, she wiggles," Zev said. "Too many philosophy courses."

Lacey turned to him. "That's not exactly a *mezuzah* hanging from your neck, rabbi."

"I know," Zev said, fingering his cross. "Like you, I wear it because it works. That is undeniable. Where its power comes from, I don't know. Maybe from God, maybe from somewhere else. The how and the why I'll figure out later. I've been too busy trying to stay alive to give it my full attention." He held up his hands. "Talk of intangibles we should save for the daylight. Now we should ready ourselves. I believe we'll soon have uninvited and unsavory company. We should be prepared."

Looking unhappy, Zev wandered away. But Joe didn't want to let this drop. He sensed a chance to break through his niece's wall of disbelief. By doing so he might save her soul.

He lowered his voice. "If the power of the cross is not from God, Lacy, then who?"

"Might not be a *who*," she said with a shrug. "Might be a *what*. I don't know. I'm just going with it for now."

" 'There are none so blind as those who will not see,' " Joe said.

"It's not blindness to not see something that won't show itself. Where's your god now?" She jutted her chin at Zev's retreating figure. "His god and yours—where's he been? This is Ascension Thursday, right? Think about that. Maybe Jesus ascended and kept on going. Turned his back on this planet and forgot about it. After the way he was treated here, who could blame him?"

Joe shook his head, feeling a growing anger mixed with dismay. He hated to hear his niece talk like this. "Are you still an anarchist too?"

"Damn betcha."

"Well now, it looks like you've got what you wanted—a world without religion, without government, without law— what do you think?"

Joe could tell by the set of her jaw and the flash of fire in her eyes that he'd struck a nerve.

"This is not at all what I was talking about! This undead empire is more repressive than any regime in human history. It makes Nazi Germany and Stalinist Russia look like Sunday school!"

"And they're here to stay," Joe said, wondering if all today's plans and preparations weren't an exercise in futility.

He wondered where Palmeri was and how long before he got here.

PALMERI . . .

He wore the night like a tuxedo.

Dressed in a fresh cassock, Father Alberto Palmeri turned off County Line Road and strolled toward St. Anthony's. He loved the night, felt at one with it, attuned to its harmonies and its discords. The darkness made him feel so alive. Strange to have to lose your life before you could really feel alive. But this was it. He'd found his niche, his métier.

Such a shame it had taken him so long. All those years trying to deny his appetites, trying to be a member of the other side, cursing himself when he allowed his appetites to win, as he had with increasing frequency toward the end of his mortal life. He should have given in to them long ago.

It had taken undeath to free him.

And to think he had been afraid of undeath, had cowered in fear that night in the cellar of the church, surrounded by crosses. But he had not been as safe as he'd thought. A posse of Serfs had torn him from his hiding place and brought him to kneel before Gregor. He'd cried out and begged with this undead master to spare his life. Fortunately Gregor had ignored his pleas. All he had lost by that encounter was his blood.

And in trade, he'd gained a world.

For now it was his world, at least this little corner of it, one in which he was completely free to indulge himself in any way he wished. Except for the blood. He had no choice about the blood. That was a new appetite, stronger than all the rest, one that would not be denied. But he did not mind the new appetite in the least. He'd found interesting ways to sate it.

Up ahead he spotted dear, defiled St. Anthony's. He wondered what the serfs had prepared for tonight. They were quite imaginative. They'd yet to bore him.

But as he drew nearer the church, Palmeri slowed. His skin prickled. The building had changed. Something was very wrong there, wrong inside. Something amiss with the light that beamed from the windows. This wasn't the old familiar candlelight, this was something else, something more. Something that made his insides tremble.

Figures raced up the street toward him. Live ones. His night vision picked out the earrings and familiar faces of some of the serfs. As they neared he sensed the warmth of the blood coursing just beneath their skins. The hunger rose in him and he fought the urge to rip into their throats. He couldn't allow himself that pleasure. Gregor had told him how to keep the servants dangling, keep them working for him and the nest. They all needed the services of the indentured living to remove whatever obstacles the cattle might put in their way.

Someday, when he was allowed to have get of his own, he would turn some of these, and then they'd be bound to him in a different way.

"Father! Father!" they cried.

He loved it when they called him Father, loved being one of the undead and dressing like one of the enemy.

"Yes, my children. What sort of victim do you have for us tonight?"

"No victim, father—trouble!"

The edges of Palmeri's vision darkened with rage as he

heard of the young priest and the Jew and the others who had dared to try to turn St. Anthony's into a holy place again. When he heard the name of the priest, he nearly exploded.

"Cahill? Joseph Cahill is back in my church?"

"He was cleaning the altar!" one of the servants said.

Palmeri strode toward the church with the serfs trailing behind. He knew that neither Cahill nor the Pope himself could clean that altar. Palmeri had desecrated it himself; he had learned how to do that when he became leader of Gregor's local get. But what else had the young pup dared to do?

Whatever it was, it would be undone. *Now!*

Palmeri strode up the steps and pulled the right door open——and screamed in agony.

The light! The *light!* The LIGHT! White agony lanced through Palmeri's eyes and seared his brain like two hot pokers. He retched and threw his arms across his face as he staggered back into the cool, comforting darkness.

It took a few minutes for the pain to drain off, for the nausea to pass, for vision to return.

He'd never understand it. He'd spent his entire life in the presence of crosses and crucifixes, surrounded by them. And yet as soon as he'd become undead he was unable to bear the sight of one. In fact, since he'd become undead he'd never even *seen* one. A cross was no longer an object. It was a light, a light so excruciatingly bright, so blazingly white that looking at it was sheer agony. As a child in Naples he'd been told by his mother not to look at the sun, but when there'd been talk of an eclipse, he'd stared directly into its eye. The pain of looking at a cross was a hundred, no, a thousand times worse than that. And the bigger the cross or crucifix, the worse the pain.

He'd experienced monumental pain upon looking into St. Anthony's tonight. That could only mean that Joseph, that young bastard, had refurbished the giant crucifix. It was the only possible explanation.

He swung on his servants.

"Get in there! Get that crucifix down!"

"They've got guns!"

"Then get help. But get it *down!*"

"We'll get guns too! We can—"

"*No!* I want him! I want that priest alive! I want him for myself! Anyone who kills him will suffer a very painful, very long and lingering true death! Is that clear?"

It was clear. They scurried away without answering.

Palmeri went to gather the other members of the nest.

JOE . . .

Dressed in a cassock and a surplice, Joe came out of the sacristy and approached the altar. He noticed Zev keeping watch at one of the windows. He didn't tell him how ridiculous he looked carrying the shotgun Carl had brought back. He held it so gingerly, as if it was full of nitroglycerin and would explode if he jiggled it.

Zev turned and smiled when he saw him.

"*Now* you look like the old Father Joe we all used to know,"

Joe gave him a little bow and proceeded toward the altar. Lacey waved with her revolver from the other side of the nave where she stood guard by the side door. She'd put on her black leather jacket and looked ready for anything.

All right: He had everything he needed. He had the Missal they'd found in among the pew debris earlier today. He had the wine—Carl had brought back about four ounces of sour red babarone. He'd found the smudged surplice and dusty cassock on the floor of one of the closets in the sacristy, and he wore them now. No hosts, though. A crust of bread left over from breakfast would have to do. No chalice, either. If he'd known he was going to be saying Mass he'd have come prepared. As a last resort he'd used the can opener in the rectory to remove the top of one of the Pepsi cans from lunch. Quite a stretch from the gold chalice he'd used since his ordination, but probably more in line with what Jesus had used at that first Mass—the Last Supper.

He was uncomfortable with the idea of weapons in St. Anthony's but saw no alternative. He and Zev knew nothing about guns, and Carl knew little more; they'd probably do more damage to themselves than to the Vichy if they tried to use them. Only Lacey seemed at ease with her pistol. Joe hoped that just the sight of the weaponry might make the Vichy hesitate, slow them down. All he needed was a little time here, enough to get to the consecration.

This is going to be the most unusual Mass in history, he thought.

But he was going to get through it if it killed him. And that was a real possibility. This might well be his last Mass. But he wasn't afraid. He was too excited to be afraid. He'd had a slug of the Scotch—just enough to ward off the shakes—but it had done nothing to quell the buzz of the adrenaline humming along every nerve in his body.

He spread everything out on the white tablecloth he'd taken from the rectory and used to cover the filthy altar. He looked at Carl.

"Ready?"

Carl nodded and stuck the automatic pistol he'd been examining into his belt.

"Been awhile, Fadda. We did it in Latin when I was a kid, but I think I can swing it."

"Just do your best and don't worry about any mistakes."

Some Mass. A defiled altar, a crust for a host, a Pepsi can for a chalice, a sixty-year-old, pistol-packing altar boy, and a congregation consisting of a lesbian atheist and a rabbi.

Joe looked heavenward.

You do understand, don't you, Lord, that all this was arranged on short notice?

Time to begin.

He read the Gospel but dispensed with the homily. He tried to remember the Mass as it used to be said, to fit in better with Carl's outdated responses.

As he was starting the Offertory the front doors flew open and a group of men entered—ten of them, all with crescent moons dangling from their ears. Out of the corner of his eye he saw Zev move away from the window toward the altar, pointing his shotgun at them.

As soon as they entered the nave and got past the broken pews, the Vichy fanned out toward the sides. They began pulling down the Stations of the Cross, ripping Carl's makeshift crosses from the walls and tearing them apart.

Carl looked up at Joe from where he knelt, his eyes questioning, his hand reaching for the pistol in his belt. Lacey didn't look at him at all. She acted on her own.

"Stop right there!"

She held her pistol straight out before her, arms rigid. Joe saw the barrel wobble. She might be tough, he thought, but she's only twenty-five. And she's only got two rounds.

But the Vichy didn't know that. They stopped their forward progress and tried to stare her down.

"You can't get all of us," one said.

Zev worked the pump on the shotgun. The sound echoed through the church. "That's right. She can't."

He sounded a lot tougher than Joe knew he was. He hoped the Vichy were fooled.

Maybe they were. They looked at each other but didn't back off. A stand-off was good enough for now. Joe nodded and kept up with the Offertory.

Then he caught a flash of movement out of the corner of his eye. One of the Vichy had ducked through the side door behind Lacey. He carried a raised two-by-four.

"Lacey!" Zev cried. "Behind—!"

She whirled, ducking, pistol raised, but the Vichy had the jump on her. The two-by-four glanced off the side of her head and slammed into her forearm. She dropped the gun and went down. But not before landing a vicious kick on the inside of his knee. He staggered back, howling with pain while Lacey, cradling her injured arm, jumped up and scrambled toward the altar.

The Vichy cheered and went on with their work. They split—one group continuing to pull down Carl's crosses, the other swarming around and behind the altar.

Joe chanced a quick glance over his shoulder and saw them begin their attack on the newly repaired crucifix.

"Zev!" Carl said in a low voice, cocking his head toward the Vichy. "Stop 'em!"

"I'm warning you," Zev said and pointed the shotgun.

Joe heard the activity behind him come to a sudden halt. He braced himself for the blast . . .

But it never came.

He looked at Zev. The old man met his gaze and sadly shook his head. He couldn't do it. To the accompaniment of the sound of renewed activity and derisive laughter behind him, Joe gave Zev a tiny nod of reassurance and understanding, then hurried the Mass toward the Consecration.

As he held the crust of bread aloft, he started at the sound of the life-size crucifix crashing to the floor, cringed as he heard the freshly buttressed arms and crosspiece being torn away again.

As he held the wine aloft in the Pepsi can, the swaggering, grinning Vichy surrounded the altar and brazenly tore the cross from around his neck. Zev, Lacey, and Carl put up struggles to keep theirs but were overpowered. The Vichy wound up with Carl's gun too.

And then Joe's skin began to crawl as a new group entered the nave. They numbered about twenty, all undead. He faced them from behind the altar as they approached. His gut roiled at the familiar faces he spotted among the throng.

But the one who caught and held his attention was the one leading them.

Alberto Palmeri.

PALMERI . . .

Palmeri hid his hesitancy as he approached the altar. The crucifix and its intolerable whiteness were gone, yet something was not right. Something repellent here, something that urged him to flee. What?

Perhaps it was just the residual effect of the crucifix and all the crosses they had used to line the walls. That had to be it. The unsettling aftertaste would fade as the night wore on. Oh, yes. His nightbrothers and sisters from the nest would see to that.

He focused his attention on the man behind the altar and laughed when he realized what he held in his hands.

"Pepsi, Joseph? You're trying to consecrate Pepsi?" He turned to his nest siblings. "Do you see this, my brothers and sisters? Is this the man we are to fear? And look who he has with him! An old Jew, a young woman, and a parish hanger-on!"

He reveled in their hissing laughter as they fanned out around him, sweeping toward the altar in a wide phalanx. The young woman, the Jew, and Carl—he recognized Carl and wondered how he'd avoided capture for so long—retreated to the other side of the altar where they flanked Joseph. And Joseph . . . Joseph's handsome Irish face so pale and drawn, his mouth stretched into such a tight, grim line. He looked scared to death. As well he should be.

Palmeri put down his rage at Joseph's audacity. He was glad he had returned. He'd always hated the young priest for his easy manner with people, for the way the parishioners had flocked to him with their problems despite the fact that he had nowhere near the experience of their older and wiser pastor. But that was over now. That world was gone, replaced by a nightworld—Palmeri's world. And no one would be flocking to Father Joe for anything when Palmeri was through with him.

Father Joe . . . how he'd hated it when the parishioners

had started calling him that. Well, their Father Joe would provide superior entertainment tonight. This was going to be *fun*.

"Joseph, Joseph, Joseph," he said as he stopped and smiled at the young priest across the altar. "This futile gesture is so typical of your arrogance."

But Joseph only stared back at him, his expression a mixture of defiance and repugnance. And that only fueled Palmeri's rage.

"Do I repel you, Joseph? Does my new form offend your precious shanty-Irish sensibilities? Does my undeath disgust you?"

"You managed to do all that while you were still alive, Alberto."

Palmeri allowed himself to smile. Joseph probably thought he was putting on a brave front, but the tremor in his voice betrayed his fear.

"Always good with the quick retort, weren't you, Joseph. Always thinking you were better than me, always putting yourself above me."

"Not much of a climb where a child molester is concerned."

Palmeri's anger mounted.

"So superior. So self-righteous. What about *your* appetites, Joseph? The secret ones? What are they? Do you always hold them in check?" He pointed to the girl in the leather jacket. "Is she your weakness, Joseph? Young, attractive in a hard sort of way. Is that your style? Do you like it rough? Are you fucking her, Joseph?"

"Leave her out of this. She just showed up today."

"Well, if not her, then who? Are you so far above the rest of us that you've never given in to an improper impulse, never assuaged a secret hunger? You'll have a new hunger soon, Joseph. By dawn you'll be drained—we'll each take a turn at you—and before the sun rises we'll hide your corpse from its light. You'll stay dead all day, but when the night comes you'll be one of us."

He stepped closer, almost touching the altar.

"And then all the rules will be off. The night will be yours. You'll be free to do anything and everything you've ever wanted. But blood will be your prime hunger, and you'll do anything to get it. You won't be sipping your god's thin, cold blood, as you've done so often, but hot *human* blood. You'll thirst for it, Joseph. And I want to be there when you take your first drink. I want to be there to laugh in your self-righteous face as you suck up the crimson nectar, and keep on laughing every night as the red hunger carries you into infinity."

And it *would* happen. Palmeri knew it as sure as he felt his own thirst. He hungered for the moment when he could rub dear Joseph's face in the reality of his own bloodlust.

"I was just saying Mass," Joseph said coolly. "Do you mind if I finish?"

Palmeri couldn't help laughing this time.

"Did you really think this charade would work? Did you really think you could celebrate Mass on *this?*"

He reached out and snatched the tablecloth from the altar, sending the Missal and the piece of bread to the floor and exposing the fouled surface of the marble.

"Did you really think you could effect a transubstantiation here? Do you really believe any of that garbage? That the bread and wine actually take on the substance of"—he tried to say the name but it wouldn't form—"the Son's body and blood?"

One of his nest sisters, Eva, a former councilwoman, stepped forward and leaned over the altar, smiling.

"Transubstantiation?" she said in her most unctuous voice, pulling the Pepsi can from Joseph's hands. "I was never a Catholic, so tell me . . . does that mean that this is the blood of the Son?"

A whisper of warning slithered through Palmeri's mind. Something about the can, something about the way he found it difficult to bring its outline into focus . . .

"Eva, perhaps you should—"

Eva's grin broadened. "I've always wanted to sup on the blood of a deity."

The nest members hissed their laughter as Eva raised the can and drank.

Palmeri watched, unaccountably fearful as the liquid poured into her mouth. And then—

LIGHT!

An explosion of intolerable brightness burst from Eva's mouth and drove him back, jolted, cringing.

The inside of her skull glowed beneath her scalp and shafts of pure white light shot from her ears, nose, eyes— every orifice in her head. The glow spread as it flowed down through her throat and chest and into her abdominal cavity, silhouetting her ribs before melting through her skin. Eva was liquefying where she stood, her flesh steaming, softening, running like glowing molten lava.

No! This couldn't be happening! Not now when he had Joseph in his grasp!

Then the can fell from Eva's dissolving fingers and landed on the altar top. Its contents splashed across the fouled surface, releasing another detonation of brilliance, this one more devastating than the first. The glare spread rapidly, extending over the upper surface and running down the sides, moving like a living thing, engulfing the entire altar, making it glow like a corpuscle of fire torn from the heart of the sun itself.

And with the light came blast-furnace heat that drove Palmeri back, back, back until he had to turn and follow the rest of his nest in a mad, headlong rush from St. Anthony's into the cool, welcoming safety of the outer darkness.

ZEV . . .

As the undead fled into the night, their Vichy toadies behind them, Zev stared in horrid fascination at the puddle of putrescence that was all that remained of the undead woman Palmeri had called Eva. He glanced at Carl and Lacey and caught the look of dazed wonderment on their faces. Zev touched the top of the altar—clean, shiny, every whorl of the marble surface clearly visible.

He'd witnessed fearsome power here. Incalculable power. But instead of elating him, the realization only depressed him. How long had this been going on? Did it happen at every Mass? Why had he spent his entire life ignorant of this?

He turned to Joe. "What happened?"

"I—I don't know."

"A miracle!" Carl said, running his palm over the altar top.

"A miracle and a meltdown," Lacey added from behind Zev. He felt her hand on her shoulder. "Rabbi, are you feeling what I'm feeling?"

He turned to her. "Feeling how?"

She lowered her voice. "That this shouldn't be happening? That there's got to be another explanation?"

Zev wondered if the lost look in her eyes mirrored his own.

"Explanations I'm running short on."

"Me too. I'm getting pushed into a place where I'm going to have to revise . . . everything. A place where I'm going to have to accept the unacceptable and believe in the unbelievable. I don't want to go there but . . ."

Lacey winced as she moved her right arm. She eased it out of her jacket and looked at it.

"Good thing I was wearing leather."

Zev inspected the large purple swelling below her shoulder. "Do you think it's broken?"

She shook her head. "I don't think so. My hand and forearm are all tingly and kind of numb, but I'll be okay."

"You're sure?" Joe said.

She grimaced. "Of my arm? Yeah. But I think that's about the only thing I'm sure of anymore." She nodded to the Pepsi can lying on its side atop the altar. "What was *in* there?"

Joe picked up the empty can and looked into it. "You know, you go through the seminary, through your ordination, through countless Masses *believing* in the Transubtantiation. But after all these years . . . to actually *know* . . ."

Zev saw him rub his finger along the inside of the can and taste it. He grimaced.

"What's wrong?" Zev asked.

"Still tastes like sour barbarone . . . with a hint of Pepsi."

"Doesn't matter what it tastes like," Carl said. "As far as those bloodsuckers are concerned, it's the real thing."

"No," said the priest with a small smile. "If I remember correctly, that was Coke."

And then they started laughing. Zev only vaguely remembered the old commercials, but found himself roaring along with the other three. It was more a release of tension than anything else. His sides hurt. He had to lean against the altar to support himself.

"It wasn't *that* funny," Joe said.

Lacey smiled. "No argument there."

"C'mon," Carl said, heading for the sanctuary. "Let's see if we can get this crucifix back together."

Zev helped Lacey slip her arm back into her jacket.

"You rest that arm," he told her.

She winced again and cradled it with her left. "I don't think I have much choice."

Zev jumped at the sound of the church doors banging open. He turned and saw the Vichy charging back in, two of them carrying a heavy fire blanket.

This time Father Joe did not stand by passively as they invaded his church. Zev watched as he stepped around the altar and met them head on.

He was great and terrible as he confronted them. His giant stature and raised fists cowed them for a few heartbeats. But then they must have remembered that they outnumbered him twelve to one and charged. He swung a massive fist and caught the lead Vichy square on the jaw. The blow lifted him off his feet and he landed against another. Both went down.

Zev dropped to one knee and reached for the shotgun. He would use it this time, he would shoot these vermin, he swore it!

But then someone landed on his back and drove him to the floor. As he tried to get up he saw Carl pulling Lacey away toward the side door, and he saw Father Joe, surrounded, swinging his fists, laying the Vichy out every time he connected. But there were too many. As the priest went down under the press of them, a heavy boot thudded against the side of Zev's head. He sank into darkness.

JOE . . .

. . . a throbbing in his head, stinging pain in his cheek, and a voice, sibilant yet harsh . . .

". . . now, Joseph. Come on. Wake up. I don't want you to miss this!"

Palmeri's sallow features swam into view, hovering over him, grinning like a skull. Joe tried to move but found his wrists and arms tied. His right hand throbbed, felt twice its normal size; he must have broken it on a Vichy jaw. He lifted his head and saw that he was tied spread-eagle on the altar, and that the altar had been covered with the fire blanket.

"Melodramatic, I admit," Palmeri said, "but fitting, don't you think? I mean, you and I used to sacrifice our god symbolically here every weekday and multiple times on Sundays, so why shouldn't this serve as *your* sacrificial altar?"

Joe shut his eyes against a wave of nausea. This couldn't be happening.

"Thought you'd won, didn't you?"

Joe refused to answer him, but that didn't shut him up.

"And even if you'd chased me out of here for good, what would you have accomplished? Most of the world is already ours, Joseph, and the rest soon will be. Feeders and cattle— that is the hierarchy. We are the feeders. And tonight you'll join us. But *he* won't. *Voilà!*"

Palmeri stepped aside and made a flourish toward the balcony.

Joe searched the dim, candlelit space of the nave, not sure

what he was supposed to see. Then he picked out Zev's form and groaned. The old man's feet were lashed to the balcony rail; he hung upside down, his reddened face and frightened eyes turned his way. Joe fell back and strained at the ropes but they wouldn't budge.

"Let him go!"

"What? And let all that good rich Jewish blood go to waste? Why, these people are the Chosen of God! They're a delicacy!"

"Bastard!"

If he could just get his hands on Palmeri, just for a minute.

"Tut-tut, Joseph. Not in the house of the Lord. The Jew should have been smart and run away like Carl and your girlfriend."

Carl got away? With Lacey? Thank God.

We're even, Carl.

"But don't worry about your rabbi. None of us will lay a fang on him. He hasn't earned the right to join us. We'll use the razor to bleed him. And when he's dead, he'll be dead for keeps. But not you, Joseph. Oh no, not you." His smile broadened. "You're mine."

Joe wanted to spit in Palmeri's face—not so much as an act of defiance as to hide the waves of terror surging through him—but there was no saliva to be had in his parched mouth. The thought of being undead made him weak. To spend eternity like . . . he looked at the rapt faces of Palmeri's fellow undead as they clustered under Zev's suspended form . . . like *them*.

He *wouldn't* be like them! He wouldn't allow it!

But what if there was no choice? What if becoming undead toppled a lifetime's worth of moral constraints, cut all the tethers on his human hungers, negated all his mortal concepts of how a life should be lived? Honor, justice, integrity, truth, decency, fairness, love—what if they became meaningless words instead of the footings for his life?

A thought struck him.

"A deal, Alberto," he said.

"You're hardly in a bargaining position."

"I'm not? Answer me this: Do the undead ever kill each other? I mean, has one of them ever driven a stake through another's heart?"

"No. Of course not."

"Are you sure? You'd better be sure before you go through with your plans tonight. Because if I'm forced to become one of you, I'll be crossing over with just one thought in mind: to find you. And when I do I won't stake your heart, I'll stake your arms and legs to the pilings of the Point Pleasant boardwalk where you can watch the sun rise and feel it slowly crisp your skin to charcoal."

Palmeri's smile wavered. "Impossible. You'll be different. You'll want to thank me. You'll wonder why you ever resisted."

"Better be sure of that, Alberto . . . for your sake. Because I'll have all eternity to track you down. And I'll find you, Alberto. I swear it on my own grave. Think on that."

"Do you think an empty threat is going to cow me?"

"We'll find out how empty it is, won't we? But here's the deal: let Zev go and I'll let you be."

"You care that much for an old Jew?"

"He's something you never knew in life, and never will know: he's a friend."

And he gave me back my soul.

Palmeri leaned closer. His foul, nauseating breath wafted against Joe's face.

"A friend? How can you be friends with a dead man?" With that he straightened and turned toward the balcony. "Do him! *Now!*"

As Joe shouted out frantic pleas and protests, one of the undead climbed up the rubble toward Zev. Zev did not struggle. Joe saw him close his eyes, waiting. As the vampire reached out with the straight razor, Joe bit back a sob of grief and rage and helplessness. He was about to squeeze his own eyes shut when he saw a flame arc through the air from

one of the windows. It struck the floor with a crash of glass
and a *wooomp!* of exploding flame.

Joe had only heard of such things, but he immediately realized that he had just seen his first Molotov cocktail in action. The splattering gasoline splashed a nearby vampire
who began running in circles, screaming as it beat at its
flaming clothes. But its cries were drowned by the roar of
other voices, a hundred or more. Joe looked around and saw
people—men, women, teenagers—climbing in the windows, charging through the front doors. The women held
crosses on high while the men wielded long wooden pikes—
broom, rake, and shovel handles whittled to sharp points.
Joe recognized most of the faces from the Sunday Masses he
had said here for years.

St. Anthony's parishioners were back to reclaim their
church.

"Yes!" he shouted, not sure of whether to laugh or cry. But
when he saw the rage in Palmeri's face, he laughed. "Too
bad, Alberto!"

Palmeri made a lunge at his throat but cringed away as a
woman with an upheld crucifix and a man with a pike
charged the altar—Lacey and Carl.

"Are you all right, Uncle Joe?" Lacey said, her eyes wide
and angry. "Did they—?"

"You got here just in time."

She pulled out a butterfly knife, flipped it open with one
hand, and began sawing at the rope around Joe's right wrist.
She was using her left only; her right arm didn't seem to be
of much use.

"Told ya I wouldn't let ya down, didn't I, Fadda?" Carl
said, grinning. "Didn't I?"

"That you did, Carl. I don't think I've ever been so glad to
see anyone in my entire life. But how—?"

"We told 'em. We run through the parish, Lacey and me,
goin house to house. We told 'em Fadda Joe was in trouble
at the church and we let him down before but we shouldn't

let him down again. He come back for us, now we gotta go back for him. Simple as that. And then *they* started runnin house to house, and afore ya knowed it, we had ourselfs a little army. We come to kick ass, Fadda, if you'll excuse the expression."

"Kick all the ass you can, Carl."

Joe glanced around and spotted a sixtyish black woman he recognized as Lilly Green. He saw her terror-glazed eyes as she swiveled around, looking this way and that; he saw how the crucifix trembled in her hand. She wasn't going to kick too much ass in her state, but she was *here*, God bless her, she was here for him and for St. Anthony's despite the terror that so obviously filled her. His heart swelled with love for these people and pride in their courage.

As soon as his arms were free, Joe sat up and took the knife from Lacey. He sawed at his leg ropes, looking around the church.

The oldest and youngest members of the parishioner army were stationed at the windows and doors where they held crosses aloft, cutting off the vampires' escape, while all across the nave—chaos. Screams, cries, and an occasional shot echoed through St. Anthony's. The undead and their Vichy were outnumbered three to one. The undead seemed blinded and confused by all the crosses around them. Despite their superhuman strength, it appeared that some were indeed getting their asses kicked. A number were already writhing on the floor, impaled on pikes. As Joe watched, he saw the middle-aged Gonzales sisters, Maria and Immaculata, crucifixes held before them, backing a vampire into a corner. As it cowered there with its arms across its face, Maria's husband Hector charged in with a sharpened rake handle held like a lance and ran it through.

But a number of parishioners lay in inert, bloody heaps on the floor, proof that the undead and the Vichy were claiming their share of victims too.

Joe freed his feet and hopped off the altar. He looked around for Palmeri—he *wanted* Palmeri—but the undead priest had lost himself in the melee. Joe glanced up at the balcony and saw that Zev was still hanging there, struggling to free himself. He started across the nave to help him.

ZEV . . .

Zev hated that he should be hung up here like a chicken in a deli window. He tried again to pull his upper body up far enough to reach his leg ropes but he couldn't get close. He had never been one for exercise; doing a sit-up flat on the floor would have been difficult, so what made him think he could do the equivalent maneuver hanging upside down by his feet? He dropped back, exhausted, and felt the blood rush to his head again. His vision swam, his ears pounded, he felt as if the skin of his face might burst open. Much more of this and he'd have a stroke or worse maybe.

He watched the upside-down battle below and was glad to see the undead getting the worst of it. These people—seeing Carl among them, Zev assumed they were part of St. Anthony's parish—were ferocious, almost savage in their attacks on the undead. All their pent-up rage and fear was being released upon their tormentors in a single burst. It was almost frightening.

Suddenly he felt a hand on his foot. Someone was untying his knots. Thank you, Lord. Soon he would be on his feet again. As the cords came loose he decided he should at least attempt to participate in his own rescue.

Once more, Zev thought. *Once more I'll try.*

With a grunt he levered himself up, straining, stretching to grasp something, anything. A hand came out of the darkness and he reached for it. But Zev's relief turned to horror when he felt the cold clamminess of the thing that clutched him, that pulled him up and over the balcony rail with inhuman strength. His bowels threatened to evacuate when Palmeri's grinning face loomed not six inches from his own.

"It's not over yet, Jew," he said softly, his foul breath clogging Zev's nose and throat. "Not by a long shot!"

He felt Palmeri's free hand ram into his belly and grip his belt at the buckle, then the other hand grab a handful of his shirt at the neck. Before he could struggle or cry out, he was lifted free of the floor and hoisted over the balcony rail.

And the *dybbuk*'s voice was in his ear.

"Joseph called you a friend, Jew. Let's see if he really meant it."

JOE . . .

Joe was halfway across the floor of the nave when he heard Palmeri's voice echo above the madness.

"Stop them, Joseph! Stop them now or I drop your friend!"

Joe looked up and froze. Palmeri stood at the balcony rail, leaning over it, his eyes averted from the nave and all its newly arrived crosses. At the end of his outstretched arms was Zev, suspended in mid-air over the splintered remains of the pews, over a particularly large and ragged spire of wood that pointed directly at the middle of Zev's back. Zev's frightened eyes were flashing between Joe and the giant spike below.

Around him Joe heard the sounds of the melee drop a notch, then drop another as all eyes were drawn to the tableau on the balcony.

"A human can die impaled on a wooden stake just as well as a vampire!" Palmeri cried. "And just as quickly if it goes through his heart. But it can take hours of agony if it rips through his gut."

St. Anthony's grew silent as the fighting stopped and each faction backed away to a different side of the church, leaving Joe alone in the middle.

"What do you want, Alberto?"

"First I want all those crosses put away so that I can see!"

Joe looked to his right where his parishioners stood.

"Put them away," he told them. When a murmur of dissent arose, he added, "Don't put them down, just out of sight. Please."

Slowly, one by one at first, then in groups, the crosses and crucifixes were placed behind backs or tucked out of sight within coats.

To his left, the undead hissed their relief and the Vichy cheered. The sound was like hot needles being forced under Joe's fingernails. Above, Palmeri turned his face to Joe and smiled.

"That's better."

"What do you want?" Joe asked, knowing with a sick crawling in his gut exactly what the answer would be.

"A trade," Palmeri said.

"Me for him, I suppose?" Joe said.

Palmeri's smile broadened. "Of course."

"No, Joe!" Zev cried.

Palmeri shook the old man roughly. Joe heard him say, "Quiet, Jew, or I'll snap your spine!" Then he looked down at Joe again. "The other thing is to tell your rabble to let my people go." He laughed and shook Zev again. "Hear that, Jew? A Biblical reference—Old Testament, no less!"

"All right," Joe said without hesitation.

The parishioners on his right gasped as one and cries of "No!" and "You can't!" filled St. Anthony's. A particularly loud voice nearby shouted, "He's only a lousy kike!"

Joe wheeled on the man and recognized Gene Harrington, a carpenter. He jerked a thumb back over his shoulder at the undead and their servants.

"You sound like you'd be more at home with them, Gene."

Harrington backed up a step and looked at his feet.

"Sorry, Father," he said in a voice that hovered on the verge of a sob. "But we just got you back!"

"I'll be all right," Joe said softly.

And he meant it. Deep inside he had a feeling that he would come through this, that if he could trade himself for Zev and face Palmeri one-on-one, he could come out the victor, or at least battle him to a draw. Now that he was no longer tied up like some sacrificial lamb, now that he was free, with full use of his arms and legs again, he could not imagine dying at the hands of the likes of Palmeri.

Besides, one of the parishioners had given him a tiny crucifix. He had it closed in the palm of his hand.

But he had to get Zev out of danger first. That above all else. He looked up at Palmeri.

"All right, Alberto. I'm on my way up."

"Wait!" Palmeri said. "Someone search him."

Joe gritted his teeth as one of the Vichy, a blubbery, unwashed slob, came forward and searched his pockets. Joe thought he might get away with the crucifix but at the last moment he was made to open his hands. The Vichy grinned in Joe's face as he snatched the tiny cross from his palm and shoved it into his pocket.

"He's clean now!" the slob said and gave Joe a shove toward the vestibule.

Joe hesitated. He was walking into the snake pit unarmed. A glance at his parishioners told him he couldn't very well turn back now.

He continued on his way, clenching and unclenching his tense, sweaty fists as he walked. He still had a chance of coming out of this alive. He was too angry to die. He prayed that when he got within reach of the ex-priest the smoldering rage at how he had framed him when he'd been pastor, at what he'd done to St. Anthony's since then, would explode and give him the strength to tear Palmeri to pieces.

"No!" Zev shouted from above. "Forget about me! You've started something here and you've got to see it through!"

Joe ignored his friend.

"Coming, Alberto."

Father Joe's coming, Alberto. And he's pissed. Royally *pissed.*

ZEV . . .

Zev craned his neck, watching Joe disappear beneath the balcony.

"Joe! Come back!"

Palmeri shook him again.

"Give it up, old Jew. Joseph never listened to anyone and he's not listening to you. He still believes in faith and virtue and honesty, in the power of goodness and truth over what he perceives as evil. He'll come up here ready to sacrifice himself for you, yet sure in his heart that he's going to win in the end. But he's wrong."

"No!" Zev said.

But in his heart he knew that Palmeri was right. How could Joe stand up against a creature with Palmeri's strength, who could hold Zev in the air like this for so long? Didn't his arms ever tire?

"Yes!" Palmeri hissed. "He's going to lose and we're going to win. We'll win for the same reason we always win. We don't let anything as silly and transient as sentiment stand in our way. If we'd been winning below and situations were reversed—if Joseph were holding one of my nest brothers over that wooden spike below—do you think I'd pause for a moment? For a second? Never! That's why this whole exercise by Joseph and these people is futile."

Futile . . . Zev thought. Like much of his life, it seemed. Like all of his future. Joe would die tonight and Zev might live on . . . as what? A cross-wearing Jew, with the traditions of his past sacked and in flames, and nothing in his future but a vast, empty, limitless plain to wander alone.

Footfalls sounded on the balcony stairs and Palmeri turned his head.

"Ah, Joseph," he said.

Zev couldn't see the priest but he shouted anyway.

"Go back, Joe! Don't let him trick you!"

"Speaking of tricks," Palmeri said, leaning further over the balcony rail as an extra warning to Joe, "I hope you're not going to try anything foolish."

"No," said Joe's tired voice from somewhere behind Palmeri. "No tricks. Pull him in and let him go."

Zev could not let this happen. And suddenly he knew what he had to do. He twisted his body and grabbed the front of Palmeri's cassock while bringing his legs up and bracing his feet against one of the uprights of the brass balcony rail. As Palmeri turned his startled face toward him, Zev put all his strength into his legs for one convulsive backward push against the railing, pulling Palmeri with him. The undead priest was overbalanced. Even his enormous strength could not help him once his feet came free of the floor. Zev saw his undead eyes widen with terror when his lower body slipped over the railing. As they fell free, Zev wrapped his arms around Palmeri and clutched his cold and surprisingly thin body tight against him.

"What goes through this old Jew goes through you!" he shouted into the vampire's ear.

For an instant he saw Joe's horrified face appear over the balcony's receding edge, heard his faraway shout of *"No!"* mingle with Palmeri's nearer, lengthier scream of the same word, then came a spine-cracking jar and in his chest a tearing, wrenching pain beyond all comprehension. In an eyeblink he felt the sharp spire of wood rip through him and into Palmeri.

And then he felt no more.

As roaring blackness closed in he wondered if he'd done it, if this last desperate, foolish act had succeeded. He didn't want to die without finding out. He wanted to know—

But then he knew no more.

JOE . . .

Joe shouted incoherently as he hung over the rail and watched Zev's fall, gagged as he saw the bloody point of the pew remnant burst through the back of Palmeri's cassock directly below him. He saw Palmeri squirm and flop around like a beached fish, then go limp atop Zev's already inert form.

As cheers mixed with cries of horror and the sounds of renewed battle rose from the nave, Joe turned away from the balcony rail and dropped to his knees.

"Zev!" he cried aloud. "Good God, Zev!"

Forcing himself to his feet, he stumbled down the back stairs, through the vestibule, and into the nave. The undead and the Vichy were on the run, as cowed and demoralized by their leader's death as the parishioners were buoyed by it. Slowly, steadily, they were falling before the relentless onslaught.

But Joe paid them scant attention. He fought his way to where Zev lay impaled beneath Palmeri's already decomposing corpse. He looked for a sign of life in his old friend's glazing eyes, a hint of a pulse in his throat under his beard, but found nothing.

"Zev, Zev, Zev, you shouldn't have. You shouldn't have."

He stiffened as he felt a pair of arms go around him, then saw it was Lacey. Tears streamed down her cheeks as she leaned against him and sobbed. She reached out and touched Zev's forehead.

"Oh, Uncle Joe . . . Uncle Joe . . ."

Suddenly they were surrounded by a cheering throng of St. Anthony's parishioners.

"We did it, Fadda Joe!" Carl cried, his face and hands splattered with blood. "We killed 'em all! We got our church back!"

"Thanks to this man here," Joe said, pointing to Zev.

"No!" someone shouted. "Thanks to *you!*"

Amid the cheers, Joe shook his head and said nothing. Let them celebrate. They deserved it. They'd reclaimed a tiny piece of the world as their own, a toehold and nothing more. A small victory of minimal significance in the war, but a victory nonetheless. They had their church back, at least for to-night. And they intended to keep it.

Good. But there would be one change. If they wanted their Father Joe to stick around they were going to have to agree to rename the church.

St. Zev's.

Joe liked the sound of that.

GREGOR . . .

"I was wrong, wasn't I!" Olivia raged, waving her arms and she stormed back and forth across the main floor of the Post office. Her get-guards flanked her, watching the windows, trying to cover her as she moved. Gregor's guards clustered near him, warily watching the others. "Yesterday, when I heard that more than one of your serfs had been killed in a single night, I thought it couldn't get any worse. But now this! *This!*"

Gregor, still too numb with shock, said nothing.

He and his guards had been on the other side of town, roaming the streets, hunting the vigilantes, when he'd heard the news. He'd rushed back to the church, not believing it could be true. But it was. He'd found St. Anthony's aflame with searing light, too bright to look at. Crosses blazed from every window and door, the corpses of his cowboys and his get lay in a tangled pile on the front steps, and from within . . . the voices of the cattle raised in hymns.

Olivia stopped her pacing and glared at him. "You allowed this to happen, didn't you, Gregor. You're trying to humiliate me, aren't you."

That did it.

"You bitch!" Gregor shouted.

He raised his fist and took a step toward her. Her guards reacted by reaching for their machetes, and Gregor's guards followed suit. As much as he wanted his hands around her throat, crushing it, twisting until her head ripped free, this was not the time or place for a pointless melee. Gregor opened his fist and stabbed a finger at Olivia.

"You conniving, self-centered bitch! Humiliate *you*? I'm the one whose local get has been virtually wiped out! If anyone's pride has been damaged tonight it is *mine*!"

"And you've nobody to blame but yourself," she snarled. "Your serfs and your get failed you, failed all of us. They deserved what they got. I see only one solution. I will have to bring in my own serfs and get to clean up your mess."

"This is what you've wanted all along, isn't it. For all I know you engineered this yourself!"

"Don't talk like a fool! I—" She stopped, held up a hand, and closed her eyes. "Wait. Wait." She opened her eyes and stared at him. "Do you see what is happening? A few of the cattle make a move against us and what do we do? We turn on each other. This is not the way."

Realizing she was right, Gregor stepped back. But he said nothing. The sting of her words remained. His get had *not* deserved to die.

"We have a situation," Olivia said. "One that must be kept quiet and crushed immediately. If word of what happened here tonight gets around, insurrections like this could spread like wildfire."

Gregor watched her. He didn't trust this suddenly reasonable Olivia.

"The thing to do is retake the church," he said. "Immediately."

"But we can't, Gregor. The slow attrition of your serfs to these vigilantes over the past weeks plus their wholesale slaughter tonight leaves us short of manpower. Of the ones we have left, half are ready to bolt. We'd better hope these vigilantes are so happy to have their church back that they'll stay there tomorrow, because we now have barely enough serfs to guard us during the sunlit hours. If these vigilantes should decide to put together a hunting party . . ."

Gregor suppressed a shudder. "They won't. They're not the vigilantes."

"You so dearly wish. Then the blame would not be on you for allowing them to roam free for so long. In fact, as I remember, you were supposed to solve the vigilante problem before this coming sunrise."

Did she have to bring that up? He'd been searching since sundown.

"It seems we've had a slight, unanticipated distraction."

She waved her hand, brushing him off. "Unlike you, I am not going to sit on my hands. I've already contacted Franco."

The word *bitch* rose to Gregor's lips again but he bit it back. Pointless to call names now.

"I'm sure you gave him a scrupulously evenhanded account of the night's events."

She offered him a tight smile. "Certainly. I requested a detachment of ferals and a group of tough, seasoned serfs. The plan is simple: tomorrow night they will firebomb the church and let the parishioners run out into the arms of the ferals."

Gregor had to admit it was a good plan: simple, direct. It would work.

"And what did Franco say?"

Her smile faltered. "He said he'd take it under consideration."

Gregor's mind reeled in shock. *Franco is hanging me out to dry! Is this what I get for my loyalty, my efforts?*

"Is he telling us to clean up our own mess?"

Olivia's eyebrows shot up. "*Our* mess?"

"Yes, Olivia. You were here when it happened. No matter how you spin it to Franco, he's still going to see it as *our* mess."

Gregor didn't know if that was true, but it didn't hurt to make Olivia squirm, get her working with him instead of against him.

"The vigilantes were your problem long before I arrived."

"And I'm telling you these are not the same people."

"A very self-serving theory."

"Their methods are different. I've been gathering information since it happened. One of my cowboys—serfs—walked in on them in the church earlier today. They didn't kill him, just pushed him around and sent him on his way. If it had been the vigilantes they would have slit his throat and hung him from a pole just like all the others."

"Maybe they've changed tactics."

Gregor shook his head. "The church problem was started by a priest and a rabbi."

"Working together? Maybe this is more of a problem than I thought."

"It is. But these two are not the vigilantes. They're worse. They're visible, and they've provided a base of operations, a rallying point for the cattle. They're doing everything the vigilantes did *not* do."

"This will not get you off the hook, Gregor."

"Will you listen to me? I'm trying to tell you there are *two* groups to deal with now, separate and distinct. And if they should band together we will be in even bigger danger."

"As I said, Gregor: theory. A theory needs proof. If you're so convinced the vigilantes are not in that church, then prove it by finding them and bringing them in. I hope you succeed."

"I find that hard to believe."

"I'm quite serious. Your serfs are becoming afraid to move about in the day. They sense a foundering ship and, like the rats they are, they're ready to jump. We can't have that. We need them to hold the day. If these people take back the day, then we might lose the night as well."

That will never happen, Gregor thought. I will not allow it.

"I will bring in these vigilantes as promised. And when I do, I'll bleed them—just enough to weaken them. Then I'll give them to the cowboys to finish. I'll let them take as long as they like to exact their revenge. And then they'll see that we take care of our helpers. And the rest of the cattle will see that resistance is futile."

He had to succeed, had to prove that the vigilantes were not connected with the church rebels, otherwise the blame for the fall of the church would rest on his shoulders. His whole future depended on finding those damn vigilantes.

"Let's hope so," Olivia said. "Meanwhile, I won't be idle while waiting to hear from Franco. I'm going to have that church watched closely in case this priest or rabbi or anyone else from inside steps out." Her eyes blazed. "I want one of them."

"For what?" Gregor asked.

"For answers. For leverage. For . . . fun." Olivia smiled. "I can be very inventive."

5

JOE . . .

Father Joe gave the dirt on Zev's grave a final pat with his shovel, then turned away. He didn't know any of the Jewish prayers for the dead, so he'd made up a prayer of his own to send his old friend on his way.

Lacey walked beside him, a shovel across her shoulder. "You were really close to him, weren't you."

"Like a brother. Closer than a brother. Brothers drag all sorts of baggage into their relationship as adults. We had none of that. We didn't even share the same culture."

"He seemed like a good man."

"He was. He had a kind, generous, gentle soul. I will miss him terribly."

Joe's throat clenched. He still couldn't believe Zev was gone. He'd feared him dead after the vampires invaded, but hadn't really believed it. Now he had no choice.

He looked around. Rifle- and shotgun-toting men stood at the corners of the little church graveyard. Joe had found spots in the crowded soil for Zev and the four parishioners who'd died during last night's fight, and this morning a crew of volunteers—Lacey among them—had started digging.

He glanced at his niece, noting the sheen of perspiration on her bare arms, the nasty-looking bruise below her shoulder. It didn't seem to be bothering her much this morning. She was in good shape and surprisingly strong. She'd held her own with that shovel.

The midday sun hung high and hot as they followed the walk around to the front of the church where half a dozen women were busy scrubbing the steps. Two more armed men patrolled the sidewalk behind them.

"Good job, ladies," Joe said.

The women smiled and waved.

"Sure looks better than it did this morning," Lacey said.

Joe nodded. They'd hurled the bodies of the vampires and the dead Vichy out the front door last night. In hindsight, that had been an error, because the morning sunlight created a terrible mess, reducing some of the undead cadavers to a foul, brown goo that stained the steps and coated the Vichy bodies.

Carl had found a front-end loader and the men used that to haul the stinking mess to a vacant lot where it was buried in a mass grave.

Lacey stared at the stains. "Lots of death last night." She turned to Joe, her eyes troubled. "Why don't I feel bad?"

"Maybe because this is war. A war like never before. In past wars the enemy gets propagandized into monsters, subhuman creatures. In this war we don't have to do that. They *are* subhuman monsters."

"And the Vichy?"

"They're just subhuman."

She continued to stare at him. "This is not the Uncle Joe I knew."

How right she was. He sensed that memories of last night's carnage and bloodshed would keep him awake for months, maybe years. But he couldn't allow himself to dwell on it. He had to move on.

"Thank God I'm not. The old Father Joe would have tried to reason with them. But I worry that many more scenes like last night will change us, make us more like them."

"So? Maybe we need to become more like them if we're to survive. In a war you have to submerge a lot of the decent impulses and empathy that made you a good partner or spouse or parent or neighbor. Especially in this war, because we're dealing with an enemy that has lost all decent impulses. You offer an olive branch and they'll shove it down your throat. Will we be changed by this? Look around you, Unk: we already are."

He nodded. "We'll all be either dead or permanently scarred when this is over. And so, in the unlikely event that we win, we'll still lose." He managed a smile for her. "How's that for optimism?"

She shrugged. "One thing's for sure. The Uncle Joe who used to say, 'Just have faith and everything will turn out fine' is gone."

Yes, he is, Joe thought with a deep pang of regret. Gone forever.

"Do you miss him, Lacey?"

"Yes and no. He was a great, easygoing guy, but he's not what we need now. And speaking of now, here comes the big question: what next?"

Good question. Joe had been thinking about that. He closed his eyes, lifted his face to the sun, and watched the glowing red inner surface of his lids.

The sun . . . their greatest ally. As long as it was out, he and the parishioners had a fighting chance. The Vichy, what remained of them, seemed cowed. A few had shown their faces in the vicinity but were quickly chased off without offering even token resistance. Every so often Joe would spot one skulking in the shadows a few blocks away, watching the church, but none ventured close.

But once the sun set, the balance would shift to the undead and their collaborators.

"I think we should start a compound," he said.

"You mean, like a fort?"

"Not so much a fort as a consolidation. Gather everyone close for mutual protection and pooling of resources."

Lacey nodded. "The Ben Franklin approach."

"Ben Franklin?"

"Yeah. What he said at the signing of the Declaration of Independence: 'We must all hang together, or assuredly we shall all hang separately.' "

"Declaration of Independence . . . I guess we did that last night."

"Damn right. But with deeds instead of words on paper."

"But as for hanging together, that's the plan—and I don't mean by our necks. The living are scattered all over town now. That leaves us vulnerable to being picked off one by one. But if we use the church as a hub and bring everybody toward the center—"

"Circle the wagons, in other words."

"Exactly. As of now we've got the rectory, the convent, and the church itself. That'll house some people, but it's not enough. We need to expand."

"You got that right."

By word of mouth and who knew how else, the news that someone was fighting back had spread. A steady stream of newcomers, anxious to join the fight, had been flowing to the church all morning. Many of them were not even Catholic. Jews, Protestants, even Muslims were showing up, wanting to know how they could be part of what was happening. Joe had passed the word to welcome everyone. This was not a time for divisions. The arbitrary walls that had separated people in the past had to be knocked down. There could be only one belief system now: the living versus the undead and those who sided with them.

"There's an empty office building across the street from the back of the church," Joe said, remembering the night he and Zev had spent there. Had it been only two nights since then? "That should hold a lot of folks. We'll start there."

"I passed a couple of furniture stores on the way here," Lacey said. She pointed south. "If I remember, they're just a few blocks that way."

"You're right," Joe said. "I know the places."

"We can raid them for bedding."

"Great idea. Once we set that up, we'll take over the surrounding houses—assuming they're unoccupied."

"Pretty safe assumption," Lacey said. "If the owners somehow survived, I can't see them hanging around for long, considering what's been going down in the church."

"But first I want to start blocking off the surrounding streets—get old cars, line them up in the intersections. That'll fend off or at least slow down any blitzkrieg-style counterattacks."

He felt Lacey's hand on his arm and turned to find her staring at him.

"You've given this a lot of thought, haven't you."

"That's just it. I haven't. I'm making it up as I go along. As I told you last night, my original intent was to hold the place for one night, say Mass, then move on."

Lacey smiled. "I was wondering what happened to that idea."

"It got lost in the crowd."

Joe hadn't counted on drawing a crowd. Now that he had, what did he do with them? He couldn't perform the loaves-and-fishes miracle. How was he going to feed them? But seeing the desperate hope gleaming in their eyes this morning, he couldn't simply walk out on them.

"So . . ." Lacey said slowly. "Beyond a compound . . . what?"

"I wish I knew."

"You realize, don't you, that we can't win."

"I don't realize any such thing."

"Hey, Unk," she said, her grip tightening on his arm. "We're only a hundred people and there are millions of them. They've got Europe, the Middle East, India, and most of Asia."

"But they haven't got the U.S. They hold the East Coast but the rest of the country is still alive."

"How can you be sure?"

"I was talking to one of the newcomers this morning. His name's Gerald Vance and he's got a battery-powered short-wave radio. He told me he's been talking to people all over the country. Philadelphia's gone but Harrisburg and Pittsburgh have only seen an occasional vampire. Same with Rochester. Atlanta fell but Alabama's fine. The Midwest and the West Coast are still in the hands of the living. So you see, it's not over."

Lacey looked away. "After seeing what's happened to the rest of the world, you could argue that it's just a matter of time."

Joe lowered his voice. "I'd appreciate it if you wouldn't talk like that. Last night was the first good thing that's happened to these people in a long time, so if you don't mind . . ."

Lacey held up a hand. "Okay. 'Never is heard a discouraging word.' But if that's true about the rest of the country, then instead of staying here maybe we should be thinking about throwing a convoy together and heading west."

Joe shook his head. He'd already thought of that.

"We're being watched. We start to assemble dozens of cars, they'll know what we're planning. They'll be waiting for us. We'll be sitting ducks on the road."

He'd seen it play out in his mind's eye. He'd envisioned a line of cars racing down Route 70 at dawn. But he'd also envisioned a Vichy roadblock, gunfire, bloodshed, disabled cars, the convoy stalled, blocked fore and aft, the sun going down, and then . . . massacre.

"We've got a better chance here. I told Vance to get on his radio and spread the word of what we're doing here. Maybe it will spur others to do the same. Right now we've set a fire. If we remain the only bonfire, I agree: we're doomed. But if we can start a trend, inspire a hundred, a thousand fires along the coast, we'll no longer be the center of attention. We might have a chance."

Lacey was nodding. "And if the rest of the country gets the message that there is hope, that resistance is not futile . . ." She grinned and raised her fist. "I always wanted to be a revolutionary."

"Well, you're going to get your wish." Joe yawned. When was the last time he'd slept? "My wish is for forty winks."

"Why don't you bed down for a while in the rectory? You catch your forty while I take some people over to that office building and check it out. We'll see how we can divide it up for living arrangements."

Joe stared at her. Where did she get her energy?

"Aren't you tired?"

She shrugged. "I've never needed much sleep. Besides, I had a nap."

"When?"

She smiled. "While you were saying Mass."

Joe sighed. "When are you going to face facts and admit—?"

"Hush." She put a finger to her lips. "I'm still not on board, but we'll argue about this some other time. Right now, there's too much work to do."

Joe watched her stride off, thinking that whoever said there are no atheists in foxholes obviously hadn't met Lacey.

LACEY . . .

Lacey gazed out the window at the lengthening shadows and rubbed her burning eyes.

Tired. She hadn't found time for another nap yet. All she needed was twenty minutes and she'd be good for hours more of activity.

Her uncle and the rest were in the process of working out a sleep schedule, assigning shifts. Some of them were going to have to live undead style, sleeping in the day, up all night, while others would keep a more normal schedule. Lacey figured she'd volunteer for the undead shift since she tended to be a night person anyway.

She turned away from the window and checked out the

room behind her. The desks had been pushed into a corner and a mattress and box spring placed in the center of the floor. Not fancy but functional, and a helluva lot more comfortable than trying to sleep on the church's stone floor.

She stretched her aching muscles. A good workout today, driving pickup trucks to the furniture stores, hauling bedding back, and lugging it up the steps to the upper floors. Toward the end of the afternoon she would have given anything for a generator to power up the elevator.

Back to the window for another look at the grand old Victorian next door. Janey had been so into Victorians, dragging Lacey around the city, pointing out this Second Empire and that Italianate until she'd caught the bug too. They'd planned someday to come down to Asbury Park, buy a place like the three-story affair next door and renovate it, dress it up like those fabulous painted ladies they'd salivated over on their trip to San Francisco last year.

Lacey felt a lump grow in her throat. Janey . . . they'd had such good times together . . . the best years of her life. She missed her. Losing her had left an cavity where she'd once had a heart.

Where are you, Janey? What did they do to you?

Lacey knew in that instant which building she wanted added next to Uncle Joe's "compound."

Why not suggest it to him now?

She ducked into the hall and started down the stairwell, only to have to back up to allow a couple of the parish men to pass with a queen-size mattress.

"I'm heading over to the church to see Father Joe," she told them.

"Give us a minute and I'll escort you back," said a red-faced, heavyset man in a plaid shirt.

Lacey waved him off. "Don't be silly. It's a hundred feet away. And the street's blocked."

Probably just wants a break from all the lifting and hauling, she thought as she stepped outside.

She checked up and down the street. Nothing moving. No one in sight.

As she started across the street she glanced again at the old house and figured, why not check it out first? If it wasn't habitable—say, a big hole in the roof or something like that—why waste her time?

But she wasn't going in there alone. No way. She'd seen enough horror movies to know you don't go into empty houses alone when there are bad guys about.

She looked around, saw a short, muscular guy in a sleeveless T-shirt crossing the street, heading from the church toward the office building. What was his name? Enrico. Yeah, that was it.

"Hey, Enrico. Want to help me check out this place next door? See if we can move people in there?"

"Sure," he said, grinning. "Let's go."

She waited for him to catch up, then together they headed for the front steps and climbed onto the porch. She tried the door, hoping it was unlocked—she hated the thought of breaking one of those old windows to get in—and smiled as the latch yielded to the pressure of her thumb. All right!

Enrico hung in the living room while Lacey hurried through the cool, dark, silent interior. The decor was not authentically Victorian—nowhere near cramped and cluttered enough—but the place hadn't been vandalized. The two upper floors held five small bedrooms and one larger master bedroom, all furnished with beds and dressers. The couch in the first-floor sun room could sleep another, once all the dead house plants were removed.

Perfect, she thought, feeling the best she had all day. This is a definite keeper. And I've got first dibs on the master bedroom.

She came down the main staircase—the house had a rear servants' stairway as well, running to and from the kitchen—and found the living room empty.

"Enrico?"

Maybe he'd done a little exploring on his own. She headed for the kitchen and stopped cold when she saw a pair of feet jutting toes-up from behind a counter. She wanted to run but knew she had to check. She hurried forward, took a look at the kitchen carving knife jutting from Enrico's bloody chest, at his dead, glazed eyes staring at the ceiling, then spun and ran.

She didn't head for the front door. Instead she sprang for the French doors and leaped onto the verandah. There she ran into three waiting Vichy and had no time to react before something cracked against her skull, sending lightning bolts through her suddenly darkening vision. She lashed out with her booted foot but struck only air, and then another blow to her head sent her down.

She had flashes of faces, one clean-shaven, one bearded, one with braided hair, snatches of voices . . .

"Got one!" . . . "Hey, she's fine! She's really fine!"

A feeling of being carried, then an impact as she was tossed into the rear of a van, the van starting to move, then more voices . . .

"We get major points for this—*major!*" . . . "Man, she's *so* fine! Shame to hafta give her to the bloodsuckers." . . . "Ay, yo, they only said they wanted a live one. Didn't say nothin 'bout havin to be a virgin, know'm sayin?"

Laughter.

"Right! Fuckin-ay *right!*"

And then the feeling of her clothes being torn from her body . . .

CAROLE . . .

Sister Carole watched a beat-up old van race along the street. She couldn't see who was driving but it was coming from the direction of St. Anthony's.

St. Anthony's . . . how she'd wanted to step inside when she'd passed by this morning. She'd heard the voices drifting through the open front doors, responding to Father Joe during Mass, and they'd tugged her up the steps to participate and . . . to see Father Joe's face once more. But she couldn't allow it. She was unworthy . . . too unworthy.

She'd seen the stains on the steps—blood and fouler substances—and had asked one of the armed men guarding the front about them. He'd told her about what had happened during the night, how Father Palmeri and other undead had been routed and killed along with their living helpers, how the church was now a holy place again.

Carole had walked on with her heart singing. Maybe what she'd been doing was not all for naught. Maybe there was a Divine Plan and she was part of it.

Then again, maybe not.

Most likely not.

The song in her heart had gasped and died.

And so she'd spent most of the rest of the day working around the house. She figured it was only a matter of time before she was caught and wanted to be ready when the undead or their cowboys came for her.

<I wish they'd come for you NOW, Carole. Then this shame, this monstrous sinfulness would be over and you'd get what you DESERVE!>

"That makes two of us," Sister Carole said.

She didn't want to go out again tonight but knew she had to.

Her only solace was the certainty that sooner or later it going to end—for her.

She set a few more wires, ran a few more strings, then headed up to the bedroom to change into her padded bra, her red blouse, her black leather skirt.

<Not again! When is it going to END, Carole? When is this going to STOP?>

"When they're all dead and gone," Sister Carole said aloud to the stranger in the bedroom mirror. "Or when I am. Whichever comes first."

GREGOR . . .

Gregor frowned as he smeared makeup on his face to hide
his pallor. He hoped it looked all right. Since he couldn't use
a mirror he had to go by feel. It would have made more sense
to have one of his get apply it, but he wanted to keep his plan
to himself.

He sprayed himself with Obsession cologne. The living
said the undead carried an unmistakable odor. He couldn't
detect it himself, but this should mask it. He rose and looked
down at himself. A long-sleeved work shirt, scruffy jeans, a
crescent-on-a-chain earring, and now, a passably—he
hoped—ruddy complexion.

"Hey there," he said in the drawl he'd been practicing
since sundown, hoping to disguise his own accent with another. "Ahm new in these here parts."

He slipped a cowboy hat onto his head to complete the
picture.

A good enough picture, he hoped, to decoy these vigilantes into picking on him as their next cowboy victim.

Gregor smiled, baring his teeth. *Then* they'd be in for a
surprise.

He could have sent someone else, could have sent out a
number of decoys, but he wanted this hunt for himself. After
all, Franco had his eye on the situation, and that mandated
bold and extraordinary measures. Gregor needed to prove
without a doubt that the vigilantes were separate from the insurgents in the church.

He stepped over the drained, beheaded corpse of the old
man who'd been brought to him earlier—what had happened to all the young cattle?—and checked the map one
last time. He'd marked all six places where the dead cowboys had been found. The X's formed a rough circle. Gregor's plan was to wander the streets within that circle. Alone.

An hour ago he'd sent his get-guards upstairs to the main

floor of the synagogue, telling them he wanted to sup alone and be left undisturbed here in the basement while he planned the night's sortie. Now he crept up the steps and let himself out a side door and into the dark.

Gregor took a deep, shuddering breath of the night air. Too long since he'd done this. Not since he'd migrated out of Eastern Europe with the others. It felt wonderful to be on the hunt again.

JOE . . .

Joe realized with a start that he hadn't seen Lacey since this morning.

"Has anybody seen my niece?" he said to a group of men standing guard on the front steps.

"Niece?" one of them said, a big black man with gray stubble on his cheeks. "I didn't know you had one. What's she look like, Father?"

"Dark hair, tattoo on her arm about here, and she's—"

"Sure," said another fellow. He jerked a thumb over his shoulder. "She was with us back there across the street in the office building most of the day. Some kinda worker, that girl."

"That she is," Joe said, trying not to sound too obviously proud. "But when did you last see her?"

"Late afternoon," said a big, red-faced man. "Said she was coming back here to see you about something."

A jolt of alarm lanced though Joe. "I haven't seen her. She never got to me!"

He tore back into the church, scanning expectant faces as he hurried through the nave—expectant because he was supposed to start saying evening Mass just about now. He ducked through the sanctuary and into the sacristy where he found Carl, getting ready for his altar boy duties.

"Carl! Have you seen Lacey?"

He shook his head. "No, Fadda. Something wrong?"

"She's missing. Gone." Joe's gut crawled. "Get your gun and a couple of the men. We've got to find her."

"But what about Mass?"

"Forget about that. Lacey comes first."

"Y'gotta say Mass, Fadda. Everyone's out there waiting for you." He stepped to the door and looked out into the nave. "Let's do this: I'll tell some of the non-Catholic guys to look for her during Mass. They can look just as good as us. They'll find her. Chances are she's probably conked out in the convent or rectory catching up on her sleep."

Joe prayed that was true. It seemed logical. Lacey could take care of herself, probably better than most of the men. She'd made it all the way down here from New York on her own, hadn't she?

Still . . . not knowing where she was gnawed at him.

GREGOR . . .

Where are you? Gregor wanted to shout. I'm right here in your kill zone. Come and get me!

He had been walking these empty streets for what seemed like hours. It hadn't been nearly that long, but his gnawing impatience made it feel that way. He'd seen no one, living or undead. He fought the discouragement he sensed creeping up on him, preparing to pounce on his back. He would not give up. He refused to return empty handed again.

He was wondering if perhaps he should set himself up as bait in another area when he heard a woman's voice call from the shadows.

"Hey, mister. Got any food?"

He jumped, not having to fake his surprise. How had she sneaked up on him like that? She was downwind, he realized, and had been hiding behind a thick tree trunk. Still, he should have sensed her presence.

His senses were on full alert now. Were the prey taking the bait? Was this woman bait herself, placed here to lure an unsuspecting cowboy into a trap?

He saw her clearly—a young woman in provocative clothes. Not that it provoked him. Only one thing could do that, and it wasn't made of cloth. It was red and warm and flowed and spurted.

Gregor made a show of squinting into the darkness. No sense in giving his night vision away and scaring off her backup—if indeed she had backup. He sensed no other living human nearby.

"Come on out where ah can see you, honey," he said, remembering to add the drawl.

The cow stepped out of the shadows into the moonlight.

"My, my, you sure are a purty one. What you doin out here alone?"

"L-looking for some food. You got any you can spare?"

"I might. What's in it for me?" Didn't want to sound too anxious.

"What do you think?" the woman said.

Gregor nodded. "I guess that's fair. Where do we make the trade?"

He felt his excitement fading. This was sounding more and more like some tawdry little sex-for-food deal. Not at all what he was looking for. Where were those vigilantes? Damn them!

"Anywhere you want," the cow said. "I just have to check on my little girl first."

Little girl? That renewed Gregor's interest. If it were true, well, he hadn't had really young blood in too long. And if it was a lie to entice some hapless cowboy looking to earn some bonus points, that was fine too. That was why he was here.

"I'll follow you home, then we'll go to my place."

Her house was only a block and a half away. Gregor felt his tension mount as she led him up the front steps to the door. He wouldn't be able to cross the threshold uninvited. If he hesitated too long, she'd guess the truth.

He waited until she'd opened the door. As soon as she stepped inside he said, "This ain't some kinda trap, is it?"

She turned and faced him. "What do you mean?"

"Well, guys like me been dyin left and right lately. I don't wanna step through that door and get jumped."

"Stop being silly and come in."

Gregor stifled a laugh as he stepped forward. Stupid cow.

She was already heading for the stairs when he crossed the threshold.

"Let me just take a quick peek," she said as she bounded up the steps, "and then we can get going."

Gregor watched her go, then closed his eyes, trying to sense other living presences. He found none. His disappointment mounted. This cow wasn't connected to the vigilantes. She was here alone.

Wait. Alone? What about the daughter she'd mentioned? Why didn't he sense her?

Curious, Gregor moved toward the stairs.

OLIVIA . . .

Olivia stared at the woman captured near the church and wanted to scream. If they weren't so short of serfs she would have bled out the three who'd brought her here.

Look at her. Crumbled in the corner like a discarded mannequin. Naked, battered, bleeding from the mouth, nose, vagina, and rectum. And worst of all, unconscious. How could she get any information from this cow if she couldn't speak? Had they beaten her into a coma? What if she never woke up? Olivia would then have to wait until they picked up another. And that would be much harder now because the church fold would be watching for it.

This is what you get when you have to depend on scum.

And what do you get when you depend on an egomaniac like Franco? Just as much. Maybe less.

Wasn't *anything* going to go right down here in this wasted little section of the coast?

Word had come from New York that Franco was refusing her request for a contingent of ferals and more experienced serfs. Franco was going to handle this matter himself, in his own way, whatever that meant.

What it meant was a slap in the face not just to Gregor, but her as well. Damn him. Damn them all. If just once she could—

One of her get-guards returned then with the bucket of water she'd ordered. Olivia pointed to the cow on the floor.

"Pour it on her. See if that wakes her."

The guard did as he was bid. The cow stirred and shivered but didn't open her eyes.

"Damn! Get more!"

Just then one of the serfs, a tawdry blond woman, tried to step through the Post Office door. Olivia's guards restrained her.

"That's her!" the woman screamed. A deep purple bruise ringed her left eye. "That's the one who suckered me! Let me at her! Just five minutes!"

"Get her out of here," Olivia said.

"No!" the woman shrilled as she was shoved back into the night. "I got a score to settle with her. She owes me!"

"*Out!*" Olivia screamed.

With help like that, she thought, who needs enemies? How we came this far I'll never know.

Another commotion at the door.

"If it's that serf cow again, slit her throat!"

"It's Gregor's get," one of her guards said. "All his guards."

"What does he want now? He's supposed to be hunting his beloved vigilantes."

Her guard looked puzzled. "He's not with them."

Olivia stiffened with shock. Gregor's get without Gregor? What on—?

And then she smiled. Had Gregor gone off and done something foolish? Something reckless? Oh, she hoped so. It would look all the worse for him when he showed up empty handed again.

"By all means, send them in. But keep close watch on them."

CAROLE . . .

As Sister Carole changed out of her slutty clothes she had a feeling something was wrong. She couldn't put her finger on it, but she sensed something strange about this one. He wore the earring, he'd reacted just the way all the others had, but he'd been stand-offish, keeping his distance, as if afraid to get too close. That bothered her. Could there be such a thing as a shy collaborator? The ones she'd met so far had been anything but.

God willing, she thought, in a few moments it would be over.

She'd followed her usual routine, dashing upstairs, being sure to take the steps two at a time so it wouldn't look strange hopping over the first.

Now she began rubbing off her makeup, all the while listening for the clank of the bear trap when it was tripped.

Finally it came and she winced as she always did, anticipating the shrill, awful cries of pain. But none came. She rushed to the landing and looked down. There she saw the cowboy ripping the restraining chain free from its nail, then reaching down and opening the jaws of the trap with his bare hands.

With her heart pounding a sudden mad tattoo in her chest, Sister Carole realized then that she'd made a terrible mistake. She'd expected to be caught some day, but not like this. She wasn't prepared for one of them.

<Now you've done it, Carole! Now you've really DONE IT!>

Shaking, panting with fear, Sister Carole dashed back to the bedroom and followed the emergency route she'd prepared.

GREGOR . . .

Gregor inspected the dried blood on the teeth of the trap. Obviously it had been used before.

So this was how they did it. Clever. And nasty.

He rubbed the already healing wound on his lower leg. The trap had hurt, startled him more than anything else, but no real harm done. He straightened, kicked the trap into the opening beneath the faux step, and looked around.

Where were the rest of the petty revolutionaries? There had to be more than this lone woman. Or perhaps not. The empty feel of the house persisted.

One woman doing all this damage? Gregor could not believe it. And neither would Olivia. There had to be more to this.

He headed upstairs, gliding this time, barely touching the steps. Another trap would slow him. He spotted the rope ladder dangling over the windowsill as soon as he entered the bedroom. He darted to the window and leaped through the opening. He landed lightly on the overgrown lawn and sniffed the air. She wasn't far—

He heard running footsteps, a sudden loud rustle, and saw a leafy branch flashing toward him. Gregor felt something hit his chest, pierce it, and knock him back. He grunted with the pain, staggered a few steps, then looked down. Three metal tines protruded from his sternum.

The cow had tied back a sapling, fixed the end of a pitchfork to it, and cut it free when he'd descended from the window. Crude but deadly—if he'd been human. He yanked the tines free and tossed them aside. Around the rear of the house he heard a door slam.

She'd gone back inside. Obviously she wanted him to follow. But Gregor decided to enter his own way. He backed away a few steps, then ran and hurled himself through the dining room window.

The shattered glass settled. Dark. Quiet. She was here inside. He sensed her but couldn't pinpoint her location. Not yet. Only a matter of time—a very short time—before he found her. He was making his move toward the rear rooms of the house when a bell shattered the silence, startling him.

He stared incredulously at the source of the noise. The telephone? But how? The first things his nightbrothers had destroyed were the communication networks. Without thinking, he reached out to it—a reflex from days gone by.

The phone exploded as soon as he lifted the receiver.

The blast knocked him against the far wall, smashing him into the beveled glass of the china cabinet. Again, just as with last night's explosion, he was blinded by the flash. But this time he was hurt as well. His hand . . . agony . . . he couldn't remember ever feeling pain like this. Blind and helpless . . . if she had accomplices, he was at their mercy now.

But no one attacked him, and soon he could see again.

"My hand!" he groaned when he saw the ragged stump of his right wrist. The pain was fading, but his hand was gone. It would regenerate in time but—

He had to get out of here and find help before she did something else to him. He didn't care if it made him look like a fool, this woman was dangerous!

Gregor staggered to his feet and started for the door. Once he was outside in the night air he'd feel better, he'd regain some of his strength.

CAROLE . . .

In the basement Sister Carole huddled under the mattress and stretched her arm upward. Her fingers found a string that ran the length of the basement to a hole in one of the floorboards above, ran through that hole and into the pantry in the main hall where it was tied to the handle of an empty teacup that sat on the edge of the bottom shelf. She tugged on the string and the teacup fell. Sister Carole heard it shatter and snuggled deeper under her mattress.

GREGOR . . .

What?

Gregor spun at the noise. There. Behind that door. She was hiding in that closet. She'd knocked something off a shelf in there. He'd heard her. He had her now.

Gregor knew he was hurt—*maimed*—but even with one hand he could easily handle a dozen cattle like her. He didn't want to wait, didn't want to go back to Olivia without *something* to show for the night. And the cow was so close now. Right behind that door.

He reached out with his good hand and yanked it open.

Gregor saw everything with crystal clarity then, and understood everything as it happened.

He saw the string attached to the inside of the door, saw it tighten and pull the little wedge of wood from between the jaws of the clothespin that was tacked to the third shelf. He saw the two wires—one wrapped around the upper jaw and leading back to a dry cell battery, the other wrapped around the lower and leading to a row of wax-coated cylinders standing on that third shelf like a collection of lumpy, squat candles with firecracker-thick wicks. As the wired jaws of the clothespin snapped closed, he saw a tiny spark leap the narrowing gap.

Gregor's universe exploded.

LACEY . . .

Lacey had been conscious for a while but kept her eyes closed, daring every so often to split her lids for a peek. It had taken all her reserve to keep from screaming when that bloodsucker had splashed a bucket of water on her.

At least they'd kept that Vichy broad, the one from under the boardwalk, from getting to her. Lacey didn't think she could handle any more pain.

She hurt . . . oh, how she hurt. Everywhere. In places and in ways she'd never imagined she could hurt. She didn't remember the details, but she knew those three Vichy must have worked her over good. Raped her every possible way.

Lacey ground her teeth. Goddamn human animals . . . *male* human animals, using their dicks as weapons.

Then she remembered Enrico. They'd used a knife on him. Maybe he was the lucky one. He'd gone quickly. She'd been brought here to be someone's meal. After she was drained they'd rip off her head and toss her body on a pile somewhere to rot. But that was better than becoming one of them.

But why were they trying to wake her? They didn't need her conscious to drain her blood. Did they have another use for her in mind? Like using her to find out what was going on inside the church?

A shiver ran through her. She was freezing here on this puddled marble floor and couldn't keep her limbs from quaking. Had anybody seen? She split her lids and took a peek.

Not much light. Only a few candles sputtering but it was enough to make out faces. The female vampire with the big hair had been ranting in French before, but now she stood silent with her six armed attendants. Guards? Lacey had heard that some of the higher-up undead traveled around with what looked like bodyguards, but this was the first time she'd seen it. Why did the undead think they needed guards, especially when everyone else around was undead?

Four new undead males wearing machetes and pistols entered. They addressed the female as Olivia and spoke in English.

"'Ave you seen Gregor, Olivia?" said a dark-haired guard with a British accent. He looked dirty, all in black, his shirt-front crusted with old blood.

Olivia replied in English. "Not since before sunrise." A small smile played about her lips. "Don't tell me you've misplaced him."

"Bloody bastard gave us the slip. We found makeup and cologne in his quarters. 'E's gone out on 'is own to find those vigilantes."

Vigilantes? Lacey thought. This was interesting. She hadn't heard anything about vigilantes. But then, she'd only arrived in town yesterday. Who was this Gregor and why was he hunting them?

"That seems rather reckless, don't you think?" Olivia said.

The Brit snarled at her. "I'm sure 'e'd never be out there if you 'adn't driven 'im to it. We were 'oping 'e'd come to see you first and we could intercept 'im 'ere, but I see we're in the wrong place."

"You certainly are."

"Look, Olivia," the Brit said, his tone becoming conciliatory. "If you've any idea where 'e might be, please tell us. We've got to find 'im. 'E could be in grave danger."

Lacey was struck by the concern in the Brit's voice. The undead supposedly cared about only one thing: blood. But the Brit seemed genuinely worried about this Gregor. Lots more than Olivia.

"Well, if he is, it's his own doing."

The Brit snarled again. "If anything happens to Gregor . . ."

"You'll be the first to know." She laughed, showing her sharp teeth.

"Bitch!" the Brit said and reached for the handle of his machete.

Olivia's guards closed around her, reaching for their own.

And then a thunderous boom rattled the windows and shook the floor beneath Lacey.

As the sound of the blast faded, the Brit and the three other undead who'd arrived with him cried out and clutched their chests. One by one they dropped to their knees.

Olivia's smile had vanished, replaced by a look of horror. Her voice rose in pitch, somewhere between a shout and a wail, as she rattled off a barrage of French too rapid for Lacey to follow. Lacey recognized the name "Gregor" but that was it.

Her guards looked as terrified as she as they encircled her, facing outward, machetes and pistols drawn. They were speaking French too, and again Gregor was mentioned.

What were they saying? Lacey wished now she'd taken French instead of Spanish.

The Brit's friends lay writhing, kicking, and gasping on their backs and bellies, but he was still on his knees, glaring at Olivia.

"You!" His voice was faint, and sounded as if someone were strangling him. "You did this! You're responsible!" He began a faltering crawl toward her.

"Keep him away!" Olivia said.

The Brit pulled his machete from his belt and tried to use it as a crutch to regain his feet. "I'll see you—"

One of Olivia's guards stepped forward then and, holding his machete like a baseball bat, took a two-handed swing. The blade sliced through the Brit's neck with an indescribable tearing sound, sending the head flying. But no gout of blood sprayed the room as the body flopped forward onto its chest and lay still next to the other three fallen undead, now equally still.

And the head . . . the head rolled toward Lacey's face. She shut her eyes, bracing herself if it rolled against her. She couldn't allow herself to move, couldn't give herself away, no matter what.

What was happening here? Undead dropping dead, fighting and killing each other. What the hell was going on? It had something to do with someone named Gregor, but what?

Lacey opened her eyes again and stifled a gasp as she found herself almost nose to nose with the Brit. His eyelids blinked and his lips were moving, as if he was trying to tell her something.

Bile rose in Lacey's throat and she squeezed her eyes shut again.

GREGOR . . .

I'm awake! Gregor thought. I survived!

He didn't know how long it had been since the blast. A few minutes? A few hours? It couldn't have been too long—it was still night. He could see the moonlight through the huge hole that had been ripped in the wall.

He tried to move but could not. In fact, he couldn't feel anything. *Anything*. But he could hear. And he heard someone picking through the rubble toward him. He tried to turn his head but could not. Who was there? One of his own kind—*please* let it be one of his own kind.

When he saw the flashlight beam he knew it was one of the living. He began to despair. He was utterly helpless here. What had that explosion done to him?

As the light came closer, he saw that it was the woman, the she-devil. She appeared to be unscathed . . .

And she wore the headpiece of a nun.

She shone the beam in his face and he blinked.

"Dear sweet Jesus!" she said, her voice hushed with awe. "You're not dead yet? Even in this condition?"

He tried to tell her how she would pay for this, how she would suffer the tortures of the damned and beg for death, but his jaw wasn't working right, and he had no voice.

"So what are we going to do with you, Mister Vampire?" she said. "Your friends might show up and find a way to fix you up. Not that I can see how that'd be possible, but I wouldn't put anything past you vipers."

What was she saying? What did she mean? What had happened to him?

"If I had a good supply of holy water I could pour it over you, but I want to conserve what I've got."

She was quiet a moment, then turned and walked off. Had she decided to leave him here? He hoped so. At least that way he had a chance.

But if she wanted to kill him, why hadn't she said anything about driving a stake through his heart?

He tried to move but his body wouldn't respond. Somehow the blast had paralyzed him. He noticed his vision growing dim, his sense of hearing fading. What was happening? He felt as if he might be drifting toward true death . . .

No! That that couldn't be. He was only paralyzed.

Through his misting vision Gregor saw her coming back. Her hands were bright yellow. How? Why?

"The only thing I can think of doing is to set you on the east end of the porch and let the sun finish you."

No! Please! Not that.

The woman rested the flashlight on a broken timber and reached for his face. He saw now that she wore yellow rubber gloves. He tried to cringe away, but again—no response from his body. She grabbed him by his hair and . . . lifted him. How could she be so strong? Vertigo spun him around as she looked him in the face.

"You can still see, can't you? Maybe you'd better take a look at yourself."

Vertigo again as she twisted his head around, and then he saw the hallway, or what was left of it. Mass destruction . . . shattered timbers, the stairs blown away, and . . .

Pieces of his body—his arms and legs torn and scattered, his torso twisted and eviscerated, his intestines stretched and ripped, internal organs reduced to large, unrecognizable smears.

As his vision faded to black in the final fall toward true death, Gregor wished his lungs were still attached. So he could scream. Just once.

LACEY . . .

A stink filled Lacey's nostrils as she noticed that Olivia's rapid-fire French seemed to be fading away. She dared another look. The Brit's face was slack now and the flesh was starting to decompose. She lifted her head to look beyond him and saw Olivia and her crew backing into a stairwell, heading down to what Lacey assumed was the basement.

As soon as the door closed behind them, Lacey raised her head further and looked around. Except for the bodies of the four dead vampires, she was alone. She'd been forgotten. But for how long?

She struggled to rise, groaning with the pain in her joints and muscles, but especially in her pelvis. She slipped on the wet floor and banged her elbow as she went down. She tried again, clinging to the wall, using it to steady herself as the room spun about her. Clenching her teeth against a wave of nausea, she rose to her feet and hugged the wall.

When the room steadied, she looked down at her bloody, naked body and wanted to retch. What did they *do* to her?

She'd deal with that later. Right now she had to get out of here and back to the church. But where was *here*? She knew from the signs on the wall that she was in a Post Office. But how did she find the church once she got out?

First things first, she told herself. Get out of this undead nest, then worry about finding your way back.

Still holding the wall, she edged toward the doors. She looked longingly at the clothes on the corpses of the dead vampires, but their rot was already seeping through the fabric. She'd rather be naked.

She spotted a clock on the wall. It read 3:12. It couldn't be that late. Then she noticed the second hand was frozen at the half-minute mark. An electric clock, and the power had been off for a long, long time.

Lacey pushed through the doors and the cool night air hit her, sending a cold tremor through her body. She kept moving, padding across the moonlit concrete to the surrounding shadows. She needed some clothes, and not just for warmth; couldn't turn up in front of the people in the church, especially her Uncle Joe, looking like this. She had to find a house, go through one of the closets—

"It's you!" cried a voice behind her. "How did you get away?"

Lacey turned and stared at the figure advancing toward her from the other side of the street. The bottle blonde from the boardwalk, dressed in lowrider jeans and a cutaway denim jacket. Her boots thudded on the pavement. Lacey saw a flash in her right hand, heard a clink, and realized she'd just flipped open a knife. The stainless steel blade gleamed in the moonlight.

Lacey said nothing. Her brain seemed sluggish. All she could think was, Not now . . . I can't handle this now.

"Guess it doesn't matter how," the Vichy woman said with a throaty laugh as she reached the grass and kept coming. "I'm just glad you did. Because we got a score to settle, you and me."

Lacey tried to remember some of the defense moves she'd learned in her martial arts classes and couldn't come up with one. So she started backing away.

"You can run but you can't hide," the blonde sing-songed. "I don't care how much they want you alive, you ain't walkin away this time."

She was closing in. Lacey held up her hands. "No, wait . . ."

"No waiting. Looks like a few of my friends had a party with you, now it's my turn. I'm gonna cut you, girl . . . cut you *good!*"

With that the blonde lunged forward with a vicious, face-high slash, and Lacey found her limbs responding on their own. She didn't need to remember the moves. Hour upon hour of practice had programmed them into her nervous system. Her right leg shot back and stiffened, her left knee bent, her hands darted forward, grabbing the blonde's knife arm at the wrist and elbow, pushing it aside, twisting it, using the woman's own weight and momentum against her to bring her down.

Her Vichy earring flashed near Lacey's face and sudden visions of similar earrings dangling over her while her three captors—

Rage detonated in Lacey. Gritting her teeth she gave an extra twist to the falling woman's arm and was rewarded by a scream of pain as bones ground together, ligaments and tendons stretched, snapped. The woman screamed again, louder. She'd be drawing a crowd soon. Lacey's hand flashed forward, landing a two-knuckle punch on her larynx. With a crunch of cartilage the screaming cut off, replaced by strangled noises as the blonde began to kick and writhe, clutching at her throat with her still-functioning left hand.

Lacey picked up the knife from the grass and stepped back, looking around. Was anyone else coming after her? She and the blonde were alone in the shadows. She watched her struggles, waiting for them to run their course.

"So," Lacey said. "You were gonna cut me, huh? Cut me *good*. I don't think so."

She checked the knife blade: tanto shaped with the front half of the cutting edge beveled and the rear half saw-toothed. Wicked. If Ms. Vichy had had her way, this blade would be jutting from Lacey's chest about now.

The choking sounds faded, the kicking and writhing ebbed to twisting and twitching. With a final spasm the hand clutching at her throat fell away and she lay limp and still.

Lacey waited another minute, then dropped to her knees

beside the dead woman. Mastering her revulsion, she began unbuttoning her cutaway top . . .

CAROLE . . .

Sister Carole trudged through the inky blackness along the street, hugging the curb, hurrying through the moonlit sections between the shadows of the trees, towing her red wagon behind her. She'd loaded it with her Bible, her rosary, her holy water, the blasting caps, her few remaining bombs, and other essentials.

<You're looking for ANOTHER place? And I suppose you'll be starting up this same awful sinfulness again, won't you?>

"I suppose I will," Sister Carole said aloud to the night.

"Hello?" said a woman's voice from the darkness ahead. "Is someone there?"

Carole froze, her hand darting into the pants pocket of her warm-up, finding the electric switch, flipping the cover, placing her thumb on the button. Wires ran from the button through a hole in the pocket to the battery and the cylindrical charge taped to her upper abdomen.

God forgive her, but she would not be taken alive.

She held her silence, barely breathing, waiting. She sensed movement in the shadows ahead, and then a young woman stepped into a moonlight-dappled section of the sidewalk. She held an automatic pistol in each hand.

"I don't want trouble," the woman said. "I just want to know how to get back to St. Anthony's Church."

Carole looked around, wary. Were others lurking in the shadows?

"I think you already know the way," Carole said.

"No, really, I don't."

Carole eyed her spiky hair. "Don't try to fool me. You work for *them*."

"I don't, I swear."

A plaintive note in the woman's voice struck Carole.

"You dress like one"—although this one's clothes did not fit her well—"and you're armed."

"The clothes are stolen. So are the guns. I've already been attacked twice today. It's not going to happen again."

Again, the ring of truth. Carole squinted through the shadows. This woman did look battered.

"Look," the woman said. "I don't want to hurt you and you don't seem to want to hurt me, so can you just point me toward the church and we'll go our separate ways."

Carole decided to trust her instincts. "I'm headed that way. You can come with me."

"Really? I don't remember seeing you there last night."

"I wasn't." Carole noticed that the woman was barefoot and limping. "You said you were attacked. Did they . . . hurt you?"

The young woman nodded, then sobbed. "They hurt me bad. Real bad."

And then she was leaning against Carole and crying softly on her shoulder. Carole put her free arm around her and tried to soothe her, but kept her thumb on the button in her pocket. You never knew . . . never knew . . .

After a few minutes the sobs stopped and the young woman stepped back. She wiped her eyes with her bare arms.

"Sorry. It's just . . . it's been a long night." She pushed one of the pistols into her waistband and stuck out a hand. "Lacey. With an 'e.' "

"Carole," she said, shaking the hand and smiling, just a little. Something likable about her. "With an .'e.' "

"Were you a member of St. Anthony's parish?" Lacey said as they started walking again.

"I was a nun in the convent."

"Get out! Then you must know my Uncle Joe. He's been a priest there for years."

Carole stopped walking and stared. Could this tough-looking tattooed young woman be related to Father Joe?

"You're Father Cahill's niece?" She couldn't hide her disbelief.

"It's true, and I need to get back to him. He's got to have noticed I'm missing by now and he'll be worried sick."

The genuine concern in Lacey's voice made Carole a believer, but sudden fear stabbed her.

"Hurry," Carole said. She flipped the safety cover closed on the button in her pocket and broke into a fast walk. "We've got to get you back before he goes out searching for you. Once he's away from the church he's in danger."

JOE . . .

They'd started the search with the church grounds—the convent, the rectory, the graveyard—and then crossed the street to the office building. Finding that empty, Joe and the five other men in the search party, all armed to the teeth, had moved through the surrounding houses and buildings. The discovery of a man named Enrico stabbed to death in a neighboring Victorian had shaken them all, especially Joe. He'd opened every door to every room in the old house with the expectation that he'd find Lacey in the same condition.

But no. No sign that she'd ever been in the house. Lacey seemed to have vanished without a trace.

Finally, at Joe's insistence, they'd returned to the office building because that was the last place Lacey had been seen.

Joe stood now at the head of the stairs in the dark third-floor hallway. He turned off his flashlight—to heighten his hearing as much as to save the batteries—and called her name.

"Lacey! Lacey, can you hear me?"

He stood statue still and listened, but all he heard were the voices of the other members of the search party on the floors below.

He felt numb, heartsick. Lacey . . . how had he let this happen? She'd made it all the way down here from Manhattan on her own, and now she was gone, snatched from under his protective wing. He could see how it had happened. She'd felt safe here with other living around, armed with crosses and guns, ready for anything. She'd let her guard down, got careless . . .

"Lacey! Please!"

And then he heard it. A sound . . . scratching . . . so soft it was barely audible. He opened his eyes, then squeezed them shut again, trying to locate the sound. It seemed to come from everywhere at first, echoing off the walls of the hallway, but as he concentrated he felt sure it was coming from somewhere ahead and to his left. He opened his eyes and flicked on his flashlight.

There. An open doorway with a red plaque saying something about *AUTHORIZED PERSONNEL ONLY*—ALARM WILL SOUND. No, it won't. It needed electricity for that. And besides, the door was already open.

Joe played his beam along the concrete steps within. They ran one way: up. To the roof. The scratching sound was louder here. Definitely coming from the top of the empty stairwell. Someone was scratching on the other side of the roof door.

"Lacey?" he called as he took the steps two at a time. "Lacey, is that you?"

He hesitated at the door, hand on the knob, afraid to turn it, afraid to see what was on the other side, afraid it might be Lacey, horribly injured. And afraid it might not be Lacey. Might be one of *them*, lying in wait for a victim.

He'd hung his big silver cross around his neck before leaving tonight. He unslung it and held it ready, to wield as either club or firebrand. But still he hesitated. This was foolish. He should call for the others, go out there as a group.

He turned and was about to call them when he heard the voice, a faint, agonized rasp.

"Help me . . . please . . . help."

"Lacey!"

Joe shoved the door open and stepped up onto the moonlit roof. Something heavy struck him at the base of his neck, sending shockwaves of pain down his arms and driving him to his knees. He lost his grip on the cross. Then a thick

quilted blanket was thrown over him. Before he could react
he was knocked flat, rolled, and trussed up like an Oriental
rug. Panicked, he kicked and twisted, but he was helpless.
He shouted for the others but knew his cries were too muffled by the fabric to be heard.

Joe felt himself lifted by his feet, dragged along the roof,
and then he was falling. They'd thrown him off the roof!

No. The cold, steely grip never released his ankles. And
now he was rising instead of falling, being carried through
the air.

But to where?

TWILIGHT MAN

PART TWO

TWILIGHT MOM

JOE . . .

Joe had lost all track of time during the seemingly endless flight. But he knew when it ended: the cold fingers released their grip on his ankles and he fell. Before he could cry out his terror, he hit hard, head first. Only the multi-layered padding of his blanket cocoon kept him from cracking his skull.

"This is the priest," said a harsh voice. "Search him and take him upstairs. Franco is waiting for him."

Joe was then rolled over—kicked over was more like it. As he felt the ropes binding him loosen, he tightened his fists and prepared to fight. But when the blanket was pulled away from his face he found himself blinded by light.

Fluorescent light. Somebody had electricity.

As he blinked in the brightness he was kicked again, in the ribs this time. He struggled to a sitting position and felt something cold and hard as steel slam against the side of his head.

"Easy, god-boy," said a new voice to his left, and someone on his right brayed a harsh laugh.

Joe groaned with the pain and clutched his stinging scalp. He blinked again, and finally he could see.

He sat on a sidewalk in a pool of light outside the brass and glass revolving doors of a massive granite building. The rest of the world around him lay dark and quiet. A red canopy blocked out much of his view above. He did notice the number 350 above the revolving doors. Surrounding him were half a dozen men wearing earrings he knew too well. The nearest held a huge revolver; most likely its long barrel was what had slammed against his head.

Vichy.

The one next to the gun-toter was playing with a knife with a nasty reverse-curve blade, twirling it on a fingertip as he said, "This supposed to be one of them vigilantes from down the shore, huh? The guy that killed Gregor?" He kicked Joe's thigh. "Don't look so tough. Hey, Barrett. What say we soften him up before passin him on to Franco?"

Vigilante? Joe thought. Zev had mentioned something about a group that was killing off the local Vichy. Was that why he'd been brought here—wherever it was?

"Not on my watch," said the one with the gun. Barrett. The same voice that had called him god-boy. He was dressed in a tan silk Armani suit with a white shirt open at the collar. It looked tailor-made for him. "He won't want damaged goods. When the damage gets done, Franco will want to do it."

Joe looked around. "Where am I?"

"In big trouble," said Barrett.

The one with the knife, bearded and denimed, brayed again. "Yeah. *Big* trouble! Wouldn't wanna be you no-how."

"Drag him up to the office," said Barrett. "We'll search him there."

A pair of the Vichy grabbed him under the arms and roughly hauled him through a glass door set beside the revolving door. They entered a vaulted lobby of polished gray-beige marble. At the opposite end, floor to ceiling in chrome and marble, was a bas relief image of a building known the world over.

The Empire State Building. I'm in New York.

They'd kidnapped him and flown him to Manhattan. For what purpose?

And then he remembered . . . *Franco is waiting* . . .

The old *Saturday Night Live* running gag about General Franco still being alive flashed through his brain, then fled in terror.

When the damage gets done, Franco will want to do it . . .

A two-way radio squawked. Joe saw Barrett unclip it from his belt. He turned away and spoke into it. Joe looked around for an escape route, but even if he could break away from the pair who held him, the lobby area was acrawl with Vichy.

After Barrett finished his call, they led him past the remnants of metal detectors that had been kicked down and smashed, past a newsstand with outdated papers and magazines, a ruined souvenir shop, a deserted Au Bon Pain, then to a bank of elevators with black and chrome doors. Only two cars seemed to be working. The others stood open, dark, and empty. After a short ride with the suit, the beard, and two others to the third floor, Joe was propelled down a hallway to a large, desk-filled room lined with computers and monitors. A few scurvy Vichy lounged around, but three other men, older, more conventionally dressed, worked the equipment. They appeared to be under guard.

"Search him," Barrett said. "And I don't mean just pat him down. *Search* him. Confiscate any contraband here and dispose of it."

He was hiding nothing, of course. He'd been armed with his silver cross back in Lakewood but that had been stripped from him and left behind.

Barrett's words filtered through to his muddled brain. *Confiscate? Contraband?* Barrett didn't fit the typical Vichy mold. He dressed like a Wall Street broker and spoke like an educated man. What was he doing here?

BARRETT . . .

James Barrett watched Neal search the priest, making sure he didn't miss anything. Neal was not the brightest bulb in the box.

But he did a good job this time, turning all the priest's pockets inside out, removing his socks and shoes.

"He's clean," Neal said.

"You'd better be sure."

"I'm sure."

They hustled him back down to the first floor for a swift, ear-popping ride toward the top of the building. The red numbers on the readout counted the passing floors by leaps of ten. Barrett had always liked that. It was the way he'd planned his career at Bear Stearns to go: to the top by leaps and bounds. But being a hotshot investment banker these days was like being a poster boy for obsolescence.

He heard Neal chuckle. He was grinning through his beard at the priest and shaking his head. "I'm glad I ain't you. Holy shit, am I glad I ain't you. I don't know what Franco's got planned but it ain't gonna be pretty, I can tell you that."

Barrett watched the priest clench his fists. He was scared. Doing a decent job of hiding it, but not perfect. He looked like he wanted to ask who Franco was but said nothing. Probably afraid his voice would crack or waver and betray his terror.

When the elevator stopped on the eightieth floor, Neal shoved him out.

"Come on, god-boy," Barrett said. "Still one more leg to go."

They guided him around a corner to the other bank. This ride was short—only six floors. At the eighty-sixth they pushed him out into the green marble atrium.

"Hold it right there!" said a voice.

The atrium held half a dozen undead. One of them stepped toward them.

"Ah, shit," Neal muttered. "Fuckin Artemis."

"Who's this?" said the vampire, tall and lean with a ruined left eye that was little more than a lump of scar tissue.

Artemis was head honcho of Franco's security and no one—at least no one living—knew what had happened to that eye. Whatever it was, Barrett hoped it had hurt. Artemis was a grandstanding prick.

"It's the one Franco's been waiting for," Barrett told him.

Artemis's face contorted in fury. "The vigilante priest?" he shouted. "And you bring him here like this?"

"He's been searched, and Franco—"

"I don't give a damn if he's been searched! You don't bring a terrorist up here and leave him a single place to hide *anything*! Here's how you bring a terrorist to Franco!"

And with that he began tearing at the priest's clothing, ripping it off him. The priest tried to fend him off but Artemis was too strong. Less than a minute later he stood naked in the atrium.

Barrett admired the priest's musculature. Especially his low back. Lots of good meat there. Big filets.

Artemis tossed the shredded clothing at Barrett.

"*Now* he can see Franco! I'll take it from here. You two get back to your posts."

"We want him when Franco's through with him," Neal said.

Artemis laughed. "Oh, I doubt that. Not in the condition he'll be in."

"Shit," said Neal as the doors pincered closed. "I hate that fuck."

Barrett said nothing. Who knew if the elevator camera was on and this little scene was being taped. Say or do the wrong thing now and you could face repercussions later.

Neal banged his fist against the side wall of the elevator car. "And I hate takin his shit."

So did Barrett. But sometimes that was what you had to put up with to get where you wanted to go. And Barrett knew where he wanted to go: to the top. He'd been on the fast track for advancement at Bear Stearns and he was looking for a way to fast-track himself with the undead. He needed a lever to convince Franco to turn him now instead of later.

He glanced at Neal. Just like the rest of the cowboys. Never a thought past his next meal and his next trip out to one of the cattle farms where he could screw anything in sight. Maybe he occasionally thought of someday, ten years from now, being turned and joining the ranks of the undead.

But ten years was too long for Barrett. He wanted an express route to undeadland. Once he was one of them he knew he could rocket through the ranks. They were all lazy sons of bitches. He'd show them how to get things done. If he could get himself turned, he'd have Franco's job within a year. He knew it.

"Treats us like fuckin dogs," Neal said.

No argument there. But that didn't mean you had to live in a kennel and eat dog food.

Most of the cowboys had moved mattresses into the offices and stayed right here in the Empire State Building. It was convenient, had light and power, and was safer than living outside where you could be bushwhacked by some angry living or one of the more feral undead who wouldn't be deterred by your earring.

James Barrett deserved better. He had an elegant Murray Hill brownstone all to himself. He'd hooked up a generator to power lights, a refrigerator, and an electric stove. The stove was important. It allowed him to indulge in his new passion: cooking.

Barrett had recognized long ago that there were two ways of living your life: as predator or as prey. He'd decided early on that he'd be a predator. And predators ate meat. One problem, though, was the lack of meat since the undead had taken over. Or so he'd thought until he realized that there was plenty of fresh meat to be had. Every night he and the cowboys were called upon to dispose of a new round of bloodless corpses. It had occurred to him what a shame it was to waste all that good red meat.

Long pork, as human flesh was known in certain parts of the world, was really quite tasty. He'd learned to butcher the meatier corpses and now had a good supply of steaks in his freezer.

But meaty corpses were harder and harder to come by these days. That was why it was such a shame to let someone like that priest go to waste.

But who knew? Maybe there'd be something salvageable left after Franco got through with him.

Somehow, though, he doubted it.

JOE . . .

Joe's knees felt soft and he almost stumbled as the scar-faced vampire pushed him up a short flight of steps. What were they planning for him? He wanted to shout that he wasn't a vigilante and didn't know who they were, but that would simply give them a good laugh.

He stepped into a glassed-in space that had once been a souvenir-snack bar area—nothing but blackness beyond that glass—then was shoved through a door onto the Observation Deck. Cool night air, propelled by a gusty wind, raised gooseflesh on his bare skin, but the sight of dozens of pairs of undead eyes watching him weakened his knees again.

He was a goner. He could see that now. As good as dead. Or worse. Fear crowded his throat, but he swallowed it. He straightened his shoulders. At least he could go out with dignity . . . as much as he could muster without a stitch of clothing.

The crowd of undead, all armed with pistols and machetes, grinned and pointed to him. The scarred one grabbed one of his arms and hauled him before another of their kind standing by the Observation Deck wall, staring out into the night. He turned at their approach, and smiled when his cold gaze came to rest on Joe.

"So . . . this is the man who has chosen to vex me."

He was almost as tall as Joe, with broad shoulders, a blond leonine mane and mustache. A jutting nose and aggressive chin dominated his face.

His excellent English did not completely hide an Italian accent. Joe noted that he was the only undead on the deck who wasn't armed.

"A big one, this vigilante priest"—he glanced at Joe's genitals—"but not exactly built like a stallion, is he."

This brought a laugh from his guards or retainers or whatever they were. Joe stared past him, focusing on the impenetrable darkness over Franco's right shoulder, and said nothing.

The vampire clucked his tongue in mock concern. "Chilly? Under different circumstances I might relish your discomfiture, but not tonight." He turned to one of the undead holding Joe. "Find him a blanket or something to wrap about him."

The one-eyed guard said, "But Franco—"

"Do it." His dead eyes lit briefly with an inner fire.

The underling stood firm. "Just hours ago he killed Gregor."

The other undead milling around nodded and murmured, as if this were a telling fact.

That name again . . . Gregor. The second time he'd heard it tonight. Joe stood there wondering who Gregor was. The only thing he knew was that he hadn't killed him—at least not knowingly. "Just hours ago" he'd been searching for Lacey. Had the same thing happened to her? Whisked away into the night. No. Lacey had disappeared during the daylight hours. Where was she then? He prayed her circumstances were better than his.

"I don't care!" Franco said. "It will be *our* blanket, you dolt! It won't conceal a cross, so you'll have nothing to worry about! Move! I've already wasted too much time waiting for his arrival."

A few moments later some sort of fabric was roughly thrown over Joe's shoulders. Apparently they couldn't find a blanket; this was like a window drape. He pulled it close around him, grateful for the shelter it provided from the wind.

"Thank you," he said, deciding to play this as cool as he could.

"Oh, don't think I did it for your sake. I did it for mine. I want your complete attention." He motioned Joe to the wall. "Come. Let me show you my domain."

Something had been nagging at Joe since he'd stepped out on the deck . . . something wrong . . . something missing . . . and now he realized what it was.

He'd been up here once in his life, in his teens, when his father had brought him. The reason for the trip had been a French exchange student staying with them for the summer. They'd gone to the Statue of Liberty that summer too. Strange. He'd grown up only a short distance from these American landmarks but probably never would have visited them if not for the presence of a foreigner.

He remembered that on his one and only visit here there'd been high safety fencing all around the Observation Deck, with tall, pointed steel tines curving inward like fishhooks. Now most of that was gone, torn away. It made sense, though: The undead weren't worried about one of their own becoming a suicide jumper, and the fence would only hinder the fliers.

Joe approached the wall, eyeing its upper edge. It ran about mid-chest high. Eternity—and perhaps salvation— waited on the other side.

As he came up beside Franco, the vampire waved his arm at the darkness. "There it is: mine, as far as I can see."

Joe's heart broke as he took in the vista, not for what he could see—moonlight glinting off the crown of the Chrysler Building off to the left—but for what he couldn't.

Darkness. The city was dark. Any light he saw was reflected from the moon or this building. Everything else was dead and dark. This wasn't the New York he'd known. This was its corpse.

"The first thing we did was kill the power," Franco said. "It has a numbing psychological effect, especially in a place like Manhattan. People here were so used to light everywhere, all the time, and then it was gone. It serves another purpose. It makes the few who are left light fires to cook, to stay warm on the cooler nights. We home in on those fires. They're like beacons to us. Manhattan is pretty well cleaned out now, but the other boroughs still teem with survivors. We hunt them judiciously, preserving them like a natural resource."

He jerked a thumb over his shoulder.

"But I keep this building alight. More psychological warfare. The tallest building in this fabled city, its most recognizable landmark, and we have it. I live here with some of my get, just one floor down. Why should I hide in a basement when I can seal off windows in this magnificent building that affords me such a unique view of my domain. I wish those Islamic thugs had left the Trade Towers alone. They were even taller. How I'd love to be standing atop one of them now."

So full of himself, Joe thought, wondering how he could turn that to his advantage.

Franco shrugged resignedly. "But I suppose the Empire State will do. Its generators power everything in the building." He pointed to the cameras ringing the deck. "It has an excellent security system to help our serfs protect us during the day. No one moves in this building without being watched and taped. I like to review the tapes now and again, and punish any slackers I catch. As an extra security measure, we've cut the power to all but two of the elevators."

He held his hand over the edge of the wall. A red glow lit his palm from below.

"But my favorite accessory is the filters they have for the

spotlights that bathe the upper floors. Red, white, and blue for July Fourth, red and green for Christmas. We use only red now. It's our color. The color of blood. More psychological warfare." He turned to Joe and smiled. "You're pretty adept at psychological warfare yourself."

"What's that supposed to mean?" Joe said, tearing himself away from the dark vista.

Franco stared at him. "I can't tell whether you're being obtuse or coy. I'm talking about your campaign against the serfs in your area."

"Serfs?"

"Oh, I forget. They like to call themselves cowboys, you people like to call them collaborators—"

"Vichy," he said, thinking with a pang of Zev. "Some of us call them Vichy."

"Vichy." Franco nodded. "I like that. It shows a sense of history, though it gives them more cachet than they deserve." He waved his hand as if shooing a fly. "But my point is, you and your minions have caused more trouble than anyone I can remember."

Again the temptation to tell this beast that Joe had no idea what he was talking about, but he suppressed it. He was good at suppressing temptation.

"It was the terrorist aspects of your campaign that worked. The serfs are such disloyal scum, and so very susceptible to fear. You had the local contingent quaking in their boots. But you made a grave tactical error when you revealed yourself and took back your church. That gave you a face, and you weren't so terrifying anymore. Or so I thought. But when you sent Gregor into true death I decided I wanted to meet you."

Joe had to ask—because he wanted to know and because he sensed that the question might unsettle Franco—"Who the hell is Gregor?"

Franco stared at him a moment. "I suppose it's possible you didn't know his name. Same with Angelica, I imagine.

But you and yours have sent two important subordinates to true death in a matter of a few days. No one has ever done that."

Angelica . . . could that be the flying undead that Zev told him about? "Those winged ones," Joe said, taking a stab in the dark. "They always give me the creeps."

"Of course they do. They're supposed to. Psychological warfare again. Strike terror into the hearts of the cattle." He sighed. "I never cared for either of them. Angelica was too impetuous and Gregor too grasping, but the fallout from their deaths has been, well, vexing. But only temporarily."

He turned back to the night with another grandiose wave of his arm.

"My kingdom. We're facing east, you know. Long Island is out that way. We're well established there."

Joe stretched up on tiptoe, leaned over the top of the parapet, and looked down instead of out. Red light from the banks of spotlights bathed his face. Beyond them, far below and out of sight, empty pavements beckoned.

Not yet, he thought. The guards were too close. They'd stop him before he got over. He eased back and watched his host.

"We've already started the cattle ranches," Franco was saying. "We fenced off large sections of Levittown and populated them with females fifteen to thirty years old. As a reward to the serfs, we set them loose in there to impregnate the cows. Soon we'll have crops of calves to raise." He swiveled his head and smiled. "More psychological warfare."

"More like rape and brutality," Joe said, reflexively raising a fist. How he wished—

His arm was grabbed and twisted backward. A glance showed the scar-eyed one behind him. All around he heard pistols being cocked and machetes drawing from belts.

"Will you stop!" Franco snapped at his guards. "He is a lone, naked, unarmed man! What can he possibly do to me? Now get back, all of you and give us some room!"

"But Franco—"

"Now, Artemis! I won't say it again!"

With obvious reluctance, one-eyed Artemis and the other guards moved off. Not too far, but far enough to give Joe a chance to do what he needed to do . . . if he had the nerve. All he needed was a way to distract Franco.

The vampire turned his gaze eastward again. "We made so many mistakes in the Old World. We failed to control the undead population. We just rolled through, letting our numbers spread geometrically. The Middle East was the easiest. Hardly a cross to be found. Same with India and China. We did what no president or shuttling diplomat ever could. We brought peace to every place we've touched. Indian undead now sup with Pakistanis, Greeks with Cypriots, North Koreans with South, and most amazing of all, Israeli and Palestinian undead hunting together." He smiled. " 'Blessed be the peacemakers.' Isn't that how it goes. I think I should be sainted. What's the term the Church uses? Canonized. Yes, I should be canonized, don't you think?"

Joe ignored the question. "You can't survive without the living, and there'll never be peace between the living and the undead."

"Oh, but there will. We'll control our population here in the Americas and we'll control yours, and eventually Pax Nosferatu will embrace the whole world. Here in the New World we will do things right, right from the beginning. The Old World and the Third World are now full of starving and dying undead." He glanced at Joe. "Yes, dying. We need very little blood to survive, but we need it every night. Go two nights without it and you are weak; go two more nights and your are prostrate, virtually helpless. Unless someone comes on the fifth or sixth night and feeds you blood—a *very* unlikely event—you will enter true death and never awaken."

"May it be ever so," Joe said, "unto the last generation."

Franco frowned. "Don't push me, priest."

"Or what?" Joe said, finding courage in the realization that he had nothing to lose. "You'll show me no mercy? I'm not expecting any."

"You don't want to plead, offer me a deal?"

Joe shook his head. He knew there'd be no deals for him. He wouldn't deal with these things.

"Then kindly stop interrupting my story. I'm getting to the good part—my part. The task of taking the New World fell to me. I decided to learn from recent history and not repeat it. As I'm sure you know, we struck on December twenty-first, the longest night of the year. I started with Washington, loosing the ferals on Camp David and the Pentagon and Langley first, then the senate and congressional office buildings next."

"Ferals?" Joe said. "What are they?"

Franco smiled, broadly, cruelly. "In time, dear priest. In a very short time you shall learn more than you wish to know about ferals."

The prospect sent a shudder through Joe. He eyed the top of the parapet again.

"I wanted to strike at the heart of the country's defenses— drive a stake through it, as I like to say—but more than anything I wanted the president. We found him. I turned him, personally, and a few days later we had him on TV, live, via satellite, putting on a show for his nation. Did you happen to catch it?"

Joe shook his head. He'd been banished to the retreat house by then. He'd seen the beginning of the broadcast but had left the room, sickened. He hadn't seen, but he'd heard . . .

"Such a shame. You missed a psychological knockout punch. The president of the United States on his knees before a menstruating White House intern, lapping her blood. Clever, don't you think? Too bad Clinton wasn't still in office—turn around being fair play and all—but apparently he's holed up on the West Coast. Your current president did a good job, though. Really got into the part, if you know what I mean. And much more effective because he is—or rather, was—a bit more dignified than Clinton."

Joe glared at him. "You sicken me. All of you."

"But that's the whole point, priest. Physical, spiritual, and civic malaise. It's a pattern I've perfected: Go for the political and religious leaders first. See to it that they are turned early in the infiltration. It does terrible things to the morale of the citizenry when word gets around that the local mayor and congressman, along with the ministers, priests, and rabbis, are out hunting them every night. They stop trusting anyone, and when there's no trust, there's no organized resistance." He looked at Joe. "Somehow we missed you when your area was invaded. Lucky you."

"Funny," Joe said, hoping he sounded brave. "I don't feel lucky."

"But you should. You've been very lucky, and you've proven yourself quite adept at turning my game back on me. I try to hammer home that resistance is futile, then you come along and show that it can work, however briefly."

"More than briefly," Joe said. "You're going to see a lot more of it, especially if you try moving west."

"Am I? Somehow, I don't think so. Not after I'm through with you. And as for moving west, I'm in no hurry. I'm going to consolidate the East Coast, get the cattle farms established"—he wagged his finger—"all the while keeping the undead population interspersed among the living to prevent any bombing attacks. Then I may skip the Midwest altogether and take California next. I haven't decided. That's not to say I haven't been active. I regularly send trucks into the hinterlands, dropping off a few ferals here and there as they go, to wreak sporadic havoc. I don't want anyone out there feeling safe. I want them looking over their shoulders, suspicious of their neighbors, jumping at the slightest noise. As I said, I'm in no hurry, and I have all the time in the world." He shook his head. "But when I do make a move, you'll be part of it."

Joe went cold inside. "If you think . . ." He paused, choosing his words. Let Franco think he'd given into the inevitability of becoming one of his kind. "If you think I'm going to help you, even after you turn me into one of you, think again."

"I sense an arrogance in you, priest. And I will see it brought down. You are mere cattle to me, yet you look at me as vermin. I won't tolerate that."

"Who do you think you're kidding?" he said, wondering if he could provoke Franco into lashing out and killing him. "You and your kind are ticks on the ass of humanity, and you know it."

But Franco appeared unruffled. "Perhaps we were, but the anatomy has changed now: we're the ass and rebellious cattle like you are the biters." He leaned closer, staring into Joe's eyes. His breath stank of old blood. "I'll bet you think that even after we make you one of us you'll be able to resist the blood hunger."

Joe couldn't help blinking, stiffening—he'd said as much to Zev just the other day—and that let Franco know he'd struck a nerve.

"You do, don't you? You really think you could resist!" He tilted his head back and laughed. "Your naïveté is almost charming. You have no idea what you face. You change when you turn, priest. Everything turns inward. You awake from death and there's only one being in the world that matters: you. All your memories will be intact but devoid of feeling. The people you loved and hated will run together and redivide into two critical categories: those who can supply you with blood and those who can't. You'll have to sate that thirst. You'll have no choice. That hunger above all. The world exists for you. All the other undead around are inconveniences you must endure in order to secure a steady supply of blood. For the red thirst is insatiable. As I told you, we need very little blood to survive but would spend our waking hours immersed in it if we could. We're lazy, we're petty, and we don't want anyone to have more blood than we do."

Please, God, Joe prayed, if You're listening, don't let me

end up like that. I beg You. He peeled his tongue away from the roof of his dry mouth and managed to speak.

"Sounds like you've got a lock on the seven deadly sins."

"Perhaps. I never thought of that. What are they? Envy, anger, greed, lust, pride, avarice, and sloth, right. I think you might be right. Except that sex becomes meaningless. How we used to laugh at those Anne Rice novels. The undead as tortured Byronic aesthetes. Ha! We'd read them aloud to each other and howl. Her fictional undead are so much more interesting than the real thing. We're boring. We care nothing for art or music or fashion or surroundings. We bore each other and we bore ourselves. The only thing we care about, the only lust left to us, is blood."

"What about power?"

"You're thinking of me when you say that, yes? I can assure you that power is lusted after only insofar as it can assure one of more blood."

Joe glanced back at Franco's guards. "These fellows seem pretty devoted to you."

"Not out of selflessness or personal regard for me, I assure you. It's self-preservation. You see, there's a secret, a momentous secret we keep only to ourselves."

"And what's that?"

"You'll know tomorrow night. You'll be one of us then. So treasure these moments, priest. This is your last night with your own blood in your veins."

Now, Joe thought, realizing he might not get another chance. It has to be now.

"Huh?" he said and stared past Franco's shoulder at the empty darkness. "Who was that?"

"What do you mean?"

Joe raised himself on tiptoe again and leaned over the parapet, pointing into the darkness. "There! I just saw him again. One of your undead flyers. A pal of yours?"

Franco whirled to follow Joe's point. "A flyer? Up here? I should think not."

The instant Franco's back was turned, Joe dropped the drape, levered himself up onto the parapet, and rolled over it. He heard shouts from behind as his bare feet landed on the narrow outside ledge. Knowing that if he hesitated even for an instant he'd either lose his nerve or be caught, he let out a cry of terror and triumph and launched himself into the air. He spread his arms in a swan dive, hoping it would carry him beyond the setbacks. He wanted to fall all the way to the street, to splatter himself on the pavement, leaving nothing but a mocking red stain for Franco to find.

The air that had felt like cold silk against his naked body when he began his fall was now a knife-edged wind tearing at his skin and roaring in his ears. He straightened his arms ahead of him, diving headfirst into eternity.

"Forgive me, Lord," he said aloud. "I know it means damnation to throw away the gift of life, but what I was facing—"

He broke off with a cry of shock as cold fingers wrapped around his ankle and Franco's voice shouted, "Your prayers are premature, priest!"

Joe looked over his shoulder as his descent slowed and angled to the left. A grinning Franco gripped him with one hand. Large membranous wings arched from his back, spreading like a cape behind him.

Joe kicked at him with his free foot but this only allowed Franco to grab that ankle as well. Joe hung helpless in his grip as they glided through the air. Franco made a full circuit of the building, landing before the same entrance where Joe had been dropped earlier.

Barrett was outside, watching when Joe landed on the pavement.

"Well, well, well. Look who's back."

Joe wanted to cry.

Franco's wings slithered and folded and disappeared into his back as he grabbed Joe by the back of his neck and hauled him to his feet.

"Clear the way," he said. "I'm taking him to Devlin myself."

Sick with fear and disappointment and frustration, Joe allowed himself to be marched through the doors and back to the elevator banks. Franco shoved him into the car and stepped in after him.

"Just the two of us," he said as a couple of Vichy tried to crowd in behind him.

Joe didn't see any of Franco's retainers. Apparently they hadn't made it down from the Observation Deck yet. Joe stared at Franco's back, noting the ripped fabric where the wings had torn through, but no sign of the wings themselves. Where did they go?

Franco stabbed a button, the doors closed and the car began to move. Down.

He was smiling when he turned to Joe. "You almost got away with that. I didn't think you had it in you." He shook his head. "If you'd succeeded we never would have learned the details of your little vigilante operation."

"What if I don't know any details?"

Franco's smile broadened. "Come now, you don't expect me to buy that."

"But—"

"Don't waste your breath. You'll tell us everything you know."

Joe swallowed. "Torture?"

Franco laughed. "How quaint! Why waste time torturing you when you'll volunteer the information after you've been turned."

The sick, lost feeling gave way to anger and Joe lunged at him. But Franco shoved him back with one hand and grabbed his throat with the other. Joe struggled for air as he was lifted off his feet and tossed against the rear wall of the elevator car.

"Don't make me laugh," Franco said.

"Do your damnedest." Joe slumped in the corner, gasping and rubbing his throat. "I'll never be like you."

"Quite right, priest. You won't be anything like me."

The car stopped and the doors opened. Franco pointed to the right. "That way."

Joe didn't move. Why cooperate in his own death march—or in this case, undeath march?

Franco said, "You can walk or I can drag you by one of your feet."

Joe walked, looking for a way out, an escape route, but the hallway was lined with doors that seemed to lead to offices or utility rooms. Franco stopped as they came to a mirror set in the wall.

"Take a look."

Joe glanced at the reflection of his bruised, naked body, his sunken eyes. Not a pretty sight.

"Enjoy it," Franco said. "This is the last time you'll ever see yourself in a mirror."

Joe noticed with a start that the reflection showed him standing alone in the hallway.

"So it's true," he murmured. "The undead cast no reflection."

"Odd, isn't it. I used to be interested in physics. You look at me and see me because light reflects off me onto your retinas. But that same reflected light is not caught by a mirror. How is that possible? They used to say it was because we have no souls but neither does the rug you're standing on, and that reflects perfectly. I tried to sit down and figure it out once but found I didn't care enough to try. As I told you, once you're turned you care about only one thing."

He grabbed Joe's shoulder and pushed him down the hall. "Enough philosophizing."

As they moved on, Franco said, "I want to explain something to you, and I want you to listen. I want you to understand this. By now you've probably noticed that there are different kinds of undead, different strains or breeds."

Joe had, but he said nothing.

"There's a hierarchy among us. No one can explain it— it's as inexplicable as our lack of reflection or where my wings come from when I want to fly—but it's there. It's as if the strain gets tainted or attenuated the further it moves from its source. My immediate get—the ones I turn—retain almost all of their intelligence; but their get retain a little less, and the get of those retain even less. And so on down the line through the generations of get until . . . until we are begetting idiots. But intelligence isn't all that is lost along the way. Human characteristics leach away as well. The distant generations of get become more and more bestial until they're like two-legged rabid dogs. We call them ferals."

Ferals . . . Franco had mentioned them in connection with the assault on Washington.

"Why are you telling me this?" Joe said. "Why should I care?"

"You should care very much. After all, we're discussing your future." He stopped before a door. "We're here."

Joe saw an AUTHORIZED PERSONNEL ONLY sign set below a small window.

"Take a look. Tell me what you see."

Joe stepped up to the glass and peered through. He saw a dimly lit space filled with pipes and large oval tanks.

"Looks like a boiler room."

"Keep looking. See anything else. Something moving, perhaps?"

The note of glee in Franco's tone made Joe's skin crawl. He searched the shadow but didn't see—

Wait. To the right. Something there, moving from the deeper shadows into the wan light of an overhead bulb. It looked like a man yet it moved like an animal, on its toes, hunched forward, fingers bent like claws. As it came under the bulb Joe saw that it was a man, or had been. Naked, filthy, face twisted into a perpetual snarl, eyes mad and . . . feral.

"Dear God!"

"God has nothing to do with Devlin there—Jason Devlin, a young, handsome software developer on his way up until a few months ago when he was run down in the basement of the Flatiron Building and killed by a feral. The feral neglected to behead him, and so Mr. Devlin awoke the following sunset as one of us—as an undead. For a few days he looked like his old self, but then he began to devolve. Remember what I told you about the bloodline weakening, attenuating. He was turned by a feral, and so he became a feral, only more so. He's one of my line, my most distant get, so I suppose I must claim him as related to me."

"How do you know?"

"Oh, I know. We always recognize our get. I keep him around for entertainment. And as an extra stick to keep the serfs in line. I threaten to feed them to Devlin if they slack off on their duties. That's about all Devlin is good for now. He didn't retain enough intelligence to distinguish between friend and foe, which means he'd be attacking serfs as well as legitimate prey, so I can't even use him as a guard dog."

Franco tapped on the window and the creature burst into motion, leaping at the door with blinding speed, screaming and clawing at the glass. Joe almost tripped backpedaling away.

"Look at me, priest," Franco said. "Look at me and listen. Remember when you said you'd never be like me? Didn't you wonder why I agreed? It's because when you look at Devlin you are seeing your future. I'm going to let Devlin turn you."

Joe couldn't speak, could only shake his head and back away, thinking, no . . . no . . . this can't be true . . . this can't happen . . . to be like that thing, that creature, that monster . . . forever . . . no . . .

"Ah!" Franco said with a grin. "That's what I've been waiting for. That look of doomed horror, the realization that your darkest nightmare is about to come true. Where is your arrogance now, priest?"

"No," Joe whispered as he found his voice. "God, no, please!"

"That's right. Pray to your god. Beg him like so many before you. But He's not going to help you. In less than two weeks you'll be just like Devlin, only a little *less* intelligent, a little *more* bestial. Won't that be an inspiration to your parishioners? But before you're too far gone, you'll have a talk with the charming undead woman I've placed in charge of your area. You'll fill Olivia in on all the details of your little vigilante operation, and then you'll be sent back to prey upon your parishioners."

"I won't!"

"Oh, but you will. And you'll take the most trusting, the most devoted first, because they'll be the easiest. Isn't this a coup? Isn't this so much better than killing you? If you simply died, you'd be a martyr, a rallying point. But this way, you're still around, and you've turned *against* them. You are *feeding* on them! Imagine how they'll feel. If you're lucky you won't survive long. I'm suspecting they'll gather together and stake you—for your own good. And theirs, of course. And then where will that leave them besides sick at heart and demoralized? Where will they be after killing their beloved Father Joe? Why, they'll go back to where they were before you came. Hiding, waiting for the inevitable."

"No! What's been started is bigger than one man! They know now they can fight you, and they'll keep on fighting you!"

Franco put his hand on the door handle. "Well, we'll just have to see about that, won't we."

He pushed the lever down and shoved the door inward. "Bon appétit, Devlin."

Joe turned and ran, sprinting down the hall, looking for an unlocked door. He heard a howl behind him as he tried the first one he came to—locked. Without looking back he leaped across the hall to the next. The knob turned, the door swung inward—a chance!—and then he was struck from behind with unimaginable force. It drove him through the doorway and into the room where he went down under a growling fury made flesh. He tried to fight back but the savagery of the claws and fangs tearing at his flesh, ripping at his throat overcame him. He felt his skin tear, felt hot fluid gush over his chin and chest, heard an awful guzzling, lapping noise as something fed off him. He tried to rise, to throw it off but he had no strength. He felt his mind growing cold, the world growing distant, life becoming a dream, a receding memory. Joe saw one last flash of light, intolerably bright and then all was darkness and nothingness . . .

7

CAROLE . . .

Unable to sleep, Carole sat at the window, watching the night, waiting for the dawn that was still hours away. Returning to the convent, to this room, her room, the room where she'd had to kill Bernadette . . . sleep was unthinkable. Even if it weren't, her bed was occupied.

Lacey, poor thing, had collapsed when she'd heard that Father Joe was missing. A couple of the male parishioners had helped carry her here—Carole had emptied her wagon and carried her duffel and her personal items herself, afraid to let anyone else near them.

They'd placed her on Carole's bed. What an ordeal Lacey had suffered tonight. Carole had gleaned a few details from her jumbled jabber on the way to the church and had shut her ears to the rest. And then to learn that her uncle had disappeared while searching for her. It was more than anyone should have to bear.

When was it going to end?

She waited, expecting to hear Bernadette's voice shout an answer, but the voice was silent. Carole hadn't heard from it since she'd reentered the convent.

She looked at Lacey, curled into a fetal position under the blanket. Father Joe's niece. She hadn't quite believed her, but the way she'd been greeted by the parishioners had left little doubt. Some of them had even recognized Carole. She'd been uncomfortable with their joy at knowing she was still alive, especially uncomfortable with their earnest questions about how she had managed to survive and how she'd been spending her time. She couldn't tell them, couldn't tell anyone.

A little while ago Carole had left Lacey and made a quick trip back to the church to see if Father Joe had been found. He hadn't. But one of the parties searching for him had returned with his large silver cross. He'd had it with him when he'd gone out earlier this evening. They'd found it on the roof of a nearby office building.

Carole had asked if she might take the cross back to Lacey and let her keep it until her uncle returned. Because Father Joe *would* return. He was too good, too strong, too faithful a man of God to fall victim to the undead. He—only a small part of her believed that. She'd seen too much . . . too much. . . . Yet she forced herself to hope. She placed the cross on the windowsill, as a guardian, as a beacon, calling him home.

She closed her eyes and listened. Silence. The convent was virtually empty. The rooms were available to the parishioners but most of them felt safer in the church—in its basement, in the choir loft, anywhere so long as they were within those walls. Carole could understand that from their perspective, but for her the convent was home. Though she felt orphaned now, it would always be home.

She turned back to the window and gripped the upright of his cross, thinking, Come back, Father Joe. We need you. *I* need you. We—

What was that? By the rectory . . . something taking to the air from the roof . . . something large . . . man-size . . .

Terror gripped Carole's heart in an icy, mailed fist. A vampire, one of the winged kind, flying away from the rectory . . .

Somehow she knew in that instant that they'd done something terrible to Father Joe.

"Oh, no!" she whispered. "No! Not him!"

She grabbed the silver cross, pulled a flashlight from her duffel, and ran for the hall. She hurried down the stairs and out into the night. Holding the cross before her as a shield, she ran across the little graveyard, trampling the fresh-turned earth of graves that hadn't been there before, and arrived at the rectory.

A small building, holding only three bedrooms and two offices, it stood dark and empty. This was priest territory and would be the last place the parishioners would think to occupy.

Carole turned the knob and the door swung open. She flicked on her flash and directed the beam up and down and around before stepping inside.

"Father Joe?" she called, knowing that if her worst fears were true he wouldn't be able to answer. "Father Joe, are you here?"

No response. No sound except for the crickets cheeping in the lawn behind her. She moved through the rectory, checking the two downstairs offices first, then the upstairs bedrooms. Empty, just as she'd expected.

Only one place left: the basement.

Knowing what she was almost certain to find, Carole feared to go there. But she had to. Too much depended on this.

She opened the door. Light in one hand, cross in the other, she started down. No blood on the steps. That was good. Maybe it had just been a flyer looking over the church complex, doing reconnaissance for the undead or hunting for stragglers. Carole prayed that was so, but expected that prayer to go unanswered like all her others.

She reached the floor and flashed her light around. She allowed her hopes to rise when she saw nothing on her first pass. But then as she moved to the rear of the space, where old suitcases and cracked mirrors and warped bureaus were sent to die, she spotted something protruding from beneath an old mattress. A step closer and she realized what it was: a bare foot, its toes pointing ceilingward. Too big for a woman's . . . a man's foot.

"Please, God," she said again, whispering this time. "Please, oh, please. Let it not be him."

She pressed the cross against the foot. No flash of light, no sizzle of flesh. Whoever it was hadn't turned yet. She leaned the cross against the wall, gripped the edge of the mattress . . . and hesitated. Her mouth felt full of sand, her heart pounded in her chest like a trapped animal. She didn't want to do this. Why her? Why did it always seem to fall to her?

Taking a breath and clenching her teeth, Carole tilted the mattress back and aimed her light at the shape beneath it. She found herself staring into the glazed dead eyes of Father Joseph Cahill.

Images leaped at her like a frantic slide show—
—his slack, blood-spattered face—
—the wild ruin of his throat—
—his blood-matted chest—

With a cry torn from some deep lost corner of her soul, Carole dropped to her knees beside him. Her arms took on a life of their own and, for some reason her numbed brain couldn't fathom, began pounding her fists on his chest. She heard a voice screaming incoherently. Her own.

After a while, she didn't know how long, she stilled her hands and slumped forward, letting her forehead rest on his bare shoulder, moaning, "God, dear God, why must this be?"

And for a fleeting moment, even as she spoke, she wondered how she could still believe in God, or stay true to a god who could allow this to happen to the finest man she'd ever known. This was it, this was the end of everything. Where could she go from here? She'd only hung on this long in the hope that he'd return. He had, but only for a few days before this—*this*!

She straightened and looked at Father Joe again, averting

her eyes from his genitals. To kill him was bad enough, but to leave him like this: naked, torn, bloodied, with not a shred of dignity . . .

Well, what did she expect from vermin?

And yet, look at his face—ignore the severed arterial stumps protruding from his throat and focus on the face. It seemed at peace, and still held a quiet dignity no one could steal.

Carole lost more time sobbing. Then, from somewhere, she found the strength to rise. She wanted to stay by his side, never leave him, never let anyone else near him, but she knew that couldn't be. She couldn't stay here and neither could he. She knew what had to be done. She had work to do. The Lord's work.

She wandered the basement until she found a dusty old sheet draped over a chair. She pulled it off and, with infinite care, wrapped it around Father Joe . . . her Father Joe. She tried to lift him but he was too heavy. She needed help . . .

OLIVIA . . .

"Someone is here. From Franco."

Olivia lifted her mouth from the bloody throat of the spindly old man strapped to the table in the feeding room.

"Who is it?"

Jules, the unofficial leader of her get-guards, shrugged. "I've never seen him before. All I know is that he says his name is Artemis and his eye—"

"I know about his eye."

Artemis . . . one of Franco's closest get. This must be important if he'd sent Artemis. It had to be about Gregor. Damn that fool.

She looked down at the quivering old man, still alive but in shock and not too much longer for this world. His blood was as thin as his scrawny body. She remembered India. She had been with the first wave through the Middle East, through Riyadh and Baghdad and Cairo and Jerusalem. Lots of blood there, but then they'd moved on to India, lovely, overcrowded India . . . she had quite literally bathed in blood in Bombay.

But here, good cattle were hard to come by of late. She wasn't sure whether that was a result of a thinning of the herd or a thinning of the number of serfs at her disposal. Franco was either going to have to send her more serfs or widen her territory.

Olivia would have much preferred another territory altogether, a peaceful one with no foment. But, thanks to Gregor's demise, she'd inherited this one and was stuck with it, at least until it was tamed.

She pointed to the old man as she rose. "You can finish him after you bring Artemis to the sleeping room. I wish to meet with him alone."

Jules frowned. "Do you think that's wise? Everything is so unsettled."

"We have nothing to fear from Artemis."

Jules turned and headed back upstairs.

Olivia paced the feeding room. She was going stir crazy down here. She hadn't left the Post Office once throughout this long, long night. She'd been about to go out earlier but Gregor's death changed that. She'd been sequestered in the basement ever since. Only half a night, but she felt humiliated. She was supposed to be the predator, the fox, the wolf, but here she was, cowering like a frightened hare in its burrow.

Yes, she was here at the insistence of her get, but she hadn't put up much of a fight. Gregor was foolish but he'd been tough. If the vigilantes had managed to kill him, they could kill her, and she might well be their next target.

She'd sent serfs and one of her get out to find the source of the explosion, to see if that was what had done in Gregor. They'd returned with a tale of a blasted house with Gregor's head spiked on a piece of splintered wood in the front yard and his body in pieces within.

These vigilantes had taken to making bombs. That was the real reason she was down here in the basement. The Post Office had thick granite walls. Even if they somehow managed to toss a bomb through the front doors—closed, locked, and guarded now—it would have no effect down here.

Jules returned and closed the door behind him. "He's next door, waiting."

Olivia nodded, took a breath, then made her entrance. She found Artemis, his back to her, standing among the beds and cots that her get had moved into what had been a storage space. This was where she spent the daylight hours.

"*Bonsoir*, Artemis."

Artemis turned. He grinned and stared at her with his one good eye.

"English, Olivia. My French is about as good as your Greek."

Olivia tried not to stare at his ruined eye. With his curly black hair and olive skin, he'd probably been handsome once. Too handsome, perhaps. But that eye—she had bathed in blood and had cut off heads, she'd ripped still-beating hearts from chests, but she found that dead eye repulsive. Olivia had lost her left little finger once—an accident with a sliding glass door—but it had grown back. She, like other undead, could regenerate most lost body parts, except of course a head or a heart. But certain types of injury did not heal.

Artemis had been a real up and comer in Franco's get until he allowed a child he'd been about to sup on to jab a crucifix into his eye. He might have lived it down if the eye had regenerated, but wounds from holy objects never healed. His puckered scar and sunken socket were eternal reminders of his blunder, and he'd sunk to the rank of one of Franco's get-guards and errand boys.

"Very well, Artemis," she said, switching to English. "But I just want you to know that I had no control over Gregor. Whatever he did, he did on his own. I am in no way responsible for what happened to him. You can tell Franco that."

Artemis laughed. "Franco did not send me here about Gregor. He wanted to let you know that he has personally broken the back of the insurrection."

"How, pray, did he do that?"

"By capturing the priest himself, the one who took over your little church here."

"Not *my* church. It was Gregor's responsibility."

"But it happened while you were here on your inspection tour. Don't worry. That is of no import to Franco."

Olivia seated herself on the bed where she spent her hours of daysleep.

"Broken their backs, has he? What did Franco think of Gregor's idea that the insurgents in the church and the vigilantes were two separate groups?"

"He gave it the amount of consideration it deserved, which is none at all. The priest didn't even bother to deny that he was part of the vigilantes."

Olivia took some small satisfaction in being right, but she wondered . . .

"How is merely capturing the priest going to break the back of this situation?"

Artemis smiled. "Franco has turned the priest—not by himself, but by one of his pet ferals. He was delivered back to his own rectory less than an hour ago. He's been hidden in the basement. Come sundown he'll be one of us and will start to prey on his own followers. And as days go by he'll become increasingly depraved looking, increasingly vicious and feral. Isn't it simply delicious?"

"Perhaps. But it's complicated. I prefer simpler, direct solutions. Why doesn't he just burn them out and capture them?"

"You know Franco. He'd deem a frontal assault unworthy of his intellect. He saw too many *Dr. Mabuse* films while he was living in Germany, I think. Sees himself as the Grand Manipulator, the Demonic Maestro, the Great Orchestrator of life and death and undeath. He must work his coups with style, with élan."

"Élan is all fine and good, but I'd much prefer to see this over and done with."

"But you're not in charge, are you?"

Olivia didn't dignify that remark with an answer. "So what are we to do then? Sit around and hope this undead priest follows Franco's script?"

"We'll be providing direction. We'll watch after sundown and give him a little help if he needs it. Sometime during the next night or two—before he starts losing his mind—we'll question him about the vigilantes. Just in case there are cells outside the church. After that, he's on his own."

"I'm not so sure I like the idea of a feral running loose."

"Good point. He may become uncontrollable. If his followers don't get him first, we may have to put him down ourselves."

Olivia had to smile. "Not much of a future for this priest. What's his name, by the way?"

Artemis shrugged. "You know, I never thought to ask."

"Well, whoever he is, he deserves everything that's coming to him."

LACEY . . .

Startled out of sleep by a hand shaking her shoulder and a strange voice whispering in her ear, Lacey came up swinging.

"Easy, Lacey," said a woman's voice. "Easy. You're safe. No one's going to hurt you."

Lacey blinked. A small room, a single candle, and some stranger bending over her. No . . . not a stranger . . . she recognized her now. The one who'd led her back to the church, who'd said she was a nun. Lacey groaned. Her head throbbed, she hurt all over, especially between her legs.

"Where—?"

"You're in the convent. Listen to me. Something terrible has happened and—" Her voice broke. She blinked, swallowed, then said. "I need your help."

Lacey glanced at the window. Still dark out there. "Can't it wait till morning?"

The nun—what was her name? Carrie? No, Carole with an *e*—shook her head. "Morning will be too late. We have to act now before anyone finds out."

"About what?"

"Your uncle."

Lacey listened in a daze, struggling to understand Carole's story, but the words seemed to congeal in the air, clumping together into indecipherable masses. Something about her Uncle Joe . . . something about him being—

"Dead? No, no! No! You can't be serious! He can't be! He *can't*!"

"He is," Carol said. A tear ran down her cheek. "Believe me, Lacey, he is."

"No!" She wanted to smash this crazy woman's face for lying to her. Her Uncle Joe couldn't be dead!

"But he won't stay dead. By tomorrow night he'll be one of them."

"Not Unk! He'd never!"

"He'll have no choice."

Lacey tried to stand but crumbled back onto the bed. Her legs didn't want to support her. "But if they can turn him . . . make him one of them, then what's the use?"

"That's exactly how they want you to feel. And that's exactly why we must move him away from here and save him from that hell."

"We?" Lacey's stomach twisted and bile rose in her throat. "You mean . . . ?"

Carole was nodding. "There's no other way."

"No! I can't!"

"I can't move him alone, Lacey. The parishioners must never know, must never find him. They must think he died fighting for them. If they learn he's become the enemy, that he's preying on them . . ."

"But put a stake through his heart? I can't!"

."You can't *not*, Lacey. Not if you have the slightest bit of regard for who he was and what he stood for and how he'd want to be remembered."

In that instant Lacey knew Carole was right. Her Uncle Joe had lived his life by a certain set of rules, not simply avoiding evil but actively trying to do good. She couldn't let these undead vermin make a lie and a mockery of his entire life. Stopping that would not be something she did *to* him, it would be *for* him.

Somehow, somewhere, she found the strength to rise from the bed.

"Let's go."

"Can you get a car?"

Lacey nodded. "We brought in a bunch of them to block the streets. There's extras. I'm sure I can get one."

"Good. Keep the lights out and drive it around to the side door of the rectory, then come inside. I'll be waiting in the basement."

The next ten or fifteen minutes would forever be a blur in Lacey's memory. Finding the keys to an old Lincoln Town Car and sneaking it around the block remained clear, but after that . . . creeping down into that dank cellar . . . seeing her uncle's lifeless, bloodless face when Carole unwrapped the top of the sheet—it was him, really, really him—and then struggling his dead weight up the stairs . . . placing him in the trunk of the car . . . hearing the clank of the tools Carole had found in the caretaker's shed as she carefully placed them on the back seat . . . slumping in the passenger seat as Carole drove them away toward the brightening horizon . . .

And thinking about her Uncle Joe . . .

The earliest memory was riding on his back, he barely a teenager and she barely in kindergarten. A flash of watching from a front row pew as he took his Holy Orders and officially became a priest. And then later, much clearer memories of long conversations about faith and God and the meaning of life with her doing most of the talking because no one would listen to her, only him, and Uncle Joe not agreeing but giving her his ear, letting her finish without cutting her off and dissing her dissidence.

And now he was gone. Her sounding board, her last anchor . . . gone, erased. She felt adrift.

The car stopped. Returning to the present, Lacey wiped her eyes and looked around. They were at the beach. A boardwalk lay straight ahead. She'd been here a few days ago.

They'd arrived at the edge of the continent . . . to do the unthinkable . . . in order to prevent the unspeakable.

"I don't know if I can go through with this," Lacey said.

Carole was already out of the car. "Stop thinking of yourself and help me carry him."

Thinking of yourself . . . That angered Lacey. "I'm thinking about *him*, and what he's meant to me, what he'll always mean to me."

"Do you hear yourself? Me-me-me. This isn't about you or me. It's about Father Joe's legacy. And if we're going to preserve that, we have to do what has to be done."

She was right. Damn her, this weird nun was right. Lacey got out of the car as Carole popped the trunk.

"Where are we taking him?"

"Up to the beach."

"Why the beach?"

"Because we can dig a deep hole quickly, and because very few people come here anymore."

"How do you know?"

"Because I watch. I watch everything. No one will find him. Now help me lift him."

Lacey glanced around. The area looked deserted but who knew what was hiding in the shadows. Her guns . . . after taking the dead Vichy woman's clothes, she'd crept back into the Post Office and lifted the pistols off a couple of the undead corpses. She wished she'd thought to bring them, but her mind had been numbed with loss.

Carole opened the trunk to reveal the sheet-wrapped form. Steeling herself, Lacey took the shoulders, Carole the feet, and they carried Joe's body up a ramp, across the boardwalk, then down the steps to the sand. Carole directed them toward a spot under the boards with about five feet of headroom, maybe a little less.

Lacey stayed with the body while Carole ran back to the car. She returned moments later with a pair of shovels and a beat-up purple vinyl book bag. The sky had grown light enough for Lacey to see ST. ANTHONY'S SCHOOL emblazoned along the side in yellow.

"What's in there?" Lacey asked, although she had a good idea what the answer would be.

Carole said nothing. She responded by pulling out a heavy, iron-headed maul and a wickedly sharpened length of one-inch doweling. She drew the sheet back from Uncle Joe's head and upper torso.

Lacey's stomach heaved as she caught sight of his torn-open throat. She'd seen only his face back in the rectory. Good thing she hadn't eaten since yesterday, otherwise she'd be spewing across the sand.

"Look what they did to him!" she screeched. "Look what they *did*!"

Carole didn't respond. Her face seemed set in stone as she raised the stake and placed the point over the left side of his chest.

"Can't it wait?" Lacey cried.

"Till when?" Carole's expression had became fierce, her voice tight, thin, stretched to the breaking point. "Tell me a good time for this and I'll gladly wait. When, Lacey? When will be a good time?"

Lacey had no answer. When she saw Carole place the point of the stake over her uncle's heart, she turned away.

"I can't watch this."

"Then I guess I'm on my own."

Sobbing openly, Lacey resisted the urge to run screaming down the beach. She kept her back to Carole and jammed her fingers into her ears while she began a tuneless hum to block out the sounds—of iron striking wood, of wood crunching through bone and cartilage. She knew she should be helping, but after what she'd already been through in the last dozen hours, pounding a stake into her uncle's chest was more than she could handle right now. She couldn't. She. Just. Couldn't.

So she stared through her tears at the ocean, at the pink glow growing on the horizon.

Finally she pulled her fingers from her ears and tried to turn, but her brain refused to send the necessary signals to make her body move. The mere thought of seeing her uncle lying there with a shaft of wood protruding from his chest . . .

She heard a noise . . . sobbing . . . Carole.

"Is . . . is it over?"

Carole moaned. "Nooooo! I couldn't do it!"

Lacey whirled, took one look at the nun's tear-stained face, and she knew.

"You loved him, didn't you."

Another bubbling sob from Carole as she nodded. "In my fashion, yes. We all did. A good, *good* man . . ."

"I don't mean loving him like that, like a brother. I mean as a man."

Carole said nothing, just stared down at the sheet-wrapped body before her.

"It's okay, Carole. It's not just idle interest. He was my uncle. I'd like to know how you felt about him, especially now that he's . . . gone. Did you love him as a man?"

"Yes." It sounded like a gasp of relief, as if a long pent-up pressure had been released. "Not that we ever did anything," she added quickly. "Not that he ever even knew."

"But you" . . . she needed the right word here . . . "longed for him?"

"God forgive me, yes. Not lust, nothing carnal. I just wanted to be near him. Can you understand that?"

Lacey shrugged, unsure of what she could understand. This was so unreal.

"I'm not sure how to say this," Carole said, "because I've never expressed it, even to myself."

"Why not?"

"Because it wasn't right. I took vows. *He* took vows. I shouldn't have been thinking of a man like that, especially a priest. God was supposed to be enough. But sometimes . . ."

"Sometimes God just isn't enough."

"It must be a sin to say so, but no, sometimes He isn't. Father Joe had something about him that made me . . . made me want, *long* to be near him. His very presence just seemed to make the world seem right. I'd see him touch some of the other sisters, the older ones—nothing but a hand on the arm or, rarely, an arm across the shoulders as they'd laugh about something. But never me. And I never knew why. Not that I wanted more, not that I'd ever lead him astray, but a simple touch, just to let me know he knew I existed, that would have made me so happy."

Lacey felt as if she were talking to some lonely preteen, and sexually, maybe that was where Carole was. She'd probably joined the convent right out of high school—maybe during high school—and she'd never progressed past that stage in her relationships with the opposite sex.

"Do you think my uncle was avoiding you?"

"Sometimes it seemed like it."

"Well, I can think of only one reason for that."

Carole looked up. "What?"

"Maybe he felt the same about you."

"Oh, no." Carole shook her head vehemently, almost violently. "He didn't. He couldn't have."

"I'm sure of it."

She wasn't sure at all, but the sweet light flaring in Carole's eyes now touched Lacey more deeply than she could have imagined a few moments ago when this seemingly icebound woman had crouched there with a stake poised over Uncle Joe's heart.

"Carole, you should have seen his face the other night after you stopped by the church. He was worried about you, wished you'd come into the church with us, but he was beaming too . . ."

Wait a sec. That was no exaggeration. Joe *had* been beaming. Maybe there'd been more going on between those two than anyone knew, least of all themselves.

"Beaming?" Carole said.

Lacey knew a prompt when she heard one. "Yeah. Beaming. He seemed really, really happy to see you and know you were still alive. He kept talking about you."

How sad, Lacey thought. The two of them could have made each other's lives so much brighter, but they'd been kept apart.

Carole sobbed again. "Now he's gone!"

"Not quite," Lacey said. "Not yet. And that's where we come in, I guess."

"How can I do this?" She wiped her eyes and sniffed. "I could do it, I know I could if he were one of them, if I could see that cold evil hunger in his eyes, I could save him from that. But look at him. Except for his throat he looks so normal, so . . . peaceful. I can't."

"But we have to," Lacey said. She realized with a start that their roles had been reversed. "Why don't we dig the hole— the grave—first, and then . . . and then we'll do it together."

Carole stared at her. "You'll help me?"

"Yes." Lacey nodded, hoping she was making a promise she could keep. "For him. For Uncle Joe."

They began to dig, together at first, then taking turns as the grave deepened.

Lacey was waist deep in the hole as the sun began to emerge from the sea. She pointed to the loose sand sliding down the walls around her.

"If that keeps up we'll never make six feet."

Carole sat to the side, taking her turn to rest. "We'll do the best we can. We need it deep enough to discourage any wild dogs from trying to dig him up."

The exertions of digging plus her earlier concussion had started blinding bolts of pain shooting through her head. That, the beating she'd endured, and the lack of food made the work agony, but she'd keep on digging till nightfall and beyond if it meant putting off what they had to do once Joe's grave was ready.

"All right," Lacey said. "We'll go down another foot, then—" She stopped as she caught a sharp, pungent odor. "What's that? Something burning?" A puff of white smoke wafted past her. "What the hell? It almost smells like—"

"Oh, dear God!" Carole cried, scrambling to her hands and knees. "Father Joe!"

Lacey looked and saw her uncle lying in the full light of the rising sun. His exposed skin was smoking and bubbling.

"Shit!"

She scrambled out of the grave and grabbed his arm, then released it in a spasm of revulsion. The flesh felt like hot wax. She looked for a place to hide him from the sun. With the light shining at this low angle, the only shady spots here were the narrow bands behind the pilings, nowhere near enough to shelter him.

"Quick!" Carole said. "The grave!"

She grabbed Joe's sheet-wrapped feet and started dragging him toward it. Lacey helped. Seconds later they tumbled him into the opening. He landed on his back, out of the sun, and immediately his skin stopped boiling. But the odor of burning flesh still rolled off of him.

"Look at him," Lacey whispered. "Look what it did to him."

They crouched and stared at him. The still-smoking skin of Joe's face and chest and upper arms was dead white and rippled and pitted like a bad stucco job.

Finally Carole said, "Why did we do that?"

"Do what?"

"Protect him from the sun."

Lacey saw what she meant. "You mean if we'd left him there, the sun might have done the job for us?"

Carole shook her head. "I don't know, but that's what seemed to be happening."

"Are you saying we should drag him out on the beach and just let him . . . what . . . boil away?"

That struck Lacey as a greater defilement than driving a stake through him. Almost like setting him on fire.

"I don't know," Carole said. "I used to be so very sure about some things, especially this sort of thing. Now . . . I don't know."

Lacey glanced again at her uncle's body, appalled by his ruined skin, and noticed something. She squinted into the shadows of the grave, still not sure.

"What is it?" Carole said.

"Look at his throat. Wasn't it all torn open a few minutes ago?"

Carole slapped a hand over her mouth. "Oh, no! It's happening already!"

"What?"

"The change! He's turning!"

"How do you know?"

"Because Bernadette . . . because I've seen it before. As they turn, the death wound heals up as if it never was."

Lacey grabbed Carole's flashlight and fixed the beam on Joe's throat. The area where it had been torn open was thickened and puckered, a different kind of scarring than the rest of his ruined skin. "That doesn't look healed up to me. Looks more like its been fused or . . ." What was the word? ". . . cauterized."

"He's turned, I tell you." Carole looked around, then picked up Joe's big silver cross from the sand. "Watch."

As Carole leaned into the grave and pressed the cross against Joe's chest, Lacey winced, expecting a puff of smoke and who knew what else. But nothing happened.

"That's strange," Carole said. "It should have burned him."

"Which means he hasn't turned."

"Yet," Carole's eyes took on a haunted look. "This doesn't let us off the hook, I'm afraid."

Lacey glanced over to where the stake and the maul rested on the sand.

"What if . . ." Her thoughts were scattering like a startled flock of birds. "What if the sun burned it out of him?"

"Burned what out of him?"

"Whatever makes you turn undead. Look, it cauterized his wound."

"And all his exposed skin as well. He would have . . . *dissolved* out there if we hadn't pushed him into this hole!"

She had a point. Joe had looked like he was melting, but Lacey wasn't giving in. She had this feeling . . .

"Okay, but what if he was out there in the sun long enough to kill him—I mean, to burn off whatever was going to make him undead and leave him really dead? It's possible, isn't it?"

Carole sighed. "Possible, I suppose. But I've never heard of anything like that."

"There must be tons we don't know about these creatures. If you agree it's possible, then why can't we leave him as he is and just fill in his grave?"

Carole shook her head. "We need to be sure. We owe him that."

"All right then . . ." Her mind ranged over the options, anything but jumping into that hole and driving a stake through that limp body. "How about we come back here at sunset? If he's not dead, we'll be waiting when he starts to dig his way out, and we'll . . . stop him."

"You want to risk that?" Carole said, eyeing her. "It will be harder, but we can stop him as he's crawling out. Just remember, it will be much worse to have to stake him while he's moving."

Lacey wrung her hands. "I know, I know. But I've got this feeling we won't have to."

"This is nothing but wishful thinking, Lacey."

"It's more than that. Please. Do it my way, just this once."

Carole sat silent for a long moment, then, "All right. I just hope we don't regret this."

Her tone was wary, but Lacey thought she detected a hint of relief.

"We won't. I've got—"

"A feeling. So you said." Carole grabbed a shovel. "But

swear to me you'll be back here with me before sunset, and that we'll watch over him all night until dawn."

"I swear."

Carole nodded and started shoveling sand back into the grave.

"Wait," Lacey said. "Let me cover his face."

She slid into the hole, careful not to step on him, and tugged up the sheet so that it covered her uncle's face.

As soon as Lacey crawled out, Carole started shoveling again. She couldn't seem to wait to cover him.

"Shouldn't we say a few words over him first?"

Lacey didn't want a prayer, but she thought they could at least say something about the man he was and the life he'd led.

Carole looked at her. "Not yet. Not till we're sure he's at rest. Truly at rest. Then we'll give our eulogies."

He awakens in crushing darkness, a damp, dusty sheet pressed hard against his face, pushing at his eyes, an anvil resting on his chest.

Air! He needs air!

Then he realizes that he doesn't. He feels no urge to breathe, no need. Why not?

Where is he? More important—who is he? The answer is there, just beyond his grasp. Reaching for it, he tries to claw at the entrapping sheet but his arms are pinned to his sides by its enormous weight. He worms one hand up across his chest to where he can grip the sheet. He pulls it down—

Sand! Cascading into his eyes, filling his mouth and nose. He's buried in sand!

He's got to get out!

His struggles become frantic. He tears through the sheet and fights the incalculable weight, working his hands and then his arms through the granules. He's strong, and soon his hands are snaking up through the sand, slowly making their way to the surface . . .

CAROLE . . .

The setting sun's blood-red eye stared at Carole from the car's rearview mirror. She flipped the dimmer toggle to cut its brightness and steered the Lincoln along Route 88. She was thinking about napalm.

Lacey fidgeted in the passenger seat and toyed with the revolver in her lap. The cowboys—or Vichy, as Lacey called them—had been conspicuous by their absence today. Maybe the undead were alarmed by the loss of the one Carole had killed last night—dear God, had it been less than twenty-four hours?—and were keeping them close by during the light hours. Even so, she and Lacey might have the bad luck of running into a party of them before reaching the beach.

Carole glanced at the barrel of the shotgun on the armrest between them. Nothing was going to keep them from Father Joe's graveside tonight.

Carole and Lacey had caught up on their sleep during the day, awakening this afternoon to find the parishioners nervous and edgy. Father Joe was still missing and they were giving up hope that he'd be found alive. Carole had told them that even if he'd been killed, he'd want them to fight on.

They'd wanted to know how, and that was when Carole had begun thinking of napalm.

It was easy to make. She'd need soap flakes. Soap wasn't edible so there'd be no shortage of flakes in the looted grocery stores. If she could get her hands on some kerosene, she'd be in business. Napalm stuck to whatever it splashed against and burned so hot it turned human flesh into fuel to feed its flames. Would the same happen with undead flesh?

Only one way to find out . . .

She heard a sob and looked at Lacey. Tears glistened on her cheeks.

"What's wrong?"

"I hope we did the right thing."

Carole knew exactly how she felt. Apprehension had been clawing at her gut all day.

"You're having second thoughts?"

"Oh, yes. Ohhhhhh, yes. I don't want to watch him digging his way out of the ground, I don't want to see his undead eyes or hear his undead voice. I don't want that to be my last memory of him." She stared at Carole. "If I believed in God I'd be praying to him right now."

Strange, Carole thought. I do believe in Him and I've stopped praying. He doesn't seem to be listening.

"Are you all right, Lacey? I mean, after what happened yesterday?"

"Do you mean after finding my dearest and closest living relative dead and helping dig his grave? Or do you mean after getting gang raped?"

Carole winced at her tone and at the images "gang raped" conjured. "Never mind. Sorry."

Lacey reached over and squeezed her arm. "Hey, no. *I'm* sorry." She sighed. "I guess I'm doing about as well as can be expected. I'm still sore as hell, but I'm healing."

"I didn't mean physically. I meant the hurt within. Emotionally. It's such an awful, awful thing . . ." Carole ran out of words.

Lacey shrugged. "Same answer, I suppose. I know I'd feel different if it had happened—the rape, I mean—say, a year ago, back in the old civilized world. I would have been thinking, 'How could this happen?' and 'Why me?' I would have felt like some sort of pariah or loser, that the world and society had let me down, that some throwbacks had smashed through all the rules and targeted me. And I would have felt somehow to blame. Yeah, can you believe that? I bet I would've. I know I'd have wanted to dig myself a hole and pull the ground over me."

Carole tried to imagine how she'd feel if places were reversed, but her imagination wasn't up to it. She nodded to keep Lacey talking. She'd heard it was bad to keep something like this bottled up.

"Are you saying you don't feel that way now?"

Lacey shook her head. "Yeah . . . I don't know. It's a different world now, a world without any rules, except maybe those of the jungle. There's no law, no order, and because of that, I don't seem to have that pariah-loser-victim feeling. And I don't feel ashamed. I feel disgusted and sickened and violated, but I don't feel ashamed. I feel hate and I want revenge, but I don't feel a need to hide. A year ago I'd have felt scarred for life. Now I feel . . . as if I've been splattered with mud—rotten, nasty mud—but nothing I can't wash off and then move on. Does that make sense?"

Carole nodded. She knew as well as anyone how the rules had changed, and she with them.

"You're strong, though. I don't know if I could bounce back from something like that."

"I wouldn't exactly call it 'bouncing.' But don't short-change yourself, Carole. You're tougher than you let on. I think you could handle anything. Let's just hope you never have to find out."

"Amen," Carole said.

Thinking of men who could do such heinous things drew Carole's thoughts back to napalm, but she pushed them aside as the boardwalk buildings hove into view. She parked and gave herself half a moment to inhale the briny air. Then she double-checked the old book bag—crosses, stakes, garlic, hammer, flashlight. All there.

Let's just pray we don't have to use them, she thought.

What they most likely would use were the two peanut butter sandwiches on home-baked bread they'd brought along. Somewhere old Mrs. Delmonico had found whole wheat flour and a propane stove.

They left the shotgun in the car, but Lacey carried her pistol at the ready as they hurried across the deserted boardwalk and down to the beach. Lacey stayed in the lead when they ducked under the boards where they'd buried Father Joe, but stopped dead in her tracks with a cry of alarm.

Carole bumped into her from behind. "What——?"

"Oh, no!" Lacey cried. "It can't be!"

Carole pushed her aside and saw what she was looking at. The grave had been disturbed.

"He's already out!" Lacey wailed.

"No. He can't be. The sun hasn't set yet."

She pointed to areas of darker sand atop the light. "But some of the sand's still damp. That means it came from deeper down. And not too long ago."

"Then someone's dug him up. It's the only explanation."

Lacey's eyes were wild. "But who? We were the only ones who knew. And why?"

She glanced around and noticed linear tracks leading out to the beach. "Look. We didn't leave those. Someone's dragged him out."

"They can't have gone too far." Carole heard Lacey cock her pistol as she started back toward the beach. "The sons of bitches . . ."

Carole followed her out and they stood together, looking up and down the beach and along the gently rolling dunes that eased toward the water. She blinked . . . was that someone . . . ? Yes, it looked like a man, standing at the water line with a towel draped over his shoulders, staring out to sea.

"Look, Lacey," Carole said, pointing. "Do you see him?"

Lacey nodded and started forward. "You think he did it?"

"Perhaps." Carole fell into step beside her. "If not, he might have seen who did."

But as they approached, the white towel began to look more like a sheet, and the back of the man's head, the color of his hair began to look more and more familiar . . .

They were twenty feet away when Carole stopped and grabbed Lacey's arm. "Oh, dear God," she whispered. "It looks like . . ."

Lacey was nodding. "I know." Her voice had shrunken to a high-pitched squeak. "But it can't be."

He looked wet, as if he'd gone for a swim. Carole stepped

forward, closed to within half a dozen feet of him. Trembling inside and out, she wet her lips. Her tongue felt as dry as old leather.

"Father Joe?"

The man turned. The dying light of the sun ruddied the pitted, ruined dead-white skin of his face.

"Carole," he said in Father Joe's voice. "What's happened to me?"

Shock was a hand against her chest, shoving her back. She dropped the bookbag and stumbled a few steps, then tripped. Lacey caught her before she fell.

"Oh, shit," Lacey whimpered. "Oh, shit!"

"Lacey?" The man, the thing that had once been Father Joe, took a faltering step toward them. "What did they do to me?"

"Wh-who?" Lacey said.

"The undead. They took me to New York. He was going to make me one of them . . . turn me into a feral, he said. I remember dying, being killed . . . at least I think I do, but—"

Heart pounding, mind racing. Carole watched him closely, looking for a misstep, listening for a false note.

She found her voice again. "You did die. We found you and you were dead. We buried you back there, under the boardwalk."

"But I'm not dead. And I'm not one of them. I can't be because . . ." He pointed west. "Because that's the sun and it should be killing me, but it's not." He raised a scarred fist. "Somehow, some way, I've beaten them."

"But you were dead, Uncle Joe," Lacey told him. Her voice trembled like a wounded thing. "And now you're not."

"But I'm not *un*dead. Standing here in the sunlight is proof enough of that. And I'm looking at you two and I'm not seeing prey. I'm seeing two people I care about very much."

Carole suspected that under different circumstances—any circumstances but these—those words would have made her dizzy. But now . . .

She shook her head, trying to clear it, trying to step back from her roiling emotions and think clearly. He sounded like her Father Joe, he acted like Father Joe, he had Father Joe's mannerisms, but something was different, something wasn't quite right. Something terrible had been done to him, and one way or another, she had to find a way to undo it.

She bent forward and snatched the book bag from where she'd dropped it on the sand.

"Carole?" said Lacey from behind her.

"Just a minute."

She opened it and reached inside.

"Carole, you're not really going to—"

"A *minute*, I said!"

Carole's fingers wrapped around the upright of Father Joe's big silver cross. "We've been saving this for you." She yanked it from the bag and held it out to him. "Here."

Father Joe cried out and turned his head, holding up a hand to shield his eyes from the sight of the very cross he used to carry with him wherever he went.

Carole felt something die within her as she watched him and realized what she had to do.

She handed the cross to Lacey who stood dumbstruck, staring at her uncle with wide, uncomprehending eyes. Lacey gripped the cross but never took her eyes from her uncle.

As Carole pulled open the book bag again, she slammed the doors, closed the windows, and drew the curtains on everything she had ever felt for the man this creature had once been. Her hand was reaching into the bag for the hammer and stake when Lacey's voice, a hint of panic in her tone, stopped her.

"Carole . . . Carole, something's happening here. Please tell me what's going on."

Carole looked up and froze. The Father Joe thing was edging toward Lacey, his face averted, his hand stretched out toward the cross.

"What's happening, Carole?" Lacey wailed.

"I'm not sure, but don't move. Stay right where you are."

Carole watched with a wrenching mixture of horror and fascination as the Father Joe thing's fingers neared the cross. She noticed that his eyes were slitted and only partially averted, as if he were looking at the cross from the corner of his eye.

The undead couldn't stand to be anywhere near a cross, yet the Father Joe thing was reaching for this one.

Finally his scarred fingers reached it, touched the metal, and jerked back as if they'd been burned. But no flash, no sizzle of seared flesh. The fingers came forward again, and this time, like a striking snake, they snatched the cross from Lacey's hand.

"It's hot!" he said, looking up into the darkening sky as he switched it back and forth between his hands like a hot potato. "Oh, God, it's hot!"

But it wasn't searing his flesh, only reddening it.

Then with the cry of a damned soul he dropped it and fell to his knees on the sand.

"What have they done to me?" he sobbed as he looked at Carole with frightened, haunted eyes. "What am I?"

Carole closed the book bag.

She'd never seen the undead cry. This wasn't a vampire. But he wasn't the Father Joe she had known either. He was something in between. Was this an accident, or some sort of trick, some undead plot to further confuse and confound the living? She'd have to reserve judgment for now.

But she'd be watching his every move.

JOE . . .

Carole took his arm and tugged him toward the boardwalk, saying, "We need to find a place where we're not so exposed."

Joe went along with her, his mind numb, unable to string two coherent thoughts together.

The afterimage of the cross—*his* cross—still stained his vision, bouncing in the air before him. The blast of light had been intolerably bright, an explosion of brilliance, as if Carole had lifted a white hot star from her book bag. The light had caused him pain, but only in his eyes. It hadn't struck him like a physical blow the way it seemed to affect the undead, staggering them back as if they were being pummeled with a baseball bat. He could look at it as one might the sun, squinting from the corner of his eye.

He could touch the cross but couldn't hold it. He looked down at his palms. The skin was reddened there, but at least it was normal looking. Not like the ruined, thickened flesh on the back of his hands and on his arms and chest. He touched his face and found thickened and pitted skin there as well.

Joe felt as if his world were crumbling around him, then realized that it already had. The life he'd known was gone, ended. What lay ahead?

He pulled the damp sheet closer around him as Carole led him up the steps to the boardwalk. Had this been his shroud? As she turned him right, Joe heard Lacey's voice from behind.

"Aren't we going to the car?"

"Let's see if we can get into one of these houses," Carole said.

She led them past the dead arcades and along the boardwalk leading to the inlet. No one spoke. Lacey looked as dazed as Joe felt. They walked past the beachfront houses, some large with sun decks and huge seaward windows, others tiny, little more than plywood boxes, all nuzzling against the boardwalk. Most of the bigger ones had been vandalized.

Carole stopped before an old, minuscule bungalow that appeared intact. Despite the low light, Joe had no problem making out the faded blue-gray of its clapboard siding. Someone had painted the word SEAVIEW in black on the door and surrounded it with sun-bleached clamshells.

Carole tried the door. When it wouldn't open, she slammed her shoulder against it. When that didn't work, she opened her book bag and began to rummage through it.

Joe turned to the door and slammed his palm against it.

The molding cracked like a gunshot and the door swung inward. He stared at his hand. He hadn't put a lot of effort into the blow, but it had broken the molding.

"How did I do that?" he muttered.

No one answered.

In a courteous reflex, he stood aside to let Carole and Lacey enter first. Only after they were inside did he realize that he should have gone ahead of them. No telling what might have been lying in wait there.

As he stepped across the threshold, he felt a curious resistance, as if the air inside had congealed to try to hold him back. He pressed forward and pushed through. The resistance evaporated once he was inside.

As he closed the door behind him, he sniffed the musty air and looked around. Typical beach house decor: rattan furniture with beachy-patterned cushions, driftwood and shells on the mantle, fishnets and starfish tacked to the tongue-and-groove knotty pine walls of the wide open living room/dining room/kitchen combo that ran the length of the house; photos of smiling people sitting on the beach or holding fishing rods. Joe wondered if any of them were still alive.

Carole pulled out her flashlight. "Let's see if we can find any candles."

"There's three in that little brass candelabra back there," he told her.

"Where?" She flashed her light around.

He pointed. "On the dining room table."

Carole shot him a strange look and moved toward the rear of the house where she retrieved a brass candelabra from the tiny dining room. She lit one of its three candles and set it on the small cocktail table situated before the picture window overlooking the beach and the ocean. Lacey pulled the curtains.

"Let's sit," Carole said.

"I can't sit," Joe told her. "I need to know what happened to me."

"We're about to tell you all we know," Carole said.

So he sat. Carole did most of the talking, with Lacey

adding a comment or two. They told him how they'd found him, how his skin had started boiling in the morning sun, and how they'd buried him.

Joe rose and started pacing. He'd held himself still as he'd listened to them, not wanting to believe their tale, yet unable to deny it, and now he had to move. He felt too big for the room. Or was it getting smaller, the walls closing in on him? He didn't know what to do with himself—stand, sit, move about—or where to put his hands . . . his body felt different, not quite his own. He'd sensed this since pulling himself out of the sand. He'd washed himself off in the ocean, hoping it would make a difference, but it hadn't. He still felt like a visitor in his own skin.

"So what am I then?" he said to no one on particular, perhaps to God Himself. "Some new sort of creature, some freakish hybrid?" He sure as hell felt like a freak.

"That is what we need to find out," Carole said.

He stared at her and she stared back, her eyes flat, unreadable. This was not the Carole he'd known, not the woman he'd been drawn to. He'd sensed a terrible change in her when he'd run into her outside the church, but now she seemed even further removed from her old self. Cold . . . and she'd been anything but cold in her other life. Had all the sweetness and warmth in her been burned away, or had she merely walled them off?

Unable to hold her gaze any longer, he looked down at himself. He was still wrapped in the damp, sandy sheet. He wasn't cold but he didn't like looking like something that had washed up from the sea.

"I'm going to see if I can find some clothes."

Anything to escape Carole's imprisoning stare. She made him feel like a specimen in a dissection tray.

He turned into the short hallway that was little more than an alcove that divided the bungalow's two bedrooms. A pang shot through his abdomen and he realized he was hungry. Clothes first, then food.

He entered the bedroom on the left and pulled open a

dresser drawer. No good. Women's underwear. A thought struck him: What if two old spinsters kept this as a summer place? Under no circumstances was he putting on a house dress. He'd rather keep the sheet.

He tried the other bureau and found an assortment of shirts and Bermudas. He tried a pair of green plaid shorts first and, though a little loose in the waist, they fit. The top shirt on the pile was a yellow-flowered Hawaiian.

After he pulled it on he looked down at himself. Not a big improvement over that old sheet. He must look like the bennie from hell. He stepped to the mirror over the dresser to catch a full view. The mirror was blurred.

This place was in dire need of some spring cleaning.

He leaned forward to wipe away the dust but his hand rubbed across clean glass. He leaned closer and noticed that the room behind him reflected clear and sharp, yet he remained a blur.

"Oh, God!"

"Unk?" he heard Lacey say from the front room. Seconds later she was at his side with the flashlight, her reflection the only distinguishable human in the mirror. "What's wrong?"

Feeling weak—from hunger as well as the horror before him—he leaned against the dresser and pointed to the mirror. "Look at me—if you can."

She gasped. "Is that . . . ?"

"That's what's left of my reflection."

Carole's image joined them in the glass. He saw her stiffen and stare.

After a moment she said, "You're not completely gone."

"No, but nobody can tell me that's not more proof that I'm no longer human. What have I become? I'm asking you both again: What am I?"

The hunger worsened. He grabbed his abdomen and doubled over.

"Joe?" Lacey asked.

"Hungry. Can't remember the last time I ate."

He turned away and stalked to the kitchen where he began to open the cabinets and paw through their contents. Mostly condiments and spices.

"Damn it all!" he shouted. "Didn't these people eat?"

"It's a summer home," Carole said softly. "Nobody leaves food over the winter."

"God, I'm starving."

"We've got food," Lacey said.

"Right," Carole said. "You remember Mrs. Delmonico, don't you?"

"Of course I do," Joe said. "I only died. I didn't lose my memory." He looked from Lacey's stricken face to Carole's stony expression and back again. "Sorry. That was supposed to be a joke."

"Oh, yeah!" Lacey's forced laugh sounded awful. "Funny!" Her smile cracked and she sobbed. Once.

"Lacey, I'm sorry," Joe said.

She held up a hand as she pulled herself together. "I'm okay. Really."

No, you aren't, he thought. Not a single one of us is anywhere near okay.

"We should eat something," Carole said. "Who knows when we'll get another chance."

Joe looked at her. "What were you saying about Mrs. Delmonico?"

"She baked some bread and made us peanut butter sandwiches."

"Peanut butter! God, I can't remember the last time I had a peanut butter sandwich."

He followed Carole and Lacey to the cocktail table. Carole pulled out the sandwiches, unwrapped them, and handed a half to Joe. Manners reminded him to wait but hunger forced his hands toward his mouth. He took a deep bite and gagged.

His gorge rose in revulsion as he turned and spat it into his hand.

"What's in that? I thought you said it was peanut butter."

Lacey sat across the table with the other half of Joe's sandwich. She'd taken a bite and was staring at him.

He nodded to her. "Tastes awful, doesn't it."

Lacey shook her head. "Tastes fine," she said around her bite.

Carole leaned forward. "What did it taste like to you, Father?"

How could he describe something so awful? "Try to imagine rancid meat . . . in spoiled milk . . . laced with hot tar . . . and you're only part way there."

With a glance at Lacey, Carole pulled the book bag up onto her lap and reached inside. With a single quick movement she removed something and held it under his nose.

"How about this?"

Joe recoiled, almost tipping over backward in his chair. It felt like pure ammonia shoved up his nose.

"Damn! What's *that*? Get it away!"

Carole showed him the flaky clove between her fingers. "Just garlic."

A queasy nausea slithered through Joe's hunger pains. He'd always loved garlic, the more the better. But now . . .

"I don't understand this!" Lacey cried. She was leaning away from the table with her eyes squeezed shut. "You can stand in sunlight and walk into a home without being invited in, but you don't cast a full reflection and you can't stand garlic. What's going on?"

Joe shook his head. "I wish I knew." Hunger gave him a vicious kick in the abdomen, doubling him over. "I do know I've got to eat. Isn't there anything else around?"

"Yes," Lacey said. She was looking past him, a strange light dancing in her eyes. "Yes, I believe there is."

She grabbed the flashlight and hurried to the kitchen. Joe heard her opening drawer after drawer, rattling utensils. Apparently she found what she was looking for because she returned to the table and stood beside him with her hands behind her back.

"Close your eyes and open your mouth," she said.

"This is no time for games, Lacey. I'm starving."

A smile appeared; it looked painted on. "Humor me, Unk. Open your mouth and close your eyes."

Joe complied, and then things started happening—fast. He sensed Lacey move closer, heard a gasp of shock—Carole?—then felt something warm and firm and wet pressed into his mouth. He'd never tasted anything like it—utterly delicious. He opened his eyes and saw Lacey close, a steak knife in one hand, and the other—

—pressed against his mouth.

Joe flung himself backward, and this time he did go over, landing on his back. He felt no pain, only revulsion at the sight of his niece's bloody thumb, and at himself the way he licked his lips and wanted more. A glimpse of Carole's white face and stricken expression over Lacey's shoulder was the final blow.

Instead of climbing back to his feet, Joe rolled onto his side, facing away from them, and sobbed with shame. He wished he could dissolve into a liquid and seep between the floorboards to hide from their eyes. For he knew how they must be looking at him—with the same revulsion as he'd felt about the undead before . . . before . . .

And worse. He realized that his hunger was gone. Just those few drops of Lacey's blood had sated him.

He groaned. He wanted to crawl out of this house and their sight on his belly like the lesser being he'd become.

No . . . he wanted to die. Truly die.

Keeping an arm across his eyes so he wouldn't have to see the loathing in their faces, he rolled over onto his back and tore open his shirt, baring his chest.

"Do it, Carole. I don't want to be this way. End it now. Please."

No response, no sound of movement.

Joe uncovered his eyes and found Carole and Lacey staring at him from where he'd left them at the table. They looked like mannequins, but their expressions reflected more shock than revulsion.

He pounded a fist against his chest, over his heart. "Please, Carole! I'm begging you. If you've ever cared the slightest for me, either of you, you won't let me to go on as the creature I am now."

Carole only shook her head.

He looked at his niece. "Lacey? Please? You can do this one thing for me, can't you?"

Tears streamed down her cheeks as she shook her head. "No. I can't. You're too . . . you."

Back to Carole: "You hate the undead, Carole. I can tell. So why won't you put this sick dog out of his misery?"

"I could never hate you, Father Joe, but I could loathe you if you . . . if you were one of them. But it's plain that you loathe yourself more than I ever could, and that . . . that means you're not one of them."

"But I'm halfway there. What if this is just some sort of transitional phase and by tomorrow I'll be fully undead."

She shook her head. "There is no transitional phase."

"You don't know that!" He was shouting now.

Carole didn't raise her voice, only shifted her gaze to the side and said, "I do. I've seen how the change goes, and you are different. You're asking one of us to drive a stake through your heart. I can't say for sure, but I doubt very much that any undead in the history of time has made such a request. The very fact that you've asked is proof that you aren't one of them."

"Then in God's name, what am I?"

"A weapon, perhaps."

A weapon? The word stirred him. Joe sat up and hugged his knees against his chest.

"What do you mean?"

"Do you have any desire to continue what you started at the church?"

Joe hadn't given it a thought. He'd been too preoccupied with figuring out what had happened to him. But now that he did think about it . . .

"I don't see how it's possible. I can't see them following an undead priest."

"You're not undead."

"I'm certainly not their Father Joe any longer."

"You'll always be—"

"No. I can't be a priest anymore. How can I when I can't ever say Mass again? I can't look at a cross or touch one without getting burned. I certainly can't taste the consecrated bread and wine—assuming I didn't burst into flame trying to say the prayers to consecrate it."

"Father Joe—"

"Don't call me that again. I am no longer a priest, so stop calling me 'Father.' It's an insult to all those who still deserve the title. From now on it's Joe, just plain Joe."

"Very well, J—" Carole seemed to have trouble with the name. "Very well, Joseph. You don't want to go back to leading your parish. Do you have any desire to go on fighting the undead?"

"More than ever."

And with those three words a whole world of possibilities opened up before Joe. He struggled back to his feet. He felt excited, the first positive emotion he'd experienced since leaping from the observation deck the other night.

Carole had called him a weapon. He could see that she was right. By some strange quirk of fate he'd become a sort of half-breed. There had to be a way he could use that against the undead. Make them pay for what they'd done to his world, to his friends and loved ones, to *him*.

"I think it's time to fight back."

While there's still time . . . on the chance that I'll become like that feral who killed me . . . Devlin.

A terrible purpose surged through him. Yes, fight back, and maybe somewhere down the road he'd meet again with Franco. If he didn't, and if somewhere along that road he met his end—his final end—well, that was all right too. In fact, he'd welcome it. He had no illusions that he and Carole and Lacey and whoever else they picked up along the way could drive the undead horde back to Europe, but when he met his inevitable end he wanted to know he'd taken as many as possible with him.

OLIVIA . . .

"My, my," Olivia asked. "Wherever can he be?" She was enjoying this.

Artemis paced between the beds in the sleeping room. "I don't know."

Immediately after sunset he had gone over to the church area to watch the rectory for the priest's emergence. He'd wanted her to come along but her get had protested. Olivia had feigned reluctance in giving in to their wishes. In truth, she had no intention of leaving this building until she was sure the vigilantes had been identified and removed. Jules, darling Jules, had gone in her place.

"Perhaps he sneaked out a back door."

"The building has only two doors and we had both covered."

"Then he must be still inside."

"He's not!" Artemis cried. "I sneaked inside to check. He was left in the basement and he's not there now. He's not anywhere in the rectory!"

How odd, Olivia thought. "Could he have sneaked out a window then?"

"Possible, but unlikely."

"Then it must be a miracle!"

Artemis halted his pacing and glared with his good eye. "Not funny, Olivia."

"And not breaking the back of the insurrection, either. So much for Franco's coup."

"He's not going to be happy." Artemis looked worried. "And as usual he'll blame everyone but himself."

"Poor Artemis."

He took a quick step toward her, index finger raised and jabbing toward her face.

"Don't think you'll get off free, Olivia. Especially when he learns how you've been hiding under a rock the whole time."

Olivia stiffened. The last thing she needed was to be on Franco's bad side, especially when she was short on serfs.

"I'm not the enemy, Artemis," she said, wrapping it in her most conciliatory tone.

"You're certainly not acting like an ally."

"Let's think about this logically. If he's not in the rectory, then he's out of it."

Artemis rolled his single eye. "Brilliant."

"Just follow along with me. If he's out, then he got out either under his own power or was carried out."

He shook his head. "I had one of your serfs watching the building all day. If his followers had found him there'd have been an outcry and lots of milling about. But he reported no unusual activity or even interest in the rectory."

"Which leaves us with one conclusion: the priest left the rectory without being seen."

"That means he's roaming the streets right now, looking to feed." Artemis rolled his eye again. "That's not good."

"Why not? Isn't that what Franco wanted?"

"He wanted the priest feeding on his followers, not random strangers. That defeats the whole purpose of this little exercise."

Olivia couldn't help smiling. "I believe it's looking more and more like I may get my full-scale attack on the church after all."

"What you'll get," Artemis shouted, "is your lazy cowardly ass out of this hole in the ground and out there looking for him!"

Olivia backed up a step. "It's too late now. Dawn's almost here."

Artemis pounded a fist against his thigh. "All right then.

First thing after sunset. Me, you, and all your get on the street, looking. We need to find him before he goes feral. If we're too late he won't be able to tell us anything about his vigilantes."

Olivia slumped on the edge of her bed and wrung her hands. Outside? Searching? She'd never thought she'd be afraid of the night, but she was.

LACEY . . .

"What was it like being dead?"

Lacey couldn't help it. She had to ask.

After bandaging her thumb, they'd sat around for hours and hours telling their stories: what had happened to Joe after he'd been abducted, Carole telling how she'd escaped the vampire who'd been after her, and Lacey skimming over her gang rape that she couldn't remember too well anyway but describing in detail the odd events in the Post Office. No one had any explanation for what had gone down there.

Then they discussed how Joe might best wield himself against the enemy.

With all the talk, Lacey had found herself gradually getting used to the unthinkable: that her uncle had somehow died and risen from the grave without becoming one of the undead—not *quite* one of them, at least. He didn't look like himself, not with that unrecognizable, disfigured face, but the more he'd talked, the easier it became to accept that, though horribly changed, he was still his old self. The undead had changed his body, but the man within remained untouched.

And with that acceptance, the death question had grown in her mind. Now, with steely predawn light turning the black of the ocean to slate gray, the conversation had lagged. So . . .

Joe shook his head. "I don't remember."

"Are you sure? Think. Wasn't there a light or a voice or a presence or some indication that there's *something* out there?"

"Sorry, Lacey. I remember that feral biting and tearing at me, and the next thing I knew I was wrapped in a sheet under the sand. That's all. Nothing in between."

"Well, I guess that proves it then: this is it. There's no hereafter."

"Oh, but there is," Joe told her.

"You were dead and experienced nothing transcendental, so how can you say that?"

"Because I believe."

As much as she loved him—and even in the strange state he was in, Lacey still loved him—she found his resistance to reason exasperating.

"After all that's just happened to you, how can you possibly still believe in a provident god?"

Joe glanced at Carole. "Tell her, Carole."

Carole's brown eyes looked infinitely sad. "I don't think I can. God seems terribly far away these days."

The simple statement, delivered so matter-of-factly, seemed to shock Joe. He stared at Carole a moment, then sighed. "Yeah, He does, doesn't He. Almost as if He's forgotten about us. But we can't let ourselves think that way. It only leads to despair. We've got to believe that there's a purpose to all—"

"A purpose?" Lacey wanted to throw something. "What possible purpose could there be to all this worldwide death and misery?"

"Only God knows," Joe said.

Lacey snorted derisively. "Which means *nobody* knows."

Joe was looking at her. "Why did you ask me in the first place?"

"You mean, about what it was like being dead? Well, think about it: how many times do you get a chance to talk to someone who's been dead—someone who's not trying to rip out your throat, I mean?"

"Just idle curiosity?"

"Not idle. You're my uncle and I just . . . wanted to know."

"Would you have believed me if I told you I saw a light, or a golden stairway, or a glowing tunnel? Or how about pearly gates and St. Peter with the *Book of Life* in his hands?"

"Probably not."

"Then why ask at all?"

"I don't know."

"I think you do. I think you're in the market for a little transcendence yourself, just like everyone else. Am I right?"

Joe's scrutiny was making her uncomfortable.

"Just because I don't believe doesn't mean I don't *want* to. Don't you think I'd love to feel that a little spark of me will continue on into eternity after this body is gone? But I can't get past the idea that it's only wishful thinking, something we, as a sentient species, have yearned for so deeply and for so long that we've surrounded that need with all manner of myths to convince ourselves that it's real."

Joe picked up the knife Lacey had used to cut her thumb, and idly ran his finger along the edge.

"All myths have a spark of truth at their core. Look at it this way: doesn't the existence of transcendent Evil indicate that there must be a counterbalancing transcendent Good?"

"You mean the undead? I'll grant you they're evil, but they hardly strike me as transcendent."

"No?" He was staring at his finger. "I just cut myself. Take a look."

He laid his hand, palm up, on the table. His palm hadn't been exposed to the sun so it was unscarred. Lacey saw a deep slice in the pad of his index finger, but no blood.

"I don't seem to have any blood."

Lacey gasped as he jabbed the point of the blade into the center of his palm.

"Father Joe!" Carol cried.

"Uh-uh," he said, removing the knife and waving it at her. "Just Joe, remember? I'm not a priest anymore."

"Doesn't it hurt?" Lacey said.

"Not really. I feel it; it's not comfortable, but I can't call it pain." He held up his hand. "Still no blood. And yet . . ." He placed the hand over his heart. "My heart is beating. Very slowly, but beating. Why? If there's no blood to pump, why have a beating heart?" He leaned back and shook his head. "Will I ever understand this?"

"You have a better chance than anyone else," Lacey said. "Obviously something else is powering your cells, something working outside the laws of nature."

"Which would make it *super*natural. And since there's no question that it's evil . . ."

"Are we back to that again?"

Carole cleared her throat. "I hate to drag this conversation back to current reality, but there is something very important we need to discuss."

Lacey looked at her and noticed that she seemed upset. Her hands were locked together before her on the table.

"What is it, Carole?"

She stared at her hands. "Blood."

Lacey heard Joe groan. She glanced over and saw him lower his ruined face into his hands.

"What blood?" Lacey said.

Carole lifted her eyes. "The blood he needs to survive."

"Oh, that." Lacey shrugged. "He can have some of mine whenever—"

Joe slammed his hands on the table. "No!"

"Why the hell not? You had—what?—three or four drops and that was all you needed. Big deal."

"The amount is not the point! A drop, a gallon, what difference does it make? It's all the same! I'm acting like one of them—becoming a bloodsucking parasite!"

"They take it by force. I'm *giving* this to you. You don't see the difference? It's my blood and I have a right to do whatever I want with it. If I were giving a pint at a time to the Red Cross to save lives you'd say what a fine and noble thing to do. But giving a few drops to my own uncle—a *blood* relative, don't you know—is wrong?"

"Your giving isn't the issue. My taking—that's the problem."

"What problem? Since I'm volunteering, there's no ethical problem. So if it's not ethics, what is it? Esthetics?"

He stared at her. "What are you? A Jesuit?"

"I'm your niece and I care about you and I want to get the sons of bitches who did this to you. With you as you are—part undead, part human—we might have a chance to do real damage. But if you're going to let a little squeamishness get in the way—"

"Lacey!" Carole said, giving her a warning look.

Joe had closed his eyes and was shaking his head. "You have no idea what it's like . . . to have loathed these vermin and then be turned into one. To spend every minute of the rest of your existence knowing you are a lesser being than you wish to be, that everything you were has been erased and everything you hoped for or aspired to will be denied you." He opened his eyes and glared at her. "You . . . don't . . . know . . . what . . . it's . . . like."

Lacey's heart went out to her uncle. Yes, she could imagine maybe only a tiny fraction of what he was suffering, but she couldn't let him surrender. He had to fight back. She had a feeling that what they decided here tonight could be of momentous importance, and it all hinged on him. That was why she had to push him.

"I don't pretend to. But we can't turn back the clock. You've been dealt a lousy hand, Unk—an unimaginably lousy hand—but right now it's the only one you've got. And it may hold some hidden possibilities that we'll never be able to use if you fold and leave the game. I know it seems easy for me to sit here on this side of the table say it, but it's a simple truth: you have to accept what's happened and move on. Take it and turn it back on them. Use it to make them pay. Make them wish they'd never heard of Father Joe Cahill. Make them curse the day they ever messed with you. If all it takes is a few drops a day of my blood—which I'm more than willing to donate to the cause—then where's the downside? They tried to make you like them but something went wrong. They failed. You're not like them—you know it and Carole knows it and I know it—and a few drops of blood is not going to change that."

Lacey leaned back, winded. She glanced at Carole who gave a small nod, just one.

Joe seemed lost in thought. Finally he shook himself and said, "We'll see. That's all I can say now . . . we'll see." He looked out at the growing light filtering through the salt-stained picture window. "Let put this aside and go out and watch the sunrise."

JOE . . .

Lacey's words tumbled back and forth through Joe's brain as he followed the two women down to the churning water.

Accept it and move on . . .

Easy for her to say. But that didn't mean she was wrong. Yet . . . how do you accept being subhuman?

Turn it against them and make them pay . . .

That he could understand. Take this aching emptiness inside and fill the void with rage, pack it in like gunpowder in a cartridge, then take aim at those responsible for what he'd become.

Carole had called him a weapon. That was what he would become.

He joined Carole and Lacey at the waterline and stood between them. Gently he placed a hand on each of their shoulders, Carole flinching but not pulling away, Lacey leaning against him. He realized he loved them both, but in very different ways.

He noticed Carole checking her watch as the sun hauled its red bulk above the rumpled gray hide of the Atlantic. Immediately he sensed its heat, just as he'd felt the fever of the setting rays last night.

Lacey turned to him. "You're okay?"

"I can tell I'm more sensitive than I ever was in life, but it's nothing I can't tolerate."

. . . than I ever was in life . . .

How indescribably strange to be able to say that.

Lacey smiled. "Maybe we'll just have find you some SPF 2000 sun screen."

"I'm just grateful I won't have to live like them—hiding in the day and crawling out only at night. I don't know if I could take that."

They stood for a while with the waves lapping at their feet and watched the birds and the surf and spoke of how the undead plague hadn't affected the beauty of the world or touched its wildlife. Humanity had borne the full brunt of the assault.

Lacey said, "Some of my radical ecology friends, if they're still alive, probably think it's all for the good—the fall of civilization, I mean."

Carole shook her head. "How could they possibly—"

"The end of industry, of pollution, overcrowding, all that stuff they hate. No more forests being raped, no more fluorocarbons depleting the ozone, all their causes made moot because the undead don't seem to be into technology."

"Only the technology that helps them keep their 'cattle' alive. Franco went on to me about how once you've turned, your existence becomes entirely focused on blood. All the other drives—for money, knowledge, achievement, even sex—are gone. The undead are immune to cold and see in the dark so they have no interest in keeping the electricity running except as far as their cattle need it to survive. Even so, I'll bet the power will be off more than it's on. Over time I can see the level of technology declining and the world devolving into some sort of pre-industrial-level feudal order. They don't seem to need technology. Or perhaps have no mind for it is better way of putting it. They already call their human helpers 'serfs.' That will be the social order: undead lords, serfs, and herds of human cattle."

"If only the Internet were still around," Lacey said. "We could communicate, organize—"

"The Internet is history, I'm afraid—with no reliable power source, few working phone lines, and a decimated server network, it's a goner."

Joe felt his skin beginning to tingle, as if the sand were blowing, but there was no breeze. He glanced at the sun and thought it looked considerably brighter than a few moments ago. Hotter too.

"Is anyone else hot?"

Carole and Lacey shook their heads.

"No, not really," Carole said.

Lacey spread her arms and lifted her face to the glow. "It feels good."

"Does anyone mind if we go back inside? It's a little too warm for me."

He turned and started back up the dunes; Carole and Lacey came along, one on either side. As they neared the house, Joe felt his exposed sunward skin—the back of his neck, his arms, his calves—begin to heat up, as much from within as without.

With the growing discomfort pushing him toward the house, he quickened his pace. Or tried to. He felt unsteady. His legs wobbled like an old man's—a drunken eighty-year-old's. Still he somehow managed to pull ahead of Carole and Lacey.

"Unk!" Lacey cried from behind him. "Unk, your skin!"

He looked down and saw that his skin was starting to smoke wherever the direct rays of the sun touched it. He broke into a lurching run.

The sun! Cooking him! Had to escape it, find shade, shelter, darkness! The very air seemed to catch fire around him, glowing with white-hot intensity. A heartbeat ago the house had been less than a hundred feet ahead, now he couldn't find it through the blaze of light. And even if he could he doubted he'd reach it on these leaden legs. His knees weakened further and he stumbled, but felt a pair of hands grab his left arm before he could fall.

"We've got to get him inside!" Carole cried close to his ear.

Other hands grabbed his right arm.

Lacey. Carole. They had him and were supporting him, tugging him forward on his rubbery legs.

They burst through the broken door and into the shady interior.

But even inside the sunlight pursued him through the doorway and sizzled through the big picture window, chased him like a fiery predator, reaching for him with flaming talons of light. He shook off Carole and Lacey and stumbled headlong on into the deeper, shadier areas of the front room.

Not enough. The reflected sunlight, from the glass table top, even the walls and floors, felt toxic, like scalding acid.

More—he needed more protection. No basements in these bungalows. He spotted the alcove to his right and veered for it. The bedrooms. He barreled into the one toward the rear. It faced north and west—the darkest place in the house at the moment. His legs finally gave way and he collapsed in a heap next to the bed. Thank God the curtains were closed. He grabbed the flowered yellow bedspread and rolled it around him, cocooning himself with the stench of his own seared flesh.

The touch of the fabric against his scorched skin sent waves of agony to his bones, but stronger than the pain was the numbing lethargy seeping through his limbs and mind. Only fear kept him from succumbing, fear that his tolerance to sunlight had been only temporary and now was deserting him. Was it a sign that whatever remnants of humanity that had lingered with him last night were ebbing away, leaving him more like the creatures he loathed? He prayed not.

He prayed especially that he wasn't turning feral. He saw the creature's ravaged face now, the one Franco had called Devlin, remembered its mad eyes, devoid of reason, compassion, or any feeling even remotely human, heard its bestial screams as it clawed at the door, remembered its talons sinking into his shoulders, felt its hot foul breath on his throat just before its fangs tore into his flesh.

And worse, he remembered Franco's parting words.

. . . when you look at Devlin you are seeing your future . . . he didn't retain enough intelligence to distinguish between friend and foe . . . so I can't even use him as a guard dog . . . in less than two weeks you'll be just like Devlin, only a little less intelligent, a little more bestial . . .

Was he losing his mind along with his tolerance for sunlight? Was his descent incomplete, still in progress? Was he still changing, devolving further into an even lower life form? Was this another step down the road toward Devlin's fate?

He heard Carole's voice from somewhere in the room.

"Joseph! Joseph, are you all right?"

He could only nod under the bedspread, and even that was an effort. He dared not speak, even if his numb lips would permit it.

"The mattress!" Carole's voice again. "Help me with it."

"Help—help you what?" Lacey said.

"We've got to tilt it up against the window. That way when the sun comes around behind the house it won't shine into the room."

Carole . . . wonderful Carole . . . always thinking . . .

The lethargy deepened, tugging Joe toward sleep, or something like it . . . the deathlike undead daysleep. He tried to fight it. He'd thought, he'd hoped that he'd escaped falling victim to the undead vermin hours, hiding from the sun, slithering around at night. Now that hope was lost. He was more like them than he'd thought or wished or prayed against, and was falling closer and closer to their foul state with every passing hour.

The nightmarish thought chased him into oblivion.

CAROLE . . .

"We almost lost him."

The two of them slumped on the front room's rattan furniture, Carole in a chair, Lacey half stretched out on the sofa.

"I know," Carole replied.

Oh, how she knew. That had been too close. Her insides were still shaking. The sight of his skin starting to smoke and cook as he was walking . . . caused by this same sunlight bathing her now in its warmth . . . she'd never forget it. Worse, the reek of his burnt flesh still hung in the air.

Lacey kicked at the cocktail table, almost knocking its glass top onto the floor. "I don't know what to say, I don't know what to think, I don't know what to do! This is just so awful. It's a nightmare!"

Carole looked down at her trembling hands. How things had changed. Early last evening she'd been ready to drive a stake through his heart. And now she wanted him to survive.

For as the three of them had talked during the dark hours, Carole had begun to sense a plan. Not her plan . . . the Lord's. She thought about all the twists and turns of the past thirty-six hours.

After leaving her partially demolished house, why had she turned left instead of right? If she'd turned the other way she never would have run into Lacey. It was because of Lacey that she'd returned to the church and the convent. And it was there that she'd been staring out her convent room window just at the instant a winged vampire had flown away from the rectory. There were so many other things she could have been doing at that moment, yet she'd been standing at the window, watching the night. She'd been holding Father—no, he doesn't want to be called "Father" anymore . . . a hard habit to break—*Joseph's* cross at that moment. Had that inspired her?

Imagine if she hadn't seen the departing vampire. She

wouldn't have searched the rectory basement and found Joseph's body. But what had inspired her to bring him to the beach? At the time she'd thought it a good place because it was deserted and they could dig more quickly in the sand.

But had Divine Inspiration been at work? For if they'd tried to bury Joseph somewhere besides the beach, he wouldn't have been exposed to the first rays of the morning sun. That brief exposure seemed to have partially undone the vampires' work. The purifying rays had healed his wound and burned away some of the undead taint. Not all— a few more minutes in the light surely would have burned away too much, leaving him truly dead—but enough so that he remained Joseph instead of something foul and evil. What had inspired Carole to pull him into the shadows of his grave just in time to save him?

Yes . . . save him. For what?

The only answer that made any sense was that Joseph had been chosen to become the mailed fist of God, a divine weapon against the undead.

But the poor man was going through the tortures of the damned to become that weapon. Pain, disfigurement, self-loathing, the debasement of blood hunger—why did it have to be this way? Why did he have to suffer so? Were these trials a fire through which he had to pass to be tempered as a weapon?

The thought of fire brought her back to the sun . . .

"How long was Joseph in the sunlight this morning?"

Lacey shrugged. "I don't know. An hour maybe? It's hard to say. Certainly no more than that."

"An hour," Carole mused. "Not much. That's an hour longer than any true vampire can stand, but maybe it's enough."

"Enough for what?"

"For the war the three of us are going to wage."

She placed her hand over the spot where Joseph had touched her shoulder at sunrise. More than an hour ago but her skin still tingled, as if his hand were still resting there.

That single touch, that gentle weight of his hand on her shoulder, meant more to her than his embrace outside the church when they'd been reunited a few nights ago.

Despite what had been done to him and how the sun had disfigured him, despite what he had become, she sensed the desperate struggle within him against the undead taint in his flesh, in his mind, in his being, and she admired him more than ever for that refusal to be dominated. He'd win, she knew he would win.

God help her, she still loved him. More than ever.

JOE . . .

He awoke in a snap. No lingering drowsiness, no stretching or yawning. Asleep, then awake, with tentacles of a dream still clinging to him.

The dream . . . more like a nightmare—or in this case, a daymare. He remembered clinging to the lip of a rocky precipice, his feet dangling and kicking over an infinity of swirling darkness. But not empty darkness. This seemed alive, and it had been beckoning him, calling to him all day . . .

The worst thing was that a part of him had longed to answer, tried to convince the rest of him to let go and tumble into that living abyss.

He shook off the memory and pushed at the fabric enshrouding him. After an instant of panicked déjà-vu—had he been buried again?—he remembered rolling himself in the bedspread this morning. He pulled his way free and found himself on the floor of the rear bedroom. The room was hot, stuffy, and dusty, but not dark. He lifted his head. Over the naked top of the double box spring he saw its mattress tilted against the west window. Orange sunlight leaked around its edges. The sun was setting but not down yet.

Not down yet . . .

A sudden surge of excitement pushed him to his feet. He stepped closer to the mattress, surprised at not feeling stiff and sore after a whole day on wooden flooring. A ray of sunlight, dust motes swirling like fireflies along its path, was poking past the right edge to light up a square on the room's east wall. Hesitantly, Joe edged his hand toward the ray. This could hurt. This could be like sticking his hand into a pot of boiling water.

He gritted his teeth. Hell, what was he waiting for? Fast or slow, if he was going to burn, he was going to burn.

He shot his hand forward and back, in and out of the ray. It felt hot but nothing like boiling water. He looked at his palm where the sun had licked it. No blisters. Not even red.

He tried it again, this time holding his hand in the light. Hot, but bearable. Definitely bearable.

Taking a breath, he tipped the mattress back, letting the light flood into the room and bathe him. He gasped at the sudden blast of heat and squinted in the brightness, but held his ground. He could do this. Yeah, he could do this.

With jubilation spurring him, he hurried out into the front room where he found Carole asleep on the couch. He stopped and stared down at her, captivated. Her face in sleep had relaxed into a soft, gentle innocence, as if the last few months had never happened. This was the Carole he'd known. He wanted to wake her but couldn't bring himself to break the spell.

He stepped back to the alcove and peeked in the front bedroom. Lacey lay huddled under the covers.

Okay, let them both sleep.

Back to the front room where he slipped as quietly as possible through the broken door and out into the light. He walked a few steps north to where sunlight gushed between the bungalow and its neighbor. He bathed in its flow, spread his arms and dared it to harm him.

"Joseph? Are you all right?"

Carole's voice. He turned and saw her approaching across the boards. Her features hadn't yet fully recomposed themselves into their harder, waking look. He wanted to throw his arms around her but knew that would be a mistake.

"Yes. Fine. At least for now. How long till sunset do you think?"

She glanced at her watch. "It set at 7:11 yesterday, so—"

"Are you sure? I seem to remember the sun setting later than that in May."

Carole shrugged. "I guess I never got around to switching to Daylight Savings Time. Not much point, is there."

"I guess not. So you keep a log?"

"In my head. It's very important to know when the sun is going to be around and when it's not."

Of course it was. And he should have known that a former science teacher like Sister Carole would be methodical as all hell about it.

"When does it set tonight?"

"About a minute later. Around forty-five minutes from now." She looked up from her watch. "You seem to be able to tolerate the first and last hours of sunlight."

"Why is that, do you think?"

"It may be due to your sun exposure before you turned. Maybe it burned some of the undead taint out of you, leaving you tolerant to the more attenuated rays of the sun."

"Attenuated?"

"As it nears the horizon, the sun's rays have to travel through more layers of atmosphere to reach you. Those extra layers absorb and refract the light. It's that same refraction that causes the sun and moon to look darker and larger when they're low in the sky."

"Well, thank you, God, for refraction." He was glad he didn't have to face the prospect of never seeing the sun again.

"Then again," Carole said, a faint smile playing about her lips, "refraction may have nothing to do with it, and you should be thanking God directly."

"Why?"

"Maybe He's given you these extra two hours as an edge over the undead. Two hours during which you can move about while they can't."

Joe thought about that. Two hours . . . if he was going to make a strike against the undead, those two hours offered the perfect windows. He didn't know about God Himself arranging this, but he knew a good thing when he saw it. He was not going to waste this advantage.

"I like the way you think, Carole. But first we need an agenda. And the first thing on that agenda should be contacting the church and letting those people know I'm still alive."

"But you can't let them see you like this, or let them know you—"

"Absolutely not. We'll have to think of something that'll keep them together and fighting on without me. Because I'll be fighting my own war. I want to take the fight to the undead, get in their faces and hit them where it will really hurt: New York."

Yes. Franco. He wanted to see that smug son of a bitch again—and when he did, it would be on *his* terms, not Franco's.

"What's this about 'my' war?" Lacey said. Joe turned to see her standing behind them, rubbing her eyes. "This is our fight too, Unk."

He smiled. "I could use the help, but . . ."

The thought of either of these two precious people getting hurt because of him . . . he couldn't go there.

"But what?" Lacey said. "You're afraid we'll get killed or something? I figure we're as good as dead if we do nothing, so we might as well go down doing something. Better than sitting on our asses and waiting for the ax to fall."

Carole rolled her eyes. "You have such a way with words."

Lacey shrugged. "Am I right or am I right?"

Joe had to admit she was right. He faced the reddened, swollen sun as it neared the rooftops. He could look at it now, and it barely heated his skin.

"Okay then," he said. "But we'll have to run this like a military operation."

"Does that mean you want to be made general?" Lacey said through another yawn.

"No. Carole's the most experienced. She should be our general."

Carole waved her hands. "Oh, no. Not me."

Lacey squinted at him. "You know much about military operations?"

"Not a thing. But I figure we need reconnaissance and intelligence. And most of all, we need to practice before we head for New York."

Lacey nodded. "Sort of like an out-of-town tryout before hitting Broadway, right?"

"Right. And I think the local nests can provide just the sort of rehearsals we'll need."

LACEY . . .

"We have to tell the parishioners *something*," Joe said. "Any ideas?"

Lacey watched him, looking for the first signs of what she knew must come. They were back in the bungalow, seated around the cocktail table in the same places as last night. A single candle set on the glass top lit their faces.

"Why don't we tell them the truth?" Carole said.

Lacey shook her head. "This is one case where the truth shall not set them free. Besides, it's too . . . complicated."

"How about a form of the truth?" Joe said. "We'll tell them that the vampires attacked me, tried to turn me, but failed. I survived but I'm badly hurt. I need time to recover and until I do . . . until I'm back to my old self"—which will be never, he thought grimly—"I've got to stay out of sight."

"Right," Lacey said, liking the idea. "You're in hiding until you heal up because they're out there looking for you, trying to finish the job they started."

"Works for me," Joe said. "How about you, Carole?"

"Well . . ." She frowned. "It's not exactly true."

"But it's not exactly false," he said.

She shrugged. "I've no objection, but if I were in their place I'd be wondering why you wouldn't want to heal up among them . . . safety in numbers and all that."

Joe didn't answer. All of a sudden he seemed distracted. Lacey watched his right hand trail down to his abdomen and press on it.

Her heart sank. The hunger . . . it was starting.

She force-fed brightness into her tone. "We'll just say that you feel it's safer to stay away. Your presence there might trigger an assault on the church, causing unnecessary casualties. When you're fully healed you'll return. But till then they must be brave and vigilant and keep up the fight, blah-blah-blah."

Joe nodded absently, both hands over his stomach now. "Good . . . sounds good."

Carole said, "Then the next question is, how do we get this message to them?"

Lacey kept her eyes on her uncle. "How about a letter, hand written by their Father Joe himself? You and I could 'find' it and read it to the parishioners."

Carole shook her head. "They don't know his handwriting. Some of them will think it's a fake. Doubt will spread, ruining the whole plan."

Carole was right. Lacey searched for an alternative. She thought of having Joe sneak up to the church at night and speak from the shadows to someone he trusted—Carl, maybe—but discarded the idea. Too chancy. Too many ways it could backfire, especially if anyone caught sight of his ruined face. They'd think he was an impostor.

Then it came to her, so obvious she kicked herself for not thinking of it immediately.

"We'll tape you! All we need is to get hold of a little cassette recorder and have you record your message. We leave it at the church for someone to find. It'll have a note saying it's from you. They'll play it and recognize your voice. No doubters then."

Carole nodded. "Brilliant. I know a Radio Shack not far from here that ought to have a cassette recorder."

Lacey looked at Joe. His teeth were clenched. He didn't seem to be listening. She grabbed the flashlight and headed for the bathroom. Not that there was any water pressure in the town's system to make the bathroom useful for its intended functions, but she needed to be away from Carole. She placed the flashlight on the glass shelf under the medicine cabinet . . . next to the steak knife she'd left here earlier just for this purpose.

Picking up the knife, she called, "Uncle Joe? Could you come in here a sec?"

When she heard him approaching, she bit her lip and sliced the pad of her left index finger. She jumped with the pain, almost dropping the knife.

Damn, that hurt!

She placed the knife in the sink and cupped her right hand under the finger.

"Something wrong?" Joe said as he came up behind her.

"Close the door, will you?"

When she heard it close she turned and held her bloody finger up to his lips. "Here," she whispered. "I know you need it."

He turned his head and stepped back. "No!"

Lacey stepped closer. "I thought we settled this last night!" she hissed. "This is something you need and something I want to give. Don't do this, Unk. I'm already cut and bleeding." She pushed her finger toward his mouth. "Take what you need."

With a groan he grabbed her hand and pressed her finger to his lips. He sucked hungrily for an instant, then pushed her hand away.

"Enough!" The word sounded as if it had been ripped from deep inside him.

"You're sure?"

He looked away and nodded. "Look . . . I'm going out. I need to do some reconnoitering, see if I can locate a nest or two."

"Want us to come along?" She opened the medicine cabinet and found a tin of Band-Aids.

He shook his head. "Better if I do this alone. I'll be less noticeable solo." He glanced at her, then away again. "Lend me the car keys."

"Carole has them."

"Can you get them for me?"

"Just ask—"

"Please?"

Lacey bit back a remark. She wrapped a Band-Aid around her finger and returned to the front room.

"Is everything all right?" Carole asked. Her eyes darted from Lacey's face, to her bandaged finger then to her eyes again.

"He needs the car to go hunt up some targets. Where are the keys?"

Carole fished them out of her sweatsuit pants pocket. "Alone?"

"He thinks it'll be better that way."

Lacey took the keys back to the bathroom. "I don't understand you," she whispered. "I thought we straightened this out last night."

"We didn't." His voice was barely audible. "I said we'd see."

"Okay. We've seen. And it was quick and simple. Now tell me, why wouldn't you get keys yourself?"

"Because . . . because Carole's in there. One look at me and she'd know."

"So?"

"Let's just drop it."

"No. Tell me."

"Because . . . because I can't bear being in her presence after doing this. I feel so . . . so *diminished*." He squeezed her hand. "Got to go."

You poor, poor man, she thought, staring at him. You've got it bad, don't you. And this is tearing you apart.

He squeezed past her and stepped into the front room. He turned right, heading for the rear of the bungalow.

"Good-bye, Carole," he said in a choked voice without looking at her. "I'll be back around sunrise."

Lacey leaned against the sink until she heard the back door open and close, then she returned to the front room.

"Carole," she said. "We've got to talk."

JOE . . .

Standing in the deep moon shadows, he watched the church from afar, listened to the hymns echoing from within, saw the daylight-bright glow gushing through the open front doors, and yearned to go inside.

But that was not to be. The huge crucifix hanging over the sanctuary and the dozens of crosses on the walls—crosses he'd helped fashion with his own hands—would blind him now, make his presence there an ongoing agony. That part of his life was over. The simple comfort of kneeling in a pew and letting the cool serenity of the church ease the cares and tensions from his soul would be forever denied him. And as for saying Mass . . .

The longing pushed a sob to the back of his throat but he forced it down. In his other existence he might have felt tears running down his cheeks, but they remained dry. The undead don't have tears. Their hair doesn't grow. They don't progress or regress, they simply are.

He was about to turn away when movement to his right caught his eye. His night vision picked out a figure—balding, with a ripe gut bulging over his belt—leaning behind a tree.

Joe, it seemed, wasn't the only one watching the church.

He bent into a crouch and moved a few yards closer. He caught the flash of a Vichy earring.

Not surprising that the undead would want to keep an eye on the church. They had to be furious and more than a little unsettled by these defiant "cattle."

With a start Joe realized that they might be watching for him.

Of course. Franco had expected him to rise from the dead in the rectory and start feeding on the parishioners. He must know by now that that hadn't happened. He'd want to know why. Never in a thousand years would he guess the truth.

Franco had to be baffled. His beautiful plan had gone awry. More than awry, it had gone bust. He had to be furious.

Joe cradled the thought, letting it warm him, feeling the best he'd felt all night.

He found a place between a couple of waist-high shrubs where he could watch the watcher without being seen. He settled onto the ground. Despite his lightweight shirt and shorts, the damp earth and cool breeze didn't chill him. He felt perfectly comfortable. Extremes of temperature didn't seem to bother him.

What else wouldn't bother him? He had much to learn about, this new existence, this altered body he'd be wearing into the future.

The future . . . what did that mean anymore? How long could he exist? Would he go on indefinitely like the true undead? And beyond that hazy future, what of his salvation? What of his soul? Did he still have one?

The possibility jolted him. What if his soul had departed after Devlin had torn him up? Was he an empty vessel now, marked and doomed to wander the earth like Cain, offensive to the sight of God and man?

Joe shifted his gaze to the dark blotch of the graveyard to the left of the church. He could almost pick out Zev's grave among the shadows.

Zev, he thought. Where are you, old friend?

How he wished he were here tonight, sitting beside him. He longed for the comfort of his wit, the honed edge of his Talmudic intellect. He wouldn't have answers, but he'd know the questions to ask, and together they might come to understand this, or at least find a path toward understanding.

Here, on his own, would he ever understand what he'd become? Was there anyone else like him on earth? He doubted it. He was sui generis.

The quote, *Alone and afraid in a world he never made*, trailed through his head. Whoever wrote that hadn't been thinking of Joe Cahill, but could have been.

Joe watched the watcher through the night. When the sky started to lighten, the Vichy slunk away from the tree and started walking south. Pistol in hand, the man kept to the center of the street, looking wary. Dear Carole, all on her own, had filled their rotten hearts with terror.

Joe paralleled his path, traveling through the backyards of the deserted houses lining the street, catching only occasional glimpses of him between the buildings, but that was enough.

Although Joe's was a much more difficult route, hopping fences and ducking through hedges, he felt no sense of exertion. He wasn't even breathing hard.

He stopped as he realized with a start that he wasn't breathing at all. He had to take in air in order to talk, but otherwise he didn't need to breathe. No blood, no respiration—what was powering his body? He didn't know, might never know.

He'd lost ground on the Vichy and hurried to catch up. The task of tailing him became dicier as he entered the business district. Too open, with no cover. Joe had to settle for huddling in a doorway and watching him. After what Lacey had told him about her abduction, he had a good idea of where the man was headed.

Sure enough, the Vichy stopped before the Post Office where he met with another pair of his kind.

And then, out of the shadows, a group of undead, seven males and a female, appeared as a group. Joe couldn't make out their faces from this distance. He couldn't hear their words, either, but he saw a lot of shaking heads and tense, unhappy postures.

He was more sure now than ever that they'd been searching for him.

With the arrival of another trio of Vichy, the first three left. The second three took up guard positions as all eight undead trudged up the Post Office steps. Joe noticed that six of the males clustered around the female while a lone male brought up the rear. Something familiar about that solitary figure, but Joe couldn't place it.

No time to think about it either. He broke into a run. Dawn was coming and he had to race the sun to the beach.

10

CAROLE . . .

Soon.

Carole sat on the bungalow's tiny rear deck and watched the sun's lazy fall toward the horizon. A beautiful end to the day. She might have enjoyed it but for the adrenaline buzzing through her.

A good day . . . as good as could be expected. In these times, a good day was when nothing unusually ugly occurred.

Joseph had made it home just after sunrise. Before dropping into a deathlike sleep in the rear bedroom, he'd spoken into the cassette recorder Carole and Lacey had looted from the Radio Shack.

Was it really looting? she wondered. Did taking something from a store that was never going to reopen make you a looter? It seemed like a silly thing to worry about, but she did.

When Carole had asked Lacey what she thought, she'd replied, "Who gives a shit?"

Maybe Carole needed to adopt more of that attitude.

Carole had returned to the church this morning and, when no one was watching, left the recorder on the front steps. It seemed to take forever, but eventually someone found it and played it for the congregation.

Cheers and tears—that was the only way Carole could describe the reaction. At least initially. It took a while for the anger to set in, but when it came it was fierce. The undead and their collaborators had tried to turn their Father Joe. A craven, cowardly, backstabbing act. The anger bound the parishioners even more closely. They'd stay on and fight harder. To the death if need be.

Carole tried to draw strength from the memory of their boisterous resolve. For soon she would have to do what she and Lacey had discussed. Part of her hummed with anticipation while an equal part recoiled.

Joseph had awakened a short while ago. He and Lacey were inside, talking. The indistinguishable murmur of their voices drifted through the open glass door, mixing with the thrum of the waves and the calls of the gulls.

Her heart kicked up its tempo as their voices faded. That meant that they were heading for the front bedroom.

Soon . . . too soon . . .

"Okay."

Carole jumped and turned at the sound of Lacey's voice.

"Now?"

How inane. Of course now. That was why Lacey was here. Carole rose unsteadily. Did she have the nerve for this?

Lacey pressed the steak knife into her hand. "He's waiting."

Carole nodded, took the knife, and headed for the bedroom. When she reached the alcove she hesitated. She wiped a sweaty palm on the pants of her sweatsuit, then forced herself forward.

I can do this, she thought. I must do this.

Joe was sitting on the bed, head down, hands clasped between his knees, looking like a man on death row. He didn't look up as she entered.

"Okay," he said, his voice hoarse. "Let's get this over—" He must have sensed something. His head snapped up. "Carole? Sorry. I was expecting Lacey."

Her tongue felt like flannel. "It won't be Lacey today."

Before he could understand, before he could protest, Carole clenched her teeth and jabbed the point of the knife into the center of her palm. She suppressed a gasp of pain as the blade pierced her skin.

"No!" Joseph was on his feet. "No, don't!"

"It's already done," she said.

"Carole, I can't." He backed away a step. "Not you."

She held out her hand, cupping her palm to hold the pooling blood.

"Yes. Me. It's only fair. I don't want to be left out."

That wasn't quite the way Lacey had put it last night after Joseph had left so abruptly. She'd said that if the three of them were going to work together, be a team, then they'd have to act and feel like a team. "One for all and all for one, and all that shit," she'd said.

Which meant they had to feel at ease with each other, and that would never happen unless someone broke through the wall of shame that had sprung up between Carole and her uncle. Joseph couldn't do it. Only Carole had the power.

Lacey had known one sure way for Carole to break through. It was radical, she'd warned, something her uncle would balk at—and Carole wouldn't be too crazy about it either—but it had to be done.

Joseph was shaking his head, his mouth working but saying nothing. She could read no expression in his scarred face, but his eyes looked terrified.

Still cupping her hand, Carole sat on the bed. She placed the knife beside her and tugged on his sleeve.

"Sit, Joseph," she said. "You've given so much, had so much stolen from you, let me give something *to* you."

"No!"

"Why will you take it from Lacey but not from me? Do you think there's something wrong with my blood?"

"No, of course not."

"They why not me?"

"Because . . ." He shook his head.

"Please don't reject me." She felt a thickness in her throat, heard a catch in her voice. "I couldn't bear it if you turned me away."

Joseph must have heard it too. He slumped next to her. "Carole . . . you don't have to do this."

"I do. I want to."

That hadn't been quite true when she'd stepped into the room, but now, this close to him, feeling his anguish, she wanted to be part of this, she wanted this bond, terrible as it was.

She held her cupped palm beneath his chin.

"Please?"

With a groan Joseph bent his head and pressed his lips against her palm. A shiver ran through her as his tongue swirled against her skin.

So close . . . she'd never dreamed they'd be this close.

Carole felt him swallow, then with a sob he pushed her hand away and sagged against her, resting his head on her thighs, facing away.

"Oh, Carole, I'm so sorry. So sorry."

She made a fist over her cut palm to stanch the bleeding. Her other hand rose of its own accord, hovered over his head for a few heartbeats, then dropped and began stroking his hair.

"You have nothing to apologize for, Joseph," she said softly. "This was not your choosing. It's not your fault."

He said nothing. For a moment she feared he might rise and leave the room, but he didn't move.

She said, "You almost told me why you didn't want to take my blood. You got as far as 'Because.' Can you tell me the rest?"

"Because . . ." He took a breath. "Because I love you."

She gasped, her hand recoiling from him as if it had been burned.

Joseph began to lift his head. "I'm sorry. I shouldn't have—"

"No—no," she said, gently pushing his head back down. "Don't move." She couldn't let him see her face right now, for she knew her heart must be shining in her eyes. "It's all right. It's . . . it's . . ."

The intoxicating feelings bursting through her . . . she'd never felt anything like this before. It was indescribable. Her words dried up and blew away like dead leaves.

I love you . . . had he really said that?

"It's wonderful," she managed.

"I'm not talking about love as for a fellow human being. I'm saying that I love you as a woman."

"All the more wonderful," she said. "Because I've felt the same way about you."

Now his head shot up and she couldn't stop it. He stared at her, mouth agape. "What?"

She could only nod. She felt tears brimming her eyelids and didn't trust herself to speak.

"That can't be," he said.

She nodded again and forced the words past the swelling in her throat. "I was taken with you the day you arrived to replace Father McMann. And as I came to know you, I came to love you."

"You mean 'loved,' don't you."

"No. I still do. More than ever."

He looked away. "You can't. That man is gone."

She touched his scarred cheek. "No. He's been changed, but he's not gone. He's still there, inside. I feel him when you're near, I hear him when you speak."

"Maybe he's there now, but I don't know much longer you can count on him being around."

"I have faith in you."

"I appreciate that, Carole but . . . I've been having a dream, the same dream yesterday and today. Hanging from a precipice over this swirling darkness that's calling to me, beckoning to me."

"But—"

He held up a hand. "I know what you're going to say, but this doesn't feel symbolic. This feels real. It bothers me that part of me wants to let go and fall into that abyss. But that's all right. I think I can handle that. What bothers me more is there's no sense of light above me trying to draw me the other way. Only the darkness below."

"I don't understand."

"Where's the balance? The darkness seems to be in control with nothing opposing it. Nothing but us."

"God is out there, Joseph, working through us."

"Not working too well, I'd say. Look what's happened to me."

She wanted to tell him that what had happened to him might be all part of God's plan, but held back. Now was not the time.

He shook his head. "All those years at St. Anthony's . . . you loving me, I loving you, *longing* for you, and neither of us knew. Imagine if things had been different . . . what a team we'd have made, Carole."

"We're a team now, at least part of one."

"Yes, but the possibilities . . . all gone now." He laid his head back on her thighs. "Gone for good."

She began stroking his hair again. "We're together now."

"But look what it took for us to find out how we felt about each other. You've been through a living hell since Easter week, and I . . . I'm not even human anymore."

"I don't care what you are. I know *who* you are."

After a while he said, "Sex is out of the question, you know."

"Yes. We both still have our vows."

"I don't mean that. I mean . . . one of the changes in me . . . one of the things they stole from me . . . I don't think I ever can."

Carole said nothing. It didn't matter.

They stayed this way a long time, Joseph lying still against her thighs, Carole stroking his hair, soothing him, murmur-

ing to him. In the world outside the horror still raged all
about them, but here, in this moment, in this place, she'd
found a sliver of peace, the closest to heaven she'd ever been.

CAROLE . . .

Lacey burst out laughing. She couldn't help it.

Joe glanced up from where he sat across from her at the
little dining room table. "What's so funny?"

"I was just thinking what a cozy little domestic scene this
is. Here's Papa Joe, sharpening stakes to drive through undead hearts. There's Momma Carole at the sink mixing up a
batch of napalm. And here's baby Lacey cleaning her 9mm
pistols." She laughed again. "We're the new nuclear family!"

Carole turned from the sink where she was stirring a
strange mix with a large wooden spoon, and gave her a wry
smile. "Nuclear . . . there's a thought."

"No, Carole," Joe said. "Don't go there."

What a change in Carole and Joe. Their meeting in the
bedroom had transformed them. They'd come out leaning
close to each other. Lacey wouldn't have been surprised if
they started holding hands, but they didn't. Joe seemed so
much more at ease in her presence, and Carole . . . well, Carole positively glowed.

All because of me, Lacey thought. Did I have the situation
and solution nailed or what? Am I brilliant or am I brilliant?

After Joe had fed, they went their separate ways. Joe took
the car to Lakewood to work out a plan of attack on the Post
Office. Carole walked down to the abandoned business district on Arnold Avenue to do what she termed some "shopping." Lacey hoped that neither of them ran into Vichy along
the way.

Her own job was simpler. Armed with a makeshift siphon,
she'd been assigned the task of finding gasoline.

That had proved a cinch. Her first stop had been the

garage behind the bungalow where she discovered an old Ford convertible with a full tank. She found a dusty five-gallon gas can, probably for a motorboat, and filled that.

Carole returned later with a shopping cart loaded with boxes of different brands of soap flakes, some lighter fluid, plus a bag of sundries from a party supply shop. She immediately set up in the kitchen and went to work filling the house with fumes.

Lacey held up one of the 9mm rounds and showed it to Joe.

"Look at this. Hollow point. They're all hollow points."

Joe shook his head. "Nasty things. I hear they make a little hole going in and a great big hole coming out."

"Why would the undead be carrying automatics loaded with these?"

"To protect against humans, I imagine," Joe said. "They're strong, they're fast, but that's not enough if they're attacked by a mob." He pointed to the round. "That's probably what the Vichy will be using against us this morning—if they get the chance."

"Let's go over the plan again," Lacey said.

She wasn't crazy about it. As much as she respected her uncle's intelligence, he'd had no military training, had never engaged in any sort of violent activity. Lacey had at least studied martial arts. That wasn't much, but it had trained her on how to size up an opponent, how to look for strategic openings. Joe's plan seemed to depend on too many variables.

"Okay," Joe said. "The Vichy guards spend most of their time hanging around on the front steps. When they're not smoking they're sleeping. They're bored and don't take their job seriously. No one's ever attacked them on duty like that and they probably think no one ever will. We're going to change that."

"Hitting them at dawn I understand, but why napalm? Why don't we just shoot them?"

"Because we're not marksmen—or, excuse me, markswomen—and we can't afford a protracted gun battle because my clock will be running. If they hold out past my sun tolerance, we'll have lost more than the battle. We won't be able to take them by surprise again. But more than that, the more bullets flying, the greater chance of you or Carole getting hit."

"But how do we know the napalm will work?"

Joe's idea was for the three of them to climb to the roof of the building across the street and each toss a napalm-filled balloon onto the Vichy as they lounged on the Post Office steps below. The street wasn't wide and it was an easy throw from the roof. Or so he said.

"Oh, it will work," Carole said from the sink. "Have no fear of that."

"But it has to ignite."

"We'll make sure one of them's smoking before we toss."

"That doesn't guarantee it will light."

Joe leaned back, staring at her. For a moment she thought he was angry but couldn't be sure. So hard to gauge emotions when a face has no expression.

"You're right," he said finally. "It doesn't." He turned toward the kitchen. "Do we have any gasoline left, Carole?"

"A little. Why?"

"Save half a dozen ounces or so. We're going to bring along a Molotov cocktail." He turned back to Lacey. "Better?"

"You mean throw that first, then the napalm?"

He nodded.

"Yeah," Lacey said. "That'll work."

JOE . . .

"Oh, no!" Joe said as he heard a thwacking noise and the car began to vibrate. He slammed a fist against the steering wheel. "Damn!"

They'd left an hour before dawn. The plan had been to loop north of Lakewood through Howell and approach downtown from the west. They were on Aldrich Road when the noise began.

"What's wrong?" Carole said. She sat next to him in the front, Lacey sat in the rear with the arsenal.

"Can you believe it? We've got a flat!"

He popped the trunk and jumped out. Of all times for something like this to happen.

"Can't we drive on the rim?" Carole said.

"Any other time I'd say fine, but we can't risk the racket it will make."

He lifted the trunk lid and was relieved to find the spare present and inflated.

Nearly half an hour later they were rolling again.

"That took too long," Carole said. "Maybe we should put this off till tomorrow."

She's probably right, Joe thought. What's another day?

But something inside wouldn't allow him to agree. He was primed and ready for a little payback. More than ready—*aching*.

"Let's see how things look," he said. "If we can't do it the way we planned, we'll call it off."

He looked at Carole and wanted to take her hand. He couldn't believe it. All these years she'd been as attracted to him as he'd been to her, and neither of them had had a clue. How sad, he thought. And how wonderful to be past that now.

They reached Lakewood just as the sun was rising. They parked two blocks from the business district and lugged their milk crate full of bottles, balloons, and guns between the buildings until they wound up in an alley across the street and half a block up from the Post Office. The three-man Vichy day shift was on the job, so to speak, smoking and lounging on the steps. One of them sat near a shotgun that leaned against a wall; the other two had holstered pistols.

Carole was looking at her watch. "We'll have to call it off. By the time we carry all this stuff up to the roof and start the attack"—she looked up at Joe—"it will be too late for you."

Joe looked at the brightening sky. Damn. She was right.

"All right. Let's head back to the car and—"

"Wait," Lacey said. "Give me a minute here."

"For what?" Joe said.

Her jaw was set and her eyes had gone flat and cold. She worked the slide on one of her pistols and stuck it into the waistband of her jeans at the small of her back.

"Lacey?"

Before Joe could stop her she stepped out onto the sidewalk and began walking toward the Vichy. He wanted to call her back but didn't dare reveal himself. With the sun lighting her back, she moved briskly, hips swaying, arms swinging at her sides. Joe could only peek around the corner and pray.

She was halfway to the Post Office before they noticed her.

"Hey, girl," one of them said, shading his eyes as he squinted into the glare. "Where you goin?"

"Just passing through," she told him.

The two who'd been stretched out on the steps were now on their feet, hands on hips, looking toward her and grinning.

"What's your hurry?" said a big-bellied one.

"No hurry," she said. "Just got places to go."

Joe watched them move out into the street to intercept her. What is she doing? he wondered. Has she gone crazy?

"Oh, I don't think so," said the first one. "I think you're gonna stop and visit."

Lacey was within half a dozen feet of them now. "Been there, done that. Hey, boys . . . don't you remember me?"

With that she reached behind her, ripped her pistol free, and began firing wildly, pulling the trigger as fast as it would allow. Joe saw the one with the shotgun take a round in the chest. His arms flew outward as the bullet punched him back. Lacey's second shot went wild but the third caught the fat one in the gut. The last Vichy was drawing his pistol when Lacey's fourth shot caught him in the shoulder, spinning him around.

Four shots, three hits, but she didn't stop there. She kept firing.

Joe leaped out from the alley and dashed toward her as she stood over the three downed men and pumped round after round into their twitching bodies. He reached her as the slide on her pistol locked back on empty.

He grabbed her shoulders and spun her to face him. "Lacey! What—?" Then he saw the tears streaming down her cheeks.

"It was them, Uncle Joe," she sobbed. "I recognized them. They're the ones who—" She closed her eyes and took a deep, shuddering breath.

Joe glanced at their blood-splattered remains. "Lacey . . . Jesus . . . are you—?"

"I'm okay. That was for Enrico . . . and me. Let's just get this done and get out of here, okay?"

Joe opened his mouth to speak—he figured he should say *something*—but his mind was blank. He settled for a curt nod. They could talk later.

Carole arrived then with her book bag full of stakes and hammers. She took one look at the bodies, then put her arm around Lacey's shoulders.

"It's all right, Lacey. You did the Lord's work."

Lacey irritably shrugged off her arm. "That wasn't any lord's work—that was mine."

Joe caught the flash of hurt in Carole's eyes and felt bad for her. Lacey's rough edges weren't getting any smoother. No time now to explain his niece to Carole.

He took the book bag from her and turned toward the Post Office. "Let's go."

He led the way up the steps. Once inside he looked around. Empty. Sunlight began to stream through the east windows.

"If there's a cellar, that's where they'll be."

Lacey pointed to a door to the left of the clerk windows. "I saw the woman and her entourage go through there."

The door was locked. No problem. Joe kicked it open. Another door, unlocked, opened onto a flight of stairs leading down into a darker space.

"We'll do as many as we can in the time we have," he said, reaching into the bag and handing out the flashlights. "But we do the woman first. From what I've seen, she seems to be in charge."

He didn't need a light of his own. The stairwell appeared well lit to him. He hurried down to where the steps made a sharp right turn at the bottom into a dank, dusty space—

—and there they were. He could see all eight of them in the cool darkness, stretched out on an assortment of beds and cots. Like a dormitory in hell. If their daysleep was anything like his the past two nights, it was like death.

Joe looked around. Concrete walls, no windows, junk piled in the near-right corner. He spotted the woman's bed on the far side of the room next to the wall and immediately moved toward her. Even if they managed to stake only one this morning, he wanted it to be her—to send a message back to Franco that nobody he sent here was safe. Eventually he wanted Franco to know that not even he was safe.

"Hey," Lacey called from behind him. "This guy's awake."

"This one too," Carole said.

Joe had been so fixed on the woman that he'd paid no attention to her six guards, arrayed around her like spokes on a wheel. He looked down at the nearest and nearly jumped when he saw wide dark eyes staring back at him, sharp teeth bared in a snarl.

Joe didn't understand. How could they be awake?

"Forget them for now. The woman first."

He stopped at her bedside and found her awake as well. She lay on her back, staring up at him in fear and wonder.

"This is really creepy," Lacey said.

Joe had to agree. What was going on here? Unless . . . maybe the gunfire outside had roused them. At least none of them was able to get up.

No time to waste. He dropped the book bag on her abdomen and pulled out the heavy maul and one of the stakes. Carole stepped up beside him and played her beam over the woman, illuminating the corner of the room like daylight.

Joe lifted the stake. This wasn't how he'd expected this to go. He hadn't counted on his victims staring him in the face as he pounded stakes through their chests.

But this was no time for squeamishness. Steeling himself, he placed the sharpened tip against her chest, just to the left of her breastbone. He'd never done this before, but he imagined that was where the heart sat. As he raised the hammer, the woman hissed and grabbed the stake with both of her hands.

Joe jumped back in surprise, releasing his own grip.

"Dear God!" Carole gasped. "She can move!"

Joe recovered and snatched the stake back from her grasp. He broke her grip easily.

"But she's weak," he said.

A deafening blast echoed through the basement and Joe felt a stabbing impact, like a punch, in his back.

A shot!

Another blast as he half turned—another blow, this time to his shoulder.

"Get down!" he shouted to Carole and Lacey. "Way down!"

He feared the ricochets in this concrete box could be almost as deadly as a direct hit. He turned and found the shooter, the pistol wavering in his hand as he aimed another shot. Joe ducked to his left, darted to the man's side, and snatched the gun from his hand.

"Hey!" Lacey cried, popping her head up. She pointed to a guard near her. "This one's going for his gun too!"

"Get it!" Joe shouted. He turned and lunged for another of the woman's guards who was lifting his automatic, moving like someone in a slow-motion movie. Joe tore it from his grasp. "Get their guns! All of them."

He saw Lacey struggling with her guard. She had a two-handed grip on the barrel. Joe was just about to step in and help when she twisted it from his grasp. He turned and saw Carole pulling a pistol from another guard's belt before he could reach it. Joe disarmed two more, then stepped over to the seventh male, the one with the cot against the opposite wall, and found him unarmed.

"You!" Joe cried when he spotted his ruined left eye.

This was one of Franco's guards, the one who'd stripped him naked before taking him to his boss. What had Franco called him?

"Artemis!" That was it. "What are you doing here?"

The good eye widened. "You know me?" the vampire rasped.

That surprised Joe for an instant, then he remembered that his face had been changed by the sun. He wished he knew what he looked like.

He jabbed one of the pistols at him. "Too bad you didn't bring Franco with you. When we finish with the lady, you're next!"

This was perfect: the woman and Franco's right-hand man in one morning. He turned and stalked back toward the guards, snatching up a couple of machetes as he reached them. "Take their machetes too. Don't leave them with anything that can be used against us."

He tossed the pistols and machetes toward the foot of the steps. Carole and Lacey did the same. He was most relieved to have the guns out of play. The bullets hadn't affected him, but Carole and Lacey's lives had been on the line.

"A little help over here," Lacey said. Her voice sounded strained.

Joe looked and saw that the woman had turned over and was trying to crawl out of her bed. Lacey was struggling to hold her back. Carole leaned in to help.

As Joe moved toward the women, one of the guards rolled out of bed and landed on the floor in front of him. Another to his right did the same. Both started a slow-motion bellycrawl toward their mistress. Joe stepped on the back of the one in front of him and rejoined Carole and Lacey.

"They're coming for us!" Lacey said, an edge of panic in her voice. She was clutching the woman's right arm while Carole held the left from the other side of the bed. The woman writhed slowly in their grasp. "Let's do this and get the hell out of here!"

"Yes, Joseph," Carole said, calm but grave. "You haven't much time."

"All right, all right." Wasn't anything going to go according to plan?

He grabbed the stake and maul. No hesitation this time. He placed the point of the stake over the woman's writhing chest, raised the maul—

Lacey let out a yelp and released the woman's right arm. "Something just touched—damn! There's one here on the floor! He's trying to grab my leg!"

She half turned and began kicking at the guard who'd crawled to their feet.

Joe stared in shock, then looked around. Others were on their way, inching toward them along the floor. This kind of loyalty and devotion was almost unimaginable, especially in the undead.

"Joseph," Carole said. She had both the woman's arms now. "Do it. Now."

Joe nodded. In a single swift move he placed the stake and hammered it home. The heavy steel head of the maul drove the point all the way through the woman and into the mattress beneath. She writhed, kicked, spasmed, then stiffened and lay still.

Done. No time to waste. Move on. First get the guard by Lacey, and then—

"What the hell—?" Lacey said.

Joe looked down. The guard at Lacey's feet was writhing on the floor. The other five were doing the same. This lasted maybe ten seconds, and then they lay as still as their mistress.

Lacey nudged one with the toe of her shoe. "Dead. They're all—" She looked up at Joe, her eyes wide. "Unk! This is what happened the other night, right upstairs. A bunch of undead guards—supposedly they belonged to someone named Gregor—they suddenly dropped dead, just like these guys. It was right after we heard a boom and . . ." She turned to Carole. "You told us you killed a vampire that night. Blew him to bits, right?"

"Right. But I never knew his name."

Lacey nodded. "I'll bet it was Gregor. You killed him across town, and his guards died upstairs in the Post Office. We killed this one, and *her* guards die a few seconds later. What's the connection? Is there some sort of spell that binds the guards to their masters? A life-and-death bond that connects them? Is that why they're so loyal?"

Memories of the Empire State Building flashed through Joe's head.

"When I mentioned to Franco how loyal his guards seemed, he told me it wasn't out of selflessness or personal regard for him—it was self-preservation."

"That was his word?" Lacey said. "Self-preservation? Well then that's it. That's how they bind their guards to them: if their master dies, they die."

Joe shook his head. "I've got a feeling it's something more than that. Franco mentioned a secret. 'A momentous secret we keep only to ourselves,' he said. If only—"

Artemis! Joe whirled and looked at the cot in the corner where he'd left the vampire. Had he died too? But his bed was empty. Where—?

"Look!" Carole said, pointing her flashlight beam at a doorway where a pair of legs were crawling through. "Someone's there!"

Joe hurried over, grabbed both ankles, and hauled Artemis back into the dormitory. He flipped him onto his back and stood over him.

"Not so fast, Artemis. We have some questions."

"Fuck you!" His voice was barely audible.

"Why did the guards die when we killed the woman?"

The vampire sneered up at him and said nothing.

Joe realized he had nothing to bargain with. Artemis knew

he wasn't going to walk away from this, so he had no reason to tell them anything.

Lacey came up beside Joe and played her light over Artemis. "Can we bring him upstairs?"

"I suppose so," Joe said. "But why?"

She looked at him. "Sunlight."

Joe glanced from her to Artemis and saw the fear in his single eye. Joe grabbed his feet again and dragged him toward the stairs.

"Good idea!"

"No!"

Joe didn't have time for threats or deals. He hauled Artemis up feet first to the main floor. The vampire twisted away from the light and flung his arms over his eyes. Joe found the brightness uncomfortable but it hadn't reached the intolerable point yet. Pulling Artemis upright, he grabbed him by the collar and belt and walked him toward the front doors. The sunlight blazed through the glass like burning phosphorous.

"Now's your chance, pal. Speak or burn. What's the big secret?"

"Fuck you! I'll be just as dead either way!"

Damn him, he was right. And a dead vampire told no tales. He spun Artemis and shoved him into a shadowed corner where he curled into a whimpering ball.

Carole and Lacey stood in the cellar doorway staring at Joe.

"Any ideas, or do we just finish him and get out of here?" he said.

Lacey stepped closer to Artemis. She spoke slowly, softly. "Tossing him out in the sun will kill him. But what if just a part of him gets in the sunlight? What will that do?"

"Yes!" Joe said. Finally—leverage. "Anyone have a knife?"

Lacey whipped out a stainless steel pocketknife. "My butterfly's gone, but this should do. Someone tried to kill me with it."

Joe unfolded the blade and began slicing at the legs of the vampire's pants below the knees. He remembered how this creature had ripped the clothes from him a few long nights ago.

"What goes around, comes around, right, Artemis?" he said through his teeth.

He pulled off Artemis's shoes, then moved around by his shoulders.

"All right, ladies. Grab his feet and we'll move his legs into that patch of sunlight over there."

"No!" Artemis wailed.

"Joseph," Carole said, giving him an unsettled look. "Do we really—?"

"Please, Carole. Time's a-wasting, and this is one of the undead who manhandled me in New York."

Artemis directed his one fear-filled eye at Joe. "New York? Who—?"

"What? You don't recognize me? I'm the priest Franco tried to turn the other night. Only he failed."

"But that's—that's impossible!"

Carole still hadn't moved. Lacey stepped in front of her. "Let's go. I'll handle it."

She grabbed Artemis by both ankles. His feeble kicks lacked the power to free him. Together she and Joe dragged the lower half of his body into the light.

Immediately his flesh started to smoke and blister. Lacey made a disgusted noise and released his ankles. His screams echoed through the building.

"Okay! Yes! Please! I'll tell! Anything you want! I'll tell! *Please*!"

Joe pulled him back into the shadows. Artemis lay in a heap, writhing, panting, and sobbing, his hands hovering over but never touching the blackened, still-smoking flesh of his lower legs. Sickened by the sight, Joe turned away for a moment. He sensed Carole watching him but could not meet her eyes.

Finally he turned back and forced himself to kneel beside the vampire. He poked him roughly on the shoulder.

"What's the secret, Artemis? Why did those guards die when we staked the woman?"

"They were her get," he gasped. "When she died, all her get died, not just her guards."

"What's 'get'?" Lacey said.

Artemis sneered. "People she turned. When Olivia died, all of her get, no matter where they were in the world, died with her."

Joe knelt there, stunned. "I don't believe you."

"Believe it, priest. It's the one thing we don't want the living to know about us."

"But you're telling me."

His smile was sickly. "What do I care? It won't matter to me, will it."

"You're telling me that anyone, anywhere, that she turned at anytime since she became undead, is now dead?"

"Yes. That's the big secret. That's why Olivia's guards did everything to protect their get-mother. Not for her sake. For their own."

Lacey squatted on the opposite side. "But that means that somewhere there's a vampire who's the ultimate source of this whole undead plague. If someone could get to him—"

Artemis was shaking his head. "No, cow. There may have been a single Prime millennia ago, but now there are many. We undead aren't immortal; it only seems that way. We age and die, but we last many centuries. Eventually rot catches up to everything, including us. It hits suddenly and over the course of a week or so we crumble to dust. But this kind of true death does not affect the get. In fact it enhances them. Only premature death kills one's get. Because we lived solitary existences for so long, we never knew about get-death. But when an ancient Prime figured it out, and started the practice of protecting getfathers, our numbers began to grow."

"Is Franco a Prime?" Joe asked.

Artemis nodded. "And my get-father." His eye narrowed. "You want him, don't you."

"Oh, yeah. If he goes, how many go with him?"

"Many. I can't give you a definite number, but every Nosferatu in the Empire State Building is his get. Not in the city, however. We've learned to mix gets within a region to avoid catastrophe. I hope you get him."

"Why?"

"I didn't want to come down here, but he made me. He hasn't treated me right since a certain unfortunate accident, and now, because of him, I'm done. Aren't I?" He shifted his gaze to Lacey and Carole. "You wouldn't consider . . . ?"

"Not a chance," Lacey said.

Joe held out his hand. "Carole?"

"Not a stake!" Artemis whined. "I don't want to be staked!"

Lacey made a face. "You rather be thrown out in the sun?"

"No! That's even worse! Look, can't you let me go? I've helped you. I've told you a valuable secret. I—"

Joe shook his head, as much to clear a creeping fog as to emphasize that survival was not one of Artemis's options. "We'll give you a choice: sun or stake. That's all you've got."

"There's another way," Carole said.

Joe looked up and saw her fishing something that looked like a candle out of the front of her sweatshirt. He seemed to be viewing her through a mist. The waxy stick had wires attached. She bent and placed it under Artemis's neck, then draped a wire over each of his shoulders.

"This is a high explosive," she said. "You won't feel a thing."

High explosive? Had she wired herself to explode? He wanted to ask but the words wouldn't come.

"Just take the two wires . . ." Carole was saying.

He watched Artemis reach up and take a wire in each hand.

". . . and touch them—"

"Fuck you all!" Artemis cried as he jammed the two wires together.

Joe managed to raise a leaden arm across his eyes and fall back—

—but nothing happened.

Carole looked down at Artemis, her expression a mask of dismay.

"You didn't let me finish." She held up a battery. "You touch the wires to opposite ends of this." She shook her head. "Your kind simply don't understand mercy or compassion, do you."

"Damn right they don't," Lacey said.

Joe saw that she held the maul and a stake in her hands. Before Artemis could react, she jabbed the point over his heart and slammed it home with two quick, hard strikes.

The vampire arched his back, shuddered, then crumpled.

Lacey pulled the explosive stick from behind Artemis's neck and handed it back to Carole. "They don't deserve a break. Any of them."

Joe was still half sitting, half lying on the floor. He tried to rise but hadn't the strength. He felt as if someone had pulled the plug on his energy.

"Something's wrong," he croaked. "I can barely move."

Carole looked at her watch. "Dear Lord! It's past your time!"

Joe fought the lethargy stealing through him. Too tired to worry. It was all he could do to hold his head up.

The world around him became a blur. He was dimly aware of voices mentioning "back door" and "employee entrance" and "bring the car around." He felt himself dragged-carried outside into a shady area that was still blindingly bright, then lifted and folded into a small space . . . a slam that sounded like a car trunk lid, then darkness . . . blessed darkness.

JOE . . .

"Carole . . . are you all right?"

Joe had awakened to find the two slugs he'd taken in the Post Office scattered around him on his mattress. He didn't know how, but his body had extruded them during daysleep.

Then he'd fed—God, how he hated the word, the concept, the act. It made him feel like some sort of jungle animal; he would never get used to it. The women had decided to alternate, so Lacey had been the donor this time. The sun was just about down, and the three of them had taken their usual positions around the coffee table.

But Joe had noticed that Carole seemed withdrawn. She looked tired, but he sensed it was more than that.

"I'm okay," Carole said without looking at him.

Lacey said, "She's been like this all day." This earned her a brief glare from Carol. "Well it's true. You barely said two words to me before we went to sleep, and maybe half a dozen since we woke up."

"Didn't you sleep well?" Joe said.

"As a matter of fact, no," Carole said.

"Bad dreams?"

"In a way." She looked up, first at Joe, then at Lacey. "Are we proud of ourselves?"

"About what?" Joe said.

"About this morning."

"Yeah," Lacey said. "We reduced the world's undead population by eight and we learned something that could turn this fight around: kill one of the big-shot undead and a whole lot of others die too."

Carole said, "What about *how* we learned that secret?"

Lacey shook her head. "I'm not following."

Carole sighed and looked at the ceiling. "Torture. Am I the only one who's bothered by the fact that we tortured that creature into giving us the information?"

"Yeah," Lacey said with an edge on her voice. Joe could sense his niece's back rising. "I guess you could say you are. They're already dead, Carole."

"No, they're *un*dead. And they very obviously feel pain."

"Hang on now," Joe said. He caught Carole's troubled gaze and held it. "We did what we had to, Carole. I didn't like it, and I'm sure Lacey didn't either, but this is war and—"

"A war for what?"

"For survival," Lacey said. "Them or us. This isn't a war of ideologies, Carole," Lacey said. "And it's not a war of religions either. This is a war for the survival of the human race."

"Even if we have to sacrifice our humanity to win it?"

Joe leaned back and kept silent. This wasn't what he'd wanted to talk to Carole about, but he sensed this argument had been brewing all day, maybe longer. Best to stay out of the line of fire unless it escalated too far.

"Ever hear of the Spanish Inquisition, Carole?" Lacey said. "That was 'humanity' at its most creative. We *invented* torture."

"You sound proud of it."

"Not at all. I look at a picture of a rack or an Iron Maiden and my stomach turns. My point is that we, as the living, don't exactly have clean hands when it comes to depravity."

"I'm not worried about humanity's hands," Carole said softly. "I'm worried about ours—the three of us. I'd like to believe that we deserve to win. But if in the process we become like the enemy, what have we won?"

"The right to survive!"

"Is that all you want?"

"No!" Lacey shot to her feet and pounded the table. "I want more! I want to see every single one of those blood-sucking parasites dead and rotting in the sun! They robbed me of the person I loved more than anyone in my life, they took my parents—maybe I was on rotten terms with them, and maybe I'll always be pissed at them for naming me Lacey, but they were still my parents—and then they took one of the few men in the world that I love and respect and tried to turn him into a monster like them. I want them gone, Carole, I want them wiped off the face of the earth, and I want them to go screaming in agony, and I'm for doing whatever it takes to achieve that!" Her voice broke and tears streamed down her cheeks as she pounded the table with each word. "Whatever—it—takes!"

Joe rose, put an arm around Lacey's shoulders, and let her lean against him. Time to make peace.

"I'm okay," she said.

"No, you're not. None of us has been okay since the invasion. We're all damaged to varying degrees, but we all want the same thing. Carole has a valid point. We need to win—we must win—but maybe there should be a line we won't cross in order to win. I think we may have crossed that line at the Post Office."

He felt Lacey stiffen and shake her head. "No lines, no limits, no quarter, no mercy."

Joe tightened his grip on his niece's shoulders. How was he going to salvage this?

"Can we leave it that we agree to disagree and hope we

don't have to cross the line again—hope that we don't find ourselves in a position where we even have to think about crossing it?"

But if that moment came, Joe wondered, what side of that line would he come down on?

Lacey shrugged, reluctantly, he thought. "I guess I'm all right with that."

Carole nodded. "So am I. I pray we're never faced with that choice again."

"Good," Joe said, sagging with relief. "You two had me worried there."

"What?" Lacey said, looking up at him with a half-smile playing about her lips. "You thought we'd break up the team? Never happen. Right, Carole?"

"Never. Our work is too important. But I thought it needed an airing."

"Well, it's aired," Joe said. "Now let me air something else." He sat and took Carole's hands in his. "How long have you been wiring yourself with explosives?"

She looked away. "A while."

"Why?"

"I think that should be obvious."

It was. But for Joe it was unthinkable.

"Carole, you mustn't . . . you can't . . ."

"I won't," she said. "Not unless all hope is gone."

"Even then—"

She faced him. "I will not become one of them, Joseph. And didn't you tell us yourself that you jumped off the Empire State Building?"

Yes, he had, hadn't he. He wished he hadn't told them. It cut off his argument at the knees. What could he say—that it was all right for him but not for her?

"But blowing yourself up . . ."

The thought of Carole being torn to pieces, bits of her splattered against the walls and ceiling of a room, or scattered up and down a street, sickened him.

Her smile was tremulous. "What better way to go? I put

my hand in my pocket, I press a button, and it's over—instantaneous, painless, and, considering the straits I'll be in at that moment, I'll probably take a few of the enemy with me."

"I kind of like that idea," Lacey said. "Maybe you can wire me and—"

Joe held up a hand. "Lacey, please." He stared at Carole. "All right. What can I say? It's something only you can decide, Carole. But I beg you, when things look blackest, when you think there's no way out and the situation can't get worse, hold off pressing that button. Give it just one more minute."

"Why?"

"Because I don't want to lose you. And who knows? Maybe in that one extra minute the situation will start to turn around. Promise?"

She shrugged. "Promise."

Joe leaned back. He'd thought he'd feel better confronting her about this, but he didn't.

He put it behind him for now and looked first at Lacey, then Carole.

"All right. That's settled—I hope. Now we should plan our next step. When do we leave for New York?"

Lacey dropped back into her seat. "New York? So soon? Are we ready for that?"

"I don't think we have much choice," Joe said. He got up and settled himself on the couch. "First off, I don't think there's another nest we can practice on. Second, after what we did this morning, I've got a feeling this area's going to be on the receiving end of a lot of attention. So while they're looking this way, gearing up to make a move against the church and the people holding it, I propose we sneak in under their radar and strike where they least expect it."

Carole was nodding. "I like it. And from the way things went this morning, I believe dawn is the best time. But I assume we'll find more than three collaborators guarding the Empire State Building."

"Lots more," Joe said. He glanced at his niece. "Too many for even Annie Oakley here to take out."

Lacey smiled. "Oh, I don't know about that."

She got up and went to the dining area. She returned dragging a large canvas mail sack. She set it beside the couch and pulled open the top. Joe started when he saw the jumble of weapons inside.

"Good Lord, Lacey, what did you do? Rob an armory?"

"Almost as good. Before we left the Post Office this morning I collected every pistol and piece of ammo I could find, from Vichy and undead alike. Even picked up that sawed-off shotgun."

Joe shook his head. "It's still not enough. We're only three and there's dozens of them. We'll need another way."

Lacey looked at Carole. "Explosives? That napalm you cooked up?"

Carole shook her head. "Nothing I can make has the detonation velocity necessary to damage a building like the Empire State."

Lacey looked glum. "Then what? If we can't get inside—"

"I think I have a idea," Carole said.

Lacey brightened. "What?"

"Just the start of one. Let me work it through first. How long have we got?"

"I'd like to leave as soon as possible," Joe said. "Hit them before they find out what we did at the Post Office. Or if they do know, catch them while they're still off balance."

"I think we should make the trip by day," Lacey said. "That way the only ones around to stop us will be living. At night we'll have to dodge the undead as well."

"But I can't help you during the day."

Lacey smiled and nudged the letter bag with a toe. "I think Carole and I can handle any Vichy we meet along the way."

Joe wasn't keen on lying helpless in a car trunk while the two women took all the risks, but he couldn't fault Lacey's logic.

"All right then," he said. "We leave at dawn. Will that give you enough time, Carole?"

"I hope so. I'll need to take the car to see if I can find what I need."

"Okay. Just get back in time so we can stock up for the trip. We need to find some gas too. The Lincoln's pretty low."

"No need," Lacey said. "There's a cool convertible with a full tank sitting in the garage. We can take that instead."

"Looks like you've got all the bases covered. Only one thing left to do before we go. Carole, drop Lacey off at the church so she can tell them what we did at the Post Office and to expect reprisals. But most important, tell them the get-death secret. Have Gerald Vance get on his shortwave and start broadcasting it around the world."

"You think anyone'll believe it?"

"I hope so. Maybe in New York we'll find a way to give the world more tangible proof."

"How?"

Joe didn't answer. He was working on the beginning of an idea of his own.

BARRETT . . .

It was a little after midnight when James Barrett stepped out of the elevator into the Observation Deck atrium. A couple of Franco's get-guards pulled pistols and started for him. Where was Artemis tonight? He was usually the first to get in the face of anyone, living or undead, who set foot on the deck.

"What do you want?"

Something in their eyes, their expressions. Was it fear? What was going down here?

"Franco said to meet him here," Barrett said.

"I'll go check," said one of the guards.

As commander of the Empire State Building's human contingent, Barrett was used to being taken straight to Franco. Why this extra layer of insulation all of a sudden?

After all, he was responsible for round-the-clock security.

He could have stayed around just on days—the really important time for security—but that meant he'd never get to see Franco, and Franco would never see him. So he caught a few winks here and there when he could and made sure he was around for at least some of the night shift.

He'd held the job for six months now. That meant he had nine-and-a-half years of servitude left. That was the deal with the undead: ten years of service and they'd turn him. Fine for the other slobs to wait that long, but not him. He'd risen as high as a living man could go in Franco's organization. He needed to take the next step, needed to be turned, and soon. But he still hadn't found the lever to boost him to that stage.

"Come with us," said the returning vampire. "But first . . ."

He patted Barrett down and removed the .44 Magnum from his shoulder holster. He stared at it a moment, then handed it back.

Barrett hid his shock. He'd never been frisked before.

"Let's go," said the other.

But instead of escorting him to the outer deck, he led him into a stairwell to the left of the elevator bank and down the steps to the eighty-fifth floor. After a short walk along a hallway, he was passed through another set of guards into a bare room furnished with only a king-size four-poster bed. Large sheets of plywood had been bolted over the windows.

Franco paced the room, his hands behind his back.

"There's been some trouble," he said without preamble, without so much as a glance at Barrett.

"Where?" It must be really serious, he thought. "I haven't heard anything."

"You wouldn't," Franco said, his eyes were on the floor as he paced. "I sent Artemis down to New Jersey a few days ago to check up on Olivia and see to it that she was staying on top of things. If she wasn't—as I was sure was the case—he was to take over. This evening I received a report from downtown that—"

He seemed to catch himself and cast a quick sidelong

glance at Barrett. What was he hiding? He knew that Artemis and a few of his get lived down in the Village. What had Franco heard?

Franco shook his head and went on. "I heard a report that made me suspect that something might have happened to Artemis. So I sent a flyer down to check." Finally he looked up at Barrett. "Artemis is dead. So is Olivia."

"Oh, shit," Barrett said. It was the best he could do. He was all but speechless.

Artemis dead? Barrett couldn't wrap his mind around it. Was there a tougher undead son of a bitch in the world? He doubted it.

"How?"

"Staked. Same as Olivia."

"Her guards too?"

"All dead."

"A massacre! Who——?"

"I suspect it has something to do with that vigilante priest. That's the only answer."

"But he's one of you now."

"His followers aren't. Maybe when they found out that we turned him, instead of being demoralized, they went berserk. I don't know."

Barrett heard opportunity knocking. Here was a chance to stand out, to maybe shorten that nine-and-a-half-year wait for immortality.

A plan was already forming. Show up down there, pretend to be another refugee, infiltrate their ranks, wait till the time was right, till they were off guard, then blow them all away.

"Want me to go down and check it out?"

Franco shook his head. "No. I need you here. I want you to gather your men from inside and outside the city and concentrate them around this building. I'm going to organize a counter strike and I don't want any interruptions. By next week I'll have gathered a horde of ferals to set loose down there. No quarter, no survivors. Then I'm going to incinerate the entire area. The flames will be visible for miles. Not one house or church or synagogue will be left standing. The rest of the living will hear and understand the consequences of resistance."

"I don't think pulling in your perimeter is such a good idea. That's like your early-warning system. You don't want—"

"What I don't want is to debate it. I did not bring you up here for a discussion. I'm telling you what to do. Now do it!"

Barrett resisted a hot retort. He held up his hands and said, "You're the boss."

As he turned and walked out, he thought, But you're an asshole.

He didn't care what Franco said, he wasn't going to pull in all the outriders. His ass was on the line here too, and if a caravan full of vampire hunters was headed this way, he wanted to know about it before they reached Fifth Avenue.

Because invariably vampire hunters were cowboy hunters too.

12

LACEY . . .

Feeling tight and on edge, Lacey sat straight and tall in the passenger seat, scanning the highway ahead and twisting to check out behind as they sped north along Route 35. Her right hand rested on the .45 semiautomatic cradled in her lap.

They'd left before dawn with Carole at the wheel. The Parkway route had been considered, but rejected. It was a wider road, but offered fewer options should they run into any Vichy. Route 35 was local, but it wasn't as if they had to worry about traffic lights or anything, and it allowed them to turn off on an instant's notice. That was good; the sun was rising into a cloudless sky, which was not so good. Lacey would have preferred a cloudy, rainy day. Better yet, foggy. Anything to cut the visibility.

As she spotted a sign that said HAZLET she felt the Fairlane surge forward. Joe—apparently he'd played around with cars as a teen—had identified this one as a '57 Fairlane; he'd checked the engine before they'd left and proclaimed it "hot," mentioning a four-barrel carburetor and other car talk she couldn't follow. She leaned left to catch a look at the speedometer.

"Ninety?" she said.

Carole nodded. She was dressed in some hideous mauve nylon warm-up she'd found last night in a neighboring house. "The road is straight and level here, and the sooner we get there, the better."

"I'll drink to that."

Carole nodded. "I don't know much about cars, but this one handles beautifully."

They merged with Route 9 and headed over a tall bridge. After that it was decision time.

"Turnpike or stay on 9?" Carole said.

Tough question. Lacey did *not* want to run into any Vichy.

"Let's think about that," Lacey said. "The closer we get to the city, the thicker the Vichy will be. But if I were a Vichy, the last place I'd look for someone traveling would be the Turnpike. It's too open. So I'd concentrate on the back roads."

"You're assuming they think that far ahead. The ones I've met so far haven't been too bright."

"But Joe said they were pretty well organized in the city. Someone with brains is probably calling the shots. I vote Turnpike."

Carole took a deep breath. "All right. Turnpike it is."

They followed the green-and-white signs and got on the New Jersey Turnpike North at Exit 11. They kept to the outer lanes.

As they roared along, Lacey felt herself starting to cook in the sunlight pouring through her side window. She rolled it down a few inches; that helped for a while, but soon she was perspiring.

She was wearing plaid cotton comfy pants and a red V-neck sweater over an extra-large T-shirt she'd found—it came from some restaurant called Pete and Elda's and apparently was a prize for eating a whole large pizza. Eventually she removed the sweater.

"If it gets much warmer we'll have to put the top down."

"I don't think that would be wise."

"Why not? Afraid of developing skin cancer in twenty years?"

Gallows humor. Even Carole smiled—a rare event these days.

Lacey pulled the T-shirt away from her skin and caught a whiff of herself.

"Damn, do I ever need a shower!"

She'd tried to bathe in the ocean but it was freezing.

"Wouldn't you love to be able to take a bath?" Carole said. "I'd give almost anything for one."

"Me too." Lacey decided Carole's cage was due for a gentle rattle. "You know, I wish I believed in the soul. I'd trade mine for one good hot shower."

"Don't talk like that," Carole said.

"It's true."

She glanced at Lacey. "You'd sell your soul that cheaply?"

"We're talking hypothetically here, and no, I wouldn't sell it that cheaply. I'd want at least *three* hot showers—long ones."

Carole looked as if she were about to reply when she glanced in the rearview mirror. Her expression tightened.

"Oh, no."

Lacey turned and looked through the convertible's plastic rear window. Two longhaired men on motorcycles had just roared out of a rest stop and were closing in on them. They wore dirty cutaway denim jackets and brandished pistols.

Vichy.

"Damn. Sorry. I guess I made the wrong call."

She reached down to the postal bag on the floor by the back seat—next to their stock of mylar napalm balloons and the canister of chemicals Carole had picked up from the town's water treatment plant—and came up with a sawed-off ten-gauge shotgun.

"Well, I was hoping this wouldn't happen, but at least we're prepared."

One of their pursuers raised a pistol and fired a round over the top of the Fairlane.

"A warning shot across our bow," Lacey said. She worked the shotgun's pump to chamber a shell. "Let's see how they like—"

Carole grabbed her arm. "Dear God, I just thought of something! What if they shoot into the trunk?"

"Joe can handle a bullet or two, as we've already seen."

Her grip tightened. "I'm not worried about the bullets so much as the holes they'll make. The sunlight will come through and—"

"Shit!" Three good minds planning this trip and not one of them had thought of that.

Another shot—this one whined past Lacey's open window. She stuck her head out and waved her empty hand. The biker on the left grinned and pointed toward the shoulder.

Lacey pulled back inside. "Pull over. But take your time. And when you think you're going slow enough, start putting the top down.

Carole looked at her. "Top down? Wh—?"

"Can't explain now. And speaking of top down . . ." She began pulling off her T-shirt.

"Lacey!"

"Just trust me."

She'd given up bras long ago. As the car decelerated, she released the roof catches and tucked the .45 into the postal bag. Then she climbed into the rear. She laid the shotgun in the sling between the back seat and the roof compartment.

She began slipping out of her pants. She still liked to wear panties but she removed those too.

The roof started to rise. The wind swirling around her body felt good as she knelt on the back seat, gearing herself up for what was to come. One of the Vichy, pistol at the ready, pulled his bike up along the driver side and looked in, probably checking out the number of occupants. When he saw Lacey his eyes went wide and he let out a whoop.

As he dropped back, Lacey said, "As soon as we stop, get out of the car and start yelling at me to put my clothes on."

"Why don't I start right now?"

"Listen to me. I want them to see that you're not armed—they'll for sure know *I'm* not. I want them off guard. So just act mad and like you think I'm crazy."

"I'm sure I can handle *that*," Carole said.

The roof was three-quarters down when the car stopped. Lacey stood and threw her arms wide.

"Guys! Am I glad to see *you*! Where the fuck you been hiding?"

The Vichy pair looked at each other, stopped their bikes half a dozen feet behind the car, and sat staring. Both still clutched their pistols.

"Not as glad as we are to see you, little lady," said the red-bearded one on the left. "And I do mean *see* you."

He gave his buddy's arm a backhand slap and they both laughed.

Lacey heard the car door slam behind her and Carole's voice cry, "Lacey! You put your clothes on right this instant!"

"Who's she?" said the other one who'd twined his salt-and-pepper goatee into a triad of greasy braids.

"Just some lezbo I hooked up with."

Redbeard grinned. "Lezzie action. Awright!"

Braids set his kickstand and got off his bike. Lacey noticed he had PAGANS written across the back of his cutaway. She also noticed the bulge behind his fly. Good. All that blood flowing away from his brain.

"Lezzie, huh?" He took a step toward Carole. "No such thing. She just ain't met the right man yet."

Oh, but she has, Lacey thought.

"Never mind her." Lacey crawled out on the trunk lid and seated herself cross legged, giving the two Vichy a panoramic view. Braids suddenly lost interest in Carole. "I'm the one in need of a little male tail, if you know what I'm saying. Been too damn long since I had a guy to do me right."

"Well then," Redbeard said, getting off his bike. He adjusted the bulge in his pants. "This is your lucky day. You get a double dose."

"Hey, I ain't got nothing against a three-way, but I need one guy to start me off right. You know, get me juiced up. Who's got the biggest dick? I want the best-hung guy first."

"That'll be me," said Redbeard.

Braids snorted. "No fuckin way!"

Here was the tough part. She had to time this just right or the whole situation would go to hell in a heartbeat. Lacey clapped her hands and forced a giggle. "Oh, this is so cool! A cock fight! Show me! Show me! Show me! I'll be the judge! No-no, wait! I'll be the package inspector!"

Laughing, the two men holstered their pistols and began fumbling with their flies. With a shaking hand Lacey reached around, pulled the shotgun from the boot, and fired at Redbeard first. The recoil almost knocked her off the trunk and into the back seat, but the blast took Redbeard full in the chest, slamming him back through a halo of his blood and into his bike. Some of the scattering shot caught Braids in his arm and he spun half around, clawing at his pistol. Lacey regained her balance and her grip on the sawed-off. She quick-pumped another shell into the chamber as she slid off the trunk to the ground, then pulled the trigger, catching Braids in the left side. His shoulder, neck and cheek exploded and he went down in a spray of red.

Lacey pumped one more shell of double-ought shot into each of them—didn't want them talking to anyone—then took their guns. She tossed the shotgun and the new weapons onto the back seat.

"Men," she said, reaching for her clothing. Loathing welled up in her. "No wonder I gave up on them. They're *such* assholes."

She pulled on the panties and comfy pants first. As she was shrugging the T-shirt over her head she found Carole glaring at her.

"What?"

"You shouldn't have done that."

"Killed them? What was I sup—?"

Carole shook her head. "You shouldn't have called me a lesbian. That wasn't right."

"It was just something to distract them, set little triple-X fantasies spooling through their heads."

Carole slipped back behind the wheel. "Still, just because I've forsworn marriage doesn't mean I'm a lesbian. A vow of chastity means no sex with men *or* women."

"I know that, Carole." She dropped back into the passenger seat and slammed the door. "Takes one to know one, and my gaydar doesn't so much as beep with you."

Carole glanced at her. "You're . . . ?"

"Yeah."

"Does your uncle know?"

"Sure does. He doesn't like it but he accepts it. Too bad you aren't, Carole. You're kinda cool."

Carole's face reddened as she put the car in gear.

Lacey laughed and gave the nun's shoulder a gentle punch. "Only kidding."

And she was. With the memory of Janey still so fresh and haunting, she couldn't think of being with anyone else. Not yet.

"This isn't going to be a problem for you, is it?"

Carole shook her head. "The convent had its fair share. It was no secret behind the doors. They kept to themselves, and I kept my mouth shut. God will be the final judge."

"I guess I have nothing to worry about then," Lacey said.

She turned and looked back at the two men sprawled in their pooling blood and felt nothing.

"Why don't I feel anything, Carole? You've killed your share of Vichy. Do you—?"

"I always got sick afterward—at least when I had to . . . do it myself . . . by hand. But what you just did doesn't bother me so much. Perhaps because it wasn't close work . . . or because it was you doing it instead of me. I know they had to die but . . ." She sighed. "Nothing in my life prepared me for this,

Lacey. I was raised to be merciful—I'm a Sister of Mercy, after all—but I don't believe the undead or their collaborators deserve any mercy from us. I've decided to leave that to God. He can decide."

"Kill 'em all and let God sort 'em out. Right." Just how Lacey felt.

"Perhaps. Still . . . I can't ignore the fact that the Vichy are still human beings. No matter what awful things they've done, they're still God's children, and I can't help thinking that if maybe someone had got to them early enough and showed them the grace of God's love, their lives would have been different."

Lacey shook her head. "Sorry. Can't buy that. Some people are just plain evil. They're born bad and they stay bad all their lives. They're like termites, undermining your house. There's no accommodating them, so if you don't want to wake up with your house reduced to sawdust, you exterminate them."

"That's what they are to you? Bugs?"

"Worse. Bugs don't have a choice in how they act."

Lacey knew she hadn't always been like this, but something started dying within her when Janey had gone missing; her parents' empty, bloodstained house had pushed it closer to the grave; Uncle Joe dead with his throat torn open had administered the coup de grâce. She couldn't imagine herself feeling anything but murderous loathing for the creatures, human and inhuman, who'd been a part of all that.

Carole hit a switch and the top began to rise.

"Leave it down," Lacey said.

Carole looked at her. "I don't think that's a good idea."

"It is. Think about it. You heard Joe: All the females of childbearing age have been trucked off to farms to be breeders. That leaves nothing for the cowboys between their stud times at the farms. They're horny as all hell. If they see two women in an open car they'll be more likely to ask questions first and shoot later, don't you think?"

"You also said we'd be less likely to run into trouble on the Turnpike."

"That was just a guess. This is based on the fact that these guys—as the two back there on the ground prove—think with their dicks."

Carole closed her eyes for half a minute—Lacey couldn't tell if she was thinking or praying—then hit the roof switch. The top settled back into the boot.

"I hope you're right."

After that, Carole kept the pedal to the metal, hitting one-twenty on the long straightaways through the flatlands by Newark Airport. The still, silent airport streamed past to the left, the equally still railyards to the right. Like running through an industrial graveyard.

The big road remained eerily empty except for one other car, half a dozen lanes away, headed in the opposite direction. Whether friend or foe, Lacey couldn't tell.

Then the roadway lifted and the Manhattan skyline hove into view to the right, pacing them as they raced along. The gap where the Trade Towers used to stand caused an ache in Lacey's chest. The hijackers and their victims were long gone, and now most of the survivors were probably gone as well. And Islam . . . Islam was gone too.

Good riddance. Lacey had no use for any religion, but she'd found Islam's treatment of women particularly offensive. A mongrel religion, cobbled from pieces of others and strung together by adolescent sex and power fantasies. Good fucking riddance.

A lump built in her throat as she thought about what her city had suffered. She'd thought nothing could be worse than the Trade Tower attack, but then the undead had come . . .

A few minutes later they were passing through Union City. She saw the weathered old sign, UNION CITY—EMBROI-DERY CAPITAL OF THE WORLD, and shook her head. Union City wasn't embroidering a thing these days.

"I can't believe this," Lacey shouted over the wind

whistling around and between them as they coasted down the Lincoln Tunnel helix. "We made it without being hassled again."

Carole glanced at her watch and shook her head. "Forty-five minutes. That must be a record."

"And that includes the time we lost with those two motor-cycle yo-yos. It's like everybody's on vacation."

"I think we might be able to take credit for some of that," Carole said. "After what we did in the Post Office, I'll bet they've drawn their collaborators closer—doubling the guard and measures like that. The upside of that is an easier trip getting here; the downside will be a much more difficult time accomplishing what we came here to do."

"Every silver lining has a cloud, right?"

Carole nodded as they threaded an E-ZPass lane and aimed for the tunnel's center tube. "Always."

Carole turned on the headlights as they entered the dark, arching maw, and just then a siren howled behind them. Lacey jumped in her seat and looked around at the flashing red lights atop two blue-and-white units that had appeared out of nowhere.

"Police?" Carole said.

Lacey eyed the cars. First off, the NYPD was long gone. Second, the four shaggy-headed silhouettes crammed into that first unit didn't look anything like cops. Probably an equal number in the unit beside it.

Eight Vichy . . . she doubted the tactics she'd used on the two bikers would fly here. As if to emphasize that point, one of the occupants in the lead cop car held an assault pistol out a rear passenger window and fired a burst into the air. The bullets shattered some ceiling tiles and the pieces rained on the cop car, denting the hood and cracking the windshield. Lacey spotted a fist flying in the rear of the car. Someone wouldn't be trying that again.

The following unit pulled alongside the first, high beams flashing on and off. Lacey rose in her seat, exposing herself to the glare, and waved.

"What do we do?" Carole shouted over the roar of the wind. Her expression was tight.

"Your turn."

"My turn? For what?"

"To show a little titty."

"*What?*"

"Yeah. I did my part, now you do yours. I'll take the wheel and—"

"Not on your life! Just shoot at them. We don't have to worry about sunlight leaking into the trunk while we're in here."

Lacey thought of that assault pistol that had fired a moment ago, and wondered if there were more of them in the units. She didn't stand a chance against that sort of firepower. Then she looked down and saw the napalm balloons.

"Slow down a little," she said as she crawled into the rear. "Here we go again."

She crouched on the back seat and pulled off her T-shirt, then she grabbed a napalm balloon in each hand.

"What are you doing?" Carole said.

"I'm about to play hide and seek. Just be ready to burn rubber when I tell you."

Could she get away with something like this again? If they were half as horny as she thought they were yeah. Maybe.

Taking a breath, she pressed a balloon over each breast, plastered a big grin on her face, then rose to her knees.

The left blue-and-white swerved as the driver hit the siren again and a couple of hands popped out the windows to wave the horn sign. The right unit did the same.

She pulled the balloon off her left breast and held it high.

The sirens wailed again.

She bared her right breast and held that balloon aloft.

Another wail.

She tossed both balloons at the cars.

"Hit it!" she yelled as she dove for the seat.

The last thing she saw as the tires screeched and the Fairlane leaped forward was one balloon splattering harmlessly on the pavement and the other breaking against the grill of the right car. The front of the car exploded, rocketing the hood toward the ceiling, and then Lacey was down, flat on the rear seat. The explosion kicked them from behind like a rear-end collision. A wave of heat rolled over them for an instant before they left it behind.

Lacey peeked over the back of the rear seat in time to see the burning unit sidewipe its companion. The second bounced off the wall with a shower of sparks, then slammed into the first as someone's gas tank exploded. The second car flipped then and landed against the first. Amid the agonized screech and groan of metal grinding against concrete and asphalt and tile, both slid to a halt across the tunnel roadway in a single, twisted, flaming mass.

Lacey shook her head. Wow. Powerful stuff.

She thought she saw something moving, a flaming man-shaped thing crawling out a window, but she couldn't be sure. Suddenly a third explosion rocked the mass. The other gas tank, she guessed.

Lacey tugged her shirt back over her head and climbed up into the passenger seat.

"That's it! The last time I strip down for these animals."

"Let's hope so," Carole said. "By the way, that was an amazing piece of indirection."

Was that a note of genuine admiration Lacey detected in her voice?

"Thank you. And my compliments to the chef on that napalm." Lacey pointed ahead at the splotch of brightness ahead in the dark of the tiled gullet. "Look. The light at the end of the tunnel."

"More Vichy there?"

Lacey grabbed the shotgun. Her stomach crawled. How long could their luck last?

But to their amazement, the Manhattan side of the tunnel was deserted. Gasping with relief, they swerved left and roared into the concrete box of an enclosed above-and-below-ground park-and-lock lot on 42nd Street.

BARRETT . . .

Neal kicked a piece of blackened metal from the wrecks and sent it spinning across the scorched pavement. He tugged on his beard.

"What the fuck?"

"What the fuck is right," Barrett said. "All seven guys gone. Just like that."

Franco was going to be pissed . . . if he found out.

The relief crews had arrived on the Manhattan side at noon to find smoke billowing from the middle tube. They'd waited till it tapered off, then drove inside. This was what they'd found.

Lights from the headlights of a couple of cars illuminated the twisted mess of metal. The ceiling and walls were scorched black for hundreds of feet in both directions.

"You think it was a hit?" Neal said.

"You mean like what happened at the Lakewood Post Office. I don't know. See any bullet holes?"

Neal shook his head. "Not a one."

Neither had Barrett.

Two carloads of cowboys reduced to crispy critters. It looked like one car had plowed into the other, smashing it against the side of the tunnel. Barrett visualized a bent side panel, showers of sparks, a gas cap tearing off, then *kablam!*

What had they been doing—drag racing through the tubes? Assholes. One car was supposed to be stationed at each end of the tunnel, but this wouldn't be the first time they'd got bored and hung out together on the Jersey end. He'd caught them at it before and this was probably another instance. Most of these guys had the attention span of a gnat.

"Well, without bullet holes in the cars—or what's left of them—how could it be a hit? Must have been an accident. Caused by terminal stupidity."

Barrett ground his teeth. He had to get out of this job. He had to take the next step. Get turned. He'd go crazy if he had to spend another nine-plus years with these assholes.

B

"Look, Ma," Lacey said. "A double threat: no hands while walking on the third rail."

Carole knew Lacey had to be as uneasy as she, walking these subway tracks, but she was doing a better job of hiding it. She briefly angled her flashlight beam at Lacey, then back to the tracks again.

"Under different circumstances I might call that a shocking display of brashness, but after yesterday . . ."

Lacey laughed.

They'd huddled in the car in the park-and-lock garage all day, venturing out only to relieve themselves. When the sun had fallen and Joseph was awake, he left alone to begin nighttime surveillance on the Empire State Building and the area around it. But he'd returned less than an hour later driving a huge Lincoln Navigator he'd appropriated from a nearby parking lot. He insisted that she and Lacey transfer to it, not because of the comfort its extra size afforded, but because of its hard top. They were already insulated by the garage's layers of reinforced concrete, but he wanted them further sealed in steel. He begged them to stay locked in during the dark hours, telling them their warm blood made them easy to pick out against the cold concrete and granite of the city. If a hybrid like him could sense them, what about the fully undead?

Carole had missed him, worried about him, but had taken his advice. She and Lacey had slept when they could, and talked when they couldn't—talked about anything they could think of. Except sex. Lacey's lesbianism made Carole uncomfortable. Or was it the fact that she felt a growing fondness for this young woman who happened to be a lesbian.

She'd been relieved to see Joseph return with the dawn. He was excited. He'd found a place where they could watch the comings and goings at the Empire State Building in relative safety and comfort, and told them how to get there.

So now it was their turn. They'd left the garage at sunrise when the undead were no threat. Only the living.

They'd walked the deserted pedestrian tunnel from the Port Authority to Times Square, and were now down on the tracks of the 42nd Street Shuttle. This seemed like the safest way to move about the city. Certainly less risk down here of running into a pack of cruising Vichy than up on the street. At least she hoped so.

Flashlight in one hand, cocked-and-ready pistol in the other; backpacks filled with sharpened stakes, hammers, batteries, and cans of salmon they'd brought from the Shore.

What a way to travel. What a way to live.

Carole knew nothing about guns, had never liked them, had never so much as laid a finger on one until a few days ago. She'd always imagined she'd be afraid of them, but had to admit she found something comforting in the weight, the solidity, the pent-up *lethality* of the semi-automatic Lacey had given her. She'd shown her how to work the safety. All she had to do if the need arose was point and pull the trigger. She prayed that need would never arise. There was no place to practice so she hadn't fired it yet, and had no idea how it would feel when she did.

"You know," Lacey said, dancing along the third rail like a gymnast on a balance beam, "it's strange. From the instant we jumped off the platform onto the tracks, I had to touch this rail. I was scared to—I mean, what if by some freak chance it was live—but I had to. Didn't you feel any of that?"

"Not at all." But seeing Lacey on the third rail made her nervous. The chance of the power coming back on was about equal to that of a subway full of commuters coming by, but still it put her on edge. "We've been told all our lives that we could never touch the third rail because we'd be fried to a cinder. At first opportunity you're up on the rail, walking along it. That's pretty much you in a nutshell, isn't it."

Lacey snickered. "I guess so. What's the psychology there? It no longer has power over me, so now I'm dancing on its grave?"

"I never placed much stock in psychology."

"But look where you're walking, Carole. What does that say about you?"

"It says nothing's changed. I was quite happy staying off the third rail when it was live, and am just as happy to stay off it now."

"Ever watch *Ren and Stimpy*?"

"Can't say that I have, although years ago at a school picnic I remember some of my students wearing badly drawn T-shirts with those words on them."

"It's a cartoon show, and in one of the early episodes they're in outer space and they come across this button with all these warnings about 'Do not press or you will destroy the space-time continuum,' or something like that. Anyway, Stimpy just *has* to press it. And when I saw that I said, Yeah, I think I'd press it too."

"Good Lord, why?"

"Well, first off, part of me would be going, Yeah, right, like this button's gonna end the space-time continuum. Uh-huh. And another part would be thinking, Really? What would *that* be like? Let's find out . . ."

"How about a part of you saying, Let's lock the door to this place and throw away the key?"

"I think when they were giving out parts I missed that one." She flashed her light at Carole and held out a hand. "Come on. I'll help you up."

"No, thank you. If one of us slips off and sprains an ankle, the other has to remain well enough to carry on."

Lacey loosed a dramatic sigh, then stepped off the rail and fell in beside her. "Spoil sport." She flashed her beam ahead. "Damn, it's dark."

Carole nodded. The light-colored tiles—she supposed they'd once been white—in the pedestrian tunnel and in the Times Square station had reflected the glow from their flashes, letting them see more than just what was in the beam. But down here on the tracks, surrounded by grimy steel girders and soot-blackened concrete walls, with no reflective surface except the polished upper surface of the tracks and an occasional puddle, the darkness seemed a living thing, pressing against them. And all those recesses and access tunnels and crawl spaces . . .

Something splashed behind them.

Carole heard Lacey gasp. Both whirled and flashed their beams madly about but found nothing moving. Carole could feel her heart pounding.

"Think it was a rat?" Lacey said.

"Could have been."

"I hate rats."

"They're just animals."

"Yeah, but I really skeeve them."

"Skeeve?"

"Yeah. Heard it from some Italian girl I knew. Means to make your skin crawl. If we see a rat, that'll be a good time for you to get used to firing your pistol. I think we can risk a few shots down here."

"I'm not shooting a rat. And neither are you. They're no threat to us, it's a waste of ammunition, and besides, they

were here first. It isn't *rodentia* you should be worried about
down here. Genus *Homo* offers the main threat right now."

They started walking through the dark again, but every so
often one of them—they took turns—would turn and flash
her light behind them.

Lacey whispered, "I remember hearing about homeless
people who used to live in the subway tunnels. I wonder if
any of them are left."

"If I were a betting woman—and I'm not—I'd say no.
Underground is where the undead go to hide from the light.
Once down here they'd sniff out the living in no time."

Lacey grabbed her arm. "Speaking of sniffing, what is
that?"

Carole felt her nose wrinkling. She knew the odor: car-
rion. "Something died nearby."

"Which means there's a good chance one of *them* is
nearby."

They followed the stench to a recess in the right wall that
led to an alcove beyond it. Carol flashed her beam down the
narrow passage. The floor was littered with the bodies of beheaded rats, some of them acrawl with maggots.

"What's with the dead rats?" Lacey whispered behind her.

"I don't know."

"We don't want to go in there."

"Right," Carole said. "But we must."

"Like hell."

"We can't leave any undead along our route. What if
we're delayed coming back and we're caught down here after sundown? We can't see in the dark; they can."

Lacey was silent a moment, then grumbled, "All right, but
let's go in with all bases covered." Carole felt a tug on her
backpack. "I'll handle the gun and flashlight—in case whatever's in there is human—while you take the hammer-and-
stake detail."

A moment later Carole had her crucifix and a stake in her
left hand, thrust out ahead of her, the hammer clutched in

her right. Lacey was squeezed beside her, manning the flashlight. Carole wished she had a third hand to hold a cloth over
her mouth and nose. The stench was unbearable.

They edged down the passage, shuffling to avoid stepping
on the dead rats, and entered a small square alcove, maybe
ten feet on a side. The first thing Carole saw was a naked
corpse crumpled in the far corner, face to the wall; the position made it impossible to determine its sex. The floor was
littered with more dead rats, most of them clustered around
the naked emaciated male figure that lay in the center of the
space. When Lacey shone the light on its face, the gummy
lids parted slowly. It let out a feeble hiss and bared its fangs.
Although this one didn't quite qualify as a feral, its appear-
ance was a long way from human.

Carole wasted no time. "Keep the light on it," she told
Lacey as she knelt beside the thing.

She touched the crucifix to its sunken belly, eliciting a
flash and a puff of smoke. That proved beyond doubt it was
undead. The creature writhed as she raised the stake—she'd
have no trouble finding a space between the jutting ribs of
this washboard chest. But just as Carole pressed the point of
the wooden shaft against its skin, Lacey let out a cry of terror and the flash beam darted around the room.

Carole turned and saw Lacey struggling as if her foot was
caught.

"It's got me!" Lacey cried. "Damn it to hell, I thought it
was dead!"

In the wildly wavering light Carole saw that what she too
had assumed to be a human cadaver had locked its fingers
around Lacey's ankle. Lacey was trying to kick herself free
but the creature clung to her like a weighted manacle. Panic
bloomed in the hollow of her gut. Were there more?

Something hit Carole's hand, knocking the stake from her
grasp. She turned back to her vampire and felt it reaching for
her. She patted the floor around her but found only dead rats.

"Lacey! The light!"

But her words didn't penetrate Lacey's stream of shouted curses as she frantically tried to free her ankle. Carole could feel things spinning out of control as events accelerated, becoming increasingly surreal, chaotic, epileptic. The creature before Carole clutched her wrist as Lacey began shooting at the one grasping her. The shots were deafening in the small space. Lacey's wildly gyrating flashlight beam raked across Carole, revealing the lost stake. Ears ringing, she swung the hammer at the forearm of the hand holding her wrist, heard a bone snap, felt the grip break. She grabbed the stake and in the dark, placed it on the creature's chest over where she hoped its heart would be, then hammered it into the flesh. Its limbs flailed, back arched, chest heaved, but Carole kept her grip on the stake, taking a second swing, the hammer head glancing off the end of the stake and grazing her hand. She clenched her teeth against the pain as Lacey fired again, the strobe of the muzzle flash giving Carole just enough light to see where to strike a third blow. This one landed solidly, driving the stake through the heart beneath it. The creature spasmed and lay still.

Carole looked around for Lacey, saw her limping away down the narrow corridor, dragging the still-attached vampire after her through the maggoty rats. Carole reached around and pulled another stake from her backpack, then followed.

"Lacey, stop."

"Carole, get this damn thing off of me!"

"I will. Just hold the light steady."

Lacey stopped moving. Carole knelt on the back of the thing, placed the point of the stake to the left of the spine, and drove it through with three swift blows. The thing shuddered and finally released its grip on Lacey's ankle.

Lacey lurched away and leaned against a steel support beam, gasping.

"I think I'm going to be sick. The undead always disgusted me, but these things . . . what the hell?"

Carole rose and leaned against the wall, waiting for her pounding heart to slow. "I think they're strays, and obviously they're starving."

"Have they been living on rats? Is that possible?"

"I don't know. Joseph said Franco told him Manhattan was empty and they were hunting in the other boroughs. I do know that we got careless."

"Yeah," Lacey said. "Sorry for losing it in there. I didn't expect . . . wasn't ready for being grabbed like that. I hope no one topside heard the shots."

So did Carole. "Let's keep moving."

JOE . . .

Joe suffers again through his daymare. Every day, the same dream, clinging by his fingertips to the lip of the same rocky precipice, his feet swinging and kicking over the same dark swirling infinity. The living darkness calling to him, beckoning, and still that same traitorous part of him longing to answer, to let go and fall . . .

No. Not fall. Go home.

Then a sudden shift. He's now standing on the ledge. And below him, clinging by their fingertips, hang Carole and Lacey. He laughs as he grinds a heel into their fingers and sends them screaming, tumbling into the abyss.

LACEY . . .

"This is creepy, Carole," Lacey said as she scanned the street from the subway stairwell. Cars lined the curbs as always, but the streets lay still and silent. "Nothing is moving. Nothing."

Except for the birds, but they didn't count.

The silence got to Lacey. She found the emptiness here eerier and far more surreal than the close call with that pair of emaciated vampires. It sent cramps rippling through her intestines.

But even so, it was good to be out of the tunnels, to feel a fresh breeze on her face, to inhale clean air. They'd found three more undead scattered in alcoves along the shuttle tracks before they reached the Lexington Avenue line, and a half a dozen more on the nine-block length of track they walked down to the Thirty-third Street station. All were emaciated, and they dispatched them without difficulty.

The morning was further along than they'd intended by the time they crept up to street level.

"We've got to head uptown a couple of blocks, then west," Lacey said.

Her uncle had laid out their route, but this was her city so it was only natural that she take the lead here.

"We'll be exposed," Carole said. "I don't like that."

"Neither do I, but the only really open spot will be crossing Thirty-fourth. After that there should be lots of nooks and crannies to hide in if need be."

They made a headlong dash to Thirty-fifth, then turned left.

"This area used to be called Murray Hill," Lacey told Carole as they hurried along the sidewalk, staying low, ever ready to duck into a doorway at the first sign of movement or sound of a car. "I guess it still is. Very tony, very high rent. At least it was."

But now it was a ghost town, pimpled here and there with piles of black plastic garbage bags, torn open, their contents pawed and pecked through by rats and pigeons, perhaps even people. Waiting in vain to be picked up by a non-existent sanitation department. Waiting for Godot.

She led Carole past the brick-fronted Community Church of New York with BLESSED ARE THE PEACEMAKERS emblazoned on its front wall.

Peacemakers . . . is that us? she wondered.

Further up on the right, on the corner of Madison Avenue, sat a brownstone church and steeple.

364 F. PAUL WILSON

"The Church of the Incarnation," Carole muttered as they passed. "I wonder . . . oh, it's Episcopal."

"Almost as good as Catholic, right?"

Carole smiled. "But not quite."

They dashed across Madison to the shadows of the Oxford University Press offices, then continued on toward Fifth Avenue. Before reaching Fifth they found the broken side doors of the City University Graduate Building. They squeezed through and climbed to the second floor. There, through huge arched windows, they had a panoramic view of the Art Deco lower levels of the Empire State Building and the intersection of Fifth Avenue and Thirty-fourth Street.

Lacey leaned forward to see if she could see the top.

"Don't get too close to the window," Carole said, pointing to the sunlight slanting through the dusty air. "Somebody might see you."

Lacey nodded, too awestruck by what she saw.

"Look. They have electricity."

Houlihan's bar and restaurant, occupying the ground-floor corner of the Empire State nearest them, was lit up inside. A neon Red Hook Lager sign glowed in the window. She'd stopped in there once to eat but had walked out. Fourteen bucks for a hamburger. Location, location, location.

"Joseph told us they were using the generators."

"I know. But it's been so long since I've seen a working electric light, I . . . it's kind of wonderful in a way. Gives me hope."

They found some chairs well back in the shadows and settled down to watch. A few Vichy hung around under the canopied front entrance, but otherwise there wasn't much activity.

"Do you think this is the right way to go?" Lacey said after a while. "The three of us attacking the Empire State Building, I mean."

"We don't know that we will be. That's why we're here now. To see if it's feasible."

"Don't get me wrong, but do you get the feeling that no matter what we find, somehow Joe's going to think it's feasible?"

Carole turned and stared at her. "I don't think I understand."

"I think you do. My uncle's got a major hard on for this Franco."

"Lacey—"

"It's true and you know it. That's all he's talked about since we did the Post Office: Franco, Franco, Franco. Here we are, possibly the only three humans in the world with firsthand knowledge of the vampires' secret—how the death of one reverberates through the progeny, wiping out all his or her get down the line—and we're all together in New York instead of splitting up and trying to make it into the unoccupied areas of the country to spread the news."

"We've been through that."

"Yeah, I know, but . . ."

It was easier to move around within the occupied zone than to get out of it. Vichy were stacked at the Delaware River crossings waiting to pick off anyone who tried. Joe's theory was that if they could knock off Franco and his get, the Vichy network would collapse in disarray—at least for a while—and they could waltz across.

Maybe.

"And remember," Carole said, "one of the parishioners has a shortwave and is probably broadcasting the news to the world right now."

"We don't know that. And who'd believe him?"

"Exactly. That's why we agreed it will be much better to be able to show than simply tell."

Another idea of Joe's: use the building's security system to videotape the deaths of Franco and his get. Then they'd have proof.

"Look, Carole, I know Franco is the head honcho and taking him down will put a serious crimp in the undead master plan, but do you get the feeling that there's more to it, that if Joe could demonstrate this get-death on another undead of equal stature, he'd bypass the opportunity and remain fixed on Franco?"

Carole's tone took on a definite chill. "You're saying that Joseph would jeopardize our lives and what we know just to get revenge on Franco?"

"You're not answering the question."

Carole looked away.

Was it simple revenge? That had to be part of it, Lacey knew, and she had her own score to settle with this monster for what he had done to her Uncle Joe. But she sensed something more than revenge driving Joe to this showdown, something she was missing.

That worried her.

"Look, Carole, you've got to admit that Joe isn't exactly the same guy he was a week ago. He was dead, and now he's not. What brought him back to life? It wasn't your God, so what was it?"

"God intervened. Joseph was supposed to become one of the undead, but he did not. God has turned the Devil's own work back on him, making Joseph an instrument of His divine vengeance."

"Buy into that if you want, Carole. I don't. I can't. And I'm a little worried about that weird dream he's been having. We know Joe's been to hell and back. I just hope he didn't bring a little of that hell back with him."

14

CAROLE . . .

By Sunday evening they were ready to make their move.

Fifty-three minutes before sundown, as soon as Joe was up and fed—Lacey's turn tonight—he got behind the wheel of the Navigator and drove down Broadway. Lacey sat up front next to her uncle; Carole had the rear to herself.

"Are we ready for this?" he said as they approached Thirty-fourth Street.

Carole wasn't sure. She hoped so.

They'd learned through three days and three nights of steady surveillance that the Vichy—the more time she spent with Joseph and Lacey, the more Carole found herself using that designation—stuck to a fairly rigid schedule of two shifts: a large contingent of perhaps twenty-five or thirty worked the days, while only a half dozen or so manned the entrance at night.

They'd taken over Houlihan's and turned the bar-restaurant into a cafeteria of sorts. It served two meals a day—breakfast and dinner—at change of shift. Using binoculars, Carole and Lacey had watched from their perch across the street as the Vichy attacked heaps of scrambled eggs every morning—the

cook had to be using the powdered kind—and pots of some
sort of stew every evening.

All three agreed that the meal break at shift change was the
time to strike. All the Vichy were concentrated in Houlihan's
then. They'd settled on dawn, Monday, for their assault.

But assault how?

Joseph and Lacey had wanted to find a way to use the napalm, rig it somehow to explode and turn the restaurant into
an inferno while the Vichy were eating their breakfast. But
the "somehow" eluded them. And even if they did manage to
come up with a way to explode it, the napalm presented too
many chances for something to go wrong. If they were only
partially successful—if they killed some but not all of the
Vichy—they'd have to abandon all hope of success. They
couldn't win a fire fight with them, and from then on the
Vichy would be warned and on full alert.

Carole had had a better idea. This was why she'd brought
along the canister of sodium fluorosilicate. She'd had a feeling they might need a more silent form of death than bullets
and napalm. She'd found canisters of the chemical at one of
the local municipal utility authorities where it was used to
purify the water supply. At a few parts per million, sodium
fluorosilicate was harmless. But ingestion of half a gram of
the odorless and tasteless powder interfered with cellular
metabolism, making you deathly ill. A gram caused convul-
sions and death. Not a pretty way to go, but probably better
than being burned alive by napalm.

Carole wished there were another way, one that could be
delivered by someone else and not multiply the number of
lives she'd already taken. But there was nothing and no one.
It was her idea, her responsibility. She couldn't shirk it off
on someone else.

The question was, how to get it into the Vichy? Obviously
via their food. This evening's sortie would accomplish
that—they hoped.

Joseph turned the big SUV onto Thirty-fourth and said,
"Let's pray that those technicians I've been watching don't

eat with the rest of them tomorrow. We need them. And besides, they appear to be innocent. The three of them seem
older than the typical Vichy, they're unarmed, and dress like
middle managers. They arrive in a group every morning,
flanked by two Vichy. They're not tied or manacled, but I get
the impression they're prisoners of some sort."

"But they could wind up sick or dead," Lacey said. "Then
what do we do?"

"Please, God, don't let them," Carole said. She had blood
on her hands, she was crimson to her elbows, but so far none
of it was innocent.

"But what if they do?" Lacey persisted.

Joseph shook his head. "I've been watching three dawns
in a row and not once have they eaten with the others. In
fact, by the time they're brought in, breakfast is just about
done, and they're taken directly inside. Let's hope tomorrow
is no exception."

Halfway between Sixth and Fifth Avenues, Joseph slowed
the car to a crawl. Carole leaned forward, peering ahead between Joseph and Lacey toward the lighted windows of
Houlihan's, glowing like a beacon in the fading light. She
searched for signs of stray Vichy who'd wandered away
from the Fifth Avenue entrance around the corner where
they usually hung out. But nothing was moving on the street
except their car.

"Damn!" Joseph said. "The earring. Would somebody do
the honor?"

Lacey fished the Vichy earring off the dashboard and
punched it through his earlobe.

"Didn't feel a thing," he said. "Are you ladies ready?"

"Ready as I'll ever be," Lacey said. "How about you, Carole?"

Carole could only nod. Her mouth was too dry for speech.
They were entering the belly of the beast.

Joseph swung the car into the curb and stopped. Houlihan's lit-up interior was empty. Dinner wasn't ready yet. The
cook was back in the kitchen.

"I'll turn the car around and wait here. Hurry. And be careful."

Carole watched Lacey shove a pair of steel bars she called "nunchucks" up the left sleeve of her sweatshirt. She turned to Carole and took a deep, quavering breath.

"Let's roll."

Carole alighted with her backpack in her hand. She'd removed the stakes and crosses and hammer and replaced them with a football-size sack of sodium fluorosilicate. A pound of the stuff. Enough to kill the Empire State Building's Vichy contingent a dozen times over.

They hurried across the sidewalk, pushed through the revolving glass doors, and headed straight for the rear of the restaurant area. The air smelled sour. The bar, tables, and floor were littered with paper plates, food scraps, and empty beer cans. Waves of glistening brown beetles scurried out of their way as they approached.

"Cockroaches," Carole whispered. "I've never seen so many."

"Maybe they feel some kinship with the clientele," Lacey replied.

They paused outside the swinging doors to the kitchen. Light filtered through the two round, grease-smeared windows.

"Okay," Lacey said. "I go first."

She pushed through the doors; Carole followed. A fat, balding, cigar-chewing man in a bulging tank top stood before a stove, stirring a big pot. He looked up as they entered.

"Who the fuck are you?" he said.

"A couple of hungry ladies," Lacey said. "Got any dinner you can spare?"

"Yo." He grinned and grabbed his crotch. "I got dinner right here."

"That's not exactly what we had in mind."

"You eat some of this, you get to eat some of what's cookin in the pot. *Capisce*?"

While Lacey talked, Carole looked around the filthy mess

of a kitchen. She didn't see a gun. The cook probably couldn't imagine he'd need one. Immediately to her right she spotted the other thing she was looking for: half a dozen ten-pound canisters of powdered eggs. One was open, its lid slightly askew.

"I'm kind of cranky right now," Lacey was saying. "I'm hungry, I've got low blood sugar, and I'm feeling premenstrual. You'll like me better when I'm not hypoglycemic."

"Ay, this ain't no *Let's Make A Deal.*" He jabbed a finger at Lacey. "You do me before you eat"—then at Carole— "and she does me after. Otherwise you can get the fuck outta here."

Lacey sighed and took a step toward him. "Oh, all right."

He grinned and started loosening his belt. "That's more like it!"

Lacey's hand darted to her sleeve and came up with her nunchucks. She whipped her hand around in a small circle, snapping her wrist and slamming one of the steel bars against the side of the cook's head. He grunted and staggered back, clutching his head. Lacey followed, swinging her nunchucks left, right, left, right, then vertically, connecting each time with either the man's head or his raised elbows. With blood spurting from his face and scalp, the cook turned away, dropped to his knees, then fell forward, covering his head with his hands and groaning.

"Stop, stop! Take what you want!"

"Warned you I was cranky. Now get flat on your belly and stay there." He complied, leaving the patterned soles of his sneakers facing Carole. Lacey turned and gave her a nod.

Carole knelt beside the open canister of powdered eggs and removed the lid. It was three-quarters full. A heavy metal scoop lay inside. She pulled the bag of sodium fluorosilicate out of her backpack and began scooping the egg powder into its place.

"You could have been nice, you know," she heard Lacey saying. "All we wanted was something to eat. Didn't your mother ever teach you to share?"

"I'm sorry," the cook moaned. "I'm sorry!"

"Now we'll have to take it."

When Carole figured she'd scooped out about two pounds of egg, she zipped up the backpack, then emptied the pound of sodium fluorosilicate into the canister. The chemical was white and the powdered egg was a pale yellow. She used the scoop to mix them into a consistent color, then replaced the lid.

God forgive her. She'd just sealed the fates and numbered the hours of dozens of men. Vicious, evil men, but men nonetheless.

"All right," she told Lacey. "I've got the eggs."

Lacey had the big chrome refrigerator door open and was peering inside.

"What have we here?" she said. She reached in and removed what looked like a pepperoni and half a wheel of white cheese. "Looks like cookie's got his own private stash!" She turned to the cook and squatted beside him. "All right. We're leaving. Don't even think about moving or making a sound until we're gone or I'll bust your head wide open and fry your brains on the grill. *Capisce?*"

The cook moaned and nodded.

Lacey looked at Carole and waggled her eyebrows. "Let go."

JOE . . .

Joe could see the kitchen doors through Houlihan's plate glass windows. He'd watched Carole and Lacey push through them only a few minutes ago, but it seemed like an hour.

"Come on, ladies," he whispered. "Come on."

The idea was to make this look like a food raid—desperate people risking their lives to take food *out*, not leave something behind. That was why he'd asked Lacey not to show a gun unless she had to. All it would take was one shot to bring the Vichy running. Let them think the thieves who'd hit them were amateurs armed only with nunchucks and knives.

Am I doing the right thing? he wondered for the thousandth time since they'd arrived in New York. He had a feeling he wasn't.

They were following his lead, trusting him with their lives. Was he, as the phrase went, exercising due diligence? He didn't know. All he knew was that once the idea of targeting Franco in his aerie had taken hold, he couldn't uproot it. He'd considered other options, but none of them held a candle to this. Because this was unquestionably the best tactic or because he'd become fixated on Franco? Part of him argued that he should have sent either Carole or Lacey west, to try to cross into unoccupied territory with the secret. But a stronger part had countered that he needed both of them along to take Franco down, and that argument had prevailed.

And he knew why. He had a secondary goal in mind, one he dared not tell Carole and Lacey. They'd never let him go through with it.

But he had another concern. Joe was noticing wild mood swings. In life he'd been prone to periodic lows that usually responded to a couple of stiff Scotches. Now he found himself experiencing surges of rage at the slightest provocation. He'd managed to control them so far. Like early this morning when Lacey had questioned him about some minor point in tonight's plan, he'd had this sudden urge to grab her by the throat and scream at her to stop asking so many goddamned questions.

He'd managed to fight it off, but that urge still frightened him. Was it the stress, the responsibility of what they'd planned, or was he edging closer to the darkness in his daymares? What if—?

Movement in the SUV's side mirror caught his attention. A Vichy, bearded and denimed like so many of them, had rounded the corner and was approaching the Navigator with a raised pistol. Then Joe recognized him: the one who'd been with the head Vichy in the Armani suit when Joe was dropped outside the front entrance.

He'll recognize me! This will ruin—

Wait. He won't *recognize me.*

Joe had forgotten momentarily how his face had been disfigured by the sun. Easy to forget when you'd never seen it, when mirrors gave back only a smeary blur.

"What the fuck is this?" the Vichy said, stepping up to the open driver window and leveling his semiautomatic at Joe. "Who are you and what the fuck you think you're—shit! What happened to your face?"

That voice . . . Joe remembered it taunting him in the long elevator ride to the Observation Deck.

I'm glad I ain't you. Holy shit, am I glad I ain't you.

"Good morning," Joe said. "Just waiting to pick up a friend. And the face? An industrial accident."

"Who gives a shit. What're you doin here, man? You think this is some kinda taxi stand?"

Joe turned his head and showed his right earlobe. He flicked the dangly earring. "Hey, I'm in the club."

"That don't mean shit. Who you waitin for?"

Joe cudgeled his brain for the name of this guy's buddy, the one in the suit who'd called him "god-boy."

"Barrett," he said as it came back to him. "He told me to meet him here at sundown."

The Vichy's eyes narrowed. "Barrett's on night duty with me. Should be here any minute." He pulled open Joe's door. "Let's go see about this."

As Joe stepped out of the car, he saw movement in Houlihan's over the Vichy's shoulder: Carole and Lacey leaving the kitchen.

Joe reached for the man's pistol and was surprised by how fast his hand moved. It darted out in a blur of motion; he grabbed the weapon and twisted it from his grasp. The Vichy jumped back with a shocked look and stared at his empty palm. Then he opened his mouth to shout but Joe's other hand reached his throat first, fingers gripping the nape of his neck while the thumb jammed against the windpipe. The man made a strangled sound. Joe pressed harder, hearing the cartilage crunch as it began to give way.

Stop, he told himself.

They'd decided no killing tonight, it might rile the Vichy too much, send them out hunting instead of staying close to Houlihan's and tomorrow's breakfast.

But this felt too, too good. And oh this man deserved dying for how he'd taunted him. Worse yet, he'd seen too much.

A crushed throat might raise too many alarms, though.

With a heave Joe lifted him off his feet and hurled him head first toward the sidewalk. The back of his skull hit the concrete with a meaty crunch; his arms stiffened straight out to either side, then fell limp beside him.

"Joseph?" It was Carole, stepping through the revolving door. She stared at the body with the blood pooling around its head. "What—?"

"Hey, Unk," Lacey said. "I thought we said—"

"In the car, both of you!" he snapped. "We've wasted too much time already!"

Their fault. If they hadn't dawdled so damn long inside, this wouldn't have happened.

The two women piled into the back seat as Joe slipped behind the wheel. He wanted to slam his foot against the accelerator and burn rubber out of here, but a quiet departure was best. When he reached Sixth he turned uptown one block, then raced east on Thirty-fifth. Mostly pubs and parking garages along this block. He pulled into a multi-level garage and parked far in the rear. If the Vichy went hunting for the thieves who stole their food and killed their man, they'd never expect them to hide just one block away.

As he shut off the engine he noticed a foul odor emanating from the back seat.

"What is *that*?" he said.

"Just some snack foods we picked up," Lacey said. "A pepperoni and what looks like provolone."

"The pepperoni—does it have garlic in it?"

"Probably, I—oops. Sorry about that."

"Throw it out."

"No way, Unk. We might never see another pepperoni again. But we'll eat it outside the car."

Joe was halfway turned around, ready to grab the damn pepperoni and shove it down her throat when he stopped himself.

He turned back and leaned his head against the steering wheel.

What's happening to me?

15

CAROLE. . . .

At dawn, and not a minute before, Joseph, Carole, and Lacey stepped out of the garage and started toward Fifth Avenue. The pistol in Carole's hand—Joseph had told her it was a 9mm Glock—felt heavy as it swung with her gait, muzzle toward the sidewalk.

They'd been waiting for Joseph when he awoke an hour ago. After Carole had fed him a few drops of her blood, they'd gone to work checking weapons and mentally preparing themselves for the coming ordeal.

While Joseph and Lacey had tinkered with their guns, Carole sidled off with her gear to a far corner of the garage to make her own preparations. In a little while they'd be entering the heart of darkness, with a fair chance of not coming out alive. Carole wasn't afraid of dying. It was *un*dying that terrified her. So while Joseph and Lacey armed themselves from the collection of weapons confiscated along the way, Carole added extra precautions to guarantee she'd never be an undead: extra charges front and back, and extra triggers. If it came to the point where all hope was lost, she'd make her exit. But not alone.

If worse came to worst, she'd be risking eternal damnation to avoid undeath. Carole shuddered at the prospect. She'd been taught that suicide was a one-way ticket to hell, but she hoped and prayed that God would understand. Death before dishonor . . . death before undeath . . . surely that was the right thing to do.

And now they were on the street, heading toward . . . what?

"All right," Joseph said as they neared Fifth Avenue. He was walking between them. "This is it. We take it slow down to Thirty-fourth. If things went as planned we won't meet any resistance. If things didn't, well, we might have to fight to escape."

Carole knew all this but let him talk. She sensed an unusual tension in Joseph. Was it because this was their D-Day, when all their planning and watching and waiting would either bring them success or death? Or was it something else?

He stopped them at Fifth and worked the slide on his gun.

"Ladies—time to lock and load."

Carole followed his example. The slide gave more resistance than she'd expected.

"Remember what I said," Joseph told them. "If anything happens to me, get out of town and do your best to reach unoccupied territory."

He leaned away and peered around the corner, then turned back to them and nodded.

"I think we're in business."

He motioned them to follow when Carole cleared the corner she saw what he meant. Down the gentle slope, past Thirty-Fourth Street, she spotted three still figures lying on the sidewalk under the Empire State Building's front canopy.

As they passed a smashed and looted Duane Reade, Houlihan's came into view. Writhing forms littered the sidewalk in front of it. One lay in the open doorway next to the revolving door. The odor of fresh coffee wafted across the street through the cool dawn air. On another day, in another place, the smell would have had her salivating, but right now her stomach had shrunk to a tight little knot the size of a walnut.

They crossed the street and now Carole could see the Vichy close up—their gray faces, their bloodshot eyes, their blue lips. She tensed and ducked into a half crouch as she caught movement to her right. One of the Vichy was convulsing on the sidewalk. Her first impulse was to run to his side and help him, but she suppressed it. She, after all, was the reason for his seizure.

Carole stared in horror at the thrashing arms, the foam-flecked lips. It was one thing to plan for their deaths, to imagine them dead. It was something else entirely to witness their death throes.

"Dear God, what have I done?"

JOE . . .

"Let's keep moving," Joe said.

He noticed Carole's sick look. He felt for her, but this was no time for Carole to start second-guessing herself. The old Father Joe might have been appalled, but ex-Father Joe was more fatalistic. It was an ugly scene, but what was done was done. No turning back now.

"Right," Lacey said. "Your window is shrinking."

Joe checked his watch. He had less than fifty minutes before daysleep took hold. They entered the building and he led Lacey and Carole on a winding course through the prostrate forms in the Empire State's front lobby.

At the elevator banks he stopped when he noticed the closed doors to the local car. He pressed the call button, then stepped back and aimed his pistol at the doors.

He motioned Carole and Lacey to the side. "Be ready to fire. This may not arrive empty."

"But this car is waiting," Carole said, pointing to a set of open doors.

"That's the Observation Deck express. At this point we only want to go to three."

The car arrived empty. Joe got on after Lacey and Carole, stabbed the 3 button, and they were on their way. Mentally he was anxious, but physically he was calm—no butterflies in his gut, no pounding heart. As if his emotions were divorced from his body. Or maybe because his body had entered a new mode of existence, one without adrenaline.

Joe pointed his gun at the doors as the car slowed to a stop on three. They parted to reveal an empty hallway. He touched his fingers to his lips and stepped out. Keeping his pistol raised before him, he approached the open double doors to the security center. He was four feet away when a heavyset Vichy stepped into view.

"About fuckin—"

His eyes widened as he saw them and he was reaching for the pistol in his belt when Joe shot him once in the chest. He staggered back, eyes even wider, and then another shot rang out, catching him below the left eye and snapping his head back. He fell like a tree to lay stretched out on the hall carpet.

Joe glanced at Lacey who had her pistol extended in a two-handed grip.

She smiled. "Just making sure."

He looked at Carol. She clutched her pistol waist high, pointed at the wall. She looked like a startled deer.

Joe stepped into the security area and found the three technicians staring at him in shock. He pointed to the fallen Vichy in the hall.

"Any more like him here?"

They shook their heads.

"No," said the oldest of the three. He looked about sixty with gray hair and a receding hairline. "But there will be soon. He was waiting for his relief so he could go get breakfast."

"His relief's not coming," Joe said. "And breakfast has been canceled."

He allowed himself a moment of congratulation. They'd

done it. They'd knocked out the Vichy and captured the Security Center.

Now they had to hold it.

"Who are you?" said the technician. He couldn't seem to pull his gaze from Joe's face.

Joe opened his mouth to speak but Lacey beat him to it.

"Just some nobodies who've come to liberate the building."

"No shit?" said the youngest, who appeared to be in his forties.

"No shit," Lacey agreed. "Who are you three and why are you working for the bloodsuckers?"

"I'm Marty Considine," said the gray-headed one. He pointed to the young one. "This is Mike Leland, and that's Kevin Fowler." The third technician was fat and wore a stained half-sleeve white shirt. He nodded but said nothing.

"As for being here," Considine went on, "we don't have much choice."

"Yeah," said the fat one, Fowler. "Not if we want our wives and kids to live."

Lacey shook her head. "You call this living?"

Leland looked away. "No. But when they slap your kid around and rape your wife in front of you, just to give you a taste of what will happen if you screw up, you get the message."

Joe felt for them, but not terribly. Everyone had suffered. He was scanning the monitors. When he recognized views of the Observation Deck, he said, "We've got one job for you, then you can go back to your families."

"And do what?" said Fowler. His lower lip trembled. "Where can we go?"

"That's up to you. Within half an hour, if all goes well, your services will no longer be needed here. By anyone." He stepped closer to the monitors. "Is there a camera in the stairwell to the Observation Deck?"

Leland began typing on a keyboard. "We've got three there. Which one do you want?"

"The highest—between the eighty-fifth and eighty-sixth if you've got one."

"We do."

"Audio?"

"Just video." He grabbed a mouse and clicked. "Here you go."

A monitor went blank, then cut back in with a view of a door marked 85 in an empty stairwell. A sawed-off shotgun leaned in the corner next to the door.

"Excellent," Joe said.

Leland squinted at the screen. "Hey, somebody's usually guarding the door to eight-five from dawn to dusk."

"We gave him the day off," Lacey said. "Any way of broadcasting from here?"

Considine shook his head. "The building has a huge TV antenna, but that's another department. We're security. We don't know squat about TV transmission."

"It's okay," Joe said, tapping the screen. "We'll tape as planned. Record that one, and then I'll tell you another one to record when I get to the Observation Deck."

"It's true then?" Considine said. "You're really liberating the building?"

"That's the plan," Joe said.

"About time. How many of you are there?"

"Just us," Lacey said.

He stared. "Three? Just three? You've got to be kidding! Are you people crazy?"

Joe shrugged. "Probably. But we're already more than halfway to succeeding. We—"

A burst of static from the hallway startled him.

"Security! Security, do you copy?"

Joe tensed. "What's that?"

"One of their two-ways."

Joe stepped out into the hall, found the little walkie-talkie clipped to the dead guard's belt, and turned it off. He returned to the Security Center and faced Carole and Lacey.

"That means at least one of the Vichy is still alive out there. Probably more."

"Well," Lacey said, "we knew from the get-go we wouldn't get them all."

"I don't like leaving you two alone here."

Considine stepped past him. Joe tensed as he picked up the fallen guard's pistol. He worked the slide and chambered a round.

"Who said they're alone? Your ranks just swelled to four."

Joe stared at him. "You know how to use that?"

Considine nodded. "Nam, pal. Eighteen months in country."

Joe liked leaving Carole and Lacey with an armed stranger even less, but sensed he could trust Considine. He didn't have much choice.

"You folks hold the fort here. Lock the door and pull that desk in front of it. Shoot anyone who tries to get in."

"Where are you going?" Considine said.

"Upstairs. I've got a date with Franco."

He glanced at Carole. She had a dazed air about her that worried him. "Carole, are you all right?"

"I'll be fine," she said. "Hurry. You haven't much time."

"I know." He stepped close to her and took her in his arms and held her. He never wanted to leave her.

"I love you," he murmured as he kissed her hair. "Always remember that. We—"

He stopped as he felt a lump between her shoulder blades, and another farther down near the small of her back. He knew what they were.

"Oh, God, Carole!" he whispered. "Don't ever push those buttons. I know they give you comfort, but I beg you, don't. Please don't."

He released her she stared at him with stricken eyes. "Only as a last resort," she told him. "Only when all hope is gone."

"Then I pray that moment never comes." He turned and hugged Lacey. "My favorite niece," he said. "One of my favorite people in the whole world. Just remember: if anything happens to me, you and Carole get these tapes to the unoccupied territories."

Lacey backed away and gave him a strange look. "Why do you keep saying that? It's like you don't think you'll see us again."

"I might not. But I'm not what this is about. I'm expendable. If I can't make it back, you two must go on without me."

He couldn't tell them the truth. He turned to go.

"Wait," Carole said, holding a zipped-up backpack. "Don't forget this."

He nodded and began slipping his arms through the straps as he ran for the elevators. The pack was hot against his back.

BARRETT . . .

Home from the night shift, James Barrett stepped into his Murray Hill brownstone and checked the long-pork filet he'd put in the refrigerator to thaw when he'd left at sunset. It had softened considerably but still had a ways to go.

He yawned. Christ, this was a boring way to live. Sleeping days, working nights. His internal clock couldn't seem to get used to it. Cooking was the only interesting thing in his life now, and even that was palling on him. Without fresh spices there were only so many ways you could cook human flesh. At least it was better than eating that slop they served the troops at Houlihan's day after day.

Not that he'd eat with the hoi polloi anyway. He needed to set himself apart, both in their eyes and in the undead's.

At least they'd had a little excitement last night with Neal getting killed and those two women stealing food from the kitchen. Neal wound up with the back of his head stove in. He was one tough mother. Barrett couldn't see a couple of women doing that. Must've had help.

He wondered if they were connected to the mess in the Lincoln tunnel. What if that hadn't been an accident?

He had put the cowboys on full alert tonight, stationed a couple of guards in Houlihan's, and sent out teams to look for someone, anyone who might be connected. They'd returned with a few stray cattle but no one who fit the cook's description.

He'd miss Neal. He was good for a laugh and for the application of a little muscle when Barrett gave him the go-ahead. But did he feel even a trace of sadness at his passing? They said when you were turned and rose as undead, you lost all your emotions. That would be a breeze for Barrett. He had no memory of feeling anything for anybody. Ever.

That was why his situation was so frustrating. He was already most of the way to undead. All he needed was the bite and he'd be there. If he could just—

His two-way squawked. Now what? Couldn't they do anything over there without him? He snatched it up.

"Yeah. Talk to me."

Nothing but faint static from the other end.

"Hey, you called. What do you want?"

Nothing again, then something that sounded like a groan, a very agonized groan.

"Hello? Who's there? What's going on?"

Again the groan, fainter this time, then nothing. Barrett tried to get a response but nothing came through. He tried calling the Security Center but no one picked up.

His chest tightened. Something was up. Remembering Neal's cracked dome, he stuck his Dirty Harry gun—his .44 Magnum—into his shoulder holster and hurried back to the Empire State.

JOE . . .

When Joe stepped out on the eightieth floor, instead of heading for the other bank of elevators to take him the last six floors to the Observation Deck, he looked around and found an exit door. He pushed through and climbed the stairs.

Outside the door marked 85 he looked around for the security camera. When he found it he waved, then reached for
the handle.

A foul miasma of rot engulfed Joe when he opened the
door. The stairwell was well lit but the space beyond the door
was dark as a tomb.

How appropriate, he thought.

His night vision was extraordinary but it wasn't up to this,
so he stepped through and found a light switch on the wall.
The hallway was strewn with office furniture. He began
searching room to room. The first two were filled with som-
nolent get-guards stretched out on mattresses and futons, but
Franco was not among them. He looked down the hall and
saw a form stretched out before a doorway. Could be a dead
victim, but if it was a get-guard . . .

It was. That could only mean Franco was inside. Joe
picked up the pistol and machete at the guard's side and
tossed them down the hall. Then he tried the door. Locked.
He reared back and kicked it in.

There, in the center of the otherwise empty room with
boarded-up windows, a four-poster bed sat like a ship be-
calmed on a still dark sea.

And in that bed . . . Joe recognized the big blond hair and
mustache, the sharp angle of the nose. A burst of fury like
nothing he'd ever experience took hold of him. He wanted to
run down the hallway, find that machete, and start hacking
away at this worthless cluster of cells. But no killing blows.
Just slicing off small pieces, one at a time . . .

Joe shook it off. These dark impulses were getting
stronger. Had to stick to the plan.

"Franco!" he shouted as he stepped over the get-guard.
"Franco, I've got something to show you!"

Franco lay on his back in gray silk suit pants and a glossy
white, loose-sleeved shirt that reminded Joe of a woman's
blouse. Slowly he pivoted his head toward Joe. His eyes
widened in surprise as his lips formed the word, *Who?*

"We'll get to that in a minute."

He lifted the big vampire onto his shoulder, something that would have been a back-wrenching task a week ago; but now, with his semi-undead strength, he found it easy. Franco struggled but his movements were weak, futile. The get-guard at the door clutched at him as he passed but didn't have a prayer of restraining him.

Joe moved down the hall, kicking in each door he passed, shouting, "Hey! I've got your daddy and I'm going to send him to his final reward. Try and stop me!"

Back in the stairwell he started up the flight to the Observation Deck but stopped halfway. He put Franco down and let him slump on the concrete steps.

"Who are you?" Franco rasped.

"Am I that easy to forget?" Joe said. "It was only a week ago—a week ago today, as a matter of fact."

He heard something scrape against the concrete under Franco. He flipped him over and saw the leathery tips of his wings struggling to emerge through the slits in his shirt. Joe pulled off his backpack and unzipped it. Rays of bright white light shot from the opening.

Blinking in the glare, Joe reached in and found the foam-rubber padding Carole had duct-taped to the lower end of his silver cross. Even through the padding he felt its heat. Averting his eyes he pulled out the cross and slammed it against one of the emerging wings. A hiss of burning flesh, a puff of acrid smoke as Franco writhed and let out a hoarse scream. Then the other wing—with the same results.

He returned the cross to the back pack and zipped it. He blinked to regain his vision; when it cleared he looked down at Franco's back. The wing tips were now smoldering lumps of scar tissue. He turned as he heard the door from the eighty-fifth floor hallway swing open. Members of Franco's get-guard began to crawl into the stairwell.

Good.

He grabbed the gasping, whimpering Franco and turned

him onto his back. The vampire stared at Joe's face, his expression terrified and confused.

"I'll refresh your memory, Franco. You allowed something called Devlin to lunch on me." Joe's anger flared again as he recalled his terror, his helplessness, and the searing pain of having his throat ripped open. "Remember?" He heard his voice growing louder. "Told me I'd soon be just like him. Remember?" He grabbed Franco by the neck and drew his face close. *"Remember?"*

He was shouting now and he wanted to rip Franco's head off.

No. Not yet.

He looked down and saw that the get-guards had reached the steps and were crawling up, their progress slow, tortured.

"Come on, guys," he said. "Move it. I haven't got all day."

Damn right. He glanced at his watch. He had maybe twenty, twenty-five minutes before he became as weak as they.

He turned back to Franco and saw that a light had dawned in the undead's eyes—realization, but not belief.

"The priest?" he whispered in a voice like tiny claws scratching stone. "You? No . . ."

"Yes!" Joe heard the word hiss out like escaping steam. "The priest. Killing me wasn't good enough. You had to condemn me to an eternity of depravity, rob me of every shred of dignity, undo every scrap of good I'd done in my entire life. At least that was your plan. But it didn't work."

"How?" The word was an exhalation.

"I'm not even sure myself. All I know is this is how it works out in the end: I lose, but you lose too."

He flinched at a deafening report and the *spang* of a bullet ricocheting off the concrete above his head. Another shot and this time the bullet dug into his hip with a painful sting.

He stood and faced them, spreading his arms. "Go ahead. It won't matter. I'm one of you."

Not true. He'd never be one of them, but no reason they shouldn't suffer some confusion and dismay in their final minutes.

More shots. Most were misses because their weak, wavering hands were unable to aim, but a few hit home. He jerked with the impacts, felt the heat and pain of their entries, but it was nothing he couldn't bear. Finally they gave it up. He smiled at the alarm in their faces.

He turned to Franco and lifted him in his arms. "Let's go."

"Where?"

"To see the sun. Don't you miss it? We're too late for sunrise, but it promises to be a beautiful day."

Franco grabbed Joe's shirt and pulled on it. A feeble gesture. But Joe was surprised to see a nasty grin stretch his thin lips.

"You idiot! Devlin was my get! That makes *you* my get as well. When I die, *you* die!"

"I know," Joe said, returning a grin he hoped was just as nasty: "I'm counting on that."

Franco's jaw dropped open. "N-no! You can't! You—"

"I can. Because I don't want to exist like this."

Joe pushed through the door at the top of the steps and emerged into the green-tiled atrium by the elevators. Sunlight, searingly bright, blazed through the huge windows of the enclosed observation area that lay a few steps up and beyond. Only a six-foot swath, no more than two feet wide, penetrated the atrium.

I'm here. I've done it.

Amazing what someone can do when they don't care if they live or die, he thought. But they can achieve so much more, achieve the seemingly impossible, when they're *looking* to die.

He forced himself to look at that swath of direct light. That was where Franco would meet his end, sealing Joe's fate as well. But first he'd wait for the get-guards to arrive. He wanted as many as possible on camera when Franco bought it.

CAROLE . . .

Carole's stomach clenched as she stared at the monitors. "What is he *doing?*"

"Just what he said he would," Lacey replied. "Getting as many get-guards onscreen before he pushes Franco into the sunlight."

"But there's a whole stairwell full of guards. Too many of them. He's letting them get too close. Why doesn't he have the cross out?"

"What can they do? After that display in the stairwell they know they can't shoot him."

"But they have those machetes."

"So? They can barely lift them. Don't worry, Carole. He's got them beat."

Carole wasn't so sure. A lucky swing from a machete could sever an Achilles tendon, or worse, a higher swing could catch Joseph's hamstrings. He wouldn't be able to stand then. He'd go down and they'd swarm over him. One of them might be strong enough to behead him . . .

Her chest tightened at the thought. She couldn't, wouldn't lose him.

"I'm going up there," she blurted.

"No way!" Lacey said. "Our job is to stay here."

Carole began pushing the desk away from the door. "No. I can help. I can use the cross to keep them back."

Lacey grabbed her arm. "Carole—"

Carole wrenched free. "Please don't fight me on this. I've got to go. I've just got to."

"Shit!" Lacey said. "Then I'll go with you."

"No." She cracked the door and peeked out into the hall. Empty. "One of us has to stay here. That's you."

Without looking back, she stepped into the hall and started for the elevators.

She heard Considine's voice behind her. "Tell her she's got to go down to one and catch an express to eighty."

"Carole—" Lacey began.

"I heard," Carole said over her shoulder.

"Keep your gun ready," Lacey called. "You see anything moving, shoot first and ask questions later."

"I will."

And she would. Joseph needed her and no one was going to bar her from reaching him.

BARRETT . . .

Barrett staggered through the Empire State lobby in a daze. His men lay strewn about like jackstraws. Blue-gray faces everywhere. Those who weren't dead were well on their way.

Obviously they'd been poisoned, but how? The water supply? The breakfast eggs? The coffee? Didn't much matter now. He just had to remember not to eat or drink anything within blocks of this building.

But *all* of his men? Surely there had to be a couple who'd missed breakfast. But he didn't know who and he had no way of contacting them. They were scattered throughout the building. He'd have to go floor to floor and door to door.

The other question was *who*. Who did this? What did they want? Were they after the cowboys, to send a message to anyone who collaborated with the enemy? Or were they after the undead too? If so, they'd be upstairs, on eight-five— where the vamps would be sitting ducks and the shit would really be hitting the fan.

Barrett turned and looked back at the front doors. His first impulse was to cut and run. As top cowboy the responsibility for all this would be laid on him. But on the other hand, he'd been looking for a chance to put himself in the spotlight. Maybe this was opportunity knocking.

He had to reach the Security Center. He could get the lay

of the land there and decide what, if anything, he could do. He headed for the elevators. As he passed the security kiosk in the main lobby he remembered it was equipped with a couple of monitors.

He stepped up to the console and dialed through the various feeds but stopped when he came to the Observation Deck. He gaped at the scene playing out on the little black-and-white screen. Some guy with a scarred-up face had Franco. The head vampire hung in his grip like a rag doll. A couple of get-guards were crawling through the stairway door. Where were their guns? Why didn't they shoot?

They needed someone to take charge up there and take this fucker out.

James Barrett grinned. His moment had come.

He searched the drawers of the kiosk looking for something to give him an advantage, no matter how small, beyond his big gun. He found some pepper spray and a couple of pairs of handcuffs. He took the spray, then pulled his Magnum and headed for the elevators.

As he approached the Observation Deck express bank, he heard a set of doors slide open. He started to step back, then reversed field. The car couldn't hold *that* many; he might be outnumbered but he had surprise on his side. So he made a snap decision and charged with both arms held straight out before him, pepper spray in his left, pistol in the right. He'd reached full speed when a woman stepped out of the car. He collided with her head on. As they fell to the floor he began firing into the car. He got off two booming shots before he realized it was empty.

Barrett turned his attention to the woman who was struggling beneath him. He slammed the heavy barrel of his Magnum against her head, stunning her. Then he rushed back to the guard kiosk and grabbed the handcuffs. She was stirring as he returned so he quickly pulled her arms behind her and snapped the cuffs on. He didn't have the keys and didn't need them to lock her into them. As for getting her out—not his worry.

He stood and looked down at her. A slim brunette. Not bad looking, but not his type. One thing he knew about her was that she didn't belong here. That meant she was with the ugly guy on the Observation Deck.

And that meant he had a hostage. Perfecto.

JOE . . .

Half a dozen get-guards were through the door now, their machetes scraping against the marble as they dragged themselves across the floor.

These should be enough to make the point, he thought as he edged himself and Franco away from them and closer to the patch of sunlight. They appeared to be in the camera's field of view.

Now . . . the moment of truth.

Questions surged unbidden into his mind. Did he really want to do this? It would end everything. No more Carole, no more Lacey. Wasn't this existence, hideous as it was, better than no existence at all?

No. Unequivocally no. He would not spend the centuries this half-breed existence might give him as a creature of the darkness and twilight. Yes, he'd have more time with Carole and Lacey, but he'd also have to watch them age and die.

Better to make a clean break, better to end his personal horror by removing another horror from the earth.

He lifted Franco and tensed his muscles to hurl him into the light.

"Get ready to burn, Franco," he whispered.

"No! Please—!"

Just then an elevator chimed to his left. The doors slid open and his heart sank when he saw Carole. He didn't want her to have to watch his death throes. But panic and rage exploded within him when he saw the grinning face hovering behind her shoulder.

Barrett.

The head Vichy propelled Carole ahead of him into the atrium. The doors whispered closed behind them.

"Well, well," he said, still grinning. "What have we here? I guess this is what we call a stand-off."

"Carole, are you all right?"

She shook her head. A thin stream of blood trickled down her temple from her scalp. Her eyes filled with tears.

"Joseph, I'm so sorry."

"It's all right."

He made a silent promise: *I'll get you out of this, no matter what it takes.*

He noticed that her arms were pulled behind her, which meant her hands were bound. In a way, that was a relief. Barrett had no idea how lucky he was. If Carole were able to get her hands into her pockets, she might have blown them both to pieces by now.

"Let her go, Barrett," Joe said.

His eyebrows lifted. "You know my name? You have the advantage over me, sir. And I'm sure I'd not forget a face like yours."

There wasn't time to get into that.

"Just let her go."

"And why would I want to do that?"

"It's the right thing to do."

"For you maybe, but not for me. I'm willing to make a trade, though. Her for him." He pointed to Franco. "Hear that, Bossman? I'm saving your ass. And I expect something in return—big time. After I straighten this out, I want to be turned. Immediately. We waive the ten-year clause. Agreed?"

"Yes," Franco rasped. "Of course."

"And I don't want to be turned by some low-level drone, either. By you or, better yet, by the guy who turned you, if he's still around. I want wings."

Franco nodded. "Yes. Anything. Anything you want."

"You want to be like them?" Joe pointed to the undead guards who were continuing their inching crawl toward him.

They'd be within striking distance in a minute. "Look at them. Slithering along the floor. They're vermin!"

"But they're the vermin who're running the show."

"Not for long. And then where will you be?"

"It's over for us, Mister Melted Face. The New World Order has arrived, and though it's not what anyone imagined, the choices come down to predator or prey. I've never seen myself as prey." He smiled. "So . . . how do you want to work the trade?"

"Joseph, no!" Carole cried.

Barrett grabbed a fistful of her hair and yanked her head back. "No one asked you! You're nothing but merchandise, so keep it zipped. I do the negotiating here!"

Joe took a step toward him. He wanted to kill Barrett, but slowly. Twist his head around an inch at a time until it was facing the other way.

"Uh-uh!" Barrett said. He held up an old-fashioned stiletto, pressed the button, and out snapped a gleaming four-inch blade. He pressed the point against Carole's throat. "Don't make me damage the merchandise."

LACEY . . .

Lacey stared at the Observation Deck feed. Joe's lips were moving and he was looking away from the camera.

"Who's he talking to?" she said.

Considine shrugged. "Maybe Franco, maybe your friend. She should have arrived by now."

The scars made Joe's face all but unreadable, especially on this small, grainy screen, but something about his body language set off warning alarms throughout her brain.

"Do you have other cameras up there?"

Leland grabbed his mouse. "One other that catches the atrium." Windows opened and closed on his computer screen, menus dropped down and rolled up. "Here we go."

The scene that flickered to life on the screen froze Lacey's heart. Carole . . . held prisoner by a Vichy.

"Barrett!" Considine said over her shoulder. "Fucking Barrett. How'd you miss him?"

"Who's he?"

"Chief rat."

Lacey pulled her pistol from her belt. "I'm going up there."

"Not alone, you're not," Considine said.

"Stay here," she said. "We need that tape."

"These guys can handle that. Going alone is what got your friend in trouble." He was already heading for the door. "Let's move."

Lacey followed him out into the hall. They were almost to the elevators when one of them chimed. The UP light glowed over the second set of doors. Considine went into a crouch and motioned her toward the near wall. Pistol fully extended, he hurried forward and flattened himself against the wall immediately to the right of the doors.

When they slid open and a scraggly-haired head peeked out, Considine shot him in the face from six inches away. Lacey heard someone inside the car shout "Fuck!" as the shot man went down in a spray of red, landing in the doorway. The doors tried to close but the body blocked them.

Considine knelt and, without turning his head, motioned Lacey down to the floor. Seconds later another Vichy burst from the car with a hoarse cry, spraying the hall with an assault pistol. As the bullets screamed over her head, Lacey returned fire along with Considine. She didn't know who hit him but suddenly he went into spin, falling one way while his weapon sailed in another. He ended up huddled against the wall, clutching his shoulder.

Considine peeked into the elevator car, then stepped over to the fallen Vichy, picking up his assault pistol on the way. He turned him over with his foot and—to Lacey's shock—shot him in his good shoulder, then once again in the stomach.

"Not exactly a kill shot," Lacey said as the Vichy screamed and writhed in agony.

Considine's face was a grim mask as he returned to the elevator and pulled the first body clear of the door.

"Not intended," he said.

"We don't want to leave any live ones."

He motioned her into the car. "That one we do. Between the messed-up shoulders and the gut shot, he's out of the fight."

The doors closed and he pressed the lobby button.

Lacey stared at him. "You've got something personal going on here?"

Considine's eyes remained fixed straight ahead on the doors. His voice was dead flat. "Back in January two of this guy's buddies held me and made me watch while he raped my wife. Said if I didn't cooperate they'd pass her around the cowboys like that until they were tired of her, then she'd be turned and sent to kill me."

Lacey swallowed. The terror, the humiliation this man had had to live with . . . she couldn't think of anything else to say except, "I'm sorry."

"And now *he's* sorry. It should take him hours to die. If I'm real lucky, maybe a couple of days, every minute of it in excruciating agony."

"My kind of guy," she said. He glanced at her. "That is, if I liked guys."

JOE . . .

Joe winced as he saw the point of the stiletto indent the flesh of Carole's throat.

"Don't hurt her,"

"Then stop dragging this out," Barrett said. "We make the switch and we all walk away free and clear." He smiled. "Until I come and hunt you down."

Joe felt his strength beginning to slip. He glanced toward the observation windows. He couldn't see the glass or anything beyond, only a featureless blaze of white. The sun was nearing the point where it would suck off his energy and reduce him to a crawling weakling like Franco and his get.

What could he do? If there was a way out of this, he couldn't see it. He could barely think.

So close to success—ending Franco and all his get, no matter where in the world they were. Ending himself.

Maybe that was the answer: shove Franco into the sun, and while his screams caused a distraction, make a leap toward Carole and Barrett.

Did he dare?

As if Barrett were reading his mind, he moved into the patch of sunlight, pulling Carole with him. Joe could barely look at them.

"No funny stuff," Barrett said.

Joe slumped. Now what?

"I sense indecision," Barrett said. "Let me offer some incentive." He held up the stiletto, twisting it back and forth to catch the light. "Always wanted one of these, but they've been illegal for decades. Found it in the house I'm occupying. Snap it open and you feel like a juvenile delinquent from a bad fifties movie. But it's a good street-fighting knife. Know why? This slim little blade doesn't get caught up in clothing. Watch."

With that he stabbed it into Carole's flank right below her ribs. Joe cried out as he saw her stiffen in pain and try to pull away. But Barrett had her by the neck.

"Don't worry," he said. "The cut's only an inch or so deep. Nothing that'll do serious damage. But it can cause a *lot* of pain." He angled the blade. "Especially when I drag the point along a rib."

Carole gasped as all the color drained from her face. Her knees buckled but Barrett held her up.

"All right!" Joe shouted. "All *right!* Just stop it! Please!"

Carole was shaking her head. "No!" He could barely hear her voice. "You can't!"

Barrett jabbed her again and this time she screamed. The

sound was like shards of glass being driven through his brain. He wanted to cry.

"Carole, he's got us. We've lost this round."

"Just as you'll lose every round," Barrett said.

"I can't let this happen, Joseph," she gasped.

What was she saying? Thank God she couldn't get her hands into her pockets.

"It'll be all right, Carole."

"Forgive me, Joseph, forgive me, Lord. I love you both."

She turned her head, lifted her left shoulder, and bit something there that looked like a knotted thread.

What's she doing?

"Yeah, I know," Barrett said. "You love everyone. That's why you haven't a prayer of winning."

Joe saw a string clenched in Carole's teeth, saw her close her eyes and jerk her head back.

"*No!*"

The explosion hit him like a falling slab of concrete, knocking Franco into him and sending them both flying. He lost his grip on Franco and slammed into the marble wall behind them, then tumbled to the floor. For a moment he lay there dazed, not sure of where he was, and then it came back to him.

"Carole!"

He struggled to his feet and looked around. Red . . . everything, including Joe, was splattered with red. The blast had shattered the observation windows and now a small gale rushed through the atrium.

Where was Carole? He staggered around, searching, but could find no recognizable trace of her. There had to be something left, something more than the bits of flesh clinging to the walls. Something glinted in a corner: a single bloody handcuff.

Gone . . . she was gone . . . as if she'd never been.

Movement caught his eye. The get-guards had been tossed around by the blast but were recovering now. They were crawling back toward the stairwell, dragging Franco with them, and licking the blood from the floor as they moved.

With a cry of rage in a voice he didn't recognize, Joe lurched toward them. His strength was leaking away like water down a drain. Had to do this while he still was able.

He grabbed Franco's ankle, ripped him free of the guards holding him, and dragged him toward the light. No hesitations, last words, no taunts, just finish the job he'd come here to do. He pulled Franco to his feet at the edge of the sunlit patch and shoved him forward with everything he had.

Franco must have been an old one because he burst into flame as soon as the light touched his skin. His scream was musical, at least to Joe. He spun as his skin charred to black and his eyes bubbled in his head, tried to lunge back to the shadows but his legs wouldn't support him. He collapsed in a flaming heap.

Joe fell back against the nearest wall and slid to the floor, arms open wide to embrace his oncoming death.

LACEY . . .

Lacey and Considine had reached the eightieth floor and were headed for the final elevator bank when the building shook. Lacey saw glass and debris rain past the windows.

A sick certainty about what had just happened nearly drove Lacey to her knees.

"Oh, no! Carole!"

"Your friend?" Considine said. "What—?"

She waved off his questions as she leaned against a wall and sobbed. Oh, Carole. Did you have to? Did you really have to?

"Look," Considine said, "I know we decided to stay off the stairwell, but if there's been an explosion up on the deck, these elevators won't be trustworthy. We're going to have to take the stairs. You have a cross?"

Lacey pulled one out of her pocket and handed it to him. "Here. But I've got a feeling we're not going to need it."

He led her to the stairwell where they were backed up by a blast of smoke when they opened it. The air cleared quickly, however, propelled by the wind blowing through the doorway. The lights were still on, and they hurried up the steps.

"What's that stink?" Considine said.

"Dead vampires. Lots of them."

"Why should they be dead?"

Lacey gave him a quick explanation of get-death.

"No offense," he said, "but I'll believe that when I see it. Sounds too much like wishful thinking."

"That's how most people will react. Which is why we wanted to catch it on tape."

On the eighty-fifth-floor landing they came upon the piled rotting corpses of Franco's get.

"Believe me now?"

"Jesus Christ. It's true." He looked at her with wide eyes. "That means . . ."

"Yeah, that we're not beaten, that the living have still got a shot. But we have to get those tapes to people who can use them."

She led the way over the stinking cadavers, stepping around them when she could, and on them when she couldn't. The door to the Observation Deck had been blown off its hinges and the wind flowing through it carried most of the stink away.

Lacey hesitated at the door, afraid to go any further, but forced herself through. The carnage—the blood, the shattered marble, the stove-in elevator doors—stopped her in her tracks.

"Jesus God," Considine said behind her. "What happened here?"

Lacey said nothing, but she knew . . . she could see the scene play out in her brain . . . Carole ran out of options and took Barrett with her.

In the sunlight she saw a pile of charred, smoking, semi-molten flesh. That would be Franco. But Joe . . . where was Joe?

"Uncle Joe?" she called. "Uncle—?"

And then she saw him, curled in the fetal position in a corner, face to the wall. He wasn't moving.

"Uncle Joe?" She hurried to him and turned him over. His eyes were closed and his scarred face was twisted into a mask of pain. "Uncle Joe, are you all right?"

He opened his eyes and sobbed. "*I* was supposed to die, not her! But I'm still here and she's not!"

Lacey didn't understand and didn't try to. He was weak as a newborn. She cradled him in her arms and they cried together. He had no tears but she had enough for both of them. They fell on his face, wetting his cheeks.

Behind them Lacey heard a clatter from the stairwell and recognized Leland's voice. "What the hell happened here?"

"I'm still trying to figure that out," Considine said. "Did you get it on tape?"

"The cameras here went dead but I switched to one of the deck cameras in time to catch Franco's meltdown. Also caught his guards dying like poisoned rats on the stairs. What happened to them?"

"Tell you later. Can you believe it? They did it! They liberated the building!"

"I'd say they damn near liberated the whole city."

"Hear that, Unk?" Lacey whispered. "We did it, you and me and Carole. And we can prove it."

Suddenly Considine was hovering over them.

"I just sent Leland downstairs. He's going to dupe the tape while Fowler finds a car for you two. We're going to put you on the road with a copy, then we're each going to get our families together and head west with our own copies. One of us has to get through."

"I don't think I can get downstairs," Joe said.

"You'll get down," Considine said. "I'm going to check the elevator. If it doesn't work, well, after what you just did, I'll carry you down on my back if need be."

As Considine moved away, Joe squeezed Lacey's arm.

"We can't leave Carole."

"Carole left us, Unk. And she didn't leave anything behind."

"Let me die," he whispered. "I want an end to this."

"I know you do, but—"

"I was Franco's get. I was supposed to die with him."

So that was the reason behind the "If anything happens to me" mantra . . . He was planning to go out with Franco.

"I guess since you're not truly undead, you're not truly his get."

"But I am. I have to die."

"No way, Unk. You're going to see this through till the end. This is just a step, but we're on our way. We're going to push these slime bags back into the sea. And you and me, we're going to be there to see it."

"Carole was our conscience, Lacey. She made us whole and kept us on track. What will happen to us without her?"

"I'll tell you what'll happen. You and I will become the Terrible Two. We'll make those fuckers wish on the hell they come from that Sister Carole Hanarty was still alive to rein us in. They think they've seen trouble today? They haven't seen a goddamn thing."

She thought she saw him smile as he closed his eyes and slipped deep into daysleep.

"Hey!" Considine called from the other side of the atrium. "The elevator's still working."

"Give us half a minute," Lacey said.

She held her uncle tighter and rocked him like a baby.

Look for

INFERNAL

A REPAIRMAN JACK NOVEL

BY F. PAUL WILSON

Now available in hardcover
from Tom Doherty Associates

Carnival Pride℠
April 2 - 9, 2006.

7 Day Exotic Mexican Riviera Itinerary

DAY	PORT	ARRIVE	DEPART
Sun	Los Angeles/Long Beach, CA		4:00 P.M.
Mon	"Book Lover's" Day at Sea		
Tue	"Book Lover's" Day at Sea		
Wed	Puerto Vallarta, Mexico	8:00 A.M.	10:00 P.M.
Thu	Mazatlan, Mexico	9:00 A.M.	6:00 P.M.
Fri	Cabo San Lucas, Mexico	7:00 A.M.	4:00 P.M.
Sat	"Book Lover's" Day at Sea		
Sun	Los Angeles/Long Beach, CA	9:00 A.M.	

ports of call subject to weather conditions

TERMS AND CONDITIONS

PAYMENT SCHEDULE:
50% due upon booking
Full and final payment due by February 10, 2006

Acceptable forms of payment are Visa, MasterCard, American Express, Discover and checks. The cardholder must be one of the passengers traveling. A fee of $25 will apply for all returned checks. Check payments must be made payable to **Advantage International, LLC,** and sent to: **Advantage International, LLC, 195 North Harbor Drive, Suite 4206, Chicago, IL 60601**

CHANGE/CANCELLATION:
Notice of change/cancellation must be made in writing to Advantage International, LLC.

Change:
Changes in cabin category may be requested and can result in increased rate and penalties. A name change is permitted 60 days or more prior to departure and will incur a penalty of $50 per name change. Deviation from the group schedule and package is a cancellation.

Cancellation:

181 days or more prior to departure	$250 per person
121 - 180 days prior to departure	50% of the package price
120 - 61 days prior to departure	75% of the package price
60 days or less prior to departure	100% of the package price (nonrefundable)

US and Canadian citizens are required to present a valid passport or the original birth certificate and state issued photo ID (drivers license). All other nationalities must contact the consulate of the various ports that are visited for verification of documentation.

<u>**We strongly recommend trip cancellation insurance!**</u>

For complete details call 1-877-ADV-NTGE or visit www.AuthorsAtSea.com

---

This coupon does not constitute an offer from Tom Doherty Associates, LLC.

For booking form and complete information
go to **www.AuthorsAtSea.com** or call **1-877-ADV-NTGE**

Complete coupon and booking form and mail both to:
**Advantage International, LLC,
195 North Harbor Drive, Suite 4206, Chicago, IL 60601**